P9-DMT-171

ACCLAIM FOR SANDRA BROWN AND

FRICTION

"[Brown] deserves her own genre."
—*The Dallas Morning News*

"Brown expertly ratchets up passion and danger as Crawford fights for his life, his daughter, and his new love." —*Publishers Weekly*

"Brown's latest packs plenty of passion into the deadly thrills." —*Romantic Times*

"The queen now of all American letters, the mark of her greatness spelled out clearly in FRICTION."
—*Providence Sunday Journal*

"Brown knows how to pace her stories so fans will keep turning the pages." —*Kirkus*

"At a time when the world is so unpredictable, it's rewarding to be able to pick up a book by one of your favorite authors and know, without a doubt, that you are going to have a good time for several hours to come." —BookReporter.com

"A masterful storyteller, carefully crafting tales that keep readers on the edge of their seats."
—*USA Today*

FRICTION

NOVELS BY SANDRA BROWN

FRICTION

SANDRA
BROWN

GRAND
CENTRAL
NEW YORK   BOSTON

Grand Central Publishing
Hachette Book Group
1290 Avenue of the Americas, New York, NY 10104
grandcentralpublishing.com
twitter.com/grandcentralpub

Originally published in hardcover and ebook by Grand Central Publishing in August 2015
First oversize mass market edition: February 2024

Grand Central Publishing is a division of Hachette Book Group, Inc. The Grand Central Publishing name and logo is a registered trademark of Hachette Book Group, Inc.

The publisher is not responsible for websites (or their content) that are not owned by the publisher.

The Hachette Speakers Bureau provides a wide range of authors for speaking events. To find out more, go to hachettespeakersbureau.com or email HachetteSpeakers@hbgusa.com.

Grand Central Publishing books may be purchased in bulk for business, educational, or promotional use. For information, please contact your local bookseller or the Hachette Book Group Special Markets Department at special.markets@hbgusa.com.

ISBNs: 9781538768723 (oversize mass market), 9781455581177 (ebook)

Printed in the United States of America

OPM

10 9 8 7 6 5 4 3 2 1

Prologue

The two stalwart highway patrolmen guarding the barricade stared at her without registering any emotion, but because of the media blitz of the past few days, she knew they recognized her and that, in spite of their implacable demeanor, they were curious to know why Judge Holly Spencer was angling to get closer to the scene of a bloodbath.

"…bullet hole to the chest…"

"…ligature marks on his wrists and ankles…"

"…half in, half out of the water…"

"…carnage…"

Those were the phrases that Sergeant Lester had used to describe the scene beyond the barricade, although he'd told her he was sparing her the "gruesome details." He'd also ordered her to clear out, go home, that she shouldn't be here, that there was nothing she could do. Then he'd ducked beneath the barricade, got into his sedan, and backed it into a three-point turn that pointed him to the crime scene.

If she didn't leave voluntarily, the pair of patrolmen would escort her away, and that would create even more of a scene. She started walking back to her car.

In the few minutes that she'd been away from it,

more law enforcement and emergency personnel had converged on the area. There was a lengthening line of cars, pickups, and minivans forming along both shoulders of the narrow road on either side of the turnoff. This junction was deep in the backwoods and appeared on few maps. It was nearly impossible to find unless one knew to look for the taxidermy sign with an armadillo on it.

Tonight it had become a hot spot.

The vibe of the collected crowd was almost festive. The flashing lights of the official vehicles reminded Holly of a carnival midway. An ever-growing number of onlookers, drawn to the emergency like sharks to blood, stood in groups swapping rumors about the body count, speculating on who had died and how.

Overhearing one group placing odds on who had survived, she wanted to scream, *This isn't entertainment.*

By the time she reached her car, she was out of breath, her mouth dry with anxiety. She got in and clutched the steering wheel, pressing her forehead against it so hard, it hurt.

"Drive, judge."

Nearly jumping out of her skin, she whipped her head around, gasping his name when she saw the amount of blood soaking his clothes.

The massive red stain was fresh enough to show up shiny in the kaleidoscope of flashing red, white, and blue lights around them. His eyes glinted at her from shadowed sockets. His forehead was beaded with sweat, strands of hair plastered to it.

He remained perfectly still, sprawled in the corner of the backseat, left leg stretched out along it, the toe of his blood-spattered cowboy boot pointing toward the ceiling of the car. His right leg was bent at the knee. His right hand was resting on it, holding a wicked-looking pistol.

He said, "It's not my blood."

"I heard."

Looking down over his long torso, he gave a gravelly, bitter laugh. "He was dead before he hit the ground, but I wanted to make sure. Dumb move. Ruined this shirt, and it was one of my favorites."

She wasn't fooled by either his seeming indifference or his relaxed posture. He was a sudden movement waiting to happen, his reflexes quicksilver.

Up ahead, officers had begun moving along the line of spectator vehicles, motioning the motorists to clear the area. She had to either do as he asked or be caught with him inside her car.

"Sergeant Lester told me that you'd—"

"Shot the son of a bitch? That's true. He's dead. Now drive."

Chapter 1

Five days earlier

Crawford Hunt woke up knowing that this was the day he'd been anticipating for a long time. Even before opening his eyes, he felt a happy bubble of excitement inside his chest, which was instantly burst by a pang of anxiety.

It might not go his way.

He showered with customary efficiency but took a little more time than usual on personal grooming: flossing, shaving extra-close, using a blow dryer rather than letting his hair dry naturally. But he was no good at wielding the dryer, and his hair came out looking the same as it always did—unmanageable. Why hadn't he thought to get a trim?

He noticed a few gray strands in his sideburns. They, plus the faint lines at the corners of his eyes and on either side of his mouth, lent him an air of maturity.

But the judge would probably regard them as signs of hard living.

"Screw it." Impatient with his self-scrutiny, he turned away from the bathroom mirror and went into his bedroom to dress.

He had considered wearing a suit, but figured that would be going overboard, like he was trying too hard to impress the judge. Besides, the navy wool blend made him feel like an undertaker. He settled for a sport jacket and tie.

Although the small of his back missed the pressure of his holster, he decided not to carry.

In the kitchen, he brewed coffee and poured himself a bowl of cereal, but neither settled well in his nervous stomach, so he dumped them into the disposal. As the Cheerios vaporized, he got a call from his lawyer.

"You all right?" The qualities that made William Moore a good lawyer worked against him as a likable human being. He possessed little grace and zero charm, so, although he'd called to ask about Crawford's state of mind, the question sounded like a challenge to which he expected a positive answer.

"Doing okay."

"Court will convene promptly at two o'clock."

"Right. Wish it was earlier."

"Are you going into your office first?"

"Thought about it. Maybe. I don't know."

"You should. Work will keep your mind off the hearing."

Crawford hedged. "I'll see how the morning goes."

"Nervous?"

"No."

The attorney snorted with skepticism. Crawford admitted to experiencing a few butterflies.

"We've gone over it," the lawyer said. "Look everyone in the eye, especially the judge. Be sincere. You'll do fine."

Although it sounded easy enough, Crawford released a long breath. "At this point, I've done everything I can. It's now up to the judge, whose mind is probably already made up."

"Maybe. Maybe not. The decision could hinge on how you comport yourself on the stand."

Crawford frowned into the phone. "But no pressure."

"I have a good feeling."

"Better than the other kind, I guess. But what happens if I don't win today? What do I do next? Short of taking out a contract on Judge Spencer."

"Don't even think in terms of losing." When Crawford didn't respond, Moore began to lecture. "The last thing we need is for you to slink into court looking pessimistic."

"Right."

"I mean it. If you look unsure, you're sunk."

"Right."

"Go in there with confidence, certainty, like you've *already* kicked butt."

"I've got it, okay?"

Responding to his client's testiness, Moore backed down. "I'll meet you outside the courtroom a little before two." He hung up without saying good-bye.

With hours to kill before he had to be in court, Crawford wandered through his house, checking things. Fridge, freezer, and pantry were well stocked. He'd had a maid service come in yesterday, and the three industrious women had left the whole house spotless. He tidied his bathroom and made his bed. He didn't see anything else he could improve upon.

Last, he went into the second bedroom, the one he'd spent weeks preparing for Georgia's homecoming, not allowing himself to think that from tonight forward his little girl wouldn't be spending every night under his roof.

He'd left the decorating up to the saleswoman at the furniture store. "Georgia's five years old. About to start kindergarten."

She asked, "Favorite color?"

"Pink. Second favorite, pink."

"Do you have a budget?"

"Knock yourself out."

She'd taken him at his word. Everything in the room was pink except for the creamy white headboard, chest of drawers, and vanity table with an oval mirror that swiveled between upright spindles.

He had added touches he thought Georgia would like: picture books with pastel covers featuring rainbows and unicorns and such, a menagerie of stuffed animals, a ballet tutu with glittery slippers to match, and a doll wearing a pink princess gown and gold crown. The saleswoman had assured him it was a five-year-old girl's fantasy room.

The only thing missing was the girl.

He gave the bedroom one final inspection, then left the house and, without consciously intending to, found himself driving toward the cemetery. He hadn't come since Mother's Day, when he and his in-laws had brought Georgia to visit the grave of the mother she didn't remember.

Solemnly, Georgia had laid a bouquet of roses on the grave as instructed, then had looked up at him and asked, "Can we go get ice cream now, Daddy?"

Leaving his parents-in-law to pay homage to their late daughter, he'd scooped Georgia into his arms and carried her back to the car. She'd squealed whenever he pretended to stumble and stagger under her weight. He figured Beth wouldn't take exception. Wouldn't she rather have Georgia laughing over an ice cream cone than crying over her grave?

Somehow, it seemed appropriate to visit today, although he came empty-handed. He didn't see what difference a bouquet of flowers would make to the person underground. As he stood beside the grave, he didn't address anything to the spirit of his dead wife.

He'd run out of things to say to her years ago, and those verbal purges never made him feel any better. They sure as hell didn't benefit Beth.

So he merely stared at the date etched into the granite headstone and cursed it, cursed his culpability, then made a promise to whatever cosmic puppeteer might be listening that, if given custody of Georgia, he would do everything within his power to make amends.

———

Holly checked her wristwatch as she waited on the ground floor of the courthouse for the elevator. When it arrived and the door slid open, she stifled a groan at the sight of Greg Sanders among those onboard.

She stood aside and allowed everyone to get off. Sanders came only as far as the threshold, but there he stopped, blocking her from getting on.

"Well, Judge Spencer," he drawled. "Fancy bumping into you. You can be the first to congratulate me."

She forced a smile. "Are congratulations in order?"

He placed his hand on the door to prevent it from closing. "I just came from court. The verdict in the Mallory case? Not guilty."

Holly frowned. "I don't see that as cause for celebration. Your client was accused of brutally beating a convenience store clerk during the commission of an armed robbery. The clerk lost an eye."

"But my client didn't rob the store."

"Because he panicked and ran when he thought he'd beaten the clerk to death." She was familiar with the case, but since the defending attorney, Sanders, was her opponent in the upcoming election for district court judge, the trial had been assigned to another court.

Greg Sanders flashed his self-satisfied smirk. "The ADA failed to prove his case. My client—"

Holly interrupted. "You've already argued the case at trial. I wouldn't dream of asking you to retry it for me here and now. If you'll excuse me?"

She sidestepped him into the elevator. He got out, but kept his hand against the door. "I'm chalking up wins. Come November…" He winked. "The big win."

"I'm afraid you're setting yourself up for a huge disappointment." She punched the elevator button for the fifth floor.

"This time 'round, you won't have Judge Waters shoehorning you in."

They were monopolizing one of three elevators. People were becoming impatient, shooting them dirty looks. Besides the fact they were inconveniencing others, she wouldn't be goaded into defending either herself or her mentor to Greg Sanders. "I'm due in court in fifteen minutes. Please let go of the door."

By now, Sanders was fighting the automation to keep it open. Speaking for her ears alone, he said, "Now what would a pretty young lawyer like you have been doing for ol' Judge Waters to get him to go to bat for you with the governor?"

The "pretty" was belittling, not complimentary.

She smiled, but with exasperation. "Really, Mr. Sanders? If you're resorting to innuendos suggesting sexual impropriety between the revered Judge Waters and me, you must be feeling terribly insecure about a successful outcome in November." Without a "please" this time, she enunciated, "Let go of the door."

He raised his hands in surrender and backed away. "You'll mess up. Matter of time." The door closed on his grinning face.

Holly entered her chambers to find her assistant, Mrs. Debra Briggs, eating a carton of yogurt at her desk. "Want one?"

"No thanks. I just had a face-to-face exchange with my opponent."

"If that won't spoil your appetite, nothing will. He reminds me of an old mule that my grandpa had when I was a kid."

"I can see the resemblance. Long face, big ears, toothy smile."

"I was referring to the other end of the mule."

Holly laughed. "Messages?"

"Marilyn Vidal has called twice."

"Get back to her and tell her I'm due in court. I'll call her after this hearing."

"She won't like being put off."

Marilyn, the powerhouse orchestrating her campaign, could be irritatingly persistent. "No, she won't, but she'll get over it."

Holly went into her private office and closed the door. She needed a few minutes alone to collect herself before the upcoming custody hearing. The encounter with Sanders—and she hated herself for this—had left her with an atypical uneasiness. She was confident that she could defeat him at the polls and retain the judgeship to which she'd been temporarily appointed.

But as she zipped herself into her robe, his parting shot echoed through her mind like a dire prediction.

———

"Crawford?"

Having arrived early, he'd been trying to empty his mind of negative thoughts while staring through the wavy glass of a fourth-floor window of the venerable Prentiss County Courthouse.

His name brought him around. Grace and Joe Gilroy were walking toward him, their expressions somber, as befitted the reason for their being there.

"Hi, Grace."

His mother-in-law was petite and pretty, with eyes through which her sweet disposition shone. The outside corners tilted up slightly, a physical trait that Beth had inherited. He and Grace hugged briefly.

As she pulled back, she gave him an approving once-over. "You look nice."

"Thanks. Hello, Joe."

He released Grace and shook hands with Beth's dad. Joe's hobby was carpentry, which had given him a row of calluses at the base of his fingers. Indeed, everything about Joe Gilroy was tough for a man just past seventy.

"How are you doing?" he asked.

Crawford forced himself to smile. "Great."

Joe appeared not to believe the exaggeration, but he didn't comment on it. Nor did he return Crawford's smile.

Grace said, "I guess we're all a little nervous." She hesitated, then asked Crawford if he was feeling one way or the other about the hearing.

"You mean whether I'll win or lose?"

She looked pained. "Please don't think of the outcome in terms of winning or losing."

"Don't you?"

"We only want what's best for our granddaughter," Joe said. Interpreted, that meant it would be best for Georgia to remain with them. "I'm sure that's what Judge Spencer wants, too."

Crawford held his tongue and decided to save his

debate for the courtroom. Talking it over with them now was pointless and could only lead to antagonism. The simple fact was that today he and his in-laws were on opposing sides of a legal issue, the outcome of which would profoundly affect all of them. Somebody was going to leave the courthouse defeated and unhappy. Crawford wouldn't be able to congratulate them if the judge ruled in their favor, and he wasn't about to wish them luck. He figured they felt much the same way toward him.

Since both parties had agreed to leave Georgia out of the proceedings entirely, Crawford asked Grace what arrangements she'd made for her while they were in court. "She's on a play date with our neighbor's grand-daughter. She was so excited when I dropped her off. They're going to bake cookies."

Crawford winced. "Her last batch were a little gooey in the center."

"She always takes them out of the oven too soon," Joe said.

Crawford smiled. "She can't wait to sample them."

"She needs to learn the virtue of patience."

In order to maintain his smile, Crawford had to clench his teeth. His father-in-law was good at getting in barbs like that, aimed at Crawford's character flaws. That one had been a zinger. Also well timed. Before Crawford could respond, the Gilroys' attorney stepped off the elevator. They excused themselves to confer with him.

Within minutes Crawford's attorney arrived. Bill Moore's walk was as brisk as his manner. But today his determined stride was impeded by dozens of potential jurors who had crowded into the corridor looking for their assigned courtroom.

The attorney plowed his way through them,

connected with Crawford, and together they went into Judge Spencer's court.

The bailiff, Chet Barker, was a courthouse institution. He was a large man with a gregarious nature to match his size. He greeted Crawford by name. "Big day, huh?"

"Yeah it is, Chet."

The bailiff slapped him on the shoulder. "Good luck."

"Thanks."

Crawford's butt barely had time to connect with the seat of his chair before Chet was asking everyone to rise. The judge entered the courtroom, stepped onto the podium, and sat down in the high-backed chair that Crawford uneasily likened to a throne. In a way, it was. Here, the honorable Judge Holly Spencer had absolute rule.

Chet called court into session and asked everyone to be seated.

"Good afternoon," the judge said. She asked the attorneys if all parties were present, and when the formalities were out of the way, she clasped her hands on top of the lectern.

"Although I took over this case from Judge Waters, I've familiarized myself with it. As I understand the situation, in May of 2010, Grace and Joe Gilroy filed for temporary custody of their granddaughter, Georgia Hunt." She looked at Crawford. "Mr. Hunt, you did not contest that petition."

"No, Your Honor, I did not."

William Moore stood up. "If I may, Your Honor?"

She nodded.

In his rat-a-tat fashion, the lawyer stated the major components of Crawford's petition to regain custody and summarized why it was timely and proper that Georgia be returned to him. He ended by saying, "Mr.

Hunt is her father. He loves her, and his affection is returned, as two child psychologists attest. I believe you have copies of their evaluations of Georgia?"

"Yes, and I've reviewed them." The judge gazed thoughtfully at Crawford, then said, "Mr. Hunt will have a chance to address the court, but first I'd like to hear from the Gilroys."

Their lawyer sprang to his feet, eager to get their objections to Crawford's petition on the record. "Mr. Hunt's stability was brought into question four years ago, Your Honor. He gave up his daughter without argument, which indicates that he knew his child would be better off with her grandparents."

The judge held up her hand. "Mr. Hunt has conceded that it was in Georgia's best interest to be placed with them at that time."

"We hope to persuade the court that she should remain with them." He called Grace to testify. She was sworn in. Judge Spencer gave her a reassuring smile as she took her seat in the witness box.

"Mrs. Gilroy, why are you and Mr. Gilroy contesting your son-in-law's petition to regain custody?"

Grace wet her lips. "Well, ours is the only home Georgia has known. We've dedicated ourselves to making it a loving and nurturing environment for her." She expanded on the healthy home life they had created.

Judge Spencer finally interrupted. "Mrs. Gilroy, no one in this courtroom, not even Mr. Hunt, disputes that you've made an excellent home for Georgia. My decision won't be determined by whether or not you've provided well for the child, but whether or not Mr. Hunt is willing and able to provide an equally good home for her."

"I know he loves her," Grace said, sending an uneasy glance his way. "But love alone isn't enough. In order to feel secure, children need constancy, routine. Since Georgia doesn't have a mother, she needs the next best thing."

"Her daddy." Crawford's mutter drew disapproving glances from everyone, including the judge.

Bill Moore nudged his arm and whispered, "You'll have your turn."

The judge asked Grace a few more questions, but the upshot of what his mother-in-law believed was that to remove Georgia from their home now would create a detrimental upheaval in her young life. She finished with, "My husband and I feel that a severance from us would have a damaging impact on Georgia's emotional and psychological development."

To Crawford the statement sounded scripted and rehearsed, something their lawyer had coached Grace to say, not something that she had come up with on her own.

Judge Spencer asked Crawford's attorney if he had any questions for Mrs. Gilroy. "Yes, Your Honor, I do." He strode toward the witness box and didn't waste time on pleasantries. "Georgia often spends weekends with Mr. Hunt, isn't that right?"

"Well, yes. Once we felt she was old enough to spend a night away from us, and that Crawford was…was *trustworthy* enough, we began allowing him to keep her overnight. Sometimes two nights."

"When she's returned to you after these sleepovers with her father, what is Georgia like?"

"Like?"

"What's her state of mind, her general being? Does she run to you crying, arms outstretched, grateful to be back? Does she act intimidated, fearful, or traumatized? Is she ever in a state of emotional distress? Is she withdrawn and uncommunicative?"

"No. She's…fine."

"Crying *only* when her father returns her to you. Isn't that right?"

Grace hesitated. "She sometimes cries when he drops her off. But only on occasion. Not every time."

"More often crying after a lengthier visit with him," the attorney said. "In other words, the longer she's with him, the greater her separation anxiety when she's returned to you." He saw that the Gilroys' lawyer was about to object and waved him back into his seat. "Conclusion on my part."

He apologized to the judge, but Crawford knew he wasn't sorry for having gotten his point across and on the record.

He addressed another question to Grace. "When was the last time you saw Mr. Hunt intoxicated?"

"It was a while ago. I don't remember exactly."

"A week ago? A month? A year?"

"Longer than that."

"Longer than that," Moore repeated. "Four years ago? During the worst of his bereavement over the loss of his wife?"

"Yes. But—"

"To your knowledge, has Mr. Hunt ever been drunk while with Georgia?"

"No."

"Lost his temper and struck her?"

"No."

"Yelled at her, used abusive or vulgar language in front of her?"

"No."

"Failed to feed her when she was hungry?"

"No."

"Failed to secure her in her car seat? Not shown up when she was expecting him? Has he *ever* neglected to see to his daughter's physical or emotional needs?"

Grace dipped her head and spoke softly. "No."

Moore turned to the judge and spread his arms at his sides. "Your Honor, this proceeding is an imposition on the court's time. Mr. Hunt made some mistakes, which he readily acknowledges. Over time, he's reconstructed his life. He relocated to Prentiss from Houston in order to see his daughter regularly.

"He's undergone the counseling that your predecessor mandated twelve months ago. A year hasn't diminished his determination to regain custody of his child, and I submit that, except for their own selfish interests, there are no grounds whatsoever for Mr. and Mrs. Gilroy to be contesting my client's petition."

The Gilroys' lawyer surged to his feet. "Your Honor, my clients' grounds for contesting this petition are in the file. Mr. Hunt has proved himself to be unfit—"

"I have the file, thank you," Judge Spencer said. "Mrs. Gilroy, please step down. I'd like to hear from Mr. Hunt now."

Grace left the witness stand looking distraught, as though she had miserably failed their cause.

Crawford stood up, smoothed down his necktie, and walked to the witness box. Chet swore him in. Crawford sat down and looked at the judge—in the eye, as Moore had coached him to do.

"Mr. Hunt, four years ago some of your behavior brought your ability to be a good parent into question."

"Which is why I didn't contest Joe and Grace being awarded temporary custody of Georgia. She was only thirteen months old when Beth died. She needed constant care, which circumstances prevented me from providing. My obligations at work, other issues."

"*Serious* other issues."

That wasn't a question. He kept his mouth shut.

The judge flipped through several official-looking

papers and ran her finger down one sheet. "You were arrested and pled guilty to DUI."

"Once. But I—"

"You were arrested for public indecency and—"

"I was urinating."

"—assault."

"It was a bar fight. Everyone who threw a punch was detained. I was released without—"

"I have the file."

He sat there seething, realizing that his past would devastate his future. Judge Holly Spencer was cutting him no slack. After giving him a long, thoughtful appraisal, she again shuffled through the pages of what she had referred to as his "file." He wondered how bad it looked with his transgressions spelled out in black and white. If her frown was any indication, not good.

Finally, she said, "You went to all the counseling sessions."

"Judge Waters made clear that each one was mandatory. All twenty-five of them. I made certain not to miss any."

"The therapist's report is comprehensive. According to her, you made remarkable progress."

"I think so. I *know* so."

"I commend your diligence, Mr. Hunt, and I admire your commitment to regaining custody of the daughter you obviously love."

Here it comes, he thought.

"However—"

The door at the back of the courtroom burst open and a figure straight out of a horror movie ran up the center aisle, handgun extended. The first bullet struck the wall behind the witness box, splitting the distance between Crawford and Judge Spencer.

The second one got the bailiff Chet Barker square in the chest.

Chapter 2

———◆———

Shots were fired rapidly, one right after another. Crawford tried to count them, but lost track in the chaos that erupted inside the courtroom.

Judge Spencer surged to her feet, shouting Chet's name in alarm.

Joe shoved Grace out of her chair and onto the floor, then ducked down beside her.

The attorneys scurried for cover beneath the tables at which they sat. The court reporter did the same.

Impervious to the scurrying and ear-piercing screams, the shooter, clad in stark white, his facial features distorted by a clear plastic mask, stepped over Chet's still form as though it weren't there, and kept coming, shooting, aiming toward the front of the courtroom.

All this registered with Crawford instantly, and he reacted instinctually by vaulting over the railing that separated the witness box from the judge's podium, forcing her to the floor, then landing on top of her.

Four shots? Five? Six? Crawford had recognized the pistol as a nine-millimeter. Depending on the size of the clip—

Sensing when the shooter rounded the witness box and stepped onto the platform, Crawford whipped his head around. The shooter had a bead on him. Crawford kicked backward. His boot heel caught the guy in the kneecap, hard enough to throw the attacker off balance. His arm went up, and the shot went into the ceiling. Still off balance, he stumbled backward off the platform, then turned and ran for the side exit of the courtroom.

Crawford came up onto one knee and bent over the judge. After confirming that she was alive, he launched himself off the platform like a sprinter off the chocks. He knelt down beside Chet, determined instantly that he was dead and, without allowing himself to think about the waste of a good man, unsnapped the bailiff's holster and yanked his service revolver from it.

A bailiff from another court barreled in through the rear door, skidding to a halt when he saw Crawford checking to make certain Chet's revolver was loaded. The bailiff went for his own weapon.

Crawford shouted, "Texas Ranger Hunt! Chet's down."

"Oh, Crawford, jeez. What happened?"

Civilians were beginning to crowd in behind the nervous bailiff. "Get those people to take cover. Notify officers downstairs that we have a shooter. He's masked, dressed in white from head to toe. Tell them not to mistake me for him."

By now he'd made it to the side exit through which the gunman had disappeared. He opened the door a crack and when nothing happened, banged it open and lunged through, sweeping the pistol from side to side. The long, narrow corridor was empty save for a woman standing in the open doorway of an office, her mouth agape, a hand to her throat.

"Go back into your office."

"What's happening? Who was that painter?"

"Which way did he go?"

She pointed toward the door to the fire stairs. When Crawford came even with her, he pushed her inside the office and pulled the door closed. "Lock it," he said through the door. "Get under your desk and don't come out. Call 911. Tell them what you saw."

He jogged down the hall toward the fire stairs.

A man from another office poked his head out into the hallway, saw Crawford, and his eyes went wide with fear. "Please, I—"

"Listen." Wasting no time on an explanation, Crawford gave him terse instructions about taking cover and staying there until given the all-clear. The man ducked back into his office and slammed the door.

Crawford slowed down as he approached the door to the fire stairs, closing the remainder of the distance with caution. He took a quick peek through the square, wired window in the top third of the door. Seeing nothing through the glass, he cautiously pulled the door open and, with his gun hand extended, made a wide sweep of the stairs above and below him. Nothing happened.

He entered the stairwell, where he paused, waiting for a sound or a motion that would give away which direction the shooter had gone. Then, from behind him—

He spun around as a deputy sheriff stepped through the corridor door. They recognized each other, which was fortunate because their weapons were aimed at each other's heads. The deputy was about to speak when Crawford placed his index finger against his lips.

The deputy, nodding understanding, motioned that he would go down, Crawford up. *Careful*, Crawford mouthed.

Keeping close to the wall, Crawford crept up the stairs to the next landing. He opened the door onto a corridor exactly matching the one on the floor below.

Aggregate flooring, walls painted government-building beige. Here and there hung a framed portrait of a dour, bygone official. Doors to various offices lined both sides of the hall.

About midway down, two men and a woman were conferring quietly, their aspects fearful. One of the men, seeing that Crawford was armed, raised his hands in surrender.

"I'm a Texas Ranger," Crawford whispered. "Did you see a person dressed all in white?" Remembering how the first woman had described the shooter, he added, "A painter?"

They shook their heads.

"Lock yourselves in an office. Stay clear of the door and don't open it to anyone except police."

Crawford slipped back into the stairwell. He heard footsteps coming up from below and figured the deputy sheriff had picked up a few reinforcements on their climb up from the first floor of the building where the Prentiss County Sheriff's Office was located. Obviously they hadn't encountered the shooter going down the stairs. If they had, there would have been considerably more noise, likely gunshots, echoing in the stairwell.

Crawford continued up. When he reached the sixth-floor landing, he stepped to the door and looked both ways through the window into the corridor. Another group of courthouse personnel was huddled together, looking frightened, but not hysterical, which they would have been had the masked gunman just raced past them.

He cracked the door and, staving off their questions about the gunshots they'd heard, identified himself and whispered instructions about taking cover, which they were quick to act on. He eased back into the stairwell and proceeded up to the next landing, which was only half a flight. It ended at the door that opened onto the roof.

In the corner adjacent to the door lay a pair of white coveralls, white cap, a pair of latex gloves, and shoe covers. Probably beneath the heap he'd find the mask, but he didn't touch anything.

Noticeably missing from the pile of castoff items was the gunman's pistol.

Leaning over the railing and looking below, he saw the deputy and several other uniformed officers stealthily making their way up. Crawford hitched his head toward the door to the roof. One of the officers backed down to the next landing and spoke quietly into the mike clipped to his epaulette, then gave Crawford and the others a thumbs-up.

Crawford knew that by now the rehearsed emergency response would have been implemented. The courthouse would be surrounded by policemen. Exits would be sealed off, anyone trying to leave or enter would be stopped. A SWAT team would have been deployed. Sharpshooters were no doubt already taking up positions on the roofs of neighboring buildings.

The gunman hadn't thought this out very well. The only way it could end for him was badly. Unless he could fly, he wasn't going to leave this building a free man. And as soon as he realized that, he might decide that he might just as well take out a couple more people before his inevitable capture. He'd already killed Chet in front of witnesses. Why not go for broke and make a name for himself as a mass murderer?

Crawford shrugged off his sport jacket and dropped it to the floor, then pushed open the exit door a crack. "Hey, buddy," he called through it. "Let's talk."

He half expected bullets to pepper the metal door, but nothing happened. He opened the door another inch or two. "I'm a Texas Ranger, but I'm not in uniform. I can show you my badge. I'm coming out, okay? I'm unarmed. I just want to talk to you. You cool with that?"

By now the other officers had joined him. One whispered, "Crawford, you sure about this?"

He gave the guy a wry grin to acknowledge the danger he faced, then stuck Chet's pistol into his waistband at the small of his back, opened the door wide enough to squeeze through, and stepped out onto the gravel roof, arms raised.

It took several seconds for his eyes to adjust to the blazing sunlight, then he immediately saw the guy. He wasn't even trying to hide. He was standing near the low wall at the edge of the roof. He was Hispanic, late twenties or early thirties, average height, pudgy in the middle.

He didn't look like anybody to be afraid of except for the pistol that he was aiming at Crawford with a shaky hand. In the other hand he held a smoldering cigarette.

Crawford kept his hands raised. "I'm gonna show you my badge, okay?" He eased his right hand down toward the leather holder clipped to his belt, but when the man dropped his cigarette and ordered, "No!" Crawford put his hand back in the air. "This is a bad idea, pal."

The man jabbed the pistol forward several times.

"You don't want to shoot me," Crawford said. "Put down the weapon, why don't you? Then nobody else will get hurt, including you."

In spite of Crawford's calming tone, the man was becoming increasingly agitated. He rapidly blinked trickles of sweat from his eyes, which darted from side to side. When they came back to Crawford, he motioned again with the pistol for him to back away.

It occurred to Crawford that he might not speak English. *"Habla inglés?"*

"Sí." Then more forcibly, *"Sí."*

The reply had sounded angrily defensive, leaving Crawford to doubt the man's command of the language. He took a step forward and made a patting motion toward the ground. *"La pistola.* Down."

"No." He brought his other hand up to cradle the pistol and thrust it at arm's length toward Crawford.

Shit! "Come on, buddy. There's no good way out of this if you don't— *No!*"

One of the officers must have come out another door accessing the roof because he had suddenly appeared in Crawford's peripheral vision. The gunman saw him at the same time. He whipped the firearm toward the deputy and pulled the trigger twice. He missed.

But the sharpshooters in place on the neighboring roof didn't.

The gunman's body jerked with the impact of each bullet, then crumpled and went entirely still.

Crawford, deflating, backed up to the wall and slid down it until he was crouching on his heels. He watched as officers in various uniforms swarmed through the stairwell door and surrounded the body leaking blood onto the gravel.

Feeling a hand on his shoulder, Crawford looked up into the face of the deputy who'd expressed concern about his going out onto the roof. "You hit?"

He shook his head.

"You got lucky." He pressed Crawford's shoulder, then left him to join the other officers grouped around the fallen man.

Crawford's head dropped forward until his chin touched his chest. "You dumb son of a bitch."

Anyone overhearing his castigating mutter would

have assumed he was addressing the dead man. They would be mistaken.

———

"Hunt?"

Crawford, who'd been staring sightlessly at the floor, looked toward the homicide detective holding open the interrogation room door and motioning with his head for Crawford to go in.

Crawford had to forcibly exert enough energy to stand up. He dreaded this like hell, but was eager to get it over with.

Inside the room, another man in plainclothes whom Crawford didn't know was standing with his back to the wall, noisily cracking his knuckles and giving a wad of chewing gum a workout. Crawford wondered what he had to be nervous about.

Sergeant Neal Lester, the senior detective who'd laconically summoned Crawford into the room, motioned him into one of the chairs at the small table and took a seat opposite him. Between them on the table were a legal tablet and a video recording setup.

Neal Lester withdrew a pen from his shirt pocket and clicked the retractor at the end of it several times as he fixed an unfriendly gaze on Crawford. Classmates from primary school, they'd never liked each other, and the mutual dislike had intensified when, in high school, Crawford had dated Neal's younger sister. The attraction had been short-lived and had never amounted to anything, but apparently Neal still had a burr up his butt about it.

"Want something to drink?" He made the question sound obligatory.

"No thanks."

"You know Matt Nugent? Recently made detective." He nodded toward the younger man who was still fidgeting.

Crawford acknowledged the quasi-introduction by hitching his chin in the detective's direction.

He grinned, showing crooked teeth. "How's it goin'?" A ridiculous greeting under the circumstances. Crawford didn't reply and returned his attention to Neal Lester, who had continued the infernal pen-clicking.

"You know the drill," he said.

Crawford nodded.

"This interview will be recorded."

Crawford nodded.

"You ready then?"

"When you are, Neal."

"Let's keep it official. No first names."

Crawford barely kept himself from rolling his eyes. One reason he'd never liked Neal Lester was because he was such a tight-ass. Even as a kid, he'd obeyed all the rules and tattled on kids who didn't.

What galled Crawford now, Neal Lester was eating this up. He was enjoying having Crawford in the hot seat.

However, personal feelings aside, the bottom line was that two men were dead, and Crawford had been within feet of both when they died. As a law enforcement officer, Neal and his nervous sidekick had a duty to perform, and that included questioning him.

He shifted in his chair, trying but failing to better fit his tall frame into the preformed plastic. "Fair enough, *Sergeant Lester*, where do we begin?"

"Inside the courtroom." With a decisive punch of his index finger, Neal started the recorder, stated the date, time, and who was present. "Why were you in Family Court today?"

"You know damn well why."

The detective's eyes narrowed. "Just answer the question, please."

Crawford drew a deep breath, then released it as he stated, "I was there for a custody hearing." Neither detective responded to that, only continued to look at him. He folded his arms across his chest. "My little girl's custody hearing. Judge Spencer was just about to hand down her decision when the shooter busted in."

"We have a transcript of the court proceedings up to that point."

"Then you don't need me to recount who said what."

"I'm curious, though," Neal said. "How do you think Judge Spencer would have ruled?"

Crawford was about to say that what he thought regarding that had no relevance to the matter at hand, but he withheld that, shrugged, and answered. "I was hoping for the best."

"Fearing the worst?"

Fine, Crawford thought. If Neal was going to be a prick, he could be one back. "Well, I sure as hell didn't *expect* the worst, which was seeing Chet Barker gunned down right in front of me."

The statement had the squelching effect Crawford had intended. To cover the awkward silence that followed, Neal repositioned the camera a quarter inch closer to Crawford. Matt Nugent cleared his throat behind his fist.

"Talk us through it," Neal said. "Be as detailed as possible."

Crawford covered his face with his hands and slowly dragged them down until only his fingertips were touching his jaw. Then he dropped his hands and leaned forward, propping his forearms on the edge of the table.

"I was in the witness box. The guy came through the door at the back of the room, shooting. All hell broke loose."

Nugent asked him to describe the gunman and he did, even though the painter's garb and mask had been collected as evidence, so they already had a basic description. "The cap covered all but a rim of his hair. He was wearing the gloves and they extended up under his sleeves. That mask was scary as shit. Barely had slits for his eyes. Two small holes for his nostrils. It mashed all his features flat. Total distortion."

He thought about it for a moment, recapturing his initial impression of the figure coming up the center aisle of the courtroom with such obvious intent. "But even without the disguise I think I would have picked up a bad mojo from this guy. He was focused on what he was doing. Determined."

Neal nodded. "You said he was shooting when he came through the door."

"Soon as he cleared it, he fired the first shot."

"Wild shot? Or did he aim?"

"The pistol was pointed toward the front of the court. He was holding it shoulder high, arm straight out." He demonstrated. "Pulling the trigger as fast as he could. Bam-bam-bam. Chet…" He paused and made a remorseful sound. "Chet rushed forward and raised his arms like this." He thrust his hands in front of him at arm's length, palms out. "He shouted at him. Stop! Something like that. Maybe he just made an exclamation. Then he went down."

"He died with valor, doing his job," Neal remarked.

"Yeah," Crawford sighed. "He'll be honored for doing so. But I doubt he'd ever drawn his service weapon. Not in the whole of his career. Then to get shot dead by some whack job in a freak show mask. It sucks."

Chet hadn't gotten up this morning foreseeing his death. Nor could Crawford have anticipated the wicked curveball Fate had hurled at him. Pinching the bridge of his nose, he sat back in his chair.

After a moment, Nugent asked if he'd changed his mind about something to drink.

"I'm fine. Carry on."

Neal clicked his pen and made a notation on the legal tablet. "So…Chet's down. What happened next?"

Crawford focused his thoughts on the scene in the courtroom. "Chaos. Noise. Screams. Joe moved like lightning, got him and Grace under cover. Everyone was scrambling, panicky."

"Not you," Nugent said. "People in the courtroom at the time have told us that you hurdled the railing of the witness box. Do you remember doing that?"

He shook his head. "Not really. I just…reacted. I pushed the judge to the floor and sorta…" He hunched forward, posing to demonstrate how he'd used his body to shield hers. "I heard bullets striking. I didn't feel anything, but I was so jacked up on adrenalin that, for all I knew, I'd been hit. What with the robe, I couldn't tell if the judge had been struck or not.

"When he rounded the witness box and stepped up onto the platform," he continued, "I turned to look at him. He had the pistol pointed straight at us. I remember holding my breath, thinking, 'This is it.' I guess my survival instinct kicked in. I let him have it in the knee with my foot."

He described the gunman's backward topple off the platform. "Maybe that panicked him. I don't know. In any case, he ran like hell and disappeared through the side exit."

Neal nodded as though that jibed with what others had recounted. "Then?"

"I went after him."

Neal glanced at Nugent, then came back to Crawford and repeated, "You went after him."

"That's right."

"Just like that."

"I didn't think about it, if that's what you mean. I just did it."

"Like you hurdled the witness box railing."

He shrugged. "I guess."

"You acted without thinking or weighing the consequences of your actions."

"Like you would," Crawford fired back, "if you were any kind of lawman."

"Well, we know what kind you are."

Crawford lunged to his feet, sending his chair over backward. He glared down at Neal, but instantly realized that a show of temper would only confirm what the bastard had implied. He turned and righted the chair, then sat back down. He looked at Nugent, who was swallowing convulsively, as though his chewing gum had slipped down his gullet and gotten stuck.

When he came back around to Neal, Neal said, "You left out a step."

Realizing what Neal was getting at, he said, "I stopped long enough to take Chet's revolver."

"Even jacked up on adrenalin, you had the presence of mind to identify yourself to the first officer into the courtroom."

"His hand was on his holster. I didn't want to get shot."

"You gave him a description of the gunman."

"A very basic one."

"You asked for backup. But without waiting for it, you took Chet's revolver and charged after the shooter. Why?"

"*Why?*"

"Well, considering your history, you might have exercised more discretion."

"Discretion could have gotten people killed."

"So could *in*discretion. Like in Halcon."

Chapter 3

Holly's attention was drawn to the end of the hallway when a door was opened and Crawford Hunt strode through. Looking disheveled and angry, he glanced at her but said nothing as he walked past on his way to the men's room.

"They'll be wanting to talk to me now," she said to her assistant, who had refused to leave her alone while waiting her turn to give her statement. "Thank you so much for staying, but go on home, get some rest. Tomorrow will be a circus, I'm afraid."

"But, Holly—"

"There's no telling how long they'll keep me."

"I can stay indefinitely. You shouldn't be alone tonight."

Marilyn Vidal had been of the same mind when she was notified of the shooting. She'd been prepared to drop everything and make the drive from Dallas to be with Holly, who had discouraged her from coming. "I'll call when and if I need you. Right now, it's rather chaotic."

"I thrive on chaos."

That was true enough, but Holly won the argument. Marilyn stayed put but had ordered Holly to keep in touch, particularly if she was required to issue a statement to the media. "Before you say anything into a microphone, run it past me."

Dennis, her former boyfriend, had also called on the office line. Mrs. Briggs had spoken to him, assured him that Holly was bearing up well, and agreed to notify him in the event her status changed or if there was anything he could do for her.

However, Holly hadn't been without a coterie of supporters. In a town of only twenty thousand, word of the shooting had spread rapidly. Judge Mason, the administrative judge of the district, had been in the neighboring courtroom at the time of the shooting, so he was immediately at Holly's side. A few friends she had made since moving to Prentiss had rallied around her, aghast over what had happened and eager to help in any way they could.

Most of the time they had been left waiting while she was being interviewed by police. But it had been a comfort just knowing they were accessible if she needed them. Eventually they'd seen the futility of hanging around and had made their departures.

Mrs. Briggs was the last holdout. "I'll be fine," Holly assured her now. "But if it makes you feel better, I'll request a police escort home."

"You absolutely should. And call me if you change your mind. I'll come over at any hour."

Before leaving, she got Holly's promise to do that, although Holly knew she wouldn't be summoning help. It had been a horrific experience, but the culprit was dead. All that remained for her to do was to give her formal statement, and then the ordeal would be over.

In the coming days, Greg Sanders would be watching to see how she responded to the crisis situation and how quickly she recovered from the trauma of it. If she showed any signs of cowardice or weakness, he would gleefully expose it.

Following Crawford Hunt out of the interrogation room, Matt Nugent and Neal Lester made their way down the hallway toward her. They had interviewed her in the Family Court immediately following the shooting, but to record her formal statement, they had asked that she come downstairs to the ground floor where, like the SO, the city police department was also headquartered.

She stood up. "My turn?"

"I'm afraid not, Judge Spencer," Neal Lester said. "We're only taking a break. We've got a lot more to cover with Mr. Hunt."

"I see."

"I know this is a hardship after what happened today. We'll get you out of here as soon as possible."

"I understand."

"One question, though. The suspect's name hasn't been released because we're having trouble locating next of kin, but his driver's license identifies him as Jorge Rodriguez. Ring a bell?"

"No."

"Not surprising," Nugent said, looking happy to have something to contribute. "He had a Texas driver's license, but it's a fake. Fairly good one, but still phony."

"He was an illegal?"

"We're looking into it," Lester replied. "But even if he was, that doesn't mean he hadn't wound up in your court sometime before today."

"It's a possibility. I've only been on the bench for ten months, you know. But the docket has been full. I've presided over a lot of trials and hearings since my appointment."

"Maybe Rodriguez was a holdover from Judge

Waters," Lester suggested. "Held a grudge of some kind."

When her mentor, the Honorable Clifton Waters, was diagnosed with terminal cancer, he had enticed her to resign from a law firm where she had practiced for several years, relocate to Prentiss, and apply for the bench he would be vacating.

It had been a chancy career move, but she'd taken a leap of faith, and it had paid off. Acting on Waters's recommendation, Governor Hutchins had appointed her. Judge Waters had lived long enough to see her sworn in. It had been a proud day for both of them.

Nugent said, "We'll send somebody over to your office tomorrow to look through court records, see if Rodriguez turns up."

"I'll make sure Mrs. Briggs knows you're coming and has everything ready."

"What about before you came here?"

"I was with a law firm in Dallas."

Lester jotted the name down in a small spiral notebook he took from his shirt pocket. "We'll ask them to run Rodriguez's name through their files, too."

She gave him a contact name. "The firm will help any way they can, I'm sure."

Out of the corner of her eye she saw Crawford Hunt emerge from the men's room. His hair was damp and had been pushed straight back off his forehead, as though he'd washed his face and then had run wet fingers through his hair. He seemed intent on walking past her again without speaking. She stepped into his path.

"Mr. Hunt, may I have a word with you?"

Neal Lester held up his hand, "Uh, judge…"

"I won't compare notes with him," she said to the detective. "I wouldn't interfere with your investigation or breech ethics by discussing his custody case. I just need to tell him…" Her breath caught as she turned and looked up into the other man's face, which conveyed all the warmth of an ice carving. "Thank you for saving my life."

The flinty gray eyes registered surprise, but the involuntary reaction lasted for only a millisecond. "The guy was a lousy shot."

Emotion welled up in her throat. "He was accurate enough when he fired at Chet Barker."

The implacable eyes flickered again, and this time one corner of his mouth tensed. "At that range, he couldn't have missed."

"He couldn't have missed me, either, if you hadn't done what you did."

"How do you remember it, Judge Spencer?"

She turned to Neal Lester, who'd asked. "When I saw Chet fall, my first instinct was to run to him, but I froze when the man continued up the aisle toward me. The mask made his face look grotesque, terrifying. Mr. Hunt came over the railing and sort of tackled me.

"I confess that the next few moments are a blur. The shots continued in rapid succession. I remember thinking that he would surely run out of bullets eventually, but I thought for certain that I would be killed before he did. His last shot must have gone into the ceiling. I've still got plaster dust in my hair." She tipped her head down to show them.

"The shot went wild when Crawford kicked him in the knee," Nugent said.

She looked at Crawford Hunt. "You kicked him?"

"Reflex."

Absently she nodded. "The next thing I remember, you were patting down my back. I don't remember what you said."

"I was feeling for blood. I asked if you'd been hit, you said you didn't think so."

"Did I?"

He gave a curt nod.

She turned to the detectives. "Mr. Hunt pushed off me. But not before telling me to stay down."

"But you didn't, did you?"

She replied to Lester's question with a rueful shake of her head. "The courtroom was in chaos. People who'd heard the shots were rushing in through the rear door. Mrs. Gilroy was crying hysterically, as was the court reporter. Mr. Hunt bent over Chet. He took his gun and shouted to another bailiff to summon officers. Then he ran out the side door."

Lester asked, "How much time had transpired between when the gunman ran off and Crawford charged after him?"

"A minute, maybe a little more. Not long."

"What happened next?"

"I can only speak to what was going on inside the courtroom." Glancing up at Crawford Hunt, she added, "I don't know what happened beyond that side exit."

The senior detective said, "We don't, either. Not everything. We were just getting to that when we decided to take a break."

A taut silence followed. Matt Nugent was the first to move. He dug into his pants pocket for change and started walking toward the row of vending machines at the far end of the hall. "Anyone else want a Coke? Judge Spencer?"

"No thank you."

"Mr. Hunt?"

"No."

"Nothing for me." Neal Lester's reply coincided with the chirping of his cell phone. He pulled it from his belt and checked the readout. "Excuse me." He moved a few yards away and turned his back, seeking privacy to take his phone call, and leaving Holly essentially alone with Crawford Hunt.

Besides that being inherently awkward, his physicality was intimidating. His boots added at least an inch and a half to his height, which was well over six feet. He had appeared in court wearing well-pressed blue jeans, a plain white shirt, black necktie, and a sport jacket.

At some point since then, he'd discarded the sport jacket, loosened his tie, unbuttoned his collar, and rolled up his sleeves to just below his elbows. His hair was defying the slick-back treatment he'd given it only minutes ago. Straw-colored and thick, it seemed to have a will of its own.

He went to stand on the other side of the hallway where he leaned with his back against the wall and glared at her. In her view, his animosity was unwarranted.

Trying to break the ice, she said, "Are the Gilroys all right? Your mother-in-law was terribly upset when she was finally allowed to leave the courtroom after being questioned."

"She was shaken up pretty bad. Last I talked to Joe about an hour ago, she still hadn't stopped crying."

"How traumatic it must have been for them."

He gave a grim nod.

"And how is your daughter?"

Visibly he tensed. "She's on a sleepover with a neighbor lady and her granddaughter. I thought it would be best if she spent the night there. She wouldn't understand why Grace and Joe are so upset, and I was tied up here."

Holly didn't miss the deliberate implication that the sleepover had been approved by him, as though he was the decision maker where his daughter was concerned. The angle of his chin challenged her to dispute that.

But at least she had gotten a few words out of him, even if they had been cursory. Believing their conversation was over, she turned her head aside.

"What about you?"

Surprised by the question, she looked back at him.

He said, "You okay?"

She was about to respond with the polite lie she'd been giving her colleagues and friends. *I'm fine, thank you for asking.* That's probably what he expected her to say. But, surprising herself, she gave an uncharacteristic burble of nervous laughter. "Not really, no." Perhaps because they'd shared the experience, she felt she could be honest with him.

His eyes were the only animate part of him as he took her in from head to toe. Meeting her gaze again, he said, "I landed on you hard. Did I hurt you?"

"No." She accompanied her quick answer with a shake of her head.

"What about that?" He hitched his chin.

"What?"

"The bruise."

"Oh." Tentatively she reached up and ran her fingertips over the tender spot just above her eyebrow. "When you pushed me down, my head hit the floor."

"Sorry."

"No apology necessary."

"You have a goose egg."

"Until my assistant called my attention to it, I didn't realize it was there."

"It'll hang on for a while."

"No lasting harm done, though. When I think about what could have been, I begin to lose it."

"Then stop thinking about it."

"Easier said." She held her hands in front of her at waist level, parallel to the floor. "I've tried to keep it from showing, but they won't stop shaking."

"That happens."

"Not to me."

"No?"

"No. Typically I don't scare so easily."

"Today's scare wasn't typical."

"I can't get the image of him out of my mind."

"He was freaky, all right."

"Honestly, Mr. Hunt? I was terrified."

He hesitated a beat, then, speaking barely above a mumble, said, "You held it together when it counted."

It was a veiled compliment, delivered grudgingly, so it seemed inappropriate to thank him for it. But she held his gaze for several seconds, and understanding was established.

Then he made a sound of impatience and gestured toward her hands. "It may be a couple of days before you lose the shakes. That's a normal delayed reaction to a crisis situation."

"Obviously you have more experience than I do with crisis situations." The moment the words were out of her mouth, she realized how ill-chosen they were. The taut skin over his high cheekbones seemed to stretch even tighter. "Mr. Hunt, I didn't mean—"

"Forget it." He cut off her apology in a clipped, cold voice. Pushing himself away from the wall, he turned to Nugent, who was walking toward them carrying a soft drink can in one hand and a package of peanuts in the other.

Crawford Hunt frowned at him. "Are we going to finish this, or what?"

As they resumed their places around the table in the interrogation room, Matt Nugent asked him, "Is that awkward?"

"What?"

"You and the judge. Facing off in court today. Now finding yourselves on common ground. Survivors of a catastrophe."

"We're not on common ground, and despite the catastrophe, I'll be real pissed off if she doesn't award me custody of my daughter. One has nothing to do with the other."

Neal punched the record button on the video camera. "I wouldn't count on that if I were you."

Crawford let the remark pass without comment. He wasn't going to be spurred into talking about his custody petition with Neal Lester.

Nugent relaunched the interrogation. "You told us earlier that when Rodriguez busted in—"

"I said when the 'shooter' busted in."

"Same difference."

"The hell it is," Crawford said. "As Sergeant Lester here will tell you, the devil's in the details. It's my state-ment you're recording, so, let's keep it accurate, please. For the record, I didn't know his name until just now. Rodriguez, you said?"

"Jorge," Nugent supplied.

Neal shot a glare at the younger detective, silently re-buking him for the gaffe, then came back to Crawford. "That information doesn't leave this room."

"Like I didn't know that?"

It seemed to rankle Neal that Crawford was also a law officer. His tone remained brittle. "Do you recog-nize the name?"

"No."

"Ever seen him before you two met on the roof?"

"No. He wasn't even vaguely familiar. Have you asked the judge? The name mean anything to her?"

"She says no," Nugent replied. "But we're going to check her court records and those of the late Judge Waters."

"Could be he held a grudge against her or Waters. Or maybe Rodriguez had a beef with the U.S. justice system in general. Have you checked—"

"We're on it," Neal said tightly.

Crawford got the hint: It wasn't his case. A Texas Ranger had jurisdiction anywhere in the state. He could join an investigation or initiate one without invitation of any other agency, local, state, or federal. But Neal was making it perfectly clear that, from where Crawford was sitting tonight, he was to answer questions, not ask them.

Neal continued, "You said that when *the shooter busted in* you were on the witness stand. Accurate enough?"

"Yes."

"What issue were you and judge addressing?"

"You told me you have a transcript of the hearing."

"We do."

"So…" He looked over at Nugent, who was shaking peanuts into his mouth. "What's unclear, Sergeant Lester?"

"The judge commended you for keeping all your appointments with a therapist."

"Right. She did. What's that got to do with anything?"

"It could have a lot to do with how you reacted to the unfolding situation."

"I don't see how."

"Don't get your back up. I'm just doing my job here."

"Right." He gave Neal an icy stare, then shrugged. "Ask away."

Neal appeared all too happy to oblige. "Why were

you mandated to get counseling before being granted another custody hearing?"

"Did you ask Judge Spencer?"

"Not yet. We plan to."

"Good. I'd like to know the reasons myself."

"Take a wild guess." Neal grinned, but it wasn't friendly.

Crawford divided another look between the two investigators, letting his irritation show. But what would be gained by stonewalling? They would only conclude that he was ashamed of the required therapy sessions. And he was, to some extent. But he didn't want them to know that.

"I didn't cope well with the sudden death of my wife. That was four years ago. Last year, I petitioned to regain custody of Georgia. Judge Waters was the presiding judge. He wanted to make certain that I could provide a stable home environment and required a year of therapy in order to determine that I was past all that."

"Define 'all that.'"

"Drinking more than I should. There were days when it was hard for me even to get out of bed in the morning."

"Classic depression."

"Classic grief." *Asshole.* Crawford was tempted to tack that on, but didn't.

"You shirked your responsibilities at work. The Rangers removed you from the Houston office and placed you here."

"Actually, I requested the transfer. Since the Gilroys lived here, and Georgia was with them, I made the move to be closer to her."

Neal looked skeptical. "Your transfer had nothing to do with the incident in Halcon?"

"By 'incident,' I gather you're referring to taking out

six of the Fuentes drug cartel including the big cheese himself?"

"Plus two law enforcement officers and several by-standers. Your actions there came under careful review."

Nugent stopped munching his snack. The only sound in the room was the soft electronic whirring of the recording equipment.

Crawford ground his jaw, letting his glare speak for him. He'd be damned before he'd go on record defending himself to Neal Lester, the self-righteous jerk.

Eventually he picked up the thread. "You were eventually cleared of any wrongdoing."

"That's right."

"But since then, you've stuck mostly to computer work. Credit card fraud. Insurance fraud. Kiddie porn rings. Things like that."

Crawford had requested to be moved to Prentiss for the reason stated, and he was assigned to work in conjunction with the law enforcement agencies of several surrounding counties. However, Neal was correct. If there was fieldwork involved, he let another Ranger assume it, while his investigations were more often confined to his desk. He refused to comment on it, though.

Neal persisted. "Nothing to say about that?"

"You more or less covered it."

Neal gave a noncommittal grunt. "If I deem it necessary, I may subpoena the therapist's record of your treatment."

That got Crawford's attention. Heat crawled all over him. "That's privileged."

"I could appeal to the court."

"No judge would force her to hand over her record of our sessions because it's irrelevant."

"If it's irrelevant, why not tell me what's in it?"

"I haven't seen it."

"Take a crack at what it contains."

It was difficult to be reminded of the darkest days of his life, to have past transgressions publicly aired. It had happened twice today. It was especially hard to sit and take this shit from Neal Lester.

But he forced himself to assume a nonchalance. "I think the therapist would tell you that I had learned to control my anger over losing Beth, that I had gotten a grip on the alcohol abuse, the depression, etcetera."

"I wouldn't be asking," Neal said smoothly, "except that it's germane to this investigation."

His abuse of authority angered Crawford as nothing else could have. "Germane my ass, Neal. You're trying to humiliate me, that's all. What I think, you're still pissed off because I felt up your sister."

Nugent gulped with astonishment.

Neal said nothing, but his eyes shot daggers.

Instantly regretful, Crawford sighed as he pushed his fingers through his hair. "That was a cheap shot. You're a prick, Neal, and you deserved it. But your sister didn't."

To his surprise, Neal actually smiled, but nastily. "I would expect no less from you. Besides, you're sitting there, and I'm sitting here. I've been placed in charge of investigating this fatal shooting incident, and it's up to you to convince me."

His tone set Crawford's teeth on edge. "Convince you of what?"

"That you were in a sound and stable state of mind when you confronted Jorge Rodriguez on the roof of the courthouse, and that your actions in no way contributed to his getting killed."

Chapter 4

———◆———

The front door was opened before Crawford could ring the bell. "Mrs. Amberson?"

"Hello, Mr. Hunt. Joe called. I was watching for you. Come in."

"Thanks for this. I'm sorry to bother you so late."

"No bother, and please call me Susan."

The Gilroys' neighbor looked younger than the title *grandmother* implied. Susan Amberson was trim, attractive, and smiled cordially as she stood aside and motioned him into the cheery entryway of her home.

She said, "After what happened today, I can understand why you'd want to see Georgia."

"Experiencing something like that…"

When he trailed off, she finished for him. "Makes you want to touch base with people you love." She smiled at him with complete understanding. "I've watched the news stories about it. Tragic. I don't know if Grace will ever recover."

"I haven't seen her yet. I came straight here after Joe said you'd agreed to let me stop by. I apologize for keeping you up."

"Frank's already in bed, but I'm a night owl. No problem at all."

Crawford assumed the referred-to Frank was her

husband. He was glad he wouldn't be required to make small talk with anyone else and was grateful to Susan Amberson for not pressing him for details about the events of the day as she led him down a center hallway toward the back of the one-story house.

"Thank you for watching Georgia all day," he said. "I hope she wasn't any trouble."

"None at all. She's a darling girl. Uses her manners."

"Good to hear. What's your granddaughter's name?"

"Amy. I tuckered the two of them out."

He followed her into a bedroom illuminated by a small lamp on the nightstand between twin beds. His heart constricted when he saw Georgia's mop of blond curls and her sweet face. Her lips were bowed. She was breathing through them.

"She snores," he said, his voice rough with emotion.

Sensing his embarrassment, she touched his arm briefly. "Take all the time you like."

She withdrew and Crawford moved to the bed where Georgia slept. In the other was a little girl of similar age and size, but his attention belonged entirely to his daughter as he gingerly sat down on the edge of the bed. Mr. Bunny, the stuffed toy she wouldn't sleep without, lay in the crook of her elbow.

For several moments, he simply stared into her face; then he reached for a lock of hair and rubbed the curl between his fingers. Her lips made a sucking motion, then she swiped her cheek with the back of her hand and opened her eyes.

Sleepily she blinked him into focus. "Daddy!"

"Shh, don't wake up your friend."

She sat up to receive his hug and return it. "Have you come to get me? Is it tomorrow yet?"

"Not yet. I just wanted to stop in and see how you were doing."

"Good." Yawning broadly, she lay back down and nestled the back of her head into the pillow.

"You like your new playmate? Amy."

"Um-huh. She's nice. We had a tea party and got to dress up in Miss Susan's hats. I wore beads, too."

"Yeah? How'd the cookies turn out?"

"We sprinkled sugar on top. Mine were pink." She yawned again. "Do you want to sleep with me?"

"I don't think we would fit on this bed."

"You're too big."

"Me? You and Mr. Bunny are taking up all the space." He poked her lightly in the belly, and she giggled. "I'll see you tomorrow. Go back to sleep, but give me a kiss first." He leaned down. She wrapped her arms around his neck and kissed him on the cheek.

"Good night, Daddy. I love you."

"'Night, sweetheart. I love you, too."

She rolled onto her side and closed her eyes. He waited until she was softly snoring again before reluctantly tiptoeing from the room.

———

Five minutes later, he joined his father-in-law in the Gilroys' kitchen. Even at this late hour, Joe was fully dressed and spit-polished. He had served three tours in Viet Nam flying F4s. At the end of the war, he'd left the air force. But the air force had never completely left him.

He motioned toward the coffeemaker on the counter. "Help yourself."

"No thanks."

"Since I know I won't sleep anyhow, I thought I had just as well have some."

They sat down across from each other at the dining table. Crawford said, "Grace went to bed?"

"Finally. I had to slip her a mickey. I ground up a pain pill she had left over from that ear infection. Spiked her chamomile tea with it."

"Can't hurt."

"Knocked her out."

"That's what she needed."

"Did you go by the Ambersons' house?"

"Just left there. Georgia woke up only long enough to kiss me good night. I'm not sure she'll remember that I was there. But it did me good to see her."

"You meet Frank?"

"Just Susan. Nice lady."

"They're good people."

The conversation stalled there. This was the way it had been since Beth had first introduced him to her dad. Once he and Joe exhausted chitchat about the weather and everyone's health, they never seemed to have anything else to talk about.

While married to Beth, Crawford had gone out of his way to be friendly and easygoing around Joe, even pretending an interest in his hobby of carpentry. But eventually, he'd accepted that he and his father-in-law would never be chums, and he was fine with letting their relationship remain civil and neutral.

Certainly for as long as Georgia had been in the Gilroys' custody, Crawford had done nothing to provoke Joe, to tip that delicate balance between them, to give Joe a reason to limit his access to her.

But now, sitting in the homey kitchen, without Grace's diplomacy acting as a buffer, he felt the brunt of Joe's hostility toward him.

"You talk to your cop friends?"

Crawford wanted to disabuse him of the notion that he would receive preferential treatment because he was a law enforcement officer himself. "As you know, Neal

Lester is the lead investigator. He and a guy new to me, named Nugent, took my statement. They knew most of it already and only wanted details from my perspective."

"Like what?"

"Like I didn't know you could move that fast."

"Excuse me?"

"When the guy came in shooting, you reacted with remarkable speed and agility."

"I guess my two-mile walk every day keeps me limber."

"Guess so. Lucky for you and Grace."

"He wasn't aiming at us." Joe pushed back his chair and got up to pour himself a refill of coffee. He returned to the table, but once he'd set the mug on it, he didn't touch it again. "What happened up there?"

Crawford knew that "up there" referred to the roof of the courthouse. "I haven't been near a TV, but I suppose it's been a big news story. Your neighbor Susan remarked on it. What's being reported?"

"That you were trying to talk the guy into surrendering. But that when he realized he was surrounded and fired at a deputy sheriff, SWAT team snipers took him down."

"That's pretty much it."

"The TV people are playing up the fact that you're a Texas Ranger."

"I'm a computer geek with a Ranger's badge."

"To hear them tell it, you're a hero."

"I don't look at it that way."

"Neither do I."

Joe had gradually been working up a lather, so that by the time he said those last three words, he was seething. He turned his head, listened for a moment, as though to make sure that Grace was still in the bedroom asleep, then came back around to Crawford.

But before his father-in-law could speak, Crawford went on the offensive. "Since I came through the door, you've been building up to something, Joe. Let's have it."

"You took it upon yourself to play John Wayne."

"I went after a man armed with a semiautomatic pistol who threatened the lives of everybody inside that building. Was I supposed to just stand by and let him walk out of there?"

"That building is crawling with officers of every kind, all day, every day."

"Well, the only officer immediately on hand was Chet, and he was dead."

"What did you say to the shooter?"

Crawford had spent the last several hours answering Neal's questions about that encounter. He resented getting the third degree about it now from his father-in-law. On the other hand, he hoped to avoid creating a rift with Joe and recognized the value of treading lightly.

"I'll be happy to recount it for you later, Joe, but right now I'm bushed. Thank you for arranging my visit with Georgia. I needed to see her. I also wanted to check on Grace. Now that I know they're tucked in and all right, I'm going home to my own bed."

When he pushed back his chair and stood up, so did Joe. He said, "It's time we took the gloves off."

Crawford raised an eyebrow.

"You know what I'm talking about," Joe said.

"Yeah, I know what you're talking about. But you've had years to get things off your chest, and you chose tonight? *Now*? Lousy timing, Joe. Can't your grievances keep for at least one more day?"

"No, because I don't want to be blamed later for not giving you fair warning."

"Of?"

The older man propped his hands on his hips in the stance of a victor. "You played my ace for me today. You scored a goal for the opposing team." He gave a short laugh. "I've been trying to come up with a way to beat you on this thing, and damned if you didn't do it for me."

"This thing being the custody dispute?"

"What *dispute*?" he sneered. "There won't be a dispute after your grandstanding today."

"I wasn't grandstanding. I was trying to prevent—"

"What you did was take a loaded weapon off a fallen officer and chase after a crazy man. Those courthouse employees that you encountered on your way up to the roof? They interviewed two of them on TV. Neither saw the man in white, but both said you scared the bejesus out of them."

Crawford turned toward the door. "Tell Grace I'll check on her in the morning."

"Hear me out."

Crawford came back around.

"I didn't like you from the minute Beth brought you to meet us."

"That's not exactly a news flash."

"I disliked you on sight."

"On sight? Why? You didn't even know me, so what did you have against me? That I was younger and stronger than you? Mr. Top Gun suddenly had competition for Beth's affection?"

"I saw right off that you weren't a man I would want to command."

"No," Crawford said. "What you saw right off was that I was a man you *couldn't* command. That's why you formed an instant dislike."

"Beth saw dashing and daring. I saw reckless. And I was right. Your recklessness got her killed."

Crawford had said as much to himself during booze-fueled self-analyses. More recently, he'd confessed his corrosive guilt to the therapist. But it was devastating to hear the words from his father-in-law's mouth and to know with certainty that, although he and Grace hadn't openly condemned him, they held him responsible for the loss of their only child.

Joe aimed his index finger at him. "Your derring-do robbed me of my daughter, but it's going to win me custody of my granddaughter. Permanent custody this time. I'm going to fight you tooth and nail. And, after your antics today, I'm assured a win."

———————

By the time the detectives finished interviewing Crawford Hunt, Holly was already exhausted just from sitting and awaiting her turn. Then she was in the interrogation room for an hour, giving her official statement and providing detailed answers to their questions, many of which related to Mr. Hunt's actions. It was nearing two a.m. when she finally arrived home.

As she'd promised Mrs. Briggs, she requested a police escort home, and, actually, she was grateful for the pair of officers who followed her in their patrol car, then walked her to her back door and saw her inside.

She lived in the guesthouse of a secluded two-acre estate belonging to a friend of the late Judge Waters. The cottage was quaint, charming, and surrounded by lush landscaping. Tall azalea bushes and dense ever-green hedges separated it from the main house, partially screened it from the street, and kept her backyard completely obscured.

Ordinarily she relished the privacy the place afforded, but as she bade the officers good-bye, she would have preferred, for tonight only, having neighbors close by. Feeling on edge and vulnerable, she shot the bolt on the back door, then went through the rooms checking closets and behind interior doors to ensure that no masked man in white coveralls was lying in wait. Her search yielded nothing, of course, and she ridiculed herself for being such a 'fraidy cat.

He's dead.

Nevertheless, no matter how many times she repeated that to herself, the image of distorted features behind a clear mask stayed with her, and she knew it would for a long time.

Still nervous, she reconsidered calling Mrs. Briggs, but talked herself out of it. She would insist on coming over, and that would make Holly feel like a ninny.

Calling Marilyn was another option. Even at this hour, she would probably be up. But Holly lacked the energy to engage with Marilyn tonight, who was overbearing even at the best of times.

In the end, she didn't phone anyone. Her fear was unrealistic. Nevertheless, she showered with the stall door open, even though it was made of clear glass. Dressed for bed, she went into the kitchen and found a bottle of whiskey in the cupboard, one Dennis had left behind. Ordinarily she didn't drink anything as strong as bourbon, but she couldn't think of an occasion that better called for hard liquor.

After making certain that all the windows and doors were locked, she took the tumbler of whiskey to bed with her, where she propped herself against the pillows and gratefully sipped it.

Jorge Rodriguez. She searched her memory for even a spark of recollection. It would be a relief to attribute the man's shooting spree to a grudge over a ruling that either she or Judge Waters had made. Finding even a tangential connection between her and Rodriguez, any fragmented reason for retribution, would have provided some closure.

As of now, however, the motive for the attempted assassination remained unknown, and that was unsettling. Even if her own peace of mind didn't require an explanation, the voting public would. Her constituents would wish to know what was behind the courthouse tragedy and if it related to her.

She had little doubt that Sanders would use it, twist and manipulate it, to discredit her. Tonight, he was probably awake, too, preparing his onslaught of open criticism and innuendo. He would want to attack while the incident was fresh, possibly launching it as early as tomorrow.

With that in mind, she finished the last of the whiskey, set the glass on the nightstand, and reached for the lamp switch. But she hesitated and momentarily considered sleeping with the light on. Just for tonight. Then, chiding herself for the silliness, she extinguished the light with a decisive snap.

But as she did so, she noticed that her hands were still shaking. The bourbon hadn't soothed her, but rather seemed to have magnified her memories of the gunman, made the images of him more distinct and frightening.

She lay tense and wakeful, her senses highly attuned.

So that when she heard the noise coming from the backyard, she sprang upright, heart racing with fear.

Chapter 5

A curtain was pushed aside, and her face appeared in the window. Automatically she reached for the switch plate.

"Don't turn on the light." He spoke only loud enough to make himself heard through the windowpane.

"What are you doing here?"

"Open the door."

"Are you insane?"

"The court-appointed shrink didn't think so. Now unlock the door."

Crawford waited with diminishing patience while she wrestled with the decision. Finally she slid the bolt, flipped the button on the knob, and opened up. He slipped inside, closed the door behind him, and pulled the curtain back into place. When he turned toward her, she took a cautionary step back.

"Relax, judge."

"I don't think so, Mr. Hunt."

"If I was here to do you bodily harm, would I have knocked?"

Behind her was an open doorway through which he could see into the living room. On the far side of it was a short hallway that he figured led to the bedrooms. A nightlight glowed from the baseboard in the hall. It cast only enough light into the kitchen to keep them from bumping into the furniture.

"Are you here alone?"

"It's four o'clock in the morning."

He brought his gaze back to her. "Are you alone?"

She hesitated, then bobbed her head once.

"Who lives in the main house?"

"An eighty-something-year-old widow."

"By herself?"

"Three cats."

"No caregiver? Nurse?"

"She insists on living alone, but having someone nearby is a comfort to her as well as to her family. She was a friend of Judge Waters. Knowing I needed a place to live, he suggested the arrangement, and it's worked out well for both of us."

He couldn't see a reason for her to lie about the occupant of the stately, southern Greek revival house. A genteel but independent widow living out her days with three cats was too clichéd not to be the truth.

He relaxed somewhat and took a closer look at the judge. Gone was the severe ponytail she'd worn in court. Her hair was hanging loose to her collarbone. Under his scrutiny, she self-consciously hooked it behind her ears. "I'll ask again. What are you doing here?"

"Were you asleep?"

"Yes."

Knowing she was lying, he just looked at her.

After several seconds, she sighed. "I tried to sleep but couldn't keep my mind off the shooting."

"Whose whiskey?"

"What?" Following his line of sight, she looked over at the bottle on the counter. "Mine."

"I doubt it."

"All right, a friend left it—"

"What friend?"

"—and I'm glad he did—"

"He?"

"—because I needed it tonight." With asperity, she straightened her spine. "I don't have to explain a damn thing to you, Mr. Hunt, but you've got a hell of a lot to explain to me. Like what you're doing here and how you knew where I live."

"I'm not a Texas Ranger for nothing."

"Don't be cute."

"Wasn't trying to be. Took me eight years as a trooper before I could even apply."

While she fumed, he took a more thorough look around the kitchen. There were the usual small appliances on the counter, an African violet in the window above the sink, a small dining table with only two chairs. Compact and scrupulously tidy. Nothing fussy. About what he would expect.

"How long have you lived here?" he asked.

"Since the day I came to town."

"From Dallas, right?" He cocked an eyebrow. "City girl gone country?"

Annoyed by that, she said, "I'll ask you one more time. What are you doing here?"

"That was going to be my next question to you. Why here?"

"I told you. The widow—"

"I mean why Prentiss? Why our humble burg here on the edge of a swamp?"

"When Judge Waters's health forced him to step down from the bench, he encouraged me to apply to be his replacement."

"Out of all the legal eagles vying for that appointment, he encouraged you. Why?"

When she hesitated to answer, he realized he'd tapped into a touchy subject. With obvious reluctance she said, "He'd known me since I was born. He and my father were good friends."

"Huh."

"What does that 'huh' imply?"

"Favoritism?"

"You should be campaigning for Greg Sanders."

"That loudmouth? No thanks."

"He does like to crow. His credentials are unimpressive and his platform shaky, so he's resorted to mudslinging. According to him, I'm too young and inexperienced."

"Well, he does have twenty years on you."

"Then his record should outshine mine. It doesn't."

He started ticking off her accomplishments. "First in your class in law school. Straight out of it, you were snatched up by that high-dollar family law firm in Dallas. Made partner in no time flat. Won notoriety for handling that hockey player's divorce. Got his ex a bundle in the settlement."

"You did your homework."

"Did I leave out anything?"

"I was hall monitor in seventh grade."

"I missed that. But it doesn't surprise me. You personify overachiever. Still, Sanders and others are thinking you only got that gubernatorial appointment because you were Judge Waters's fair-haired child." Again, his gaze wandered over the light strands framing her face. "Stating the obvious would be too easy."

She stiffened her backbone again. "The governor made up his own mind. In any case, I'm not going to debate this with you, Mr. Hunt. In November, I'll be elected on merit."

Their encounter earlier tonight in the hallway of the

police station had been the first time he'd seen her without the black robe she'd worn into court. She'd been dressed in a gray pants suit and a blue blouse, a tailored, no-frills outfit in keeping with her profession, something a sober lady judge would wear under her robe of office.

But for all the severity of her suit, he'd been surprised then by how much smaller she looked without the robe. Now, barefoot, wearing a faded, oversize t-shirt and an unbelted cotton robe, she looked even more diminutive. Without the trappings of judgeship, there wasn't much to her.

But there was no shortage of authority in her bearing or tone of voice. "You still haven't told me why you came here, Mr. Hunt."

His gaze was reluctant to leave the hem of the t-shirt that didn't quite reach her bare knees, but he forced it to. "I want to ask you some questions, and I don't trust phones. To say nothing of phone records."

"Records or not, you and I shouldn't be speaking privately."

"Why not? Afraid we'll get in trouble with Neal? Or are you intimidated by Nugent? A hard-nosed detective if ever I saw one."

Ignoring the insult toward the younger officer, she said, "They're conducting an investigation. We could unintentionally influence each other's account of what happened today."

"They took your statement, right?"

"Yes."

"And I gave them mine. We told our stories and we didn't compare notes beforehand. It's okay for us to talk about it now."

"Possibly. But in regard to your custody hearing, it's unethical for us to talk privately. Don't you realize that by coming here, you've compromised—"

"How were you going to decide today? Me or my in-laws?"

She looked him in the eye for several seconds, then lowered her gaze to somewhere in the vicinity of his collar button. "I don't know."

"Bullshit."

Her reestablishment of eye contact was sudden and angry. "*Not* bullshit, Mr. Hunt. I was going to give everything said in court today careful review before rendering a decision."

He placed his right hand over his heart. "Lady justice is nothing if not fair."

With obvious vexation, she took a firmer stance, which was hard to pull off with bare feet. "Precisely. I *am* fair. I wouldn't want to make a decision that could possibly damage your daughter's—"

"Her name is Georgia."

"Georgia's welfare. She is my main concern. Not you, not her grandparents. Georgia. My hope is that your relationship with the Gilroys will remain amicable, that both parties will graciously accept the outcome of the proceedings. Any resultant animosity could have an adverse effect on Georgia. Everyone, especially the court, wants to avoid that. Which is why arguments for both sides should be carefully weighed, looked at from every angle, and deliberated long and hard before a ruling is handed down."

He didn't say anything for a time. Then, "Rousing speech, judge. A real rah-rah. You should save it for a campaign fund-raiser. But I'm not buying a damn word of it, especially the part about deliberating long and hard. You had made up your mind about my petition before you came into that courtroom today, hadn't you?"

"No."

He made a skeptical sound.

"Fine. Believe what you want." She pointed toward the door. "But do it somewhere else. Please go."

"Or what?"

"Or I'll call the police."

Technically, he was the police, but he huffed a laugh. "Not a chance. Bad publicity. Bad for your campaign. More negative attention drawn to you after today?" He shook his head. "Un-huh. Your rival Sanders, Governor Hutchins, people in general are already speculating on whether or not the shooting was your fault."

As though he'd literally struck her below the belt, she protectively crossed her arms over her middle and tucked her hands beneath her elbows. "Don't say that."

Clearly she'd already considered the possibility that she was somehow responsible, and it bothered her greatly. But he couldn't soft-soap this to spare her feelings. The stakes for him were too high. When the investigation into the shooting incident was laid to rest, he wanted there to be no misgivings about the action he'd taken today. If there were, he didn't have a chance in hell of getting Georgia back.

So he pressed. "Did Jorge Rodriguez have a beef with you?"

"Not that I'm aware of."

"Come on, judge. It's just you and me now."

"You're suggesting that I lied to the police?"

"Everybody lies to the police."

"I don't. I had never heard of Jorge Rodriguez until tonight. Why would I lie about it?"

"That's easy. In November you want to be elected on merit. If there's something really ugly—"

"Get—"

"—you wouldn't want it exposed when we're coming up on voting season."

"—out!"

"No scandal involving an illegal, then?"

"No!"

Nugent had disclosed that she claimed not to recognize the suspect's name, but Crawford had wanted to gauge her truthfulness for himself. If she was lying, she was damn good at it. He didn't detect any of the classic giveaways.

She was, however, raging mad, and, despite his chest-thumping of a few minutes ago, if she ordered him to leave, he would have to go.

"Okay then," he said, "you didn't know Rodriguez. So why'd he do it?"

Some of the starch went out of her. Wearily she shook her head, dislodging the hair that she'd hooked behind her ear. She took a deep breath, which shifted the topography under her t-shirt, making him aware of it.

"I have no idea," she said softly. "I wish I did."

Dragging himself back on track, he said, "According to Neal and Nugent, they questioned dozens of people, and nobody claims to have seen Rodriguez before he entered your court. Even without the mask, he would have been noticed roaming the courthouse dressed in painter's overalls."

She raised her hands at her sides to indicate that she was clueless.

He continued. "It's reasonable to assume that he was familiar with the building. For starters, he knew there are no security cameras except at the entrances and exits. He also knew he could bring a pistol in with him." Dryly he added, "I'll bet the budget for heightened security will be approved now."

"I was surprised when I moved here and learned that there wasn't a metal screening at the entrance."

"It's always been voted down in favor of spending on something else."

"Unfortunately for Chet."

"Yeah."

"Could he have been the intended target?" she asked.

"I seriously doubt it. I've known him since I was a kid. He was the first black deputy in this county. Did you know that?"

She shook her head.

"Spent most of his career serving as bailiff." Reflecting on the man, he heard himself say, "He winked at me."

"What?"

"I just now remembered. After swearing me in, as he was turning away, he gave me a little wink."

She smiled. "That sounds like him. Although, strictly speaking, as a court official, he shouldn't have been showing any partiality."

"No. But it meant a lot to me." They said nothing for several moments. Then, shaking off the melancholy that had settled over him, he said, "Anyway, I can't imagine Chet Barker having an enemy in the world. I think he just got in the way."

"Of me," she said in a quiet voice. "You think I was the target, don't you?"

Her doleful expression implored him for an honest answer, but he let his silence speak for him, and the logical conclusion noticeably upset her. She turned her head aside and pulled her lower lip through her teeth in obvious distress.

"Look," he said, "it's all conjecture at this point. Even if you were his target, for whatever twisted reason, he can't hurt you now."

"All the same, I would like to know what I did, or didn't do, that made him want to kill me. What did I do to provoke payback that extreme?"

"Could be you had nothing to do with it."

"You just said you thought I was the target."

"No I didn't. *You* did. But maybe Rodriguez, or whatever his name was, wasn't motivated by you, the court, or anything that we can put a label on. Maybe he was just a head case whose hobby was killing small animals. It was only a matter of time before he graduated to human beings, and the courthouse made for good theater."

"Especially the final act."

"Especially the final act. He got the attention he sought. Which is why local politicians, the media, and the public will be asking questions, and the police will be scrambling to provide satisfactory answers. They'll have to justify taking him out the way they did."

"*Was* it justified?"

"I had identified myself as a law officer and ordered him to put down the weapon. He not only refused, he fired two shots at a uniformed officer, and he probably would have gone on firing if those SWAT officers hadn't stopped him. No, judge, it went down the way it had to. It's just…"

He thought back on those fateful moments. although measured in time by mere seconds, it had been a history-changing, life-ending event. He'd been there. He'd witnessed the whole thing. Yet he still didn't understand why that young man had placed himself in such a near-perfect situation to get killed.

His consternation must have been apparent, because the judge's expression invited him to share what was on his mind, and before he knew he was going to, he did. "I wish I could have had a few more seconds with him, you know? Maybe I could have talked him into putting down the pistol. Or I could have convinced the deputy to back away and let me handle it. Or—"

"Or you could have been killed."

That statement snapped him back into the present, and to her, and to the reason he'd come here in the first place. "Right. I could have been killed. Which makes me sorry I went after him in the first place. But I did. And because I did, I'm in the big thick middle of it, and I don't want to be. I've been through a mess like this once before." He paused for emphasis. "As you well know."

She looked down at the floor. "It's an unfortunate circumstance for you, and I'm sorry over it."

"Oh, I'm sure you're all torn up."

Hearing in his tone that he meant just the opposite, she raised her head and looked at him. "Why do you doubt it?"

"Because my being gung-ho today gives you the perfect out."

"I don't know what you mean."

"Sure you do." He advanced on her a step. "If you had to rule on my petition right now, this second, would you award me custody of Georgia?"

She parted her lips to speak, but nothing came out.

"That's what I thought," he said with a snicker. "After today, you can deny me custody of my little girl and walk away with a clear conscience."

His conclusion angered her. "After this," she said, passing her hand back and forth between the two of them, "I won't even be deciding your case. I'll have to recuse myself and give it over to another judge."

"Even better. You can wash your hands of the whole thing." He made a show of dusting his hands. "While I will have to start all over with a new judge. More therapy, probably. More bullshit, definitely. And more time without Georgia."

"Which is no fault of mine," she said, raising her voice to match the level of his. "*You* were the one who dictated all that inconvenience to yourself when you showed up at my back door."

She was right, of course, but he'd be damned before conceding. "Okay, since you're out of it, you can tell me what your decision would have been."

"I told you before—"

"That you don't know."

"That's right."

"Like hell you don't. While you were flipping through my 'file,' pretending to ponder your decision, you already knew what you were going to say. Right? *Right?*"

"I don't know what my decision would have been, and how dare you come here demanding to know."

"I'm demanding it because I've been put on notice by my father-in-law."

That brought her up short. She paused long enough to take several quick breaths. "Notice?"

"Joe told me tonight that he plans to fight my petition in earnest. He's proclaimed us enemies. We're no longer—How did you put it? 'Amicable'? Screw that. It's gloves off. War officially declared. If that's the way he wants to play it, fine. But I want to know from you if I'm going to be wasting my time—to say nothing of attorney's fees—engaging in a battle that I've already lost."

"I'm sure he was just overwrought."

"Jet jockey Joe? Un-huh. He doesn't get overwrought."

"He would today. Mr. Hunt, anything said in the aftermath of what we experienced this afternoon should be tempered—"

"Dammit, I hate that."

"What?"

"You talking to me like you're sitting behind a podium, robe zipped up, a goddamn gavel in hand.

Tell me straight out, no fancy talk, no legalese. Just one person to another. Were you going to rule in favor of them or me?"

"We'll discuss it—"

"Now! Now is when we're going to discuss it. Was I gonna win or lose?"

"I can't—"

"*Tell me!*"

"Stop bullying me!"

Her voice cracked on her shout, and it shocked him into silence.

"You weren't the only one affected today," she cried out in that same creaky voice. "I'm sorry for your situation. Truly, I am. I'm sorry that my kind, genial, and well-meaning bailiff, who you knew since you were a kid and winked at you, died protecting me. I'm sorry that your mother-in-law can't stop crying. I'm sorry that I don't know what prompted that man to do what he did, and if his motive has some connection to me, I'm even sorrier about that."

She leaned back against the counter and used both fists to wipe tears off her cheeks. Then she opened her hands and stared down at her palms. "I'm also sorry that I can't stop shaking, and that I seriously considered sleeping with the light on tonight, showing a cowardly streak I didn't even know I had."

Choking up entirely, she paused to swallow several times, taking hard gulps of air. "But the man in the mask was horrifying, and it was awful to see Chet die, and—" She covered her face with her hands and began to sob.

"Aw *shit*," Crawford muttered. He slid his hands into the back pockets of his jeans and left her to wallow in several moments of heavy crying. Finally, he said, "Hey. Don't do that."

"I can't help it."

"Yeah, you can."

"No I can't. I was so afraid. Not just for me, but for…for…"

"Come on now, stop crying."

"—for all of us. He was so—"

"Scary. I know. I was scared, too."

"No, you weren't."

"Hell I wasn't."

She continued to cry into her hands.

"Try not to think about it anymore, okay?"

She nodded but she didn't stop weeping.

Removing his hands from his pockets, he pulled a paper napkin from the holder on the dining table. "Here. Wipe your eyes." She didn't see the napkin he extended her, so he walked over and gently nudged her arm. "Use this."

Blindly she groped for the napkin with one hand, then held it against her eyes. But her crying didn't abate; in fact, the wracking sobs increased.

Uncomfortable with the situation, Crawford shifted his weight from one foot to the other. "Come on now. This isn't helping anything. Get it together."

"I'm trying. I can't."

"Everything's okay." He moved a step closer and lightly placed his hands on her shoulders. Patting them, he said, "It's all right."

"I know, but—"

"You're safe. We're all safe. Hear me? *Safe*."

His soothing words must have reached her because a few seconds later, her neck went boneless, and her head dropped forward. She hiccupped into the damp napkin, used it to blot her eyes and wipe her nose, then lowered her hands from her face. "I'm sorry."

"No problem. Better now?"

She nodded and when she did, her forehead brushed against his chest and then rested there. His hands stilled on her shoulders, then moved to encircle her neck, his fingertips gently kneading the back of it. She set her hands at his waist and leaned into him. A deep inhale caused her whole body to shudder.

"Shh." He hugged her closer and sent his fingers up into her hair until he was cupping the back of her head in his hand. His other slid down her back and began stroking her spine. On one downward trip, it slid past the small of her back and settled on the curve of her hip. And stayed there.

Suddenly neither of them was breathing.

After what seemed an endless time of absolute stillness, she tilted her head up.

Crawford looked down into her brimming green eyes and thought, *Oh fuck.*

Chapter 6

Crawford growled into his cell phone, "Yeah?"

"It's Neal Lester. I need to talk to you."

Crawford pried open his eyes only wide enough to read the clock on his nightstand and was surprised to see that it was after ten. "About what?"

"Were you asleep?"

"That's what you called to ask me?"

"Don't be a smart-ass."

Crawford rolled onto his back and placed his forearm over his eyes. "I had a rough night. That happens after seeing two men gunned down. I'm funny that way."

All of yesterday's events came crashing into his mind. The last in that pileup of disturbing recollections was of him having carnal knowledge of Judge Holly Spencer.

He pressed his thumb and middle finger into his eye sockets and stifled a groan. *Christ.*

Neal asked, "How soon can you be up and dressed?"

"Depends. Why?"

"I'll tell you when I get there."

An instant later Crawford was holding a dead phone. Swearing, he struggled to sit up and swung his feet to the floor, propped his elbows on his knees, and held his face in his hands as he prayed that he had only dreamed that erotic interlude with Her Honor. But then memories of it began to crystallize, taking on shape, sound, and substance.

Her. Him. Ignition. Blast-off.

His doorbell pealed. He dropped his hands between his knees. "You have *got* to be kidding me." The bell rang again. He pulled on his underwear and stamped through his house to the front door, jerked it open, scowled.

"I was parked at the curb when I called." Neal hitched his thumb over his shoulder at the unmarked sedan. "May I come in?"

Crawford turned his back and stalked away, but left the door standing open. Neal asked, "Where are you going?"

"To pee."

Crawford didn't look back, leaving his unwelcome guest to his own devices. He used the toilet and splashed cold water on his face. He picked up yesterday's jeans from off the floor beside the bed where he'd shucked them in the wee hours. He was still buttoning up when he reentered the living room.

Neal had closed the door but had remained standing just in front of it. In stark contrast to Crawford's rumpled appearance, he was a paragon of neatness—hair carefully parted, clothes wrinkle-free, shoes shined, so closely shaven, his face reflected light.

Crawford said, "Kitchen's this way."

By the time Neal joined him, he had the coffeemaker's water tank filled and was scooping grounds into the filter. Rudely, he asked, "What, Neal?"

"The ME said if we want to view the body before he performs the autopsy, we'd better get over there."

Crawford's hands were momentarily arrested in motion, then he dumped the last scoopful of grounds, clicked the filter basket into place, and punched the start button on the machine. Only then did he turn around. He gave Neal a once over. "Huh."

"What?"

"You don't look like a man who's lost his mind. But I think you must have. You spent hours last night doing everything you possibly could to piss me off, then you show up this morning and pretend we're partners? Get out of my house."

Neal's mouth formed a thin, grim line that barely moved as he said, "It wasn't my idea to bring you in. The request came from the chief himself."

"If he wants a Ranger, have him call the Tyler office, see who's available. I requested a few days off, and my major said I could take all the time I needed."

"I know, but the chief said—"

"You got the perp. All that's left to do is ID him, and you don't need me for that. I'm going back to bed. Or maybe I'll go for a long run or a swim. I'll clip my toenails. The one thing I'm *not* doing is accompanying you to the morgue to look at your dead guy."

"I figured you would say that."

"You figured right."

"Hear me out before you refuse."

"I already refused."

"The chief thought maybe you'd recognize Rodriguez if you got a better look at him."

"He was a total stranger to me until our standoff on the roof. I didn't recognize him yesterday. I won't today. Bye."

"The chief says it won't hurt for you to look at him again."

"Won't help, either."

"We won't know that for certain until you do. You didn't see Rodriguez close up. If you do, it might joggle a memory."

"It won't. And I've got other things to do."

Actually, he didn't. He had an outing with Georgia planned for later this afternoon, but until then, he was at loose ends. But under any circumstances, he wanted nothing to do with an investigation under Neal Lester's direction. If the local PD wanted the Texas Rangers' help, they could get another one. The sooner he distanced himself from yesterday's incident—incidents—the better.

However, true to form, Neal was taking his job as the police chief's messenger boy seriously. He remained standing in the center of the kitchen, looking pained but stubbornly duty-bound. Crawford turned away to take a mug from the cabinet. "Want coffee?"

After an abrupt *no thanks*, Neal said, "We've been unable to confirm that Rodriguez is his real name."

"That's a problem, all right."

"His prints weren't flagged."

"No priors, then."

"No. But he had a fake ID. No green card, work visa, nothing like that in his wallet. He had less than thirty dollars cash, no credit cards. No cell phone. In this day and age, it's practically unheard of not to have a cell phone."

"Unless you're someone who doesn't want to be captured by police with one in your possession."

"You said you didn't think he spoke English very well."

"That was only a guess. He might have been fluent and was just pretending not to understand me. Maybe he was so jumpy that his knowledge of *inglés* deserted him. A man trying to pull off such a boneheaded stunt wouldn't be thinking clearly or intelligently."

"Why do you think it was a boneheaded stunt?"

Crawford cocked his eyebrow. "You don't?"

"Of course I do. But I'd like to hear why you think so."

"You haven't got that much time."

"Look, be an asshole. That's what I expect from you. I'm not here because I want to be. Believe me."

"Oh, I believe you, Neal. You look downright constipated."

"But as long as I was sent on this errand, you could give me something to take back to the chief."

Crawford was about to tell him that he didn't care if he had only his dick in his hand when he returned to the chief, but the coffeemaker was just now beginning to burble. As long as he had to wait on it, he thought, *What the hell*, and decided to air something that had been puzzling him.

"The guy has just gunned down a man in front of witnesses."

"Right."

"He's fleeing the scene of a capital crime."

"Right."

"Why go to the roof?"

"Because two law enforcement agencies are located on the building's first floor." The matching annexes for the PD and sheriff's office were connected to the first floor of the courthouse, extending back from each side of it to form a large letter U.

Crawford said, "Even so, going down is a much better option than the roof, where there's only one means of escape. And another thing, he lights up a smoke."

"Camel unfiltered." Neal shrugged. "He needed a jolt of nicotine."

"No doubt, but…I don't know." Crawford idly scratched his bare chest and turned his head to gaze out the window above the sink. It looked like rain. He might have to change what he had planned for Georgia that afternoon.

"What else?" Neal probed.

"The guy virtually guaranteed that he would be either captured or killed. Those were his only two options."

"Suicide."

"Also after which he would be dead."

"What are you getting at?" Neal asked.

"Why the costume?" Musing out loud, he elaborated. "If escape was all but impossible, if he was doomed to wind up either in handcuffs or a body bag, why bother with the disguise?"

"For the scare factor?"

"Possibly," Crawford murmured. "If so, it worked."

His thoughts shifted back to Judge Spencer's meltdown. For hours, she had managed to delay her reaction to the fright she'd experienced in the courtroom. She'd contained it well until his bullying, as she'd called it, had cracked her restraint. Emotions had burst out of her and the overflow had been unstoppable.

His attempt to comfort her had been awkward because, up till then, they'd never touched, not even to shake hands. Then, from that tentative, consoling pat, they had proceeded at warp speed to desperate, clutching, grinding fucking.

"You with me?"

Crawford cleared his throat and turned back to Neal. "Sorry, what?"

"Are you sleepwalking?"

"No, I was just mulling over what you were saying."

"Which part?"

Neal posed the question like a snotty know-it-all, which was the way he'd been as a kid, and the way Crawford continued to regard him. "Look, sergeant, if you don't like the way I'm conducting the conversation, feel free to get the hell out of my house."

Neal stood his ground. "I repeat. None of the

government agencies in the courthouse—city, state, or federal—had an appointment scheduled with a Jorge Rodriguez. He had no outstanding traffic ticket to pay. No tax bills."

"Maybe he was there to get married."

Neal didn't so much as blink at the quip, much less smile.

"Think before you rule it out, Neal. JP's office is on the fifth floor. Some men will go to great lengths to avoid tying the knot."

Although badgering the detective felt good, Crawford's heart wasn't really in it. He was remembering the purpose with which Rodriguez strode toward the judge's podium. "He was there to kill." He looked at Neal and stated with unqualified conviction, "I don't know who he was, or why he went about it so stupidly and suicidally, but he meant to kill."

The coffeemaker hissed and spat one last time. Crawford filled his mug and leaned against the counter, sipping thoughtfully. Though he told himself to shut up about the incident and to tell Neal to go take a flying leap, he heard himself ask, "You get him on security camera coming in?"

"He entered through the main entrance at one forty-one. Here's something interesting. He wasn't carrying anything."

Dammit, that was interesting. "No gym bag, sack, backpack?"

Neal shook his head. "So either he'd stashed his costume on a previous visit in preparation for yesterday, or he was wearing the painter's garb under his street clothes."

"No way," Crawford said. "He didn't have time to switch back into street clothes after leaving the painter's stuff in a pile. He would have gone out onto the roof wearing very little or in the buff."

"Damn. You're right." Neal thought it over. "I suppose the cap, gloves, shoe covers, and mask could've been stashed in his pockets when he entered the building."

"Maybe," Crawford said, but he wasn't convinced of that. "Anything else?"

Neal shook his head. "Once through the door, he got lost in the shuffle, one of many flowing into the building around that time. Prospective jurors."

"Yeah," Crawford said. "I was waiting at the end of the hall for our two o'clock court time. All of sudden the fourth floor corridor was crawling with people."

"The jurors were on their way to Judge Mason's court, two doors down from Judge Spencer's. Rape case with extenuating circumstances. Both attorneys had asked for a large jury pool from which to select."

"Must have been fifty, sixty of them," Crawford recalled. "Most came up on the atrium stairs instead of using the elevators."

"Rodriguez could have blended, then easily slipped into that closet unnoticed. Cameras on the roof got him coming out that door at two twenty-eight. No disguise, but he's carrying the pistol, which he set on the wall at the edge."

The security cameras had verified the sequence of events as Crawford remembered and had related them in his statement, but they failed to enlighten him as to Rodriguez's purpose. In fact, when Neal finished talking through it, Crawford was left with even more gnawing questions. It was second nature for him to want to plug up the holes of missing information.

But mentally he slammed shut the door on his curiosity.

"Answers will come with a positive ID," he said. "In the meantime, you'll have to keep playing the guessing game." He raised a toast with his mug. "Good luck."

"The chief wants—"

"No."

"He's cleared it with your major lieutenant in Houston."

"I'll talk to him and unclear it. Which should make you happy. We wouldn't be simpatico changing a flat tire together. Wasn't it you, just last night, who took issue with my tactics?"

"I was out of line."

Crawford snuffled over the detective's stilted apology. "Never mind, Neal. My feelings aren't hurt. I don't give a shit what you think of me."

"Then I won't play diplomat here. I don't like you or your Dirty Harry brand of cop. But," he said, taking a breath, "it's not up to me, and others hold you in high esteem."

Crawford knew what it had cost the guy to say that. He almost felt sorry for him. But he remained unmoved. "Thank the chief for the vote of confidence, but you'll ID Rodriguez without me. If you feel like you need another Ranger—"

"That's not the point."

"Then what's the point?"

"You were the only person on the roof with this guy, the only one who exchanged words with him."

"You have everything in my statement, including my admission that I responded instinctively, and, as you were quick to point out, I did so without weighing the consequences of such a rash action. Which I now regret."

He could tell Neal was shocked to hear him say that.

"Not for the reason you think," Crawford said. "I took the correct action. I stand by that. I regret it for an entirely selfish reason."

"Want to share?"

He saw no reason not to. "Charging after that gun-man has almost certainly scotched my chances of getting Georgia back. At the next hearing, my father-in-law is going to remind the judge of my reckless disregard for my own safety. What judge is going to entrust a little girl's future to Dirty Harry?"

Especially a judge who's been slam-bam-thank-you-ma'amed by him.

Thinking back on those moments in her kitchen, he wondered if maybe he had read Holly Spencer all wrong. When she raised her head from his chest and looked up into his face, what if her watery-eyed, parted-lips expression wasn't evidence of lust but revulsion?

Hell, maybe she hadn't been telegraphing *Take me and take me now*. Instead, that look might have been a warning that if he didn't remove his grubby paw from her ass, she was going to scream the house down.

But she hadn't.

He'd acted on the signals as he'd read them. When he'd crushed her against him and lifted her off her feet, she hadn't protested. When he'd lowered her onto the living room sofa and she'd raised her hands toward him, it wasn't to stave him off, but to fight with him for ownership of his belt buckle to see who could get it undone faster.

But in the glaring spotlight of retrospection, he doubted that she would remember it quite like that. He hadn't had the crying jag, she had. He wasn't the one who'd been in desperate need of a comforting hug, she was. If he'd stopped it there, he might have been okay.

But...so much for that.

The best thing he could do now was to stay the hell away from her and leave the unanswered questions about Rodriguez for someone else to answer. He didn't need to get in any deeper.

Irritably, he wiped away the sweat trickling down his torso, a byproduct of his memories of their tussle on her small sofa. Grumbling, he said, "I'll call your chief and square it, but even he can see how this creates a conflict of interest for me. If I want my kid, it's best I sit this one out. You know your way to the door." He turned to the sink and tossed the dregs of his coffee down the drain.

"So that's a no?"

"Between you and me, that's a fuck no."

"Then how should I rephrase it to Mrs. Barker?"

Crawford came around. "Who?"

"Chet's widow." Neal reached into the breast pocket of his sport jacket and took out a letter envelope. "This was hand-delivered to the department this morning by one of her relatives. It's addressed to you, but sent in care of the chief, who took the liberty of reading it before asking me to pass it along."

He extended the envelope toward Crawford, who actually recoiled from it. Neal laid the envelope on the dining table. "Basically it says how highly Chet thought of you. He felt you were unfairly criticized over…Well, you know." Neal's expression turned sour.

"She goes on and on for several paragraphs, reiterating how highly Chet praised you. Your skills. Courage. Blah, blah. You get the idea. Anyway, she appeals to you to get to the bottom of the courtroom shooting and provide her with an explanation for her husband's death…which came about here only a few months away from his retirement."

Crawford looked down at the pastel blue envelope. His name was written on it in a fine script. He closed his eyes and mumbled a chorus of swear words.

Neal said, "I'll help myself to coffee while you're getting dressed."

Chapter 7

The morgue was in the basement of the county hospital. The medical examiner, Dr. Forest Anderson, was a fifty-something bachelor who loved forensics and French cooking. When he wasn't busy pursuing one interest, he was elbow deep in the other, which explained why he was almost as wide as he was tall.

In addition to being obese, he had high blood pressure and diabetes, and often joked that his autopsy would be one for the textbooks, and that he regretted he wouldn't be around to observe it.

As he waddled toward the table on which the cadaver lay covered, he said, "One bullet entered his back, burst through his heart. He never felt it."

Matt Nugent had been waiting for Neal and Crawford when they arrived. The three of them lined up along one side of the table. The ME moved around to the other, the cadaver's left, and folded back the sheet as far as the navel.

Over the course of his career, Crawford had seen a lot of bodies, but the dispassion of death never ceased to shock him. It was the ultimate equalizer. Whether one died violently or peacefully in his sleep, death left the remains cold, gray, and eerily motionless.

He took a few seconds to bolster himself, then looked at the dead man's face.

"This one would also have been fatal," Dr. Anderson continued. "It went through the neck from the back, severed the spinal column, exited here." He pointed to the area where the Adam's apple should have been.

Crawford's ears had begun to ring. His blood seemed to have come to a boil. He forced himself to breathe evenly through his nose.

"The third shot entered the torso from the back, lower right side, exited through the gut on the left. Until I look inside, I won't know the damage it did, but I'm guessing it was extensive. Those SWAT guys don't mess around when it comes to saving a fellow officer."

Standing beside Crawford, Neal maintained a stoic professionalism. No one acknowledged that Matt Nugent was swallowing noisily.

Anderson said, "Good thing none of them went for a head shot or his face might not be intact." He looked across at them. "No one's come forward to ID him?"

Neal answered for the group. "Not yet."

"Autopsy may shed some light on his last few hours," the doctor said, rocking back and forth on feet that were comically small compared to the rest of him. "Contents of the stomach. Drugs and alcohol in his system. I haven't found any needle marks yet, but heavy users can be clever. I'll be thorough."

"We count on that." Neal took a step back and motioned for Crawford to take his place nearer the head of the table. Crawford did so and bent over Jorge Rodriguez to closely examine his face. Needlessly. The instant he'd looked at him, he'd seen all he needed to see.

He straightened up and stepped away from the table. "I don't know him."

The younger detective stopped swallowing long enough to ask, "You're positive?"

"Positive. I'd never seen this man before yesterday." Then, backing away, he said, "I'll be outside."

———————

Crawford was pacing the length of Neal's car when the two detectives exited the hospital a few minutes later. Neal told Nugent that he would meet him at the police station after he drove Crawford home.

They rode in silence for several blocks. Finally Neal said, "It was worth a shot."

Crawford stared out the passenger window. He had aimed the AC vents directly at himself, and they were blasting cold air, but it wasn't enough. He felt hot and itchy from the inside out. "As I was leaving, I heard the ME ask what time you were coming back."

"I asked Judge Spencer to take a look at him, too."

Crawford looked over at him. "Is that necessary?"

Neal shrugged. "His name wasn't familiar to her, but she may recognize his face. Worth a shot."

"You're repeating yourself."

Neal said querulously, "I didn't want you along any more than you wanted to be there."

"But you have the chief's size twelves up your anus."

"Because the city leaders' are up his. Already the department's been put on notice that the Hispanic community is gearing up for a full-fledged protest, crying racial profiling, even though two of our SWAT guys are Hispanic. And then there was that appeal from Chet Barker's widow."

"Which is the only reason I agreed to come with you."

"Mrs. Barker wants answers. We all do. Everyone was hoping that when you saw Rodriguez up close, you'd say, 'Oh, *that* guy. Now it all makes sense. I know why he did it.' But you didn't, so your services are no longer needed. You did Mrs. Barker a personal favor. You're off the hook." Neal stopped at a traffic light and turned toward him. "So what's eating you?"

Under his breath, Crawford said, "Nothing."

Neal continued to scrutinize him until the light turned green. No more was said until he pulled the car to the curb in front of Crawford's house. Crawford pushed open the door, eager to get out. "Good luck." He closed the car door and tapped the roof twice, hoping that Neal would consider the matter closed and drive away without asking any more questions.

If anyone pressured Crawford now, he feared he would implode.

———————

Holly arrived at her office later than usual, having stopped by the Barkers' house to hand-deliver a condolence card for the recent widow. She had intended to drop it with whomever answered the door and promptly leave, not wanting to impose on the family's grieving. But Chet's daughter had invited her to come inside. "Mama will want to see you, Judge Spencer."

For the next hour, she had shared remembrances of Chet with members of his family, including Mrs. Barker, and had been touched, in view of their personal tragedy, that they expressed concern for her safety and well-being.

By the time she reached her office, two policemen sent by Sergeant Lester were set up at a portable table, searching through her court records and case files for any mention of Jorge Rodriguez.

"Nothing so far," Mrs. Briggs told her. "And I myself ran a search of his name before they even started."

"Judge Waters put all his records on thumb drives before he retired," Holly told her. "Be sure they see those, too."

"I've already handed them over. I also spoke with someone in the Dallas firm and brought them up to speed. Everyone there is worried about you. Frankly, so am I. Forgive me for saying so, but you look completely done in."

"I just came from a visit with Mrs. Barker." She knew her eyes must still be red from crying.

"Why don't you go home? Why did you even come in today?"

"Actually I prefer being here and staying busy to sitting at home, dwelling on yesterday. I'm fine."

The older woman looked skeptical, but didn't argue. "You've had numerous calls from media. As instructed, I referred them to Sergeant Lester."

"Thank you. For everything."

"And Ms. Vidal has called here three times."

"She's left messages on my cell phone, too. I'll call her now."

Holly went into her private office and closed the door. Once seated behind her desk, she fortified herself with several swallows of water straight from the bottle before using her cell phone to call Marilyn Vidal.

In her gruff smoker's voice, Marilyn answered after the first ring. "Why haven't you returned my calls?"

"I'm calling now."

"The local Dallas stations carried the story this morning. The *full* story. You underplayed it when you called me last night. For God's sake, Holly, that maniac could have killed you."

"I didn't want you to worry. The truth is that I was very fortunate my life was spared. I can't overstate how horrible it was. To see my bailiff killed right in front of me…It was ghastly."

"I'm so sorry. Do you feel like talking about it?"

She didn't. But Marilyn was orchestrating her campaign. It was only fair that she understand her present state of mind. She talked Marilyn through it, starting with the appearance of the gunman in the courtroom and bringing her up to the moment.

She omitted any mention of Crawford Hunt's visit to her home, of course, having placed that subject off limits even to herself. She refused to think about it.

"Jorge Rodriguez might have been seated in the gallery during a proceeding, but he was never a principal in any case I presided over. At least none has been found under that name."

Marilyn, never one to mince words, said, "That's both good and bad."

Holly understood exactly what she was driving at. "No direct connection between us has been established. Therefore, no fingers are pointed at me."

"Which is the good part," Marilyn said. "The bad part? The kook's motive is left wide open to wild speculation." She mulled it over for several seconds, then said, "I'll have to give some thought to how we address that. In the meantime, how are you holding up personally?"

"I'm all right."

"Pull the other one, Holly."

"I have some residual shakiness," she admitted. "I've been told that might hang on for several days. I didn't sleep well." Not one wink after her guest's departure. He'd left her sprawled on the sofa, covered by little more than an orgasmic blush and suffering from acute mortification.

"Do you have someone staying with you?"

Yanked back into the present by Marilyn's question, she replied with a subdued no.

"Have you considered calling Dennis?"

"No."

"Maybe—"

"No, Marilyn."

"You're probably right. That might be perceived as a sign of weakness, and we can't have that."

Holly had made that determination on her own last night. She envisioned Marilyn grinding out her cigarette, sympathetic but unfailingly pragmatic.

"Let me think about how best to handle this."

"It's not up to us to handle it, Marilyn. The police are handling it."

"They have their agenda and we have ours. Have you been approached by the media for a statement?"

She told her what Mrs. Briggs had reported. "But last night before I left the police station, the lead investigator discouraged me from discussing the incident publicly until the culprit has been positively identified and his next of kin contacted. As of now, to my knowledge, that hasn't happened."

"Again, good and bad. You need to be out there, visible, courageously carrying on. But I had just as soon you not be photographed while you still have the shakes."

"They're not that bad, Marilyn. It's just that you don't get over something that traumatic in a few hours. At least I don't."

"Of course not. I understand. Take today. Get a grip. I'll be in touch."

With that she was gone. No sooner had Holly disconnected than Mrs. Briggs came in carrying a large vase of red roses. "These just came for you."

Holly opened the small envelope attached. "Greg

Sanders," she said without inflection. "Expressing his concern and sending best wishes."

Mrs. Briggs snorted her disdain. "Did you see this morning's paper?"

"Where he advocated tighter courthouse security, and cited all the times he's made personal appeals to the county commissioners for funding? Yes, I saw that."

"And the other part?" her assistant asked in a softer tone.

Holly left her desk chair and walked over to the window. "Could yesterday's tragedy have been spawned by some deep, dark secret in my past?"

"He didn't come right out and pose the question, but that was the gist of it."

"He's too clever to say anything libelous. But the thought has been planted in the general public's mind."

"In yours, too, I think."

Holly continued to stare at nothing out the window. "Until I know better, I'll continue wondering if I was responsible for it. If I learn I was, it will haunt me forever."

"Despite what you say, you're not fine. Please go home. Pull the covers up over your head and—" Mrs. Briggs was interrupted by the telephone on Holly's desk. She answered on the second ring. "Judge Spencer's office. Yes, she's right here." Extending the receiver toward Holly, she said, "Sergeant Lester."

Holly returned to her desk and took the receiver. Mrs. Briggs left, pulling the door closed behind her. Holly said, "Hello, Sergeant Lester."

"I told her it was him so you'd take the call."

Her stomach dropped. She closed her eyes. But the image persisted of him looking down at her while standing beside the sofa, hastily buttoning up his fly. He'd walked out before taking time even to tuck in his shirttail or buckle his belt. Neither of them had spoken a word.

"I'm hanging up," she said.

"Wait. Don't."

"Never pull another trick like this."

"Listen to me."

"There's nothing to say."

"Little you know, judge. There's a lot to say."

"Good-bye."

"We've got to talk."

"No, we don't. We definitely do *not*. Don't call me again."

She hung up before he could say anything else. With a cold and clammy hand, she replaced the receiver on the phone. Then, folding her arms on her desktop, she laid her head on them and tried to control her breathing, which was as difficult to do as it was to block the memory of her and Crawford Hunt tugging at their clothing, clumsily adjusting limbs as they sought purchase on the narrow sofa, of her groaning with frustration, of him swearing with impatience until he was moving deep inside her, when the tenor of their groans and swearing had changed entirely.

After one solid rap on the office door, Mrs. Briggs pushed it open. Holly sprang upright. From the threshold, her assistant looked at her with a mix of puzzlement and concern. But Holly's expression must have looked like a silent order for her not to pry, not even to inquire what was the matter.

Mrs. Briggs cleared her throat. "I hate to disturb you, Judge Spencer, but you asked for a half hour's notice before you were due at the morgue."

Chapter 8

———◆———

Crawford kicked aside an empty paint can as he made his way up the weed-choked path, wondering what had happened to the paint that belonged to the can. It hadn't been applied to the house, which looked more ramshackle than it had the last time he was here.

As he stepped onto the porch, the rotting planks bowed beneath his weight. Through the screen door, he saw Conrad waving for him to come inside.

"Make sure to pull that screen closed all the way so flies don't get in."

Crawford went in. "Sure wouldn't want flies spoiling this place."

The older man cocked his head to one side. "Was that intentionally snide?"

"Nothing gets past you." Crawford motioned behind him. "Why are you leaving the door open? Is your AC busted?"

An oscillating fan was circulating moisture-laden air through the cluttered living room. The man in the recliner had stripped down to dingy white briefs and a wife-beater with stained armholes. His feet were bare.

"The compressor started making a funny racket yesterday, so I cut it off."

"Did you call a repairman?"

"Thursday's the soonest he can come."

"It's stifling in here."

"Well, nobody invited you or is insisting that you stay." Conrad aimed the remote control toward the TV and ramped up the volume.

Crawford took the remote from him and punched the off button.

"Hey, I was watching that."

"How many times have you seen it?"

Conrad was fond of World War II movies, especially the ones filmed in black-and-white where granite-jawed GIs smoked Lucky Strikes and referred to the enemies as Krauts and Japs.

Crawford tossed the remote onto a stack of old suitcases that passed for a coffee table. "The ending never changes. Our side wins."

"Now you've gone and spoiled it."

As Crawford pulled a chair from beneath the dining table and dragged it closer to the recliner, he discreetly looked around for empty liquor bottles or other signs of bingeing. But he hadn't been exaggerating when he'd remarked that nothing got past the old man.

"Sixty-two days and counting," Conrad boasted. "In case you were wondering."

"I wasn't."

Crawford sat down and tilted his chair back until it was supported by only two legs. He stacked his hands on top of his head. "Too many times to count, you've climbed on the wagon only to fall off again. So if I'm skeptical, tough."

"I'm staying sober this time."

Crawford made a scoffing sound. "Did you find Jesus?"

"Snide, skeptical, *and* blasphemous. You're on a roll."

"Conrad, you wouldn't know how to function sober."

"I'm sober now, and I'm functioning passably well."

"But drunk is your norm. How many years did you stay soused?"

Conrad screwed up his face, which was much more lined than it should have been for a man of sixty-eight. "Let's see. What year is this?"

Crawford rolled his eyes.

"That was a joke," Conrad said.

"Hilarious."

"I remain gainfully employed, too."

"Still out at the sawmill?"

"Sweeping up. Hot and dusty work, but it's wages."

"Why aren't you there now?"

"It's my day off." The old man took a moment, during which he eyed Crawford up and down. "You've been keeping yourself busy."

"You heard about yesterday's shooting?"

"Couldn't help but." He gestured toward the TV. "Dominated the news. Tuning in between my movies, I caught most of it." He made a rueful sound. "Sorry as shit about Chet. I knew him from the time he was a rookie deputy sheriff. Sent him a box of cigars when he got appointed bailiff. I saw him just about every time I went into the courthouse."

"Did I ever tell you about the time he caught me and some other boys sneaking in the exit door of the movie theater?"

"No. What'd he do?"

"He let the others go. I was the only one he called out. Just stood there staring for the longest time, then said, 'You go that route, get in trouble, you got nobody to blame but your own self.'"

"Straightened you out?"

"Worked better than jail, and I guess he knew it would."

"He was a good man."

"Yeah, and if he hadn't taken that bullet yesterday, I might not be here."

"Ah," Conrad wheezed. "Survivor's guilt. That why you dragged your butt out here? You want me to convince you that Chet's time was up, that's all there was to it, and that you can stop feeling bad about it."

The front legs of Crawford's chair landed hard on the floor when he got up and moved to the open window, ostensibly to try to catch a breath of breeze, when, in fact, he needed to speak frankly, and that was difficult to do when looking directly at Conrad. Oceans of whiskey had left his eyes threaded with red lines, but they were windows into a mind with the snapping precision of a steel trap.

In his prime, Conrad had been a feared and respected state prosecutor. His future brimmed with promise. Then his wife left him and moved to California with her lover. To blunt the pain of her desertion, Conrad turned to drink. But he could never consume enough to ease his heartache.

Soon, drowning his sorrow became his occupation, and he worked at it full-time and to the exclusion of everything else. With absolute apathy, he watched his life unravel. He squandered his career and future to become the town drunk, an object of ridicule.

The old alcoholic nursed no delusions about himself. With brutal candor and abasement, he owned up to his personal failures. Which made him as ruthlessly candid about other people's mistakes and misjudgments. He took no prisoners, he cut no slack. While Crawford scorned the old man for wasting his life, any time he sought an unvarnished assessment of a dilemma, he knew he'd get it in this run-down house.

"Well?" Conrad prompted. "I was in the middle of a

bloody beach assault. Did you interrupt all that excitement only to stare out the window? What's going on? Why the sad-sack face?"

"What I did yesterday could screw me royally."

"Going after the shooter, you mean?"

"Yes."

"How so?"

"For starters, with my in-laws." Crawford told him about the confrontation with Joe Gilroy. "I went over to their house late last night to check on Grace. Joe was polite for about two minutes, then he let me have it. He's never been a big fan of mine. Now, I've given him an excuse to make me out a hothead."

"Oh, and we all know better."

His sarcasm brought Crawford around to face him. "Why I bothered coming out here to talk to you—"

"You bothered because you know that I won't coddle you, that I'll tell it to you like it is."

"Then stop editorializing and get on with it."

"Happily. Based on what I know of Joe Gilroy, I wouldn't piss on him if he was on fire. I despise judgmental hard-asses like him. But in this instance, much as it pains me to say it, he's right. Going after that gunman, you could have gotten yourself killed, and that would've made your daughter a double orphan."

"I thought of that," Crawford admitted. "But not until later. After it was over."

"You acted in the heat of the moment."

"Conditioned reflex."

"Conditioned, my ass," Conrad snorted. "You were born with it."

"You agree with Joe, then? I'm reckless by nature."

"Let me finish, will you? *On the other hand*," Conrad said with emphasis, "what were you supposed to do? Let a madman with a pistol run amok in a building full of people? You're a Texas Ranger, for God's sake. Even off duty, you're not off duty. No lawman worth his salt is. Am I right?"

The answer being obvious, Crawford saw no need to respond.

The former prosecutor continued. "By all accounts, you saved Judge Spencer's life. No matter what your father-in-law does to try to color her opinion of you, he'll be peeing into the wind. The judge isn't going to forget how you shielded her with your own body. Stop worrying on that score. You've won her favor."

Speaking in an undertone, Crawford said, "Don't be so sure."

There was nothing wrong with the old man's hearing, either. He perked up and fixed on Crawford the shrewd stare that had cowed lying defendants. "What's that mean?"

"Nothing."

"Then why'd you say it?"

"Forget it."

"Has the judge got some reason to dislike you?"

"No." His overly loud denial caused Conrad's eyebrows to climb up his wrinkled forehead. Gesturing impatiently, Crawford said, "All I meant was, don't be fooled by the soft packaging. She's tougher than she looks. She was raking me over the coals but good when the guy rushed in with pistol blazing."

Conrad sighed. "Lunatics on shooting sprees are going for records these days, trying to outdo each other. If you hadn't reacted as you did, he would have killed the judge, and, more than likely, you and many others."

Crawford turned back to gaze out the window. "Maybe."

"Everybody's saying."

"Everybody's saying a lot of shit. Doesn't make it true."

Conrad waited several moments, then asked, "Does your little girl know that her daddy's a hero?"

"She doesn't care. It's enough for her that I'm Daddy. Anyway, I'm not a hero."

"That's arguable. You risked your life protecting others. You confronted the guy up on the courthouse roof."

Crawford said nothing to that.

"Have they figured out who he was?"

Crawford shook his head.

"Well, that's not your problem."

"It wasn't until about an hour ago."

Conrad made a snuffling sound. "I get the feeling we're just now getting to the heart of the matter."

Coming back around, Crawford told him about Neal's visit to his house that morning. "He delivered a message from the police chief, along with a letter from Chet's widow." He related the gist of it. "Next thing I know, I'm accompanying Neal to the morgue, when what I should've done was to kick him out of my house."

"Why didn't you?"

"Because of the letter from Mrs. Barker. Besides—"

"Ha! Figured there was a 'besides.' I've been waiting for it."

"I watched Chet die," he said tightly. "I watched the guy on the roof get blown to hell. Naturally, I wanted answers to all the questions left open."

"Naturally." Conrad waited, then asked softly, "You find any answers in the morgue?"

Crawford said nothing, just looked back at him, and Conrad immediately read meaning in his expression. His rheumy eyes narrowed to slits. "I see. Well, then, that breakthrough was worth you making the trip downtown. Neal Lester must be happy."

"I didn't share."

Without breaking their eye contact, Conrad lowered the footrest of his recliner, sat up straight, and scrubbed his bristly chin with his hand. "You didn't tell—"

"Or even let on about it."

Conrad eyed him, finally saying, "Usually, when someone withholds information from the authorities, it's to protect something or someone." He waited for Crawford to address that, and when he didn't, he went on.

"I won't ask what it is you know, because I don't want to hear anything that I might have to testify to in court at a later date. But whatever it is, you need to tell the police immediately."

"Why?"

"Duty. Justice. Or obstruction thereof. Just a few of the reasons that spring to mind."

"If I keep it to myself, no one will ever know."

"*You* will. Can you live with the secret, whatever it is?"

Crawford looked aside, cursing under his breath.

"I didn't think so," Conrad said.

"If I cough up what I know, I'll be placing myself in the epicenter of a shit storm."

"You're already at the center."

"A bigger shit storm," Crawford said. "An F-five shit storm."

"Which could prevent you from getting custody of your kid."

"Damn fucking straight."

Conrad took a couple of moments to assimilate that. "Okay. I get that. But what happens if you *don't* tell?"

Crawford drew in a deep breath and released it slowly. "Potential for an even greater disaster."

"How much greater? Life or death greater?" Then he said, "Never mind. It's written all over you. Somebody else could die."

"*Could*," Crawford stressed. "Maybe not. I don't know."

"But that's what you're scared will happen." This time when Crawford didn't respond, Conrad gave him a cagey grin. "Now I get why you came out here today. You want me to do the dirty work for your conscience."

Crawford placed his hands on his hips. "Does what you just said actually make sense to you? Because to me that sounds like the rambling of a drunk."

"I am a drunk. I admit it. But I'm not the one impeding a police investigation."

"I'm not impeding anything."

"That's splitting hairs, and you damn well know it." He leveled a hard look at Crawford. "As a peace officer, as a law-abiding citizen, you know what you've got to do. You knew before you walked through that door. You just want me to be the angel on your shoulder who whispers it in your ear."

"Angel? That's a laugh. Why would I come to *you* asking about matters of conscience?"

"So that when things go south, you'll have me to blame for dispensing rotten advice. Soon as that shit storm starts swirling around you, you'll curse me for being a drunken fool who you had the bad judgment to listen to. You'll get to hate me for being the one who urged you to do the right thing." He paused, then added, "Not that you need another reason to hate me."

"You got that right." Crawford turned abruptly and pushed so hard on the screen door that it swung wide and banged against the exterior wall.

"Son! Come back here."

As Crawford thumped across the porch, he called over his shoulder, "Thanks for the fatherly advice."

Most of his visits with Conrad—who, even in his private thoughts, he referred to by his given name, certainly not Dad—ended badly, which was why they were few and far between, and only when Crawford initiated one. A condition of him acknowledging Conrad at all was that Conrad was never to contact him. He'd lost that privilege years ago.

Once his mother had obtained a divorce and was free to remarry, she'd retrieved Crawford and taken him to live with her and her new husband in California. He'd resented that he hadn't gotten a vote in the matter, and it had hurt even more that Conrad hadn't put up a fight to keep him.

The severance had been permanent, the father-son relationship destroyed. But as he sped away from Conrad's place, their conversation kept repeating in his mind like an earworm.

And, damn the derelict, he had been right in every respect. Crawford had needed to hear the old man advise him to do what he already knew he had to do, which was why it rankled so badly. The reprobate had taken the moral high ground ahead of him.

Fortunately, he was due to pick up Georgia, who would neutralize his anger. She always put things into perspective. Her giggles could reduce the importance of even the most serious problem.

"It looks like rain," Grace remarked when she met him at the front door. Crawford agreed, but wasn't going to let the weather cancel his and Georgia's outing. Instead, he helped her into her rain gear.

Now, as they walked hand-in-hand toward the swing set, she said, "This is silly, Daddy."

"I promised you a trip to the park playground, and do I ever break my promises?"

"No."

"No. So here we are."

"But it's raining!"

"Naw, this is barely a sprinkle. Besides, even if you get wet, you're not going to melt."

He lifted her onto the seat of the swing and began pushing her. Her squeals and laughter were like music to his ears. Because of the inclement weather, they had the playground to themselves. They moved from one piece of equipment to another, until they'd made three circuits.

As he carried her back to his SUV, she looked down at her bright pink rubber boots. "I got them muddy."

"They're made to get muddy."

"Grandma might get mad."

"You can blame me."

"Grandpa says you're to blame for everything."

Crawford never criticized Georgia's grandparents within her hearing because he never wanted to be accused of trying to drive a wedge between them. Nor did he ever try to fish from her what they said about him when he wasn't around.

Now, however, he was about to make an exception, because Joe had vowed to fight him, and it could be a dirty fight. As he helped Georgia buckle the straps of her car seat, he asked, "When did Grandpa say that?"

"Today while we were eating lunch. He was talking to Grandma."

"How did he sound?"

"Loud."

"Loud? Like he was mad?"

"Kinda. Grandma shushed him and said they would talk about it later. What are we going to do now, Daddy?"

Pinching the tip of her nose, he proposed an ice cream treat.

"At McDonald's? They have a playground inside."

"Mickey D's it is."

While she played, he shot video of her on his cell phone. It pierced his heart every time she called to him, "Daddy, watch me!" before going down the slide or climbing the rungs of the jungle gym.

He had a vague memory of a skinny, gawky, tow-headed him standing on the end of a diving board, toes curled over the edge of it, staring down into the deep end of the pool, and hollering, "Dad, watch me!" as he took the leap.

But he wasn't certain if that blurred image and others like it were actual memories of him and Conrad or childish yearnings that had gone unfulfilled.

He and Georgia played a game of I Spy while they ate their gooey sundaes. He returned her to the Gilroys supercharged on sugar, damp from being rained on, mud-spattered, and tired. But happy.

"Promise to eat your supper even though you had ice cream."

"I will."

"And don't argue with Grandma when she says it's bedtime."

"Okay."

"You're a good girl. Give me a kiss."

She hugged his neck especially tight. "I love you, Daddy."

Clutching her to him, he whispered into her hair. "I love you, too," and renewed his determination to get her back. No matter what.

At dusk Crawford wheeled into the courthouse parking lot, found a vacant spot, and turned off his motor. Then for the next two hours, he sat there, staring through his rain-streaked windshield at the employee exit while his restless fingers beat out an impatient tattoo on his steering wheel.

His butt had grown numb by the time Holly Spencer emerged from the building. He quickly got out of his SUV and splashed through puddles to intercept her between rows of parked cars.

She was walking head down against the rain, fiddling with her key fob, so she nearly walked into him before she saw him. She drew up short.

He said, "You'll have to do better than hang up on me. I don't give up easy."

She tried to sidestep him, but he made a counter move and blocked her path.

"Get away from me."

"I told you that we need to talk."

"And I told you that we don't."

"Look, it's got nothing to do with...that."

He didn't need to spell out what "that" referred to. She winced before saying, "If it's about your custody case—"

"It isn't. It's about the shooting."

The gravity of his tone stopped her two-stepping attempts to go around him. Unmindful of the rain, she raised her head and looked into his face.

"It's serious, and I kid you not, judge. We gotta talk."

She hesitated, then said, "All right. If it's that important, call me tomorrow. I'll be in my office by nine. Tell Mrs. Briggs—"

"Not good enough. We need to talk tonight. Now."

She glanced over her shoulder at the looming red granite structure of the courthouse, as though wondering who might be watching them from any of the dozens of windows. When she came back around, she said, "Out of the question, Mr. Hunt. We shouldn't even be seen—"

"I get it, judge. It's unethical. And after last night, it's also not easy to look each other in the eye." He took a step closer and spoke in an undertone. "But what we did on your couch pales in comparison to this."

He stared into her wide gaze, trying to impress on her how imperative it was that she hear what he had to tell her. He started backing away. "I'm in the black SUV two rows over. Follow me. Okay?"

"I—"

"Follow me."

His insistent tone coaxed from her a small nod of reluctant acquiescence.

Chapter 9

He drove to the same park where he and Georgia had played that afternoon. With nightfall and rain combined, he had counted on no one else being there. The parking lot was empty, but a single, pole-mounted vapor light shed a sickly yellow glow over it, so he parked at the edge of the lane beneath the trees where the darkness was deeper. She pulled in behind him.

He got out of his SUV and walked to her car. She unlocked the passenger door and he slid in, rapidly closing the door to keep out the rain. He raked back his wet hair. As he ran his hands up and down his thighs, drying them on his jeans, he caught her watching him with a wariness that was unflattering and irritating as hell.

"I'm not going to jump you, if that's what you're worried about."

The meager light shone through the rain that trickled down the windshield, casting fluid patterns across her face. Her eyes looked like those of a lost child trying to put up a brave front, a blend of apprehension and defiance.

"What's so important that we needed to talk tonight, Mr. Hunt?"

"Stop calling me Mr. Hunt. We're not in court. Besides—" He broke off before saying anything more, but both knew why using last names was now ludicrous.

The last time they'd seen each other, he'd been tucking himself back into his jeans while she was trying to cover herself with the hem of her t-shirt. Which, he remembered well, proved inadequate.

"I'm waiting," she said coldly.

"We'll get to it in a minute." He gestured toward her forehead. "The swelling's gone down, but the bruise has spread."

"It only hurts when I touch it."

"Any others show up today?"

"A doozy on my shoulder."

He didn't apologize a second time for tackling her to the floor. "Otherwise how are you?"

"I'm all right."

"You don't look it."

With exasperation, she said, "I'm as all right as a person could be under the circumstances."

"Which circumstances? Last night or—"

"Going to the morgue."

"First time for you?"

"Yes. And I hope my last. I didn't think it necessary, but Sergeant Lester was insistent."

"He relayed a message from the chief of police?"

"How'd you know?"

"I got one, too, along with a hand-delivered letter from Chet's widow." He gave her the broad-strokes version of the note's contents, leaving out the accolades to himself. "I wanted to distance myself from the shooting and the resulting investigation. But it was impossible to refuse an emotional appeal from her."

"I went to see her today. The house was overflowing with her children and grandchildren, friends. She has a staunch group of supporters."

"But her husband is dead, murdered."

She nodded, and didn't speak for several seconds,

then returned to talking about the morgue visit. "It was a wasted trip. I didn't recognize Rodriguez. Sergeant Lester told me that you hadn't, either."

Crawford shook his head, but left it at that, not quite ready to address the subject. He needed to win her trust first. Right now, she was backed against the driver's door, her body language telegraphing that she didn't trust him as far as she could throw him.

"Look," he said, "I know I told you that we wouldn't talk about last night."

"And we won't."

"We—"

"If that's what you brought me here to discuss, you've wasted this cloak-and-dagger setup." She gestured toward the surroundings beyond the car windows.

"If we don't clear the air about it, it's always going to be there."

"Not if we cancel it."

He gave her a look. "Sorry, but unless you know a trick I don't, it's not something you can take back."

"We rid our minds of it."

"Deny it happened."

"Not deny. Beyond deny. It. Never. Happened. Period. By an act of will, we—"

"Cancel it."

"Yes."

"Okay."

"So you agree?"

"Yeah. Fine."

But he didn't believe that was a workable plan, and obviously she didn't, either. Under his stare, she lowered her head and massaged the space between her eyebrows with the pad of her middle finger.

"What about the whiskey drinker?" he asked.

"He's not a factor."

"He's an ex?"

"Yes."

"Husband?"

"Significant other."

"How significant?"

"We were never officially engaged, but we had an understanding."

"Of?"

"Marriage in the future."

"So what happened?"

She raised her head, looking piqued. "What difference does it make to you?"

"It makes a difference because I don't want a jealous ex coming after my ass with criminal intent."

"He isn't like that."

"If he's got a pair, he is. When it comes to a woman, all men are 'like that.'"

"Not Dennis."

"Dennis." The name left a bad taste in his mouth. "What sets Dennis apart from the rest of us?"

"He's not a caveman," she said. "He's reasonable. Refined."

"Huh. In other words, right there on the borderline with wimpy."

Her angry breathing was beginning to fog up the windows. "I'm done talking about this."

"I'm not. In fact, it's just now getting interesting."

"Get out of my car, Mr. Hunt."

"Is Dennis local?"

"Frisco," she said tightly. "It's a community outside—"

"Dallas. I know. Did distance break you up?"

She seemed disinclined to answer, but he waited her out and finally she said, "When I accepted the job with Judge Waters, Dennis and I were aware of the strain the distance might impose on our relationship."

"Plain English, please. I'm not the law review board."

"Do you want to hear this or not?"

He spread his hands apart, inviting her to continue.

"Dennis and I were committed to making it work."

"Except it didn't."

"No, the separation began to widen, and in more ways than geography. We saw less and less of each other. It was a long drive to make just for a weekend."

"Depends on the weekend." Catching the innuendo, her eyes snapped to his, but before she could take exception, he pressed on. "Dennis couldn't have relocated here when you did?"

"He has a senior position with a medical supply company. High-tech surgical equipment. I never would have suggested that he leave it."

"You never considered passing on the chance of getting the governor's appointment?"

"Absolutely not."

Huh. An unequivocal no. She couldn't have loved Dennis all that much. Which gave Crawford a misplaced feeling of satisfaction. As he'd said, when it came to a woman… Apparently he was of a baser bent than Dennis. "How long ago was the breakup?"

"A few months."

"Do you keep in touch?"

"No."

"Was the split hostile?"

"No. Very civilized and congenial."

"Right. Dennis isn't a caveman."

She took a deep breath, he believed in order to control her vexation. "As I told you at the start of this inane and totally unnecessary conversation, Dennis is no longer a factor in my life."

"Okay." Crawford had heard what he needed to hear and was willing to let the subject drop there.

Then she asked, "What about you?"

"Regarding what?"

"Are you in a relationship?"

"No."

"Have you been since your wife died?"

"No."

She held his gaze until he relented with a shrug.

"None that lasted longer than twenty minutes." He waited a beat before adding, "But until last night, they lasted longer than ninety seconds."

Angry, possibly embarrassed, she turned her head aside to look through the windshield.

Feeling rather like a heel for having said that, he said, "Since Beth, no involvements. I've seized on a few random opportunities. Never when Georgia is around. Never in my house. And never without protection."

At that last, she turned and gave him a pointed look.

He sighed. "Right."

"Don't fret. You're safe."

"The pill?"

A small nod, then she looked forward again. Possibly a whole minute passed before she spoke. "Sergeant Lester told me that you had loved your wife very much."

That goosed him. "You and Neal talked about Beth and me?"

"In passing."

"When?"

"Today at the morgue while we were waiting for the ME to conclude a call."

Crawford hated the thought of Neal and her talking behind his back, analyzing that dark period of his life, and forming unenlightened opinions. "What was the context of this little chat? Did it make for stimulating conversation?"

"Not in the way you're implying. Sergeant Lester

didn't disclose anything I didn't already know. I'm aware of how deeply you were affected by your wife's death."

"Of course you are. You've got a whole file on my bereavement. Beth died, and I became drunk and disorderly." *Just like my old man did when my mom left.* It had been on the tip of his tongue to add that. Fortunately, he caught it just in time and, in fact, decided he would be better off closing the subject.

He tamped down his anger and turned his head to look out the passenger window. In the rainy darkness, he could barely make out the shapes of the playground equipment. "Wettest day in recent history, and I've come to the park twice."

"Twice?"

"Earlier today I brought Georgia here to play."

"In the rain?"

He turned back to her and gestured that it hadn't mattered. "We had fun anyway. She has this little rain outfit. Pink, of course. She likes all things pink. Anyhow, she fretted about getting the boots muddy."

"That's what they're for."

"That's what I told her."

They exchanged a private smile, which put him right back in her kitchen, when his arms were around her and he could feel her against him from knees to collarbone, feel her unbound breasts against his chest, and that perfect fit at the notch of her thighs that had stopped their breathing but sparked white-hot sex.

Her thoughts must have revisited that moment, too, because there was a sudden shift in the atmosphere inside the car. The air became denser. Every raindrop striking the windshield sounded extraordinarily loud and emphasized the awkward silence that descended over them.

Finally she said, "If that's all…"

"It's not."

"Then what?"

"Your visit to the morgue." He paused. "You took a good look at the body?"

Grimacing, she nodded.

"And?"

"And nothing. I didn't recognize his face any more than I did the name Jorge Rodriguez."

He watched her closely for several seconds, then said, "Will you do me a favor?"

"Within reason."

"Close your eyes and describe the shooter to me."

"Why?"

"I want to hear your description, in your own words, in detail. Every single thing you remember about him." When she hesitated, he said, "I know it's a bitch of a favor to ask."

"Last night you were urging me to put him out of my mind."

"If this wasn't vitally important, I'd still be urging you to do that. But it is important."

She regarded him with puzzlement, but he must have conveyed the seriousness of the request. She closed her eyes and took her time to conjure up the image. "When he barged through the door, the first question that flashed through my mind was, 'Why is that person dressed like that?' But then he fired the pistol and it registered with me what was happening."

"Which hand was the pistol in?"

"His right."

"Hair color?"

"Dark. But only a mashed-down fringe of it showed beneath the cap."

"Straight hair? Curly?"

"Straight."

"What kind of shoes was he wearing?"

"There were disposable covers over them."

"Good so far. What else stands out in your memory?"

"Such as?"

"Any detail."

She gestured with frustration. "There weren't any details to be seen. He was completely covered."

"Was he wearing a wristwatch?"

"I don't know. The gloves extended up beneath his sleeves. His facial features were indiscernible because of that horrible mask. Nose, lips, everything was pressed flat."

"What about his neck?"

She thought on that. "Only an inch or so of skin was exposed between the high collar of the coveralls and the cap. The cap was pulled so low it covered the tops of his ears."

"But the lobes were visible."

"Yes."

"The right one was pierced."

She frowned and opened her eyes. "Was it? I didn't notice that."

Crawford's heart skipped. "You didn't?"

"No."

With quiet emphasis, he said, "You didn't notice because his ear wasn't pierced. But the man in the morgue, his was."

Her lips separated on a soft gasp. "It was. It *was*. Oh my God." She raised her fingertips her lips. "But that would mean…"

"Yeah," he sighed. "The man killed on the roof wasn't the shooter."

Chapter 10

What the fuck happened?"

Joseph Patrick Connor, known to his friends as Pat, wiped greasy sweat off his forehead. "Listen, I—"

"Oh, I'm listening. Count on that." The other man's voice was like a rumble of distant thunder that warned of the violence packed into an approaching storm. It originated from a wide chest over which were folded arms as sturdy as sticks of firewood. His stare could have peeled paint.

Wilting beneath it, Pat said, "Most of it worked out just like we planned."

"Not even close to most of it. Your target is still breathing."

And so am I. The fact that he was alive was a priority to Pat, but he didn't want to say that out loud and risk a swift change of his breathing status, which he figured was flimsy at best.

He glanced over his shoulder at the two men posted on either side and just behind his chair. He was seated at a small table on which were a half-empty bottle of ketchup and a weapon restricted to law enforcement and military maneuvers. In most states, anyway.

A half hour earlier, he'd been pouring himself a

Jack and Coke when the two bodyguards—for lack of a better word—shouldered their way through his back door into his kitchen. He recognized them from previous meetings, but he'd never been introduced to them by name, which was of piddling significance because it became immediately obvious that they weren't paying him a social call.

With each claiming one of his arms, they'd marched him out of his house to a waiting car and put on the blindfold he'd come to expect. They rode in silence, henchmen programmed to carry out a duty, no discussion, no questions asked.

Pat didn't think he had a prayer, and was actually surprised when they arrived at their destination. His clothes were completely sweated through by then, but perspiration was proof that he was still alive. For the time being, anyway.

The abduction wasn't entirely unexpected. He'd known he would be "summoned" sooner or later, and he'd dreaded the inevitable face-off. But the real deal was even worse than his imaginings. He'd been brought to this place a few times before, but he hadn't developed a liking for it. In fact, it gave him the willies.

He could have used at least one belt of the sour mash he'd been pouring when roughly escorted from his house.

"Well?" the man boomed, startling Pat into remembering that he hadn't responded to the last statement.

He made another swipe across his forehead, but by now his palm was as damp as his hairline. He squirmed in his chair, muttering under his breath, "I don't know why I agreed to do it in the first place."

"Do you need me to remind you, Pat?"

Distrusting the steadiness of his voice, Pat shook his head no. He didn't need a reminder of how desperate his situation had been. Was still. The man was waiting for an explanation for his failure. "For one thing, that mask was for shit. It distorted my vision."

"You didn't try it out beforehand?"

"Sure I did, but, I don't know, I think my breath must've steamed it up or something. Then, all the way around, it was a lot harder than I thought it would be. It was harder than *you* thought it would be."

"How many times had we gone over it?"

"I know. But shooting Chet Barker wasn't part of the plan. You didn't want a bloodbath, you said. But he was blocking my path. I didn't have a choice. Having to kill him threw me. Put me off my stride, you might say."

He paused, waiting for a reaction. A murmur of understanding. A grunt of agreement. Something. But the other man gave him nothing to hang a hope for longevity on. He might never get back to that Jack and Coke. He'd made a bargain with the devil, and he hadn't held up his end.

He wanted to cry. He didn't, but he developed a stutter. "B...b...but I stepped over Chet and carried on. Marched right up to the podium."

"They're saying Crawford Hunt saved the judge's life. True? Or does that just make good press?"

"It's true. When I rounded the witness box, he was on top of her, shielding her head and upper body. Then he levered himself up just a little and looked over his shoulder at me. I aimed, but the shot went wild when he hauled off and kicked the crap out of my left knee."

"Not hard enough to displace it. You could still run on it. Which is what you did, you gutless slob. You ran before you finished the job."

The two brutes behind him moved in a bit closer. He halfway expected to get a stiletto between his shoulder blades. Maybe he'd be lucky and feel nothing more than a slight sting.

But nothing happened, so he continued. "I…I guess I did panic there for a second or two. I didn't want to get caught. Last thing you wanted, too, I'm sure. I needed to get the hell out of there and strip off the costume. So I regained my head and stuck to the plan. Did exactly what we'd talked about."

"The guy, the one killed by the police, how did he wind up with the pistol?"

"He must've come along as soon as I dumped the stuff and slipped into the sixth-floor hallway. I never saw him, but he might have seen me. We'll never know. Anyway, the pistol was there for the taking, and he couldn't resist." He paused, and then rushed on hopefully. "Which worked out better for us. Right?"

He swiveled his head around to consult the stone-faced man looming over his left shoulder. "Right?" Coming back around to his inquisitor, he said, "The PD thinks they got their man, and that dead Mex'can ain't gonna sit up and tell them any different."

The man across the table from him barked a laugh that was so unexpected, it was like a karate chop across Pat's windpipe. "That's the only reason I haven't killed you already. This does work out better."

Pat nearly swooned with relief. He might get to have that drink after all. "So, then, we're square?"

The laugh might never have happened. In fact the man across from him had never looked more menacing. "No, we're not square, Pat." Leaning across the table, he brought them nose to nose. "I wanted to tell you straight to your face that you're still living *only* because I need your lousy ass."

"T…to do what? Try again?"

"To heap on some misery first. And then, when I say so, finish it."

Chapter 11

T he person in the morgue wasn't the gunman," Crawford said, speaking slowly, eliminating any lingering uncertainty on Holly's part.

She was staring at him, aghast. "How can that be?"

He exhaled heavily and dragged his hand down his face. "I don't know. Wish to hell I did."

She covered her mouth with her hand and kept it there for at least half a minute. He gave her time to try and think through the unthinkable. Finally she said, "If you're right—"

"I am right."

"—the ripple effect will be—"

"The Big Bang of fuck-ups."

Wetting her lips anxiously, she said, "Maybe you're mistaken. Maybe I am. He had a pierced ear and I just didn't notice."

"Believe me, I've been grasping at straws, too, trying to convince myself that I'm wrong, but you just proved I'm right. Immediately when I mentioned his ear was pierced, you questioned me. You didn't do that on a single other feature."

"But—"

"Listen to me, Holly." Her eyes went wide. He didn't

know whether it was because of the tone he'd used, or because he'd called her by her first name, but he had her undivided attention. "I was closer to him than anybody. That nanosecond before I kicked him, I was looking straight at him. I would swear on Georgia's head that there was no hole in his right ear."

"On the roof, you didn't notice the discrepancy?"

"The sun was in my eyes. Besides, I was too far away from Rodriguez to notice his pierced ear."

"He wasn't wearing an earring?"

"No. And my focus was on that twitching gun hand, not his earlobe. After he was down, others crowded around him. I didn't. I didn't look at him again until this morning at the morgue and instantly realized the mistake. I thought I was going to hurl."

She gave him a searching look. "You can't blame yourself."

"Can't I? Rodriguez, or whatever his name was, didn't kill Chet. He didn't do anything wrong except pick up a pistol that didn't belong to him and carry it out onto the roof when he went to smoke."

"He *brandished* the pistol at you, even after you had identified yourself as a lawman. He fired the gun at the deputy twice, and it's a miracle that he missed."

"You're right. But it's clear to me now that everything he did, he did because he was scared. He'd been caught with a pistol that didn't belong to him. When I told him to drop it, it was stupid of him not to. Then that deputy appeared, and he panicked." Looking aside, he added under his breath, "Stupidity and panic are lousy reasons to get yourself killed."

"You didn't kill him."

"I didn't fire the bullets, but I set him up as the target."

"You did your best to help him. It wasn't your fault."

Crawford would be arguing that point till they sealed

his own casket, but for right now, he had to deal with the problem, which had far-reaching repercussions to him personally, as well as to Holly Spencer. How it affected her was more urgent.

"What scares me," he said, "is that this has given the joker a high, boosted his confidence, and he was brazen as hell to begin with."

She gave a small shake of her head. "I'm not following you."

He looked at her for a moment, realized her perplexity, then said in a quiet voice, "One of those ripple effects you mentioned obviously hasn't reached you yet, and it's a tsunami. Whoever came into the courtroom yesterday wanting to kill you is still unknown and at large."

As that sank in, he watched her changing expressions and knew before she spoke that she would negate it. "Two detectives spent hours today combing through the records and transcripts of all my cases. They also went through Judge Waters's dating back to 2012, and all my records from the Dallas firm. They didn't find anything."

"Because they were looking specifically for a connection to Jorge Rodriguez."

"Even so, nothing raised a red flag."

"Which only means we've got to dig deeper, and this time we won't have a name to go on."

"That could take weeks."

"Or longer. Before we turn up even a lead, you—" He stopped to amend what he'd been about to say. "You should assume that your life is in danger and act accordingly."

"That's a lot to assume."

"Be smart. Assume it."

"'Act accordingly' doesn't sound like something you would ordinarily say."

"It isn't. That's official jargon. I'd rather give it to

you a little more hard-core, but I'm afraid you'd take offense. I only hope the message came across."

She looked away from him and, for a time, said nothing. Then, "You've thought all along that the shooting was an act of revenge."

"I haven't changed my mind. This wasn't random. It was carefully planned. Calculated. He had the painter's outfit stashed somewhere inside the building, probably in the closet across the hall from the courtroom. He put it on over his clothes and waited until court convened."

"Then came in shooting."

"But not willy-nilly. If he'd been a nutcase just wanting to kill people, he'd have sprayed the gallery with that semiautomatic. He could've taken out six, eight people in seconds. But he didn't. He was determined to get behind that podium even if it meant going through Chet."

"He didn't expect you to protect me."

"Maybe, but in any case, he figured out real quick that his only safe option was to flee. He ran from the courtroom, into the stairwell, and made it look like he'd gone up to the roof. After dumping the disguise, he slipped back down that half flight to the sixth floor, went into the corridor, and blended in when all hell started breaking loose.

"It was either a brilliant plan or the dumbest I've ever heard of," he went on, "but the bottom line is that someone bore you a grudge so deep, he was determined to kill you, even at great risk to himself. Any ideas?"

"I told you last night, none."

"Think!"

She whipped her head around to face him again. "I have! That's all I've been thinking about. But I swear to you, there hasn't been any drama in my life. Not on that scale."

"What about your political opponent Saunders?"

"I had an unpleasant exchange with him yesterday."

"Where? About what?"

She described their brief encounter at the elevator. "I suppose you could read a threat into his parting remark. It sticks in his craw that I got that appointment over him."

"Wait! He was a contender for that judgeship?"

"There were several applicants, but Greg Sanders was my most challenging rival."

"And you're just now telling me this?"

"It wasn't relevant till now," she said, matching his annoyance.

"Right. Okay. Sanders goes on the list."

"What list?"

"The short list of possible suspects."

"He wasn't the shooter," she exclaimed. "Greg Sanders has at least six inches height on him."

"He could have contracted somebody."

She thought about that, but shook her head. "I think you're wrong. That isn't his style. He wants to defeat me, crushingly, but he wants to take credit for it. He wouldn't do it anonymously. He would rather his victory get live TV coverage on election day."

"Okay, but he still goes on the list. So does Dennis."

"I told you, our breakup was friendly. No hanging up on each other, no harsh words or threats, no hostility. Nothing like that."

Crawford intended to check him out anyway. Her ex may not be as reasonable and refined as she believed. "There's nobody else you've crossed swords with, professionally or personally?"

She shook her head.

"Even going back a few years? Parents? Siblings?"

"No siblings. Both parents are deceased."

"Friends you've had a falling out with?"

"No. To my knowledge I don't have an enemy who would make an attempt on my life."

He tried to stare a contradiction out of her, but she didn't flinch. He had to take her word for it. "All right," he said, "our culprit remains a question mark. So first thing, tonight in fact, we've gotta find a place to stash you for a few days."

"Excuse me?"

"Is there someplace you can lay low? Keep out of sight?"

"What are you talking about? I can't go into hiding!"

"Hell you can't."

"Hell I will! If you feel security is warranted, I'm sure the police will provide it."

"The Prentiss PD?" he asked.

"Or the sheriff's office."

She still wasn't seeing the big picture. "Holly, anyone within the Prentiss PD or sheriff's office is a *suspect*. Everybody who was in the courthouse when the shooting occurred is a *suspect*, and that includes dozens of law enforcement officers. Anyone who was ostensibly trying to apprehend the shooter could have *been* the shooter."

She pulled her lower lip through her teeth. "How many police personnel were off duty yesterday?"

"Doesn't matter. Anyone on the payroll could still provide a plausible explanation for being in the building."

"Yes, but Neal Lester would carefully screen—"

"Neal's included."

"*What?* He's the lead investigator."

"Who better to pull off something like this?" At her horrified look, he gave a soft laugh and instinctively reached across and squeezed her thigh. "Relax. Bad joke. It wasn't Neal. He's not nearly that creative. Wrong body type."

"Wrong hair color."

"Besides, what motive would he have?" Reluctantly, he lifted his hand off her thigh. "All the same, I wish someone else was investigating this thing. Neal's a political animal, more bureaucrat than cop. He's a suck-up because he wants to be in the chief's chair one of these days, and until then he wants to be in the chief's lap. His priority will be to cover his ass first, not yours."

"How do you think he'll react when you tell him?"

"He'll have to wash his underwear. Then he'll take it to the chief, and, knowing how the grapevine works within the department, it'll be all over the place in no time. Which means that the perp will get wind of it, and he'll go underground, and we'll be screwed in terms of catching him." Lowering his voice to a murmur, he said, "Until he tries again."

She hugged her elbows. "It hasn't been established that I was the target."

He wasn't going to argue that point again. "Whoever he was, and whatever his intention, he killed Chet. I want the son of a bitch, and I'll get him."

"I thought you wanted to distance yourself from the investigation."

"I did. I do. But my chances of getting Georgia went to shit the moment I ran after that gunman. Don't bother," he said when he saw she was about to counter. "We both know it's true. I'm in, even if I didn't choose to be. Neal won't like it, but if he balks, I only have to remind him that I don't need his sanction, and, anyway, his chief solicited me. First order of business is to see that you're protected."

"I can't put my work, my life, on hold indefinitely."

"Your court is still a crime scene. You couldn't go about your routine anyway."

"I could use another courtroom temporarily."

"You could. But you'd be placing not only yourself in danger, but everyone around you."

Her shoulders slumped. "Like Chet."

The statement subdued them and nothing was said for a moment.

When Holly spoke again, she reverted to argument mode. "I can't disappear from the public eye. I'm running for office."

"Your life was threatened. Everyone will understand if you take a few days off to regroup."

"And have Greg Sanders paint me a coward?"

"That would only reflect badly on him."

She lowered her head. "I could drop out of the race altogether."

"Then you'd really look like a coward."

"It wouldn't be solely because of the courtroom shooting," she said quietly.

"What other reason do you have for even considering it?"

She gave him a look that said he knew the reason. And he did. He shifted in his seat, looked away, came back to her. "I thought we'd *canceled* it."

"As you said, it's not something you can take back."

"No, but it doesn't have to dictate your future. I'm not gonna rat you out. Nobody will know."

"We will."

Her tone was disturbingly reminiscent of Conrad's *"You* will," which prompted him to argue all the harder. "You'd be crazy to throw away your career over it. At a stretch it lasted for all of two minutes. We didn't even kiss, for crissake!"

"Like that excuses it?"

"No, but it's not like you languished in lust."

"It doesn't matter whether it lasted a few minutes or all day. You can't breach ethics just a little."

"Sure you can."

His flippancy annoyed her. "You are a principal in one of my pending court cases. It was a no-no for us to even talk privately, much less…" Then she paused, and, when next she spoke, it was barely audible. "Is that why you did it?"

"Pardon?"

She took a deep breath and looked him straight in the eye. "Is that why you came to my house? Is that why you did it?"

He had hoped she wasn't leading up to that. But by repeating it, she'd made herself perfectly clear. He began to simmer. "Is that why *I* did it? *I?*"

"Well, you knew that was the one compromise I couldn't possibly get beyond. Not if I had a grain of integrity. I couldn't preside over another custody hearing after…after…"

"After screwing me on your sofa?" He snuffled a laugh and nodded his head knowingly. "I wondered when you'd get around to it."

"To what?"

"To laying the blame on me for laying you," he said, seething now. "I could turn it around and ask you the same question, judge. Why'd *you* do it? To let yourself off the hook, maybe?" He sputtered a bitter laugh. "I can hear your ruling now. 'The court can't award this man custody of his daughter. He's reckless, unstable, and immoral. He can't control his impulses, his temper, or his dick.'"

"That is so unfair."

"No, I'll tell you what's unfair. When you go all weepy and clingy, it's unfair to blame a guy for acting on your *please fuck me* eyes."

They glared at each other with such intensity, they didn't see the man's approach and nearly jumped out of their skins when he knocked loudly on the driver's window.

Holly slapped her hand over her chest as though to keep her heart from leaping out. She reached for the button to lower the foggy window, but then realized she had to start the car engine first.

When the window went down and Neal Lester's face appeared, Crawford swore viciously.

Neal, wearing his sternest expression, looked at Holly first, then across at Crawford. "Well, this is interesting."

Chapter 12

———◆———

They caravanned to an all-night café on the outskirts of town. Crawford was in the lead, Holly behind him, Neal bringing up the rear. Neal had dictated the order so they couldn't peel off and avoid the meeting, although neither had any intention of doing so.

Customers consisted mostly of long-haul truckers, seated on counter stools, hunched over platters of deep-fried food. Crawford, still in the lead when they filed in, claimed a booth, motioned Holly into one side of it, slid in beside her, and tried not to look peeved when she put the maximum amount of space between them.

Neal sat across from them and, after ordering three coffees from the indifferent waitress, said, "I'll listen to your explanation for the tête-à-tête, then decide if I need to bring Nugent in and relocate us to an interrogation room at headquarters."

Holly took umbrage. "It wasn't a tête-à-tête."

"I'm the lead investigator of a murder investigation. You're material witnesses. What were you doing together in the park?"

"I get the feeling you didn't come upon us by accident," Crawford said.

"No. I saw the two of you talking on the courthouse parking lot."

"Hmm. Refresh my memory. What's the maximum sentence if convicted of talking on a public parking lot?"

Crawford's taunt had an effect. Neal had to unclench his jaw to speak. "When you left one behind the other, I followed."

"Why didn't you just flag us down?" Holly asked.

"Because, judge, your conversation had looked covert, and I wanted to know why."

He was forestalled from saying more when the waitress returned with their coffees. They declined menus. She ambled away. The coffee mugs went untouched as Neal began speaking low and angrily, now addressing Crawford.

"I followed you as far as the entrance to the park. But just as I got there, I had a series of calls that I had to take and respond—" He stopped suddenly. "I don't need to explain myself to you. But you need to explain yourselves. You slipped away under cover of darkness and—"

Crawford laughed. "Sorry. It's just that I've never heard anyone actually say 'under cover of darkness' with a straight face."

Neal went on doggedly. "Yesterday you two were adversaries. Tonight you were fogging up car windows. For thirty-three minutes, to be exact." He shot a glance at Holly. "It's unethical for you to be discussing his custody petition, and the only other thing you have in common is the shooting." Back to Crawford, he said, "If your clandestine meeting pertained to that, I need to know." He sneered. "Or were you just trying to get under her skirt?"

Holly's body jerked as though he'd shot her. "How dare—"

"Your dead guy in the morgue wasn't the shooter in the courtroom."

Crawford's blunt statement overrode Holly's outrage, and, as he'd intended, it completely defused Neal. It robbed him of wind and left him looking like a guy who'd just realized that his solid footing was in fact a trapdoor.

Crawford kept his expression implacable, doing or saying nothing to ease Neal's shock or to help him absorb it. The detective looked over at Holly. "What's he talking about?"

"Precisely what he said," she replied tightly, "and I'm afraid he's right."

Neal brought his attention back to Crawford. "When did you make that determination?"

"The instant I saw him in the morgue."

"How?"

Crawford told him.

Neal appeared moderately relieved. "A pierced ear?" he guffawed. "That was your big *voilà*?"

"Small detail. Big *voilà*."

Neal began to look more concerned and, as Crawford and Holly had done, began trying to construct an explanation. "Amid all the confusion, you just didn't notice the hole in his ear before."

Crawford explained how he could have missed seeing it when on the roof. "But I'm as sure as I can be that the man in the courtroom did not have a piercing. Your cadaver does. They're two different men." Remembering kicking the gunman, he said, "Look at Rodriguez's left kneecap. If it has a bruise, I'll admit to being wrong. If there's no bruise..." He raised his hands palms up. "It wasn't Rodriguez who had a bead on me."

Neal wet his lips, cut his eyes back and forth between

Crawford and Holly and ended on her. "You said you're 'afraid he's right.' That means you're not sure."

"Mr. Hunt tested my memory of the shooting from the time the gunman barged through the door." She gave him a brief rundown. "I was spot-on regarding every other detail. When he mentioned a pierced ear, it prompted an immediate response, which substantiates what Mr. Hunt had discovered."

"It was a trick question," Neal argued. "You can't back him up with one hundred percent certainty?"

She maintained her chilly tone. "This I am one hundred percent certain of. If I didn't believe he was right, I wouldn't be sitting here."

Even if Neal was unwilling to take Crawford's word for it, he seemed to regard the judge as unimpeachable. His face paled under the fluorescent lighting that hummed from the water-stained ceiling. He pulled a paper napkin from the table dispenser, blotted a sheen of perspiration from his upper lip, then wadded up the damp napkin and tossed it aside. "Why didn't you tell me when we were in the morgue?" he asked Crawford.

"On the outside chance that I was wrong, I wanted Judge Spencer's confirmation. I contacted her by phone, but she hung up on me. I had no choice except to ambush her tonight on the courthouse parking lot and insist that she listen to what I had to tell her. That was the reason for our secret meeting." He paused, then said, "You owe her an apology."

Looking a bit sickly, Neal said, "I apologize, Your Honor. The insult was aimed at Crawford, not you."

"Then you also owe Mr. Hunt an apology."

He knew Neal would rather have his tongue cut out, but the judge had pulled rank and given him little choice.

His eyes not quite meeting Crawford's, he said, "The remark was uncalled for."

"Your sincerity is overwhelming, Neal. Not that I give a damn about winning your approval. The only thing I'm after is Chet's murderer. And it wasn't Jorge Rodriguez."

"When I inform the chief that our SWAT team fatally shot the wrong guy, he'll demand to know why. Can you give me any kind of reasonable explanation for your screwup?"

"Hold on, detective," Holly said before Crawford could speak. "The man we know as Rodriguez threatened Mr. Hunt with a loaded pistol. He opened fire on a deputy sheriff. Whether or not he was the gunman in the courtroom, he had to be stopped."

"Thanks, judge, but I don't need you to defend me," Crawford said, his eyes fixed on Neal. "I don't know what happened between the courtroom and the roof, but you saw the videos from the security cameras up there. Rodriguez was acting squirrely. He paid for bad choices with his life, and that's a goddamn shame. But it's history. Can't be undone. Your job now is to figure out—"

"Kindly don't tell me what my job is."

"—where the switch was made, why it was made, and how. Was Rodriguez a dupe set up to take the fall? Or did he just pick a bad time to lift a pistol that didn't belong to him, and then panic when confronted? And the really looming question is, since he wasn't the shooter, who was?

"Until you have answers to all those questions, Neal, you're gonna have an outraged public, plus every cop in the long chain of command straight up to the chief gnawing on your ass. Now, throw me under the bus if it makes you feel better. Have at it. I've survived worse.

But until you solve this thing, it's *your* butt that's going to be dog chow. How's it feel to be lead investigator now, asshole?" He hooked his hand around Holly's elbow. "Let's go."

"Wait."

Crawford paused in the act of sliding from the booth and dragging Holly with him.

Neal's pride was wrestling with his better judgment, and the latter won out. "What do you know?"

"Not a damn thing."

"Then what do you think?"

Crawford hesitated, then scooted back into the booth. When he and Holly were resettled—not as far apart, he noticed—Neal gestured to him that he had the floor.

"I *think* the shooter had the painter's outfit stashed inside the closet across the hall from the courtroom. He put it on in there and waited until court convened. How long he waited, I don't know. We figured he slipped in undetected among all those jurors, but he could have been hunkered down in there for hours. CSU has gone over that closet?"

"It's a custodial closet. Dust cloths, push brooms, mop buckets."

"In other words, trace evidence out the wazoo."

"Bags full."

"We might not be able to put him in the closet, not conclusively enough to satisfy a jury. But we won't have to. His DNA will be all over the painter's outfit. Of course, we need a suspect before that does us any good," he added grimly. "Have you tracked down the supplier?"

"Of the painter's clothes? Didn't seem necessary. We thought we had our perp. I'll put Nugent on that."

Crawford wondered if Nugent was competent to handle the assignment. He didn't believe he was clever enough to qualify as a suspect. "Wherever our shooter is tonight, he's second-guessing leaving all that stuff behind."

"Why did he?" Holly asked.

Crawford thought it through. "Maybe he heard me in the stairwell and realized I was making my way up. Better to leave the disguise and hope for the best than to be caught with it. Same with the pistol. He risked being apprehended unarmed, but he knew there would be a shakedown of everyone evacuated from the building." Looking at Neal, he said, "I'm betting there were no fingerprints on the gun."

Neal shook his head. "Clean. Serial number filed off. We're waiting on ballistics."

"I doubt you'll get a link to any other crime."

Neal nodded glumly. "Anybody who'd file off the serial number..."

"What about Jorge Rodriguez?" Holly addressed the question to Crawford. "Do you think he was somehow involved?"

"My gut tells me no. You?"

Neal, to whom he'd addressed the question, looked back at him with perplexity. "I thought we'd determined that he was in the wrong place at the wrong time and made a fatal error in judgment, but had nothing to do with it."

"That's one possibility, but we haven't determined a damn thing. Maybe you should start thinking outside the box, Neal. Like maybe the poor son of a bitch was set up as a dupe, a decoy."

"There's absolutely nothing to support that theory."

"There's nothing that nullifies it, either. We should at least test every theory, don't you think?"

"*We*? I thought you couldn't wait to get away from this investigation."

"I've got Mrs. Barker to answer to," Crawford said. "As well as your chief. Remember? You want to complain about my participation, take it up with him."

Neal squirmed with dislike over the reminder, but he couldn't dispute it.

Crawford said, "You still need to ID Rodriguez ASAP so you can either eliminate a connection to the perp or establish one. And something else—"

"You're telling me how to do my job?"

"I wouldn't dream of it. But you need to put everyone who was in the building at the time of the shooting under a microscope. Thoroughly question every person who was evacuated. And you can't use Prentiss PD or sheriff's office personnel to conduct the questioning."

"That's disqualifying over a hundred officers."

"Plus one."

"Who?"

"Where were you at the time of the shooting?"

Neal glared at him.

"Only kidding. But in addition to visitors and people who work in the courthouse, you have to question every law officer and public official. Every-damn-body."

"Do you have any idea the fallout this is going to create?"

"That's the least of my concerns. It should be the least of yours."

"Well, unlike you, I don't like the hot seat and do everything I can to protect my reputation."

"That's one point you don't have to sell me on, Neal. Ordinarily I wouldn't give a rat's ass what your priorities are. But Chet's killer is at large. To say nothing of the threat our unsub poses to Judge Spencer. I'd say that's more important than fallout. But that's just me."

That sank in. The detective no doubt had more words for Crawford, but he pulled himself together and addressed Holly. "You'll be under police protection until the perp is captured."

"As I've told Mr. Hunt, I won't go into hiding. First because of the message it would send to my opponent and constituents. But primarily because I don't want to give my attempted assassin the satisfaction of seeing me afraid."

Neal heard her out, then said, "I'm sorry, judge, but I know the chief, mayor, all your colleagues, and especially the governor will agree that you should keep a low profile and have 'round-the-clock bodyguards. I'll get Matt Nugent on that immediately."

"I've handled it."

"What?"

Neal and Holly had responded in unison, but Crawford directed his explanation to Neal. "I called our Houston office on the drive between the park and here. Two Rangers have already been dispatched."

Neal looked like he could have bit a nail in two. "On whose authority?"

"Mine. Which is the only one required. But, figuring you'd get your back up about my interference, I got clearance from my major lieutenant, who, along with the lieutenant in Tyler, happily agreed to your chief's request that I work the case. We're back to that, Neal. Sorry you got me out of bed this morning?" He continued before Neal could form a comeback. "Anyway, it's done. Rangers will be posted to guard her house."

"What about inside?"

"Forget it," she said succinctly.

"Nowadays, public officials in major cities, including judges, have guards with them constantly," Crawford said.

"This isn't a major city."

"We're not arguing about this, judge."

She backed down, but only to an extent. "All right. But I draw the line at having officers in the house. I made a call on the way here, too. A friend is coming to spend a few days with me."

"What friend?"

She replied coolly to Crawford's brusque question. "Someone I trust implicitly."

He wanted to ask who that implicitly trusted individual was, but Neal spoke first. "That's good." He glanced at his wristwatch and winced when he read the time. "Before it gets any later, I have to go ruin the chief's night."

Crawford said, "I'll see Judge Spencer home and stay with her till I'm no longer needed." He sensed her disapproval of that plan but didn't give her an opportunity to object. Effectively settling the matter, he got out of the booth.

"One thing before you go," Neal said.

Crawford looked down at him, and the smug tilt at one corner of the detective's lips signaled that he wasn't going to like what was coming.

"Your father-in-law called me this afternoon."

Even braced for something bad, Crawford was shocked to hear that. However, he kept his expression as uninterested as possible.

"Mr. Gilroy told me that you had refused to talk to him about your confrontation with Rodriguez up on the roof. He asked if I thought that was odd."

"Do you?"

"Do I think it's odd?" Neal shrugged. "A bit."

Trying to keep his anger under control, Crawford said, "I was under no obligation to talk to Joe about it. But the reason I declined to discuss it last night was because I had just wrapped up with you. I was beat and wanted to go home."

"That's the only reason you didn't share?"

Crawford tipped his head to one side. "Something on your mind, Neal?"

"I more or less wrote off Joe Gilroy's call because of the bad blood between you two."

"*But?*"

"*But* if what you say is true, and Rodriguez wasn't the gunman, then how you handled the situation takes on graver importance. Your reckless chase might have cost an innocent man his life."

Holly had factually cited all the reasons that Rodriguez was responsible for his own tragic death. And Neal was goading him because it was within Neal's petty nature to do so.

But his implication went straight to the heart of Crawford's misgivings about the swift action he'd taken. However, he'd be damned before he gave any indication of it. He said, "You can cover the tab."

By the time Neal caught up with him and Holly outside the diner, Crawford was giving her instructions. "Check your backseat before you get in the car. Don't leave the parking lot until I'm behind you. I'll be right there."

Holly said a terse good night to Neal, then turned and headed for her car.

As Neal was about to leave, Crawford halted him with a raised hand. Glancing toward Holly's retreating back, he said softly, "This is sensitive. I didn't want her to hear it." He hitched his head toward the corner of the building.

They fell into step. As soon as they rounded the corner, Crawford hauled off and slugged Neal in the mouth. The detective reeled backward, barely managing to stay on his feet, his hands cupped over his gushing split lip.

Crawford shook blood off his right hand. "You make another crack like that one about her skirt, *ever*, and I'll make stew meat out of your balls."

———•———

When they reached Holly's house, Crawford stepped out of his SUV, giving the surrounding shrubbery careful scrutiny. They met at the back door. She unlocked it. As they went in, he stepped around her. "Wait here."

Sliding his pistol from the holster at the small of his back, he went into the living room and made a visual sweep of it, avoiding looking directly at the sofa. He took the short hallway to her bedroom, which was traditional and tidy. He checked the closet and beneath the bed.

One glimpse into the bathroom told him there was no place in it for a grown man to hide, but he went in anyway because the compact space smelled deliciously of her. Hanging on a hook on the back of the door was the robe she'd been wearing last night. On his way out he brushed his hand across it, the texture sending a shaft of desire through him.

When he reentered the kitchen, she was standing at the open refrigerator. "Water?"

"Please."

She passed a bottle to him and took one for herself. As he tilted his toward his mouth, he caught her looking at the fresh blood on the knuckles of his right hand. "I barked them on the door of my truck."

She looked doubtful of that but didn't question him.

He moved to the sink and washed his hands with hot water and liquid soap. After drying them on a paper towel, he took off his jacket and draped it over the back of a dining chair. He pulled the holster from his waistband and set it on the table.

She followed his motions, her gaze lingering on the holstered pistol.

"Goes with the job," he said.

"So does a uniform."

"I wear it sometimes. But I can be plainclothes."

"Do you always wear that?" she asked, nodding down at the pistol.

"It's always handy. I keep it out of Georgia's reach when she's at my house." Thoughtfully, he ran his fingertips across the elaborately decorated butt of the official-issue pistol. "I wasn't wearing it when I went to court yesterday. But if I'd had my weapon, I wouldn't have had to waste valuable time getting Chet's. Chet might, in fact, be alive. Maybe I could have apprehended the shooter, and Rodriguez would have finished his cigarette in peace. The perp would be behind bars tonight, and Rodriguez would be somewhere besides the morgue."

She breathed deeply and let it out slowly. "I think we'll always be asking ourselves how things might have gone *if only*."

He nodded, but discovered he didn't have anything further to contribute to that train of thought, so he said nothing as they stood there looking at each other, a few cubic feet of kitchen space separating them. Just like the night before.

With apparent unease, she clasped her hands at waist level. "Marilyn should be here soon."

"Marilyn?"

"Marilyn Vidal. My campaign manager."

"Your trusted person?"

She nodded.

He was greatly relieved to learn that it wasn't Dennis who was on his way to spend the night with her. Admitting to that would be admitting to inappropriate feelings of jealousy. Instead he aimed for professional objectivity. "You explained the circumstances to her?"

"I didn't go into all of it over the telephone. She wanted to rush right here last night. I told her it wasn't necessary. But when you began talking about guards, I called her back and told her that I would appreciate her company and offered her my guest room."

"What's she like?"

"A steamroller."

"She didn't quail at the threat of danger?"

Holly gave a soft laugh. "She's tougher than anyone you could have placed in here."

Besides me.

"Marilyn and I have a good working relationship," she was saying. "I doubt we'll make ideal roommates." She glanced at the wall clock. "She should be here soon."

"You said that already. Anxious to get rid of me?"

"I didn't mean it that way."

"I think you did."

Exasperated, she said, "All right, maybe I did. This is awkward."

"Like returning to the scene of the crime."

She glanced guiltily toward the living room.

Crawford said, "You let what Neal said get to you."

"He isn't stupid. He knew we didn't have to conduct our conversation about Rodriguez in a parked car."

"Nothing we told him was a lie, Holly."

"No, but in terms of spin, it was a Tilt-a-Whirl. He thinks—"

"Doesn't matter what he thinks."

"It does if he thinks we've slept together!"

"We haven't."

She gave him a withering look. "Your language is just more vulgar than mine."

"And much more accurate."

Whatever you wanted to call what they'd done, he was ready for an encore, which said a lot about his character. Neal's crude remark had pissed him off, but mostly because it came so close to being the truth. He wanted under her skirt, and he wanted her under him.

She was all buttoned up again in her judge's clothes, proper suit and blouse, but he remembered the feel of the comfy t-shirt she'd been wearing last night, how crushable the fabric had been when he took a handful of it and pushed it out of his way. The skin of her inner thighs had been even softer than the cloth, and between them, softer yet.

"I'm hungry," he grumbled as he stepped around her and moved toward the refrigerator. "Do you have anything to eat?"

"Help yourself."

He inventoried the contents of the fridge and found deli ham and sliced cheese in a drawer. He set them out on the counter. By the time he'd chosen the condiments he preferred, she'd taken a loaf of bread from the pantry.

"Make a sandwich for yourself," he said.

"I'm not hungry."

"Eat anyway. Plates?"

She indicated the cabinet where he could find them, then listlessly removed two slices of bread from the wrapper and stacked them on the plate he slid along the counter toward her. "You should leave before Marilyn arrives."

"We've exhausted all the reasons why you should have someone with you." He slapped a slice of ham onto the bread and slathered it with mustard.

"But it looks like—"

"What?" He stopped trying to wrestle a slice of Swiss cheese out of the package and turned toward her. "What does it look like, Holly? Like I'm trying my damnedest to keep my hands off you? To keep from thinking about it? To cancel it? Like that's gonna happen," he scoffed. "But is that what this looks like? Because that's what I'm doing. The other thing I'm doing is trying to protect you from a guy who wants you dead." He stopped, took a breath. "Now, for the last time, I'm here because you shouldn't be alone."

"I shouldn't be alone with *you*."

"Too bad. You are."

"Someone else could have been sent to guard me."

"They're being sent. In the meantime, I was readily available."

"Because you—"

"Because I don't want another dead woman on my conscience!"

Chapter 13

$H$is shouted statement left them in a sudden and tense silence. They continued looking at each other for several seconds, then, cursing under his breath, Crawford turned away and finished building his sandwich.

Holly made one for herself and carried her plate to the table. He waited until she was seated before sitting down across from her, then hungrily tucked in.

She picked at the crust of bread. "You're referring to Beth."

"I don't want to talk about it. Besides, you know everything. It's in my 'file.'"

"I know that she died in a car crash, a terrible accident."

Placing his elbows on the table, he bent over his plate and muttered, "Officially."

"You disagree with that ruling?"

"My father-in-law does. He'll tell you what he thinks about Beth's accident. Ask him." Raising he head, he looked across at her, his eyes cold and hard. "Or have you already?"

"Not specifically."

"Well, save your breath. I can tell you, he blames me."

"According to the accident report, Beth was doing

over eighty miles an hour. The car spun out of control and hit a utility pole."

His eyes lost focus and seemed to be looking at the gruesome scene. "I was told she died on impact. I guess that's something."

Speaking barely above a whisper, she said, "I'm sorry."

"Thanks."

"Georgia was spared."

"She didn't have a scratch. A miracle, really."

Holly asked, "What part of the police report do you dispute?"

"None of it. But there's more to an accident than the physics of the collision. There's the human factor, and in this instance, it was huge."

Yes, there had been extenuating circumstances surrounding the deadly crash. Holly knew what they were, but she wanted to hear what he had to say about them.

He ate the last bite of his sandwich, washed it down with a swallow from his bottle of water, then wiped his mouth with the back of his hand. When the silence between them stretched out, he gave her a surly look. "What?"

"Talk to me about it."

"Why?"

"Is it too painful for you to talk about?"

"No."

"Then…" She raised her shoulders.

He exhaled a long breath tinged with impatience. "Beth would never have left the house that night, would never have been on the road, speeding, plowing into a light pole, if she hadn't been frantic to get to me. She didn't even change Georgia out of her pajamas, just took her from her crib, strapped her in her car seat, and split."

All that was a matter of record. The court-appointed

psychologist's report had given the facts nuance. She had assessed that the guilt he felt over the death of his wife, as misplaced as it was, had been as profound and debilitating as his grief. In the counselor's opinion, he had finally forgiven himself.

But evidently he hadn't. Not completely. The scars of guilt were permanent. He had merely learned to live with them.

"Tell me about Halcon."

He assumed a thoughtful air and stroked his chin. "Well, let's see, what would you find interesting about Halcon? Here's something. Nobody seems to know why the city fathers kept the Spanish pronunciation but dropped the accent mark above the *o*."

She frowned at his lame attempt to divert her.

Irritably, he pushed back his chair and carried his empty plate to the sink. "You can read all about the gunfight online."

"I have."

He turned around, still surly. "I'll bet you have. Before or since the hearing?"

"Before. I wanted to know exactly what had happened out there because everything that's happened since harked back to that showdown between you and Manuel Fuentes."

He watched her for a moment, then tilted his head to one side. "Why a judge?"

"Pardon?"

Folding his arms, he leaned back against the counter. "I'll trade you one for one, Your Honor. I'll answer a question about Halcon in exchange for an answer from you." When she hesitated, he said, "Until Marilyn gets here, we've got nothing better to do."

Then he turned his head and looked through the door leading into the living room and, beyond it, the bedroom. When he came back to her, he asked roughly, "Do we?"

Although she experienced a rush of heat, she assumed her courtroom voice. "I get to go first."

"Fine."

"It was said that Fuentes had become an obsession with you. Is that true? Were you that determined to get him?"

"'No matter what the cost.' That's a direct quote from the *Houston Chronicle* write-up about the shootout."

"Which put Halcon on the map."

"And me in dutch." He took a moment to collect his thoughts, then began speaking matter-of-factly. "Fuentes had been on the radar for years, pumping drugs into the U.S., pumping weapons into Mexico, and making incalculable profits from both transactions. He was ambitious, audacious, and ruthless, eliminating anyone he perceived as an enemy or competition.

"His methods of execution were more grisly than you can possibly imagine. Medieval. And he circulated graphic photographs of his handiwork to terrorize and intimidate. We'll never know exactly how many people he and members of his cartel killed. Countless, literally. He had to be put out of business."

"And you had to be the one to do it?"

"It's my turn. Why'd you go after the appointment when Judge Waters got sick? Why not remain a highly paid attorney like your dad?"

"You've gone online, too, I see."

He raised his shoulder in a pseudo admission.

"Before or after the hearing?"

"I wanted to know who I was coming up against," he replied. "Get a sense of the person inside the robe." After a beat, he added, "But even having formed a basic profile of Judge Holly Spencer, you were a...surprise."

Their gazes held until she lowered hers. "Dad was a lawyer, yes. A very successful defense attorney in Dallas."

"A pal of Judge Waters."

"They had forged a friendship while at Tulane."

"But you went the way of the judge, not your dad. Why?"

"Actually, it's my turn," she said. "Before that day in Halcon, did you ever meet Fuentes face-to-face?"

"No. Nobody knew where he lived, and I'm guessing he was migratory, too smart to stay in one place for any length of time. I figured he was guarded by a veritable army. I studied him, and pegged him as a peacock, an egomaniac. He was a savvy self-promoter who manipulated the Mexican media. He thumbed his nose at law enforcement agencies on both sides of the border. He seemed untouchable. He thought he was."

He flashed a malicious smile, his gray eyes glinting. "I figured that's how we'd catch him. He would become overconfident, strut one too many times, and when he did, we'd be there."

He uncrossed his arms and placed his hands on the counter behind him, bracketing his hips. She tried to avoid looking at the intriguing surface area between, but it was difficult not to look, gauge, recall the feel of him expanding her, filling her.

He asked, "Why Judge Waters's footsteps and not Daddy's?"

She reached for her bottle of water and began playing at twisting the cap off and on. "My father lived the cliché. In middle age, he left my mother for a much younger woman."

"How old were you?"

"Fourteen."

"How'd that go? The affair, I mean."

"For him? Very well. He and the woman married, and stayed married until he died."

He frowned. "Could she be the secret enemy behind the shooting?"

She shook her head. "I've never even met her. At Dad's funeral we pretended the other didn't exist."

"Did they have children together?"

"And ruin her trophy-wife figure? No way."

"What about his estate?"

"Everything went to her, so she isn't begrudging me an inheritance, if that's what you're thinking. His will was airtight. In any case, Mom and I didn't contest it. Six months after he died, his recent widow relocated to Chicago and linked up with a big-shot hedge fund guy." She gave the cap another twist. "Fuentes came out of hiding to attend a party."

"That's not a question."

"Humor me."

"He came to Halcon for his niece's *quinceañera*."

"Her fifteenth birthday party."

"A big deal in the Hispanic culture. A girl's coming-out. We figured Fuentes would attend to honor the memory of his late brother, the girl's father. He'd been killed by an El Paso narc officer the year before."

"You were put in charge of the ambush."

"I campaigned for it."

"You'd only been a Texas Ranger a little over a year."

"But I'd spent eight years with the DPS."

"Not setting speed traps."

His eyebrows shot up. "You did a lot of online reading."

She smiled. "You were in the Criminal Investigations Division."

"Mostly in the drug program."

"You stopped traffickers."

"Small-timers. A few middlemen. I wanted to cut off the head of the snake. Soon as we heard about the upcoming party for Fuentes's niece, I moved to Halcon, spent months keeping my head down, eyes and ears open. Worked in a hardware and feed store as my cover."

"Was Beth with you?"

"It's not your turn."

She just looked at him. He relented. "No. She was pregnant, and the situation was too dangerous. If my cover was blown, Fuentes would've killed her, too, probably before he came after me, just to make a point. We were living in Houston at the time. I drove home to see her when I could."

"Were you with her when Georgia was born?"

He cleared his throat. "Yeah." Lowering his head, he stared down at the toes of his boots and for several moments seemed immersed in the memory. "I was right there. Soon as the cord was cut, the doctor handed Georgia to me." He laughed softly. "I didn't know something that little could make that much racket."

His head came up in time to catch Holly's smile, and he returned it.

But he immediately turned serious again. "It was hard to leave them, to go back to Halcon. Beth begged me not to. We fought about it. But Fuentes was still wreaking havoc. I had a job to finish."

"Was Beth ever reconciled to that?"

"No," he said gruffly. "I don't think she was."

Then, in a sudden shift of mood and topic, he asked her if her mother had ever remarried.

"She never even went on a date. Dad's leaving had shattered her self-confidence. Until the day she died, she was a very unhappy woman, and her unhappiness wasn't merely from a broken heart."

"What else?"

"Dad knew all the loopholes and used them unscrupulously in the divorce settlement. Mom didn't have the wherewithal to fight him. I was too young. He walked away without a care. For my mom and me, it wasn't so breezy. When Dad declined to help finance my education, Judge Waters broke off all contact with him."

"And came to your aid."

"He helped me obtain a scholarship. The rest you more or less know."

He gave her a thoughtful look. "I also come from a broken home. My mom lives in California with husband number two."

"Do you see her? Does Georgia?"

"Every other year or so. Mom's not what you'd call a nurturer, and Georgia doesn't see her enough to know her. By name only, really. Which is fine with me."

"And your father?"

"He's a son of a bitch."

"Like mine."

"Worse."

She laughed lightly. "I've called mine worse, believe me. But," she said, emphasizing the qualifier, "he did me a favor. He directed my career choice."

"Ah, family law. Your specialty." His eyes narrowed to slits. "I get it now. You're fighting a personal crusade. You want women to get a square deal out of their lying, cheating, leaving, thieving husbands."

"I'm fighting a personal crusade for fairness. Neither party should be disenfranchised, especially by lawyers' tricks."

"When you preside over a divorce or a custody hearing, your experience doesn't bias you in favor of women?"

"No."

"Come on. Just a little? You don't enjoy scoring points against dear ol' dad?"

"That's not why I sought the appointment, not why I want to be a judge."

He tilted his head as though he doubted that.

"What happened that day in Halcon?"

Returning to that subject, his goading smile dissolved. "I'd handpicked six men from three different agencies. These six were seasoned officers. Badasses. In their way, just as ruthless as Fuentes. They were as committed to ending his career as I was."

"You wanted him dead or alive."

"That was understood. Either way, he'd be a jackpot." He lapsed into thought, and it was several moments before he continued. "One guy was planted inside, working for the party caterer. The rest of us put a net around the town. We waited all friggin' day, and it was hotter than hell. I was beginning to think we'd go home empty-handed, that Fuentes wouldn't show.

"But then late in the afternoon, a rattletrap panel truck pulled up to the back door of the party hall. It looked like a heap, but under the hood was the souped-up engine of a race car. Fuentes climbed out wearing a suit worth five thousand dollars, ten times that much in gold and diamonds, and ostrich boots with silver-tipped toes."

"A peacock."

He nodded. "Four bodyguards accompanied him inside. Two stayed with the truck. We moved into posi-tion, planning to take out Fuentes when he returned to the truck. Of course we didn't expect him or his men to lay down their weapons and surrender when ordered to. We knew there would be a gunfight. We just hoped to neutralize them before they could do too much damage."

"But things didn't go according to plan."

"No. The son of a bitch must've figured that if any heat was around, we'd be waiting on him as he left. So he didn't go out the way he'd gone in. He went out the front entrance, the last thing we thought he'd do."

"Why?"

"The party hall was at the end of a cul-de-sac. I didn't think he would let himself get boxed in."

"A logical conclusion."

He gave a harsh laugh. "Yeah, well, Fuentes defied logic. We were in positions behind the building, jazzed, locked and loaded, when our guy on the inside started frantically whispering in my earbud that Fuentes was heading out the front door.

"I had a millisecond to decide. Scrub it, or go after him? But if we missed him then…" He shifted his eyes slightly and met hers directly. "I didn't even complete the thought. That's all the consideration I gave it before engaging."

He'd reacted just as spontaneously in the courtroom, but she kept the observation to herself.

"I left my cover and ran full out toward the front of the building," he said. "When I rounded the corner, I saw Fuentes and his four guards walking quickly toward a limo, one of the cortege that had brought the honoree and her family from the church service to the party.

"I called out to Fuentes by name and identified myself. He spun away, like he would duck back into the building. I already had my weapon up. I went for a head shot." He raised his shoulder, letting the gesture speak for him. "He was dust. But all hell broke loose. My inside guy came barreling out through the entrance. One of Fuentes's bodyguards shot and killed him instantly.

"By now, all of us were in an exchange. Fuentes's men inside the panel truck were killed, but not before

mortally wounding a DEA agent. He died in surgery."
He closed his eyes and rubbed them with his thumb
and index finger. "Tough as boot leather, but a really
likeable guy. He had a new joke every day, although he
couldn't tell one worth a damn. Always gave away the
punch line."

He dropped his hand from his eyes but kept his
head lowered, staring at the floor. "Final body count:
six of them, two of us. That's not counting the three
partygoers who were killed in the crossfire."

Holly said quietly, "They were killed by Fuentes's
men, not yours."

"True. Ballistics proved it. But my more outspoken
critics dismissed that as a minor detail. The point was
that if I hadn't initiated the shootout, there wouldn't
have been any collateral damage at all. And they're
right." Looking over at her, he added, "I was as much
of a peacock as fucking Fuentes. I wanted a showdown
with him, and I got one. A damned bloody one."

"You were injured."

"Wasn't referring to that."

"I know, but you *were* shot."

"In the calf. Hurt like a mother. Entry near my shin-
bone. Out the back. I didn't know at the time if it was
serious or superficial. In either case, I wanted an ortho-
pedic surgeon to work on it, not the hack in Halcon
who we figured was on Fuentes's payroll and was likely
to cripple me for life. CareFlight took the seriously
injured to the nearest trauma center, which was in
Laredo. EMTs determined that my injury wasn't life-
threatening, so I was ferried by chopper to Houston."

"Meanwhile, Beth was notified that you had been
wounded."

"And requiring surgery. But she wasn't given any
details. She must've pictured me barely holding on,

bleeding to death, brain swelling out of my skull, something. Anyway, she grabbed Georgia and—" He stopped. "This is where we came in, judge. My turn to ask a question."

"All right."

"How much of this did you know yesterday when we went into court?"

She had been expecting a question about herself, not his custody hearing. She took several seconds to form her reply, then quietly confessed to knowing all of it. "Not the fine details, but most of it."

"Um-huh," he said, as though unsurprised. "And how much bearing did Halcon have on your decision?"

"I didn't make a decision."

"If you had."

"I can't quantify—"

"Yeah you can."

She got up and carried her untouched plate of food to the counter. "We're not going to talk about this. I've told you so repeatedly, starting with our first conversation last night in the hallway of police headquarters. Remember? I said then—"

He interrupted her by moving suddenly to bring them face-to-face. "I remember everything you said, Holly. But mostly I remember wanting to look at you while you said it."

The declaration left her speechless, breathless, and, later, she wondered what would have been said or done next if his cell phone hadn't rung.

Without looking away from her, he let it ring three times before yanking it from his belt. "Yeah?" He listened, then said, "I'll be right out."

As he returned his phone to his belt, he said, "Rangers are here and in place. What kind of car does Marilyn drive?"

She told him.

"Where's your phone?"

She took it from her handbag, handed it over, and gave him the security code. He accessed her contacts and entered two names and cell numbers.

"Under Rangers. Don't forget." He returned the phone to her. "Keep it with you at all times and call one of them immediately if you see or hear anything. That's what they're there for. If you change your mind and want one of them inside the house, just ask."

"It won't be necessary."

"Doesn't have to be necessary. Don't be ashamed to ask if only for your peace of mind. No shame in sleeping with the lights on, either."

"I probably will."

They exchanged a quick smile. After reattaching his holster and slipping on his jacket then he opened the door. "Lock and bolt this behind me."

"I will."

"You gonna be all right?"

"Of course. I won't be alone for long."

"Okay then, good night."

"Good night."

He stood there straddling the threshold for several seconds, then mumbled something as he pushed the door shut and, with some quick maneuvering, managed to cage her against the adjacent wall, his hands pressed flat to it on either side of her head.

"Don't," she said.

"Why not? I had just as well. What have I got to lose? After the screwup with Rodriguez, the whole friggin' mess, I don't have a snowball's chance in hell of getting Georgia back, do I?"

"I can't—"

"Do I?"

"You—"

"*Do I?*" When she made no further attempt to answer, he nodded. "Figured as much. Even if you could get past all the other, you'll never get past what happened on that couch in there."

"That has no bearing—"

"Bullshit."

"I'm as much to blame for that as you."

"That's not what you said earlier tonight. You suggested I'd had an ulterior motive."

"That was wrong of me. I know you didn't plan it. I know you regret what we did."

"Hell I do," he growled. "I only regret what we *didn't*." Keeping his hands on the wall, he pressed into her softness with unmistakable implication, bending his head, and claiming her mouth with his.

For crissake, we didn't even kiss, he'd said.

He rectified that now, fiercely and possessively, and she let him. Leaving her arms at her sides, she went limp against him and allowed him complete access to her mouth. His tongue was wild and willful, reminiscent of the urgency of last night's coupling.

And then it gentled. Passion was replaced by tenderness, and that was even more undoing. The sweeps of his tongue became less aggressive, but much more intimate. Then, with a moan, he withdrew his mouth from hers, but only to bury it in her hair. His arm encircled her waist to secure her more firmly against him. She closed her arms around him and made a corresponding move to the evocative pressure he applied between her thighs.

They stayed that way, just holding each other, until he pulled his head up and looked into her eyes for several seconds, then pushed away from the wall and went out the door, pulling it closed behind him with a bang of finality.

———

Pat Connor's hand was shaking as he used the burner phone he'd been given expressly for this purpose— to impart bad news, should any arise. His call was answered after two rings. "What?"

The gruff voice alone was enough to make Pat cringe. "I thought you should know. Starting first thing tomorrow, everybody evacuated from the courthouse yesterday will be questioned again."

"How do you know?"

"Grapevine. Came from the chief of police about an hour ago. There's a lot of bellyaching in the rank and file. They're gonna question all law enforcement personnel. Judges. City officials. Everybody. The real kicker? They're bringing in outside officers to conduct the interviews."

There was a sustained silence on the other end and, when Pat couldn't stand the strain any longer, he said, "I figure there's only one reason they'd be going to all that trouble and pissing people off."

"They know they got the wrong man."

Pat saw the wisdom of keeping his trap shut. He'd done what he had been ordered to do, which had been to keep his eyes and ears open for any further developments. Maybe delivering this heads-up would get the man off his back.

That hope was dashed when he was told, "Keep yourself easy to find."

Chapter 14

———◆———

Crawford rolled to a stop alongside a dark-colored SUV similar to his own. The driver lowered the tinted window, and a face like that on a Native American nickel appeared. "Hey, Crawford."

"Thanks for coming."

"They killed the wrong guy? That's a pisser."

"Tell me."

"Her judgeship inside?"

"And alone for the time being, so don't blink."

In addition to his harsh features, Harry Longbow's name attested to his heritage. He traced his lineage to the Comanche, the fierce horsemen tribe of the Texas plains, whose raids on settlers had kept them at odds with early Texas Rangers. The Rangers had endured. Harry joked that he wouldn't hold that against the agency, if the agency wouldn't hold his gene pool against him. He'd been one of Crawford's hand-chosen few in Halcon.

"Is that Sessions?" Crawford nodded at the other vehicle parked at the far end of the street.

"He was itching to come along. Wife's redecorating and has him looking at wallpaper and carpet samples."

Wayne Sessions was just as seasoned an officer as

Harry, with whom he often partnered, but he was also a whiz on the computer, and was never without his laptop. Both were good men to have at your back.

Crawford alerted Harry to Marilyn Vidal's imminent arrival and gave him the make of her car. "Any other vehicles, consider suspicious. Nobody lives on this lane except Judge Spencer and an elderly lady in the main house. Oh, she's got three cats. Pass that along to Sessions. Don't mistake a prowling feline for our perp."

"Last thing you need, us blowing away an old lady's cats."

Crawford saluted him as he drove off. The streets of Holly's neighborhood were empty, nothing appeared even remotely threatening, but the farther he got from her house, the more powerful his urge to turn around and go back. As reliable as the other Rangers were, he wanted to be the one watching over her, protecting her.

"Professional objectivity, my ass," he muttered. Not since Beth had he kissed a woman like that. Not since Beth had he wanted to. Which was exhilarating and troubling in equal measure.

For the past four years he'd been paying self-imposed penance for the role he'd played in the fatal accident that took Beth's life. When he got lonely, he figured he deserved to be. But what he knew now that he hadn't known twenty-four hours ago was that self-denial was easy only if you were indifferent to what you denied yourself. Denying yourself something you wanted like hell was torture.

After he'd stopped the excessive drinking and getting into bar fights, well-meaning friends began encouraging him to date and offering to set him up with suitable women, saying things like, "Beth wouldn't want you to live the rest of your life alone."

To which he usually responded, "How the hell do you know what Beth would want?"

Although it was a quarrelsome comeback to a banality, it was also a valid but unanswerable question. No one, not even he, knew what Beth would want for his future without her. But whatever, self-denial seemed key to his atonement.

As he'd admitted to Holly, he'd taken women to bed, but only when a convenient opportunity presented itself, and, on those occasions, his involvement had ended with his climax. He'd never bothered to follow up with any of them because he simply had no interest in doing so. And he made damn sure his one-night stands didn't result in unhappy consequences. For anyone.

Last night he hadn't thought about any of that. Not Beth. Not consequences, none of it. He'd touched Holly and desire as unstoppable as an avalanche had overwhelmed him, and it hadn't been assuaged by that hard-and-fast in her living room, which was no sooner begun than it was over.

He wanted more of her, and not just *that*. He wanted more of *her*. The hell of it was, she was completely, totally unattainable. Because if he continued pinning her against walls and kissing her like he wanted to, he could kiss good-bye any chance he had of getting Georgia back.

He couldn't let that happen. Nothing, or no one, could interfere with his determination to be Georgia's full-time daddy. The sun would burn itself out before he shrugged off his kid the way his old man had.

Acting on that resolve, he pulled his SUV onto the shoulder of the road, shoved the gear into park, and reached for his phone. He'd programmed her number on his speed dial. She answered on the second ring.

"Hello?"

"It's me."

"I saw your name."

"Your friend there yet?"

"No. Is something wrong?"

"Yeah." Crawford covered his eyes with his hand. "I don't want to want you, Holly. But I do. God knows I do."

She didn't say anything, but her breathing turned unsteady.

"The bitch of it is, I can't have you. Not if I want custody of Georgia."

"I understand."

She didn't. But he let her believe that she did. Neither said anything for the longest time, but they kept the line open, listening to each other breathe. Finally he rasped, "Good-bye, Holly."

"Good-bye—"

She clicked off, but he could swear that she'd caught herself just before saying his name.

———

"Crawford Hunt. It has a nice, masculine heft. What's he like?"

Marilyn Vidal, despite her glamourous-sounding name, was squarely built and didn't embellish her plain features by wearing makeup or jewelry. She operated her business from Dallas but had worked in nearly every state, saving foundering candidates for various political offices, but only if she felt strongly about their winning potential. She couldn't be bothered with losers, didn't tolerate whiners, didn't suffer fools.

She gave extra points to clients who could lie with equanimity and eloquence.

Holly wasn't inclined to lying, and she certainly

didn't do it well. Marilyn's question about Crawford Hunt filled her with ambiguity. This morning she had vowed to throw away the robe she'd been wearing last night, but when she stepped from the shower only a few minutes ago, it was that robe she'd reached for and wrapped herself in.

She'd also resolved to discard her sofa at the earliest opportunity so she wouldn't have to see it each day and remember what had taken place on it. But here she was, curled into the corner of it, hugging to her chest one of the throw pillows that had been haphazardly knocked onto the floor as they'd tried to make room.

There was much she could tell her campaign manager about Crawford Hunt—that he wore soft, frayed, button-fly jeans, that the dark blond hair that grew over his shirt collar was thick but surprisingly soft, that he made an erotically animalistic sound when in the throes of passion, and that his recent telephone call—essentially telling her to have a nice life—had left her feeling disconsolate, not relieved, as she should have been.

But of course she said none of that. In reply to Marilyn, who was industriously pacing the width of the sofa, she said, "He's...I don't know...cop-like."

She rubbed the space between her eyebrows, which, she realized, she'd been doing a lot lately, and it was a habit reserved for when she was especially stressed. Marilyn had been under her roof for all of ten minutes, and already she regretted having her as a houseguest.

Marilyn seemed to drain those around her of their vitality, then absorb it, giving her a surplus. It was hard to say whether or not that siphoning of energy was intentional or a trait of which Marilyn was unaware. Holly suspected the former.

In light of yesterday's events, she had arrived even

more super-charged than usual. As she filled a highball glass with vodka, which she'd brought with her, she said, "When I got here, I was surprised not to find media camped out on the lawn."

"This is a small town, Marilyn."

"Which made big news yesterday."

Holly conceded that with a weary nod. "Mrs. Briggs was busy all day fending off calls from reporters. I finally released a statement that didn't divulge any sensitive information. Essentially it said that I had nothing to add to the police spokesperson's brief."

"We'll change that tomorrow. It's time you came out from under cover and made a public statement about the whacked-out Michelin man who shot up your courtroom. You don't get an opportunity like this in every campaign."

"That 'opportunity' cost two men their lives."

"Right. It's high drama, and you need to take advantage of it. It's a shame you didn't alert someone to your visit with the widow. That would have made great press."

She regretted now telling Marilyn about her condolence call. Her expression must've indicated her disapproval of Marilyn's callousness.

"Okay, okay," she said, waving her unlit cigarette. "I'm an insensitive bitch, but it's been a day and a half since the shooting. We need to start making hay."

"I can't compromise the ongoing police investigation."

"What's to investigate? It's not like there's a big freaking mystery here. They got the guy."

Holly didn't correct her. Like the rest of the world, Marilyn would learn of the mishap tomorrow. Holly anticipated an explosive reaction from her campaign manager, and she was too frazzled to deal with it tonight.

Marilyn was pouring her second vodka. "Tomorrow, you need to appear looking appropriately saddened, but resolved that nothing like yesterday's tragedy will ever happen again. 'Not in my courtroom. Not in my county.' See where I'm going? Make it an issue of your campaign."

"In other words, exploit it."

"Hell, yes, it's exploitative. But…Here." She slid an issue of the local newspaper from the outside pocket of her bulging briefcase and placed it on the coffee table. "I saw this in the convenience store when I stopped for cigarettes. Greg Sanders is exploiting the hell out of it."

In the photo accompanying the front-page story, her opponent was captured with his fist raised high above his head.

"He looks like a fire-breathing evangelist," Holly said. "I believe the picture was taken as he was sowing seeds of uncertainty about my past, which suddenly has become shady. It's a scattershot attack. There's no basis whatsoever for any of his sly implications. Who would take him seriously?"

"Voters."

"Did you read the quote from Governor Hutchins? He stands by his decision to appoint me."

"Of course he does. In typical public official fashion, he's covering his ass." Marilyn fixed her with a stare. "Is your heart still in this, Holly? Do you want to keep that bench or not?"

"Of course I do."

"Then you had better get your butt in gear."

"For heaven's sake, Marilyn, cut me some slack. If I'm less than my sparkly self, it's because I'm tired to the point of collapse. I've had a grueling two days. I'm—"

"Oh, boo-hoo. I'm not your mother. I'm not your

best friend and confidante. I'm your campaign manager. You're paying me to see to it that you win."

"I will win."

"Not if you stay soft on something as earthshaking as a goddamn fatal shooting in your courtroom." Slapping her fist into her other palm, she said, "Yes, your opponent's ranting is ridiculous, but you must confront it. If you don't, it will look like there *is* something shady in your past."

She stopped and eyed Holly speculatively. "I'm trusting that's not the case. You and Waters...?"

Holly merely glared.

"Okay. Your relationship was as pure as the driven snow."

"It was."

"But Sanders isn't going to spring a nasty surprise, is he? A mental disorder during your teen years? Raging kleptomania? A love child? Illicit affair?"

Holly's cheeks grew warm as she became aware of the sofa beneath her. But she shook her head in reply to Marilyn's question.

"Well then, you need to go on record stating that you have no idea why this obviously unbalanced individual did what he did, but it sure as hell had nothing to do with you personally. You're outraged over the death of your bailiff. *Your* bailiff. Make his murder a personal loss. You're heartbroken."

"Which it was, and which I am."

"Then say so! It's too bad Sanders beat you to the punch by setting up that fund for his widow and grandkids."

"It was tasteless grandstanding."

"Of course it was, but it gave him a platform." She took a drink of vodka. "What we need is theater. We need—"

"What I need is sleep." Holly replaced the throw pillow and stood up. "I can't talk about it anymore tonight. Your Honor is calling a recess and going to bed."

"I'm going to stay up for a while, thinking."

"The guest room is tiny, but I think you'll have everything you need. Good night." She turned and started down the hall toward her bedroom.

"Would he be of any use to us?"

Holly stopped and turned back. "Who?"

"The Texas Ranger. Would he be any good on camera?"

Holly panicked at the thought of Marilyn approaching Crawford and talking about "theater" to advance her campaign. "Absolutely not."

"He's a hero."

"But not a glory-seeker. The opposite, in fact. He's shunned the limelight, too, and he's adamant about protecting his daughter from it."

"Oh," Marilyn said, frowning. "That's no fun, then."

"I assure you, it's not the least bit fun. Leave him alone."

Still frowning thoughtfully, Marilyn unconsciously placed the cigarette in her mouth and reached for her lighter.

Holly added sternly, "And don't smoke in my house."

———

"Crawford, I wish you'd called first. I've already put Georgia down."

Grace answered the door dressed in a robe and slippers. It wasn't that late, but even so, she looked unusually haggard, ill at ease, and none too glad to see him. She didn't invite him in.

"How is she?"

"Fine. But I let her stay up past bedtime to finish a new DVD. By the time it was over, she was nearly asleep. Joe had to carry her to bed."

"Then I won't wake her up. Actually, I came to see Joe."

"Right now isn't a good time." His mother-in-law began twisting her fingers together. "We were on our way to bed. We haven't quite recovered from yesterday."

"Neither have I."

"Then don't you think it's probably best if we…"

"What?"

"If we keep some distance."

"Why?"

"Because Joe has been on a tear, and nothing good will come out of you two going at each other."

"I couldn't agree with you more. But I'm not sure Joe is of the same mind. Or else why did he call Neal Lester and raise questions about my 'odd' behavior?"

"Let him in, Grace."

Joe's harsh voice cut through the darkness behind her, and a second later he stepped into view. In contrast to Grace's deshabille, he was as stiffly starched as ever. Crawford wondered if he slept that way.

Reluctantly, Grace moved aside, making room for Crawford in the entryway, then, after getting a pointed look from her husband, she excused herself and retreated in the direction of their bedroom at the back of the house.

He and Joe squared off. Crawford said, "You're rattling sabers, Joe."

"I warned you of a fight."

"Between you and me. Why'd you take it to Neal?"

"Your refusal to talk about your exchange with Rodriguez—"

"I didn't refuse. I postponed talking about it."

"—left me asking some hard questions about how you handled that situation."

"Why didn't you come to me with those questions?"

"I considered them to be a matter for the police."

"Like hell you did. It was a cheap shot to get to me. Unworthy of you, Joe."

"I'll use any means to keep Georgia."

"That's what worries me. You've lost your perspective, and Georgia will be the one to suffer for it."

"How do you figure that?"

"Have you been talking trash about me in front of her?"

"I don't have to answer to you."

"Where Georgia is concerned, you do."

"Not while I still have legal custody. Besides, I speak only the truth about you, and your daughter needs to hear it."

"You think you're going to win her affection by bad-mouthing me?"

"Tell you what, you can raise that issue the next time we're in court."

"Tell *you* what, Joe," Crawford fired back, "not a fucking chance. I won't do anything that necessitates Georgia being in on a hearing. I can't believe you would drag a five-year-old into a pissing contest between you and me."

"That's what you think this is?" He snorted.

"Isn't it? One of the main reasons you're contesting my petition is simply to spite me."

"Not so. I want what's best for my granddaughter."

"Save it for the judge. Save it for when you're under oath. If you're spoiling for a fight, I'll give you one. But let's conduct it in a court of law."

Crawford took a step closer to him. Joe held his position, but since he was shorter, he had to tilt his head back in order to look into Crawford's face. "*But*, if you keep saying in Georgia's presence that I'm to blame for everything—"

"You are! Beth would be alive if not for you."

"If you insist on making our fight personal, I'll oblige you. For four long years I've taken your crap for Grace's sake. For Georgia's sake. But push me hard enough, and you'll lose not only Georgia but something you value even more."

"There is nothing I value more."

"Oh, but there is."

Crawford spoke softly but emphatically, and, for the first time since he'd known the man, Joe looked uncertain. But the chink in his armor closed up as fast as it had appeared. He thrust out his chin. "How dare you threaten me, you—"

"Daddy?"

Crawford jerked his gaze off his father-in-law. Georgia had come from her bedroom into the hallway and was regarding them warily. She had sensed the anger between them, causing her to hesitate rather than to run and greet him as she normally would have.

He sidestepped his father-in-law and pasted on a smile. "Well, if it isn't Miss Sleepyhead."

"Are you and Grandpa mad?"

"No. We were just talking." In her nightie, with her fair curls tousled, she looked so sweet and vulnerable, it made his heart ache. He scooped her up and carried her into her bedroom, settling into the rocking chair with her on his lap, cupping his hand around her bare toes. "I heard you got a new DVD."

She snuggled against him and nestled her head on his chest. "Grandma brought it for me when we went to Walmart."

"Is it about a princess?"

"She lives in a castle. But it's got holes in the roof and mean birds fly through them and scare her."

"She lives there by herself?"

"Her mommy's in heaven like mine."

She rarely talked about not having a mother, but any time she did, it was like being speared in the gut, the soul. "What about her daddy?"

"He's funny. He has whiskers."

"Whiskers? Maybe I should grow some. How would you like that? Big, bushy whiskers." He delighted in her giggle. Nuzzling her neck where she was ticklish, he said, "You're my princess, and I love you."

"I love you, too, Daddy. Are you really gonna grow whiskers?"

She offered her opinion of that by wrinkling her nose, looking so damn cute, he laughed out loud. For the next quarter hour, he held her close. Just yesterday, he'd gone to court, hoping that it would end with him moving her permanently into her new bedroom. It would remain vacant a while longer.

"I have a big surprise waiting for you the next time you spend the night with me," he told her.

"What is it?"

"I can't tell or it won't be a surprise. But I'll give you a hint." He whispered in her ear. "It's pink."

She made a few guesses, then yawned hugely.

"Bedtime for you, young lady." He carried her over to the bed and tucked her in.

She rolled onto her side and mumbled into the pillow, "I already said my prayers."

"Okay," he whispered and kissed her cheek. "Sleep tight."

In the hallway outside her bedroom, Joe was waiting like a sentinel. The implication that Georgia needed to be protected from him made Crawford livid. But he didn't give in to it, mostly because he figured Joe would enjoy seeing him upset.

"Joe, prepare yourself for a bombshell." He told him about Rodriguez not being the shooter.

Joe maintained his military stance, but he blinked rapidly several times. "How did you discover that?"

"That's a matter for the police," Crawford said, taking pleasure in throwing Joe's words back at him. "The only reason I'm telling you tonight is because the news will probably break in the morning. You and Grace may be called on for comment."

Joe looked him up and down with scorn. "Jesus Christ. The calamity you're capable of never ceases to amaze me."

Crawford went around him and opened the front door, looking back in order to deliver his parting words. "Don't push too hard, Joe, or I swear to God, you'll be sorry."

Chapter 15

———◆———

Overnight, Neal Lester must have done as Crawford suggested and had the ME check Rodriguez's knee cap for a bruise, because Houston and Tyler TV stations aired the story about the "egregious error" during their local break-ins of the national morning shows. A public information officer from the Prentiss PD owned up to the mistake.

"It's been determined that the man killed by SWAT officers on the roof was not the individual who opened fire in Judge Spencer's courtroom minutes earlier."

Just like that, Crawford's hero status was corrupted.

He didn't care. *Hero* wasn't a label he was comfortable with anyway. But it chafed that he had made news again at all. After the shootout in Halcon, he'd hoped never to have notoriety again in his lifetime.

He knew that a long and tedious day lay in store, but at least Holly was safe. When he checked in with Harry, he was told, "Not so much as a mouse fart all night."

"Later today, after some locals have been cleared, we'll let them take over."

"The major told Sessions and me to stay on it till you say otherwise."

"Thanks."

Preferring to work alone and from his own office rather than in police headquarters where everyone would be walking on eggshells, he drove to the DPS building. One lone news van from the Tyler station was in the parking lot. The resourceful reporter and his cameraman leaped from it when he alighted from his SUV. They jogged alongside him as he strode to the employees' entrance. He didn't say anything into the microphone poked at him, not even "No comment."

Inside, state troopers and civilian personnel alike looked at him with either wariness or blatant curiosity. One of the clerks who worked in the driver's license division timidly approached him at the communal coffee bar and told him that her prayer circle had put his name on their list. He thanked her, although he was afraid to ask what they were praying for—his absolution or damnation.

No sooner had he sat down in his cubicle than his cell phone rang. He looked at the caller ID, saw that it was Conrad's landline number, and cursed under his breath as he answered. "You had better be dying."

"You're not that lucky. In fact you're about the most luckless bastard I've ever come across."

"Started when I was sired by you."

"Isn't there a commandment about honoring your parents?"

"You're not supposed to contact me unless it's an emergency."

"In my opinion this qualifies. Your roof guy was the wrong guy. That was the secret eating on you yesterday, right? You gave it up?"

"Yes and yes."

"I admire your integrity."

"What do you know about integrity, except possibly how to spell it?"

His father bypassed that. "As you predicted, the flub has caused an F-five shit storm, and you're at the center of it."

"Told you."

"Neal Lester is catching his fair share. Is he blaming you?"

"Behind the scenes. But he can't dispute that Rodriguez refused to disarm and opened fire on a deputy. He's got it on security camera video."

"So now what?"

"I ride it out and do everything I can to catch the would-be assassin."

"Beats sitting in front of a computer all day."

"I do important work at this computer, and it's not life-threatening."

"You could die of boredom."

"There is that," Crawford said under his breath.

"What was that?"

"Nothing. I gotta go."

"Need any help?"

"With what?"

"The shooting case."

"Help from you?" Crawford chortled. "No."

"I could do research."

"Into what?"

"Possible suspects. How many enemies can the young judge have?"

"She says none she knows of."

"Could be she's lying."

"Could be, but I don't think so."

"Anybody who was in the courthouse at the time—"

"We're aware of that, Conrad."

"That's a total of—how many?"

"Over two hundred."

Crawford had been disheartened by the head count

when Neal emailed the list of names to him late last night. They were fortunate in that many who'd reported for jury duty that Monday morning had been dismissed before two o'clock. Otherwise the number would have been even higher.

"Two hundred." Conrad whistled. "Any leads?"

"We're pursuing a few."

"Don't try to bullshit a bullshitter. You've got nothing."

Actually he did have something, a small niggling inconsistency that he needed to bring to Neal's attention. His current conversation was preventing that. "Bye, Conrad."

"You know, this reminds me of a case I had."

"Ancient history."

"A woman got knifed to death on a Sunday morning in the basement of her church where she was making the flower arrangement for the altar. No apparent motive. Every suspect was a church member. Hand-waving, foot-washing holy rollers. Where do you start looking for a killer among that flock?"

"Conrad, I don't have time for—"

"Guess who killed her?"

"I don't give a damn. Good-bye."

"I'm a good snoop."

"You're a good drunk. You're a *really* good drunk."

"I haven't touched a drink in—"

"Sixty-two days and counting."

"Which makes it sixty-three."

"I'm busy."

"That's why you should let me do some legwork for you."

"Don't call me again."

He hung up before Conrad could say anything else. He called Neal's cell but got voice mail, then dialed the

PD and asked to be put through to the Crimes Against Persons unit and eventually got Matt Nugent on the line.

Crawford went straight to the reason for the call. "How many names on your list of people who were evacuated from the courthouse?"

"Counting everybody?"

"Everybody."

"Two oh seven."

"Okay," Crawford said, "now break out the police department and sheriff's office personnel, plus all other courthouse officials and their staffs. How many names does that leave?"

"Hmm." Nugent did the calculation as he'd done when Neal sent him the list. "Seventy-five."

"Right. Should be seventy-six. We're short one civilian name."

Crawford could hear Nugent redoing the subtraction. "Borrow one," he murmured. "Geez, you're right."

"If you see Neal before I can reach him, have him call me." He clicked off and swiveled his chair around, about to go after a hot refill of coffee, only to discover his lawyer standing in the opening of his cubicle.

Crawford was startled to see him. "What brings you by?"

"Can we talk where the walls don't have ears?" Then, looking up at the open space between the cubicle and ceiling, he said, "Where there are actually walls?"

Mystified by William Moore's unexpected visit as well as by the attorney's uncharacteristically subdued manner, Crawford forgot about the fresh cup of coffee and led Moore to a storage room, which was presently empty. He closed the door to give them privacy.

Crawford said, "I didn't initiate this meeting, so don't even think about adding it to my billable hours."

"This one's on the house."

That was even more ominous. Ordinarily a two-minute phone call was prorated.

Moore gnawed the inside of his cheek as though trying to decide how best to jump in. Crawford waited and finally the lawyer asked, "How do you think it would have gone yesterday? If all hell hadn't broken loose during the hearing, what do you believe the outcome would have been?"

"My petition would have been denied."

The lawyer nodded as though that coincided with his prediction. "As your counsel, I advise you not to go on record with your opinion of the ruling, Judge Spencer, anything relating to the custody issue. From now on, if anyone asks about that, refer them to me."

"Dispensing free advice? Unlike you, Bill. What's going on?"

Lowering his voice, Moore said, "Neal Lester called me this morning. Plain and simple, he was on a fishing expedition."

"About me?"

"Seems he isn't quite satisfied with your explanation of why you charged after the gunman when he ran from the courtroom."

"Shouldn't that be obvious?"

"Should be. But it isn't to him. He's also unconvinced of how the roof confrontation played out, particularly now that you, and only you, he emphasized, claim that Rodriguez wasn't the gunman."

"The judge—"

Moore held up his hand. "He told me she corroborated the pierced ear thing, but with a degree of doubt that was 'palpable.' His word."

Crawford thought back on their lengthy conversation in the diner. "What he sensed wasn't palpable doubt. She was pissed off."

The lawyer arched his eyebrow in silent query.

"At Neal for a lewd crack he made."

Moore held his stare, eyebrow still raised.

"Okay, and at me."

"For something that occurred while you and she, the presiding judge over your custody hearing, were alone together in a parked car for thirty-three minutes?"

Crawford swore under his breath. He hadn't slugged Neal nearly hard enough. "Did Neal say 'under cover of darkness'?"

"Close."

"It was all my doing, Bill. Not hers."

"Your gallantry makes me even more nervous. I won't ask what you two were doing in that car, because I don't want to hear it. Just like I wish I hadn't heard the crack you made yesterday morning about taking out a contract on her if she didn't rule in your favor."

Crawford laughed. "Come on, Bill. That was a joke."

"Sergeant Lester might not see the humor in it."

Crawford's smile gradually relaxed. "Wait. Are you saying...? Neal's hinting that I had something to do with the attempt on Holly's life?"

Again, the attorney's brow shot up. "So it's Holly now?"

"Answer the goddamn question."

"Yes. He danced around that possibility."

"And you're taking it seriously?"

"As death and taxes. So should you."

Crawford stared into his lawyer's unblinking eyes, then placed his hands on his hips and walked a slow circle in the confined space. When he'd made a complete three-sixty, he said, "I don't have time enough to list all the reasons why that's freakin' ridiculous. Not the least of which is that I'm working the case with him."

"You know the adage about keeping your enemies closer. I'm sure Neal knows it, too."

He went on to tell Crawford in more detail, and using direct quotes, everything that Neal had theorized. He was still talking when Crawford's cell phone buzzed. Harry Longbow. He held up a finger to stop Moore mid-sentence. "I've got to take this." Then into his phone, "Hey."

"You have a TV on?"

"No."

"You're not gonna like it."

Five minutes after getting the call, Crawford wheeled into a parking space in the courthouse lot. As he jogged toward the main entrance, he was somewhat mollified to see that a temporary barricade had been set up and that deputy sheriffs were screening everyone before allowing them in.

Based on what Bill Moore had told him, Crawford halfway expected to be stopped and frisked, but he was saluted by one of the deputies as he stepped over the barricade. Neal, the son of a bitch, must not have shared his stupid suspicions with everyone.

Crawford wended his way through the media people already gathered in the cavernous lobby. Six floors overhead, sunlight was streaming in through the dome windows. One beam was acting like a spotlight on the podium behind which a building custodian was fiddling with the microphone, causing it to pop and screech.

Harry and Sessions were in what appeared to be a heated discussion with Neal while Nugent stood nearby, gnawing on his fingernail. When Crawford reached them, Sessions, an average size, average looking man with an above average IQ and jaw-dropping sharp-shooting skills, brought him into the argument.

"Harry and I followed Judge Spencer here and into the building. Now he's saying that we can back off, that he's got it covered."

Crawford turned to Neal. "First of all, they stay. The more uniforms visible, the better. Second," he said with additional consternation, "none of us should be needed. What the hell were you thinking? Why didn't you veto this plan?"

"Judge Spencer didn't consult me beforehand. I knew nothing about it until the media began showing up. I delayed the start until we could get men into place, but if I had called it off, the negative PR—"

"Don't talk to me about PR, Neal, or I'll reopen your swollen lip." He was gratified to see that it was twice its normal size. "What men? Who's in place?"

"Policemen that Nugent and I had already screened and cleared of any involvement with the shooting."

Crawford was dubious of anyone cleared by Nugent, but the screening itself would have put a dissatisfied would-be assassin on notice. He'd have to be crazy to make another attempt on Holly's life in the courthouse when it was crawling with law enforcement officers and people with cameras.

But then, he'd have had to be crazy to do what he'd done two days ago.

At the barricade, uniformed officers were checking press IDs and searching handbags, backpacks, and camera bags before letting anyone through. But the atrium was open to every floor. Employees and visitors were moving along the circular galleries, either going about their business or watching the activity on the ground floor with avid curiosity. Officers were posted along the railings on every level, but in Crawford's estimation, they were too few in number.

He turned to the other two Texas Rangers and said under his breath, "I don't like it." The look he gave them was a silent signal. They moved away and went in different directions to reconnoiter.

Turning back to Neal, Crawford asked, "Where is she?"

"Directly behind you."

Crawford turned. Holly was making her way across the lobby toward them. She was dressed in a cream-colored suit with a snug-fitting jacket, thigh-hugging skirt, and high heels. She looked great.

He wanted to strangle her.

With her was a woman who was shaped like a bale of cotton. Her salt-and-pepper hair was cut close to her scalp, and she walked as though going into combat. In his present mood, she virtually was.

As Holly approached him, her smile looked forced. "Good morning. I'm glad you're here so I can introduce you to my campaign manager, Marilyn Vidal. Marilyn, this is Ranger Crawford Hunt."

The woman thrust out a square hand with stubby fingers. As they shook, she gave him a once-over. "You certainly look the part."

"Part of what?"

"The Texas Ranger. Square jaw, steely eyed glint and all." She smiled, revealing teeth that looked like old piano keys. "But since you're not in uniform, you could use a cowboy hat. I don't suppose you have one handy? Preferably white. And maybe one of those gun belts that you wear around your hips and tie to your thigh?"

He subjected her to the glint she had admired, then said, "Excuse me," and stepped around her in order to get nearer to Holly. "Judge Spencer, this is a really bad idea. You should have notified Sergeant Lester or me before scheduling a *public event*." He pressed the last two words between his teeth.

"I'm a public figure in a political race. As I've told you, repeatedly, I can't cower and hide."

She was using that lofty judge tone that made him want to shake her and then remind her that, twelve hours earlier, her cool mouth had been hotly fused with his, kissing him like there was no tomorrow.

Instead, he said, "You don't have to hide. But you're making it too easy for any crackpot with a grudge or a cause."

The campaign manager used her wide shoulders to wedge herself between them. "I don't see any reason for concern. There are cops all over the place."

"I'll only be speaking for a few minutes," Holly said.

"He only needs a few seconds," he said. "As you of all people should know."

By now Neal had joined the huddle. Ignoring Crawford, he said, "Judge Spencer, we've got the situation under control. But the sooner we get it over with, the better." He motioned her toward the lectern.

Crawford was relieved to see that policemen had formed a circle around it, facing outward toward the crowd. Crawford sidled up to one. Pat Connor was a veteran of the department. Paunchy, a bit long in the tooth, Connor was now relegated to guarding the courthouse. But at least he was another pair of eyes.

Crawford said to him, "You see anything hinky, Pat, you signal me."

"Sure thing. Where will you be?"

"Right over there." Crawford tipped his head toward the periphery of the media cluster. But before he could move away, Marilyn Vidal hooked his elbow and steered him to the lectern. "You stand here."

He wanted to ask just who the hell she thought she was to order him around. But he was aware of all the onlookers as well as the live microphone. Besides, although he hated being in the spotlight, he was glad to be standing close to Holly, on her right and slightly behind her. From that position he could survey the crowd.

The din subsided as Marilyn Vidal stepped up to the microphone. She introduced herself and thanked everyone for coming on short notice. "Despite the harrowing incident that occurred in Judge Holly Spencer's courtroom on Monday afternoon, she wanted to address you this morning. Some, including myself, tried to dissuade her from appearing publicly so soon after an attempt was made on her life, but she insisted that I call this press conference.

"She'll make a statement, but I've refused to let her take questions." She raised her hands to stave off the murmurs of disappointment. "You'll have your chance with her at a future date. I promise. Without further ado, I'll turn the podium over to Judge Spencer."

Holly took the campaign manager's place at the mike. She also began by thanking the reporters for being there. "The incident in the courtroom *was* harrowing. I think I speak for everyone who was there that we feared for our lives. Tragically, we who work here in the courthouse lost a highly regarded colleague, Deputy Sheriff Chet Barker."

She went on to commend him and underscore that he'd sacrificed his life in the performance of his duty. "What occurred afterward on the roof was an additional tragedy. But the man who was mistaken for the gunman in the courtroom did fire twice upon a uniformed officer, and this after having been ordered several times to place his weapon on the ground. There's been a lot of speculation about what went wrong and who was to blame. But I want to go on record as saying that I owe my life to Texas Ranger Crawford Hunt."

Crawford, stunned by the statement, cut his gaze over to her, but otherwise didn't move.

"Had he not reacted swiftly and without any regard for his own safety, the number of casualties could have been much higher. Many more could have fallen victim to the man who was later killed by the SWAT officers, or to the individual who eluded capture and remains at large. I want to publicly express my gratitude to Ranger Hunt now."

She turned and extended him her right hand. He looked down at it, then into her eyes. He took her hand, gave it two abrupt shakes, then dropped it, all the while maintaining his rigid stance while photographers' lights exploded like fireworks.

Holly turned back to the microphone and began addressing something that her opponent had alleged, but anger had deafened Crawford to what she was saying. He had no choice except to hold his temper until she wrapped up. Fortunately, the rest of her remarks were brief.

As she stepped away from the podium, the harridan with the bad hair stepped forward to congratulate her on how well she'd done. Neal, who was standing outside the circle of policemen guarding the lectern, was rushed by several reporters asking questions about the progress of the investigation.

Marilyn Vidal planted herself in front of Crawford. "You were fantastic. No conceit, no false modesty. Perfect. Let's go have a drink."

"'Fraid not." He curled his hand around Holly's biceps. "There's an urgent matter that I need to discuss with Judge Spencer."

He gave neither woman time to protest before turning

Holly around and marching her toward the hallway off the lobby where the restrooms were located. Realizing that they were being watched, she went along without protest, acting as though she'd expected to be led away like a child being placed in time-out.

Pat Connor had followed them. When they reached the hall, Crawford told him, "Keep everybody away from here."

"Sure thing."

He propelled Holly forward until they were at the end of the corridor, where she pulled her arm free of his grasp and faced him. "I know what you're going to say."

He bent down and whispered, "What the *fuck*? That's what I was going to say."

"I know you're angry. I knew you would be."

"Which is why you didn't tell me or Neal or anybody else about this press conference beforehand."

"If I had, you would have said no."

"Damn right."

She took a breath for both of them and continued in a less heated manner. "I was against exploiting any aspect of the incident and had made that clear to Marilyn. But this morning's reports about Rodriguez changed my mind. The slant was critical toward you."

"I'm a big boy, Holly. I do my job. I don't care about the slant of some reporter trying to earn his spurs."

"Well, you should. The fact that you had saved my life was little more than a footnote. The chip on your shoulder might prevent you from being bothered by that—"

"I don't have a chip."

"Only the size of Rushmore. Your bravery deserved to be commended, not questioned."

"Thanks, but you can keep your commendations. I

hate the attention. Regardless of that, calling a press conference in a place where it was damn near impossible to guard you—"

"I was guarded."

"Not enough."

"Nothing happened."

"Not this time. What about the next?"

"There'll probably never be a next."

He placed his hands on his hips. "You've decided that?"

"Well, I can't think of anyone who would want to kill me. Marilyn says it was more than likely an isolated incident, unrelated to me."

"Oh, Marilyn says. *Marilyn* says? You're willing to gamble your life on what Marilyn says? Is she worried about you, or losing to Sanders?"

"It's a valid concern. But even if it weren't for the upcoming election that will determine my professional future, I can't remain in hiding forever."

"Who said anything about forever? Just till we catch him."

"What happens if you don't?"

"We will."

"If you don't?" she pressed. "Who will determine when it's safe for me to resume my work, the campaign?"

"I can't give you a date."

"Exactly! How long am I to keep my life on hold?"

"You won't have a life if—"

"Stop yelling at me!"

"Crawford!"

"*What?*"

He and Holly sprang apart and turned toward the lobby end of the corridor, where Neal Lester, full of self-importance, was striding past the policeman Connor.

With Neal was a man wearing a Euro-looking suit and a worried frown.

Holly made a startled sound. "Dennis?"

Lithe and long-legged, he outdistanced Neal in order to reach her and draw her into an embrace. Speaking into her hair as he hugged her close, he said, "God, I've been wild with worry about you."

Chapter 16

A half hour later when Crawford walked into the Crimes Against Persons unit, Neal was seated at his desk talking on his cell phone. Nugent was pecking on a computer keyboard, but he paused long enough to point Crawford toward a vacant chair.

He slumped in it, crossed his ankles, and gazed out the window while waiting for Neal to finish. When he disconnected, he said to Crawford, "My wife."

Crawford hitched his chin in acknowledgment, but he was thinking *Pity the woman* and couldn't help but wonder if Neal had ever made love to her with the lights on.

"Where have you been?"

"Seeing Harry and Sessions off. These policewomen you put on the judge—"

"Solid. We know the shooter wasn't female."

"Okay. Then I called Georgia. I hadn't had a chance to before now." Leveling a stare on Neal, he added, "It's been that kind of morning."

"Did she see you on TV?"

"No. Grace had the presence of mind to shoo her out of the room while the press conference was on. Thank God."

"Why would you object to her seeing you? You're the Rhinestone Cowboy."

"Didn't ask to be."

"Didn't you? Going after the bad guy in such a courageous fashion, earning accolades from Judge Spencer."

"You got a bee up your butt, Neal? If so, let's talk about it."

The detective held Crawford's challenging stare for several seconds, then opened the case file on his desk. "The ex-fiancé's full name is Dennis White."

"They were never officially engaged."

Neal gave him a quick look, then referred again to the file, moving his pen down the bullet point list of facts. "Master's degree in business from SMU. President of the alumni association. Runs the United Way campaign for the international pharmaceutical company where he's regional director of sales."

"Overachiever."

"Makes six figures annually *before* bonuses."

"You'd think he could afford socks."

Neal raised his head. "What?"

"He wasn't wearing socks."

"I didn't notice."

Crawford merely shrugged.

"Anyway, he checks out," Neal said.

"You've already concluded that?"

"Well, I had ample time to interview him while we were searching the building high and low for you and Judge Spencer. Your private conversations in out-of-the-way places are becoming a regular thing."

"You should make up your mind, Neal."

"How's that?"

"Which is it I'm trying to do? Get under her skirt or kill her?"

Neal tossed down his pen. "Bill Moore told you."

"It was a chickenshit implication."

"Was it?"

"You think I contracted Rodriguez to kill the judge, and then set him up to get shot?"

"I didn't say that."

"That's what it boiled down to."

"If you were in this chair, wouldn't you entertain some suspicions? Of everybody in the judges' court records and case files, here and in Dallas—and detectives both places have gone through them twice—guess who stands out as the most resentful of court-ordered mandates? Right. Crawford Hunt. And it's your claim alone that the shooter's ear was pierced."

"*Wasn't* pierced."

"Whatever. Nor did Judge Spencer recall you kicking the gunman. So, based on things attested to *only by you,* I've got a hell of a mess going on here."

"Gee, Neal, I hate messing up your tidy career. I'm sure Judge Spencer regrets it, too. After all, it's only her life that's at stake. Which is why I was reading her the riot act about calling that press conference. She was giving it back to me. That's what you caught us doing in that out-of-the-way place."

Neal said nothing, merely glowered as he rocked back and forth in his chair and used his tongue to dab at the split on his swollen lower lip.

Crawford was willing to let it rest for a while. Grudgingly he asked, "Anything else on Dennis White?"

"He claims their breakup was amicable. At the time of the shooting, he was conducting a sales meeting. Thirty people present. Which I would call a solid alibi. Although they're no longer a couple, he thinks the world of her. To his knowledge she doesn't have any enemies. Uh…"

He consulted his notes again. "It's incomprehensible that anyone would want to harm her. It made him ill to think of the trauma she suffered. He's been trying to shake loose from his schedule to get down here and see for himself that she was all right."

"It took him three days to shake loose from his schedule? Doesn't sound 'wild with worry' to me."

"Busy man."

Lousy boyfriend, Crawford thought. Even for an ex.

"Greg Sanders?" he asked.

"Cleared."

"Just like that?"

"No, not just like that. I had two different detectives question him."

"What did he think of that?"

"They said he was cooperative, that he understood why he might have fallen under suspicion. Anyway, having left the courthouse shortly before two o'clock, which he says Judge Spencer herself can verify, he joined his wife at Golden Corral for a late lunch. Restaurant employees and Mrs. Sanders corroborate."

Neal had recited all that tongue-in-cheek. Crawford said, "I don't think he was the shooter, Neal, but he and Holly Spencer are rivals in a grudge match. He's a defense attorney. Rubs elbows with criminals on a daily basis."

"I've got somebody looking into all that. Have to tell you, though, it doesn't feel like him."

It didn't feel like him to Crawford, either. As Holly had said, it wasn't the blowhard's style. Crawford was brooding over that when his attention was drawn to the door, where a man had appeared accompanied by a uniformed officer.

The civilian was around fifty years old, although his severe buzz cut was almost solid gray. Deep squint lines showed up white against an otherwise ruddy, wind-scoured complexion. Whoever he was, he spent a lot of time outdoors. He was dressed in a golf shirt and sport jacket over khaki pants.

The policeman pointed them out to him. He thanked the cop, then started walking toward them, every foot-fall evincing self-assurance.

"Who's this guy?" Crawford asked.

Neal turned his head and, upon seeing the man, shot to his feet, sending his desk chair rolling backward.

The man stopped in front of Neal's desk. "Sergeant Lester?"

"Yes, sir."

"Chuck Otterman."

The two shook hands across Neal's desk, then Neal introduced Nugent and lastly Crawford. Otterman's handshake reminded him unpleasantly of his father-in-law's. Less a social courtesy than an arm-wrestling match.

Neal ordered Nugent to fetch the man a chair, but Crawford stood up. "He can have this one."

Otterman thanked him, rounded the desk, and took a seat.

Crawford backed up onto the corner of a nearby desk where he could take the measure of the man without being too obvious about it. Otterman was a stranger to him, but as soon as Neal saw him, he'd reacted with immediate recognition and surprise.

Now the detective gave a nervous little laugh. "We don't typically see VIPs in this division, Mr. Otterman."

"I'd hardly call myself a VIP."

Turning to Crawford, Neal explained. "Mr. Otterman is overseer of the gas drilling company." Going back to the man, he said, "I attended a luncheon where you spoke. You were very persuasive as to why natural gas is the answer to our energy crisis. You changed a lot of minds that day."

During Neal's explanation, Otterman had removed a fifty-cent piece from his pants pocket and was now deftly rolling it back and forth across the backs of his fingers. In response to Neal's statement, he said, "There are still a few die-hard tree huggers who are critical of my outfit in particular and the industry in general."

"Progress usually meets with some resistance."

Crawford was beginning to understand why Neal, being Neal, was kowtowing to Chuck Otterman.

The Lerner Shale spread over one hundred square miles in southeastern Texas and neighboring Louisiana. Prentiss County lay in the center of it. Over the past few years, natural gas companies had paid well for land leases and drilling rights, and, in the case of many, speculation had turned into filthy lucre.

Many local residents had expressed concern over fracking and the detrimental effects that the drilling and extraction process might have on the environment, but they had been outnumbered by those enjoying the up-tick in the local economy.

With it, however, came a corresponding spike in crime. Roughnecks went where the work was. Many took advantage of living away from home, free of wives, girlfriends, and other shackles of domesticity. They brawled, gambled, drank, and womanized in excess. On days off, they were the contemporary equivalent of cattle drive cowboys coming into town to blow their paychecks on various vices and essentially to raise hell.

Law enforcement officers were frequently summoned to the man camp, a village of temporary dormitories that housed the roughnecks, either to settle disputes or mop up after one that had ended with bloodshed.

Crawford figured that one of Otterman's men had gotten sideways with the authorities.

Neal pulled his chair back to his desk and sat down. "To what do we owe this honor, Mr. Otterman?"

"This morning's news." He shot a significant glance toward Crawford, flipped the coin, and caught it in his fist. "It was a shocking turn of events. Floored me, if you want to know the truth."

Neal asked, "Any particular reason why?"

"Because I was in the courthouse at the time of the shooting."

The statement stunned even Crawford. No one spoke for a moment, then Neal stammered, "I...I didn't notice your name on the list of people evacuated."

"My name wasn't on the list."

"That explains it," Nugent exclaimed, as though he'd just discovered gravity. He grinned across at Crawford, who immediately had the attention of the other two as well.

He held Otterman's gaze for a beat, then addressed Neal. "Nugent and I discovered a discrepancy in the number of people evacuated and the number questioned before being released."

"And you kept this information to yourself?"

"I've been busy," he said in terse reply to Neal's superior tone. *Fending off your illogical allegations.* Neal probably would have rebuked Nugent for failing to pass along the information, but Otterman picked up there.

"I'm sorry for creating confusion." He had resumed fiddling with the coin. "I thought, as everyone else did, that the man killed on the roof was the culprit. End of story. This morning when I found out differently, and realized that a madman was still at large, I knew I had to do my civic duty and admit to leaving before I was accounted for."

Neal shook his head with perplexity. "The entire courthouse was secured within minutes. How did you manage to leave undetected?"

"Before you answer that one," Crawford said, "I'd like to know why you were there in the first place."

Otterman shifted in his seat to look more directly at Crawford. "To meet with an assistant DA."

"Why?"

"In the hope of getting charges against one of my employees dropped or reduced."

"What'd he do?"

"It's alleged that he assaulted a man with a tire iron."

"But he's innocent."

Crawford's droll tone caused the other man to smile, but it wasn't a pleasant expression. "No. He beat the crap out of the guy. But the guy had it coming."

"How so?"

"He'd caught his wife in bed with my roughneck. But instead of laying into him, the man started in on his wife."

"Your roughneck came to her defense with a tire iron," Neal said.

"That's right."

"Cool."

That from Nugent, who'd been hanging on to every word. Crawford wasn't so caught up in the tale as he was in Otterman's calm telling of it. He couldn't pinpoint what bothered him, but something was off, possibly the man's arrogance. Most people entering any law enforcement agency did so with a degree of self-consciousness. Not so with Mr. Otterman. He was supremely cocksure.

He caught Crawford watching his play with the coin and chuckled. "I used to smoke four packs a day. This took its place. No nicotine, but it gives me something to do."

If he figured to steer Crawford away from the topic, he figured wrong. He asked, "Which assistant DA did you meet with?"

"I'll take it from here," Neal said, giving Crawford a look that would drive nails. "We appreciate your coming forward, Mr. Otterman. However, this department prides itself on how quickly it responded to the emergency, implementing an evacuation plan we'd rehearsed. It would be helpful to know how you managed to escape our security."

"I didn't. I was herded out like everybody else."

"Under police guard?"

"That's right. They were hustling everybody along. People were nervous, afraid. The officers were trying to keep panic to a minimum. We were told they were taking us to an area of safety where we would be 'sheltered' until the gunman was apprehended." He shrugged. "I didn't have time to be sheltered. Once we got clear of the courthouse, I went my own way."

"You just walked off?" Nugent asked.

"No. An officer stopped me. He ordered me to stay with the group. But when I told him who I was, he let me go."

Crawford asked, "What was his name?"

"I have no idea. He didn't tell me, and I didn't ask."

"Because you were in such a big hairy hurry to get away from there minutes after a fatal shooting had occurred."

Otterman's hand closed tightly around the coin and his left eye squinted fractionally more than the right one. "I don't care for your accusatory tone."

"Neither do I," Neal said.

Crawford forced himself to smile. "No accusation, Mr. Otterman. It's just that officers wear name tags."

"I didn't notice his name tag."

"Can you describe him? Ethnicity? Short, tall?"

"Youngish. Average height. Caucasian. He was in uniform."

"PD or deputy sheriff?"

"Policemen wear blue?"

Crawford bobbed his head.

"Then he was a policeman, but I can't be more specific than that. I'm sorry."

"What floor were you on when the shooting took place?"

"Crawford."

Otterman raised his hand to stave off Neal's attempt to intercede. "It's all right, Sergeant Lester." To Crawford, he said, "I was on the third floor, where the district attorney's offices are located. By the way, the assistant DA I met with was Alicia Owens."

He pocketed the coin as he stood. "I think that about covers it." He smiled at Nugent. "I'm glad I could clear up that discrepancy in the head count." Then to Neal, "I hope you catch the suspect soon."

Neal came to his feet. Nugent followed his example. Crawford remained with his behind propped on the corner of the neighboring desk.

Neal said, "Thank you for coming forward, Mr. Otterman," and reached across his desk to shake hands.

Otterman nodded and turned toward the door.

Crawford said, "I'd like you to take a look at Rodriguez."

"What?"

"Why?"

Otterman and Neal had spoken at the same time, but Crawford ignored the detective and replied to Otterman. "We haven't confirmed his identity. We don't know what he was doing in the courthouse on Monday and—"

"Now you never will."

The remark was meant to be snide, and, although Crawford knew it was aimed at him, he let it bounce off. "If you took a look at him, maybe you would remember seeing him in the courthouse. It could be the clue we need to tie up those loose ends." When Otterman failed to respond immediately, he added, "Just a thought. Since you're so into civic duty, and all."

He had intentionally created a dilemma for the man. If Otterman agreed, it would be a concession to their authority, and Crawford felt that he didn't like conceding authority to anyone. If he declined, he would have two strikes against him, because, in spite of Neal's bowing and scraping, much could be made of the fact that Otterman had left the scene of a capital crime.

"Of course, I'll take a look," he said genially. "Unfortunately, it will have to wait until tomorrow. I have a meeting at three thirty this afternoon. A group is flying in from Odessa."

Neal jumped on that. "Tomorrow is soon enough, Mr. Otterman. What would be a convenient time?"

"Nine o'clock."

"I promise not to keep you any longer than absolutely necessary. Thank you for coming in today. Nugent will walk you out."

Nugent was twitchier than usual as the two made their way to the door. As soon as they had cleared it, Neal launched into Crawford. "What is the matter with you? Are you determined to self-destruct and take me with you? You just pissed off the man in charge of the largest economic boom this area has seen in generations."

"What's the matter with *you*?" Crawford fired back. "You're a cop. Or you're supposed to be. You can't back down from someone because you're afraid of rubbing him the wrong way. If he'd have been anybody else, you probably would have arrested him for obstruction."

"But he's not *anybody else*. You honestly think he's a suspect? Let's forget for the moment that he's got the wrong hair color and a different body type. Does he come across as a man who would dress up like Halloween? *Really?*" By the time he got to the last word, his voice was practically a screech. "Asking him to look at Rodriguez? What's that about except a waste of everyone's time?"

"We don't know that."

"If he looks at him and says, 'Never saw him before,' what have you gained?"

"Nothing. But we'll be no worse off, either."

"Except that we'll have offended a very influential man."

Crawford placed his hands flat on Neal's desk and leaned over it. "He strolled in here like royalty and admitted to leaving a crime scene, like it was no big deal. Chet was dead, and this asshole went on his way because he didn't have time to hang around and answer a few questions. Fuck if I care we hurt his feelings."

He straightened and raked his fingers through his hair. "Besides, you're missing the point of why I asked him to come to the morgue. I don't expect him to recognize Rodriguez."

"Then why bother him?"

"I want to watch him when he *denies* recognizing Rodriguez. If he's lying about it, I'll know. I don't think he was the shooter, but…Hell, I don't know," he said, irritably rubbing the back of his neck. "Something."

"Such as?"

"I don't know. But put someone on finding out who the cop was that let Otterman leave. Have him suspended for a nice long time. Give him weeks to rethink that decision.

"And assign somebody to start digging into Mr. Chuck Otterman's life for the past five years or so. Have it mapped good. Work history. Family stuff, too. Divorce. Child custody. Like that."

"Why me? You're the expert on all that."

Instead of taking the bait, Crawford said, "Good place to start would be the law firm that Holly left to come here."

"That's been done already."

"Have it done again, this time looking for Otterman." He turned and stalked toward the door.

"Where are you going?"

Over his shoulder, he said, "To lunch."

Chapter 17

————◆————

Marilyn was on her third Bloody Mary. Dennis was nursing a glass of iced tea. Their entrees hadn't yet arrived. Holly couldn't wait for this lunch to end.

They were seated at a window table in the country club dining room, dubbed by Dennis the only decent restaurant in Prentiss unless you were carbohydrate-loading. It was a pleasant room overlooking the golf course and a pond with a backdrop of solid pine forest.

But Holly was too keyed up to enjoy the room, the view, or the company. Marilyn, who'd insisted on treating them to lunch, had driven her own car from the courthouse so she could smoke, leaving Holly to ride with Dennis, which had afforded them some time to themselves.

At first, their conversation had revolved around the shooting, but once he had been assured that she wasn't injured beyond a few bruises, and that she was coping as well as she could with the aftermath and everything it entailed, they drifted toward more personal topics.

When she asked if he was seeing someone, he sheepishly admitted that he had a new romantic interest, which didn't surprise her. Dennis was handsome, successful, charming, and intelligent. Yet she wondered what had ever attracted her to him. He now seemed very...polished.

He rarely got agitated. He never raised his voice. The most heated argument she ever remembered them having was over her decision to relocate to Prentiss, and that had been more of a discussion of the pros and cons rather than a quarrel.

Their reunion had been as civilized and dispassionate as their relationship, including their breakup. No theatrics, no pyrotechnics. When she saw him, the only bump her heart had given was one of anxiety over what Crawford would do, say, and feel about Dennis's unheralded arrival. Neither his opinion nor his reaction should have mattered, but somehow they did.

She didn't wish Dennis any ill will, and it was clear that he felt the same toward her, but once they had more or less established that, they had little to talk about. Holly was eager for him to be on his way back home and firmly fixed in her past, so she could get on with her present.

When her cell phone chimed from the pocket of her handbag, she seized on the distraction. Checking the caller ID, she saw that it was her assistant. "Mrs. Briggs would never interrupt our lunch unless it was important."

She excused herself and left the table in a rush, wanting to catch the call before it went to voice mail. "I'm here," she said as she moved past the hostess stand into the foyer.

"I apologize for calling during your lunch."

"No problem. What's going on?"

"Mr. Joe Gilroy is here. He doesn't have an appointment, but he says it's important that he speak to you as soon as possible, and he doesn't want to do it by phone. What shall I tell him?"

She glanced into the dining room, where Marilyn was talking with animation and Dennis was laughing. Holly said, "Please ask him to wait. I'll be right there."

The pair of policewomen who'd taken over for the Texas Rangers had been sitting at a table not far from Holly's party. One had followed her into the foyer. She asked her now if she could please have a lift back to the courthouse in their squad car.

"Of course, Judge Spencer. After lunch?"

"No, right now. Just let me say good-bye to my friends." Holly reentered the restaurant. As she approached the table, Dennis stood up and pulled out her chair. "I'm sorry," she said, "but I can't stay."

"What? Why?" Marilyn's tone had a demanding edge.

Dennis said, "You haven't even eaten."

"Someone's waiting for me in chambers. I need to get back right away."

"I'll drive you."

She placed her hand on Dennis's arm. "The policewomen are giving me a ride. Stay and enjoy your lunch."

"Will I see you later?"

It was on the tip of her tongue to ask what would be the point. Instead, she smiled up at him. "I appreciate your coming all this way to check on me. Truly. It was sweet of you. But, as you can see, I'm fine. You have other things to do, and so do I."

He caught the underlying message of the statement and smiled back, actually looking a bit relieved.

She kissed him on the cheek, then said to Marilyn, "I'll see you at my house later."

"Not too much later. We've got a lot of planning still to do."

Holly shouldered her handbag, smiled at Dennis for what would most likely be the final time, and joined the policewomen who were waiting for her at the hostess stand. She rode in the backseat of their squad car. They saw her into the courthouse and up to the door of her chambers.

In the anteroom, Mrs. Briggs was seated behind her desk. Joe Gilroy was sitting in an armchair with a briefcase on his lap. He stood up when she walked in. They shook hands, and he thanked her for seeing him without an appointment. She motioned him to follow her into her private office and closed the door.

Once they were seated and she was facing him across her desk, he opened the briefcase and took out several paper-clipped sheets. "I filed all the necessary documents with the county clerk."

He slid the documents across the desk toward her. "She informed me that I need your signature. That's why I asked to meet with you as soon as possible. This needs to be served without delay."

Holly had recognized the documents immediately. Unfortunately, in a family dispute they were too often necessary to protect one party from another. Which is why she could only gape at Joe Gilroy with incredulity.

He had filed for a temporary restraining order against Crawford Hunt.

———

Crawford went looking for Smitty and found him in the second topless club he checked. This one was a bit more upscale than the others. Between eleven and three o'clock each weekday, it served free lunch to anyone who bought a minimum of two drinks.

When Crawford asked the bouncer if the boss was in, he demanded to know what business Crawford had with him. With his badge and unflinching stare serving as incentives, the bouncer told him that he would find Smitty in his office at the back of the building.

Crawford entered the club through a maroon velvet curtain and moved along the buffet, noting that the chicken wings looked dry and the pizza slices had begun to curl up at the edges. However, the few patrons sitting at the edge of the stage weren't there for the food, but rather to ogle the two dancers, whose performance was uninspired at best. One of them even yawned as she swayed.

On the far side of the club, he entered a dimly lit hallway, followed it past the restrooms, and went through a door forbidding entrance to anyone except employees. He passed two storerooms where cases of liquor were stacked chest high. A dressing room door stood open, revealing a woman in a bathrobe, seated in front of a lighted mirror, admiring her image as she talked on her cell phone. Finally Crawford came to a closed door with "Manager" stenciled on it.

Through it he heard Smitty shouting, "Look at you, for crissake! Who wants to pay to see a black eye?"

Then a woman's voice. "When I'm on stage, you think they're looking at my *eyes*?"

"Who did it? A customer or a boyfriend?"

"What's it to you? You don't own me."

Crawford knocked once, then pushed the door open. Smitty was standing behind his desk, hands on hips. A young woman was slouched in the chair facing the desk, a landscape of litter.

Smitty groaned when Crawford strolled in. "Oh, perfect. Fucking perfect. Just what I need today." With disgust, he looked down at the girl and waved her away. "Get out of here. Go buy some makeup that'll cover that. You can't control men and their urges, you got no business in this line of work. It happens again, you're out on your ass."

"Oh, I'm so sure," she drawled. "My ass is a crowd pleaser."

She sauntered toward the door, pausing as she came alongside Crawford. Cheekily she winked the eye that had been blackened. "Who are you, cutie?"

"I'm a bootlegger."

"Seriously?"

"*Out!*" Smitty bellowed.

She slammed the door behind her. Smitty plopped into his desk chair and smoothed down his greasy comb-over. "Bitch knows I won't fire her. Her ass *is* a crowd pleaser."

Crawford took the chair the woman had vacated. "What I saw of it in those jeans, it looked pretty good."

"She goes on at ten tonight. You can see all of it then. Drink?"

"No thanks."

Smitty reached for a bottle of gin on his desk and poured some into a cloudy glass. He shot the drink, then snarled, "Well? What brings ya? I don't recommend the wings."

"I saw them."

"So?"

"Chuck Otterman."

Smitty froze in the act of pouring a second drink, then carefully returned the bottle to his desk.

Crawford said, "Ah. I see you know him."

"I didn't say that."

"You didn't have to."

After leaving the courthouse, Crawford had contacted the DPS office and asked a trooper to get him the nuts-and-bolts on Chuck Otterman. The trooper had called him back less than five minutes later with the particulars—date of birth, Social Security and driver's license numbers, and so forth. Otterman also had a concealed handgun license. His permanent address was in Houston, his temporary address a PO box in Prentiss.

"Email me all that."

"Already have."

"What's he been doing the past thirty years or so?"

"Completed two years of junior college but left without a degree. Seems to have worked every day of his adult life in oil and gas," the trooper reported. "Probably doesn't have a carpeted office because he likes the on-site work. Moved around, never staying with one outfit for more than a coupla years."

"Anything to indicate why?"

"Nothing on the surface."

That was a curiosity Crawford would check out.

However, Otterman appeared blemish-free. He'd been married once in his twenties, divorced less than two years later, no fuss or muss, no children. He paid his alimony on time, he was current with the IRS. No major debts or liens against him. No arrests.

Crawford asked the trooper a few more questions. Although the answers didn't raise suspicions, he still smelled a rat. Which is why he'd tracked down Smitty, who was a source of information, the kind that couldn't be found using computers and search engines.

"Chuck Otterman. What do you know, Smitty?"

"I know that you should do yourself a favor. For *once*. I've seen the news. Yesterday, a hero. Today?" He made a face and waggled his hand. "Not so much. Except for the judge. Now she—"

"Otterman."

"Crawford, how long have we been friends?"

"We've never been friends. Occasionally I pay you for information. I always take a long, hot shower after."

The club owner slapped the area of his heart. "That hurts, that really does."

Crawford propped one ankle on his opposite knee and rested his linked fingers on his midriff, settling in. "That young lady with the good ass didn't seem all that surprised that you had a bootlegger calling on you in the middle of the afternoon. Five minutes, you're shut down while me and some boys with badges do a thorough investigation of the revenue you bring in off alcohol. Nobody goes on at ten o'clock tonight."

It was a valid threat. Del Ray Smith's business wasn't entirely legit, or even mostly legit. Crawford figured that he kept at least two sets of books, and knew for a fact that Smitty conducted a brisk trade with bootleggers, bookmakers, and pimps.

He had started out in his teens as a petty crook and had progressed to grand larceny before he dropped out of eleventh grade. After being released from his second stint in Huntsville, he'd decided he needed to improve his act.

He scraped up enough money for a down payment on a ratty beer joint on the Prentiss County line. From that he'd grown his business until it now encompassed five nightclubs with dancers that he proudly advertised as "Totally Nude." Apparently the redundancy escaped him.

Crawford's threat caused Smitty to pat down his comb-over again. "I've got nothing to hide."

"True. Your corruption is transparent."

All innocence, he said, "Corruption?"

"You're a tax dodger, a facile liar, a moral cesspool. You know, and I know, that you'll eventually sell out. So let's cut to the chase, okay? Tell me what you know about Otterman."

"Better idea. Why don't you let me treat you to a lap

dance, then you go home, go fishing, to the movies, go see your kid. Something. Anything. You don't want to tangle with Otterman."

"Why not?"

"I'll throw in a happy ending to that lap dance. This girl—"

"I'm losing my patience. What do you know about Otterman?"

Smitty raised his hands to shoulder height, palms out. "Nothing."

"Smitty."

"Swear to God. His roughnecks are good for my business. *Real* good for my business. I don't want you and your nosing around to scare them off."

"Is Otterman himself a customer?"

"No."

Crawford looked at him, said nothing.

"Okay, occasionally."

Crawford didn't blink.

"Jesus," Smitty said under his breath. "He's a *good* customer, all right?"

"Does he favor one club over another?"

"Tickled Pink."

"How often is he there?"

"Three, four nights a week."

"Does he go to see a particular girl?"

"No. Swear," he added, when Crawford registered doubt. "He rarely even watches the show. He sits in one of the big booths and just meets with people."

"What people?"

"I don't know. People." He shot Crawford a querulous look as he decided on that second gin after all and sloshed some into the glass.

"What kind of people? Young, old, men, women? Down-and-outs? Well-heeled?"

Smitty chugged the gin and belched noxious fumes. "Men. All kinds."

"What do all these kinds of men talk to Otterman about?"

"How the hell should I know? The weather." Under Crawford's baleful stare, he squirmed in his squeaky chair. "Look, I don't meddle, okay? Or eavesdrop. Otterman buys name-brand booze and lots of it. My interest in him stops there."

"Heavy drinker?"

"No. He buys the hooch for his guests. Never seen him any way except cold stone sober."

"Fights?"

Smitty hesitated, then said no.

"Fights?"

The club owner rolled his eyes, then, at a look from Crawford, gave it up. "I've never seen him engaged in one, but he's…let's say…respected."

"Feared."

"I didn't say that. You can never quote me as saying that."

"But nobody crosses him."

"Not more than once, anyway. Draw your own conclusion."

It wasn't a conclusion, but it was a good guess that Otterman wasn't above knocking heads together, or having henchmen to do it for him. "Does he carry?"

"Wouldn't know. Haven't looked."

Smitty was probably lying about that, but Crawford let it pass. If Otterman had a CHL, it was to be assumed he was armed. "What else?"

"That's it. He tips twenty percent, doesn't cause me any trouble, and I don't cause him any, and that's the way I want to keep it. So if that's all…" He looked at Crawford hopefully.

"You know a guy named Jorge Rodriguez?"

He shook his head. "Don't get many greasers in my clubs."

"Why's that?"

Smitty raised a shoulder. "Maybe it has to do with the Virgin Mary."

"The Virgin Mary?"

"You know, beans are into all that."

Crawford didn't pursue that illogical train of thought. "I want to know who these men are that Otterman meets with."

Smitty made a strangling sound of righteous indignation. "You want me to spy on one of my best customers?"

His act didn't impress or deter Crawford. He'd seen it before and knew it was all for show. He stood up and headed for the door. "Same as always, I need the info yesterday, and I'll pay based on how good it is."

"I'm no snitch."

"Smitty, if the price was right, you'd sell your mother as a sex slave to a gang of vandals."

"Already did," he called to Crawford as he went out. "They brought the sorry bitch back."

Chapter 18

————◆————

It was late afternoon by the time Crawford returned to police headquarters. He found Neal at his desk. When he saw Crawford, he said, "Long lunch."

"I'm a slow eater. Got anything on Otterman?"

Neal related the basic information that Crawford had already obtained. He sat down at Nugent's vacant desk and swiveled the chair from side to side. "Strike you as funny that he doesn't stay with any one outfit for very long?"

"Not particularly."

"Hmm. Did you check the video from the entrance security camera?"

"He came into the courthouse by the main entrance just shy of one forty. ADA Alicia Owens confirmed that they had an appointment at one forty-five. He was five minutes early. She was twenty minutes late. During the course of their meeting, they were alerted to the situation on the fourth floor and evacuated along with everybody else. We see him being herded through the west side exit on the ground floor."

"You find the cop who let him leave?"

He told Crawford his name, but Crawford didn't know him. "He's earnest, but green," Neal said. "Understandably, Otterman intimidated him. He's being dealt with by his superior."

"How harshly?"

"That's another department. Not my business."

Crawford wanted to jerk him up by his necktie and ask what his business was if not finding Chet's murderer. "Otterman ever been in any of our district courts?"

"No."

"As a witness?"

"Not as a witness, not as a juror. No association what-soever," Neal said. "We checked all. Double-checked Judges Waters and Spencer. No record of him at her former firm. Nil. Zilch. *Nada*. Zero. Told you so."

"You want me to back off him."

"You took the words right out of my mouth."

"If the morgue visit doesn't produce anything, I will. Anything on the gun?"

"Far as we can tell, it was virgin except for the missing serial number. We're checking local dealers for recent purchases, but it could've been bought anywhere."

"The painter's get-up?"

"Sold at nearly every hardware, paint, and big box store in the country. You can also order that brand from various online outlets. Shipments to Texas in the last six months amount to thousands, and that's after being narrowed down by size, style, and lot number from the manufacturer. Also, he could've bought it in any one of the other forty-nine states and brought it here."

"Gloves?"

"Same thing. We've got them by the boxful over there in that cabinet."

"Readily available to any cop."

"Also to any medical worker, housewife, food han-dler, hairdresser, germophobe. Let's see…"

"Okay, I get it," Crawford said with irritation. "The mask?"

"Not as widely distributed as the other items, but

available in party and costume shops, as well as off the Internet. We're still trying to track sales to this area. And, before you ask, we've conducted eighty-something interviews of people who were in the building."

"Judging by the look on your face…"

"Everyone questioned has a logical, easily confirmed explanation of what their courthouse business was, and can account for themselves when the shooting took place."

"Still leaves a lot of folks not yet questioned."

"True, but so far nothing even mildly sinister or suspicious has come to light. No ties to Judge Spencer except for one woman. Judge Spencer granted her a divorce six months ago. No kids involved. It was settled to each party's satisfaction. Her ex moved to Seattle. On Monday afternoon he was at his job at a fish-packing plant. She was in the courthouse because she was summoned to jury duty."

"People lie, Neal."

"People also tell the truth. This lady still had her summons."

"Nothing new on Rodriguez?"

"Nobody's missed him. At least, no one has come forward to claim the body."

"Doc Anderson confirmed there was no bruise on his knee?"

"No bruise."

"Told you."

"But no one can substantiate that you kicked the guy." He sat forward, propping his forearms on his desk. "Our main person of interest remains *you*."

Without inflection, Crawford said, "I don't fit the gunman's description, and I have an alibi."

Neal was still holding his stare when Crawford's cell phone vibrated on his belt. He read the caller ID and clicked on. "Hello, Grace."

"You're not alone," Holly said.

"Neal Lester and I are comparing notes on the case."

"You're in the building?"

"That's right. What's going on? Georgia good?"

"I need to see you."

"Okay."

"In private."

His heart hitched. "I can do that. When and where?"

"I'm in my office, but wait until the building clears out before you come up."

"Sure thing. I'll be there."

Disconnecting, he said to Neal, "Grace invited me over for lunch tomorrow."

———

"One of the policewomen offered to go after food, and she brought back about fifteen pounds of barbecue plus a half dozen sides."

The thought of food made Holly ill. "Start without me," she said to Marilyn, who had already called numerous times, asking when she could expect Holly at home. "I'll be there as soon as I can get away."

"You said that hours ago."

"I've had a lot of catching up to do. It's been a busy afternoon."

"Greg Sanders has had a busy one, too. He was on the six o'clock news."

"So was I."

"Yes, but your appearance was a rerun of the press conference. That's old news. We need something fresh." On a burst of inspiration, she said, "I'll bring the feast to your office. We'll talk turkey over ribs."

"Absolutely not," Holly said. "Mrs. Briggs left me

with a stack of documents and correspondence to sign. Besides, how many vodkas have you had?"

"Who's counting?"

A soft knock sounded on Holly's door. "My last appointment is here, Marilyn. I have to go. Don't you dare get behind the wheel of a car."

She hung up just as Crawford came through the door and closed it behind him. Since his clean-shaven court appearance, he'd grown a scruff. His jacket was wrinkled, his necktie loose and askew, his dark blond hair completely ungoverned.

He looked wonderful. She wanted to climb him and hang on.

"Hi."

"Hi."

She followed his gaze down to the cell phone still in her hand. Setting it on her desk, she said, "Marilyn."

"Who's high on my shit list."

"For calling the press conference? I never would have agreed to it if I hadn't thought it was important to defend your actions."

"So you've said. But you took an unnecessary risk."

"So you've said. No need to rehash it."

He tugged his crooked tie into place, rolled his shoulders, shifted his weight. After several moments of awkward silence, he asked, "Where's Dennis?"

"Home by now, I suppose."

"Your home?"

"His home."

"Huh. Short visit."

"He only came here to see for himself that I was all right."

He made a derisive sound. "You're nearly gunned down, he rushes to your rescue, wild with worry, three days later."

She smiled. "You made rather obvious your aversion to him."

"What gave me away?"

"You stormed off without a word to anyone."

He looked angry, then chagrined, then angry again. "He sailed in and acted like he owned you."

"He hugged me."

"He held you."

"What's the difference?"

"Where he put his hands."

"He and I were together for a long time. We're familiar."

"He's familiar, reasonable, and refined. But I've got a caveman mentality. When he put his hands on you, I wanted to rip out his throat. Mine are the only hands I want touching you."

"You don't have a claim."

His eyes narrowed. "I kinda do." He started walking toward her, and for each step forward he took, she took one back until she came up against her desk. "That unreasonable, unrefined fuck on your sofa gave me a claim."

The rumble of his voice, and the words themselves, caused her heartbeat to accelerate, and, while she knew she should stop this, she couldn't bring herself to.

By now he had her trapped against her desk, his wide chest filling her field of vision, his scent, his raw, unpolished maleness, wreaking havoc on her.

"This plan to 'cancel it,'" he said, "how's that working for you?"

"Not very well."

He placed the heels of his hands on her hip bones and curved his fingers around her bottom. "For me either."

In a hushed voice, she said, "I wish I still had it to look forward to."

His eyes searched hers. "Do you remember it the way I do?"

"How do you remember it?"

"To tell you, I'd have to get really graphic."

"Blushing terms?"

"Gutter terms." He leaned in closer and whispered, "Wanna hear how tight you were?"

She closed her eyes momentarily. "Crawford."

"Sorry. I know. Wrong place, wrong time, wrong everything." He exhaled a gust of frustration, removed his hands, and backed away. "So wrong we can't even talk about it. But at least I got you to call me by my first name."

She moved away from the desk so she wouldn't be tempted to pull him back to her. "Last night you told me good-bye."

"I meant it. Last night."

"It's the right decision, Crawford."

"It's the only decision. For both of us. Except..." He looked her in the eye, sighed, muttered a swear word. "Except, if that one time with you was going to be the only time, I wish I'd taken it slow."

She ducked her head and sensed that he, too, looked away.

Eventually, he cleared his throat. "We've got business to talk about. Does the name Otterman mean anything to you?"

"Chuck?"

His head went back with surprise. "*Chuck?* You know him?"

"Of course."

"Why 'of course'? Have you locked horns?"

"Not at all. In fact, just the opposite. He's a supporter. He's contributed to my campaign."

He looked at her with bafflement, then laughed, then

dragged his hand down his face. "Oh, that's beautiful. It'll give Neal a woody."

"Why?"

"Doesn't matter. Private joke." His hand dropped to his side in an attitude of defeat. "Why'd you need to see me?"

"Sit down." She indicated a chair facing her desk.

He looked at her incisively. "No, this sounds like news I'd rather hear while standing."

"It's bad."

"That's the only kind of news I've been getting lately. Let's have it."

The blow couldn't be softened. She didn't even try. "Joe Gilroy has filed for a temporary restraining order against you."

For several seconds he looked at her as though she'd spoken in a foreign language, then he tilted his head in misapprehension. Finally, when he'd fully processed what she'd told him, his facial features tightened with rage. Through his teeth, he hissed, "Son of a bitch." He turned and started for the door.

Holly, anticipating just such a reaction, beat him to it, placing herself between him and the door and pressing her hands flat against his chest. "Crawford, think! If you blaze over there and confront him, you'll be doing just as he wants you to. He'll call the police, and it will be written up as a domestic disturbance."

"Another entry to my *file*. That stinking, fucking file."

"Exactly! You'll be playing right into his hands, making his case for him. Is that what you want?"

"No. I want to kill him."

She gave him a look that caused him to rethink that declaration and set him to cursing. Abruptly turning away from her, he began prowling her office like a caged lion, taking in the aspects of the room. He picked up the crystal paperweight on her desk and hefted it in his palm. For a moment she feared he would hurl it through the window.

"Nice office." He tilted his head back to look at the chandelier in the center of the ceiling. "Is this where you make all those judgments against people? Is this where you roll the dice to determine their futures?"

"Don't do that."

Brimming with contempt, his eyes cut to her. "Why not?"

"Because I won't be your whipping boy when it's not me you're angry at. Besides, I won't be making any judgments regarding you. I recused myself from your custody case."

Chastened, he returned the paperweight to the desk with inordinate care. "Since when?"

"I dictated the letter first thing this morning, before the press conference. Mrs. Briggs had it typed on my letterhead and ready to sign before I left for lunch. She hand-delivered it to Judge Mason. He's the administrative judge for this district."

He relaxed his stance and his shoulders, but resumed the prowling.

She went on. "I told Mr. Gilroy that he would have to take the TRO to another judge for signature, but I asked him why he felt one was necessary. He told me about your unannounced visit to their home last night."

"I've never had to announce my visits before. I always did just as a courtesy. Fat lot of good having manners has done me."

"He claims you threatened him with 'you'll be sorry.'"

"I did, and he will be if he keeps up this kind of bullshit."

"There wasn't any physical contact last night?"

"If he said there was, or ever has been, he's lying."

"No, he acknowledged that you hadn't touched him. In which case, I urged him to reconsider."

"To no avail, apparently."

"He…" This was the part she had most dreaded telling him. "He claims you pose a threat to Georgia."

He stopped pacing and looked at her, obviously at a loss for words.

"Not in an abusive sense," she said. "He fears you might take her."

"Kidnap her?"

"That was the word he used."

He snuffled a mirthless laugh. "If I'd had intentions of doing that, I'd have done it a long time ago."

"I said as much. But he argued that the events on Monday could have an impact on you professionally. Your mishandling of the situation, and the fallout from it, could cost you your career."

"Mishandling?"

"He said all this, Crawford. I didn't."

"Discounting Neal, neither has anyone official. I never even discharged a weapon."

"I noted that. However, in Mr. Gilroy's view, the action you took might eventually come under internal review, and this time, he said, your agency—or any agency—might not be as lenient as they were after Halcon. If you were fired or forced to resign from the Rangers, you'd have nothing to lose by taking Georgia and disappearing."

"Except that it would make me a criminal. A fugitive. Even if I chose that for myself, does Joe believe I would do that to Georgia?"

"I don't know what he believes, Crawford. But I told him that *I* believed he was completely wrong. Unfortunately I didn't change his mind, didn't even make a dent. He left here to seek out another judge."

He rubbed his hand across his mouth. "What kind of repercussions will there be for you?"

"For recusing myself?"

"For giving me warning of the TRO."

"If Joe Gilroy learns of it, he could file a grievance against me."

"Christ, Holly. I don't want any of my crap to land on you."

"I don't want you to be provoked into an altercation with your father-in-law."

He glanced at the door. "If you hadn't stopped me, I would have been in his face by now."

"Which is what I feared and why I gave you the heads-up. It flirts with violating ethics, but in good conscience, I couldn't let you completely destroy your chances of getting your daughter back."

"How destructive is it for you? What reason did you give for recusing yourself?"

"Giving a reason isn't required. A judge can simply say he/she can't hear a particular case. That's it. However, what I put in the letter to Judge Mason and the governor—"

"The governor?"

"I felt he should know. I called his office, but he's out of state at a conference, so I emailed him, explained the situation, and attached a copy of the letter to Judge Mason."

"You have the governor's email address?"

She made a gesture downplaying that. "What I said in the letter was that since you had saved my life, and that, by necessity, you and I are closely linked to the investigation, sustaining objectivity is virtually impossible. Which is the truth."

"If not the whole truth," he said softly.

"If not the whole truth," she echoed in a whisper. "Plain

and simple, I broke the rules. Even if no one else ever knew about what happened between us, I would."

Their gazes held for several seconds, then he turned away from her and went over to the bookcase wall. Placing his hands on the edge of a shelf above his head, he braced himself against it, his head dropping forward between his shoulders. He remained like that for a full minute. She supposed he was trying to absorb everything that this development signified.

Finally, addressing the floor, he said, "Temporary restraining order. In other words, I'm an imminent threat."

"You should be talking to William Moore about it."

He looked at her over his shoulder. "I'm talking to you."

With reluctance, she nodded. "The TRO goes into effect immediately when you're served."

"And then I have to go to court and defend myself against Joe's crock of shit."

He did, or the full restraining order went into effect automatically, and it could remain in effect for years. Of course, he knew that, so she refrained from saying anything.

"How long before the hearing for the full restraining order? It usually takes, what? Two, three weeks?"

"Sometimes sooner, sometimes longer."

"And Prentiss County is currently short one courtroom," he said wryly. "Between now and the hearing, whenever it is, the TRO remains in place."

"We don't know for certain that another judge granted it."

"Best odds?"

"Not in your favor, I'm afraid. Even though there's been no physical abuse, your father-in-law is alleging harassment and threats of violence. With a child's safety and welfare at stake…"

"The judge will sign." Turning to face her, he added, "And they'll waste no time serving me."

"Honestly, I thought you might already have been served, so by telling you, I'm not going that far out on a limb." She took a step toward him. "Crawford, you know that you must abide by the order. I beg you to. If you violate it, the consequences will be severe."

"I know the consequences. I could go to jail. Hell, I've slammed people in jail for violating a TRO."

"Beyond that, a ruling in favor of the Gilroys would be practically guaranteed at the hearing. As an offender, you could be kept away from Georgia for years. So please, promise me that you'll comply with the terms."

"How bad are they?"

"Until the hearing, you can't get within one hundred yards of Georgia, the Gilroys, or their property. No contact whatsoever. Not even by phone. Any attempted contact will be considered a violation."

"Jesus."

"I'm sorry. I know it's difficult to hear this, to hear yourself spoken of in terms of an 'offender' but—"

"Screw all that," he snapped. "Joe, the court, can call me any damn thing they please. What about *Georgia*? What's she gonna think when I suddenly disappear from her life? She'll think her daddy abandoned her."

His chest rose and fell with emotion. "Whether or not you believe it, whether or not my in-laws like it, my little girl loves me. The last thing we talked about was the surprise I have waiting on her at my house. Now? Christ!" He made an angry swipe through the air with his fist. "I'll never forgive Joe for this." Stepping around her, he headed for the door. "I gotta go."

"Where are you going? What are you going to do?"

"I don't know. Get drunk maybe."

Panicked, she grabbed his sleeve and held on even as he tried to shake her off.

"I won't let you leave when you're in this frame of mind."

"You'd do well to let me go, Holly. When I'm in this kind of mood, I tend to act out."

"If you act out, you'll lose Georgia forever."

He threw off her grasp. "That's funny coming from you," he sneered. "I'd have Georgia now if you had given her to me instead of wasting time enumerating my past transgressions. 'Here's your daughter, Mr. Hunt. Go in peace.' Bang the gavel. We're outta there. But, no, you had your judgmental points to make."

She shrank away from him. She knew the harsh words were spoken in anger and supreme frustration, but that didn't make them any less hurtful. Or any less true. They hovered there between them, widening the chasm that circumstances had already created.

He was the first to move. His motions abrupt, he gave the heavy doorknob a vicious turn, yanked the door open, and strode out.

———

"They were together tonight. Alone."

"Who?"

Pat Connor nodded a greeting to another police officer as he walked past carrying a Whataburger sack. Once the cop was out of earshot, he whispered into the burner phone. "The judge and Crawford Hunt. They had a closed-door session in her chambers for over half an hour. He came out looking like he could either fuck or kill somebody. Not necessarily in that order."

He'd thought that was a rather clever turn of phrase,

but there wasn't so much as a snicker on the other end of the call.

"When was this?"

"Just now. He took the atrium stairs down. Fast. Practically at a run. He left the building. I followed him out and watched him drive away."

"Where's the judge?"

"Still in her office."

"They might have been discussing the investigation."

"Alone? Neal Lester's here. So's Nugent. Why wouldn't they have been in on the meeting? And something else."

"Well?"

"This morning after the press conference, he dragged her off for a whispered conversation." Pat related everything he'd seen and overheard, leaving out the part about how he nearly messed himself when Crawford Hunt had singled him out. "Told me not to let anybody interrupt them. But Neal Lester showed up with her boyfriend, and that put a stop to it."

Several moments lapsed, then Pat was asked, "Did he see you see him?"

"Tonight, you mean? Yeah, as he blew out of the judge's office. We made eye contact. He bobbed his head, like 'how you doin'?' but he didn't say anything." Pat waited and when nothing was forthcoming, he asked, "What do you want me to do now?"

"See to it that Neal Lester knows about their meeting. Mention it to him in passing. Casually. But stress that Hunt was angry when he left her."

"I don't know," Pat whined. "I don't want to stick my neck out too far on this thing."

The man's chuckle was sinister. "Too late to be worried about that."

Chapter 19

—————◆—————

Crawford didn't keep liquor in the house. After Beth died, he'd started drinking to dull the pain. It had no effect, so he drank more. Getting the DUI had been a wake-up call. He'd seen how close he was to becoming like Conrad, and he was not going to be like him. Not in any respect. Now, when he drank at all, he limited himself to one and went out for it.

He sat at the bar of a popular watering hole, slowly sipping the straight bourbon while ignoring the clamor around him—half a dozen TVs all tuned in to the same baseball game, the clack of billiard balls, the drone of conversation, the wailing lament of a country song being piped through the sound system.

If his cell phone hadn't been on vibrate, he would have missed the call. He checked the caller's name and hesitated, but only for half a second before deciding in favor of answering. Keeping his tone bland, he said, "Hey, Neal. What's up?"

"You bastard."

"Excuse me?"

"It was you, wasn't it?"

"Something wrong? You sound plumb overwrought."

"You leaked his name to the media, didn't you? *Didn't* you?"

"Whose name?"

"It's on the ten o'clock news. I'm watching it. A 'new person of interest' in the courthouse shooting. Chuck Otterman."

Crawford couldn't help but smile over Neal's distress. He signaled the barkeeper to switch one of the TVs over to a Tyler station. On the screen was a reporter doing a live standup in front of the Prentiss County Courthouse. The audio was muted, but Crawford could guess what he was saying, because he'd practically spoon-fed it to the guy.

Neal's lame approach to the investigation and his kowtowing to Otterman had left Crawford feeling that a shake-up was in order. A Houston station would have had ten times the viewers, but Tyler was closer, and its audience more homegrown. Therefore interest was greater about the goings-on in rural Prentiss. Using the burner phone he kept handy in the glove compartment of his SUV, he'd placed an anonymous call to the station's news hotline and asked to speak to a reporter.

Sticking to the facts, Crawford told him about Otterman's coming forward and admitting to leaving the crime scene, about his being asked by the "team of investigators" to view the body of the man erroneously suspected of the shooting. He hadn't answered any of the questions put to him by the reporter, who was hyperventilating by then. He'd been purposefully evasive and made himself sound nervous about leaking information, hoping the tactic would whet the reporter's appetite and ensure a deeper probe. His pot-stirring obviously had worked.

Neal was still ranting. "You were his 'unnamed source,' weren't you? You tipped them. I know it."

"They wouldn't broadcast an anonymous tip without having it corroborated."

"The reporter called me to substantiate it two minutes before air time. *Two minutes!*"

"Then what are you yelling at me for, when it was you who confirmed Otterman's involvement?"

"All I confirmed was that he'd done his—"

"Civic duty. He's a model citizen, all right."

"In fact, he is."

"Then he's got nothing to worry about, does he?"

"No, but you do. I'm going to have your ass over this. I'm going to have it mounted on the wall of my den."

"Have you cleared that with the missus?"

"How am I going to explain this snafu to Mr. Otterman?"

"Jeez, Neal, I don't know. But you've got, uhhh, ten hours and forty-eight, no forty-nine, minutes to figure that out. Wasn't the convenient time for him nine o'clock tomorrow morning?"

"Fuck you."

"See you at the morgue."

Crawford clicked off, having succeeded in upsetting Neal and hopefully shaking Otterman's equanimity. But it was a minor triumph that did little to cheer him. Rather than goose Neal into conducting a more aggressive investigation, the detective would more than likely become more stubbornly conservative.

Otterman was probably as solid a citizen as Neal believed him to be. Crawford couldn't pinpoint why the guy had got under his skin, but his initial response had been dislike and mistrust. His gut instinct about people had been too reliable to start dismissing now. He would continue going with it until it was proven wrong about Otterman.

Before concluding that he was absolutely innocent,

as Neal already had, he wanted to gauge Otterman's reaction when he looked at Rodriguez's corpse, and wait to see what, if anything, Smitty turned up on him and his unexplained meetings.

He left his drink unfinished. Rather than lifting his spirits, it was only making him more depressed. In contrast to the air-conditioned bar, the atmosphere outside felt particularly sultry. He was clammy with sweat by the time he climbed into his SUV. He blamed the heat index for his lethargy—not the wounded look on Holly's face when he'd left her with that harsh accusation vibrating between them.

Talking dirty to her one minute, lashing out at her the next. If she hadn't known it before, she knew it now: Refined, he wasn't.

Feeling bone-tired and dejected, he let himself into his house through the back door, draped his jacket over a kitchen chair, slid his necktie from around his neck, and, without even bothering to unbutton his shirt, pulled it off over his head as he made his way down the hall toward his bedroom.

As he passed the open door to Georgia's room, he did a double-take.

Then he stood there, stupefied, his brain trying to register what his eyes were seeing. Blindly he felt for the wall switch and flipped on the light.

The bedroom had been turned inside out, upside down, destroyed. The mirror between the upright spindles of the dresser had been splintered into a million shards, the picture books ripped to shreds, the stuffed animals disemboweled, the princess doll dismembered and decapitated. The bed linens had been sliced to ribbons. Red paint, flung onto the pink walls, looked obscenely like blood spatters.

The violation made him sick. He forced down the gorge that surged into his throat.

He did a quick walk-through of the other rooms, but nothing else had been disturbed, which upset him more than if his entire house had been trashed. The offender knew him well, knew what he valued most, knew how to strike where it would hurt the worst, and scare the shit out of him.

Any attempted contact will be considered a violation, he remembered Holly saying. But he hadn't been served yet, so with "screw that" haste, he called the Gilroys' house. Grace answered.

"It's me," he said. "Is Georgia okay?"

"Crawford. Uh—"

"*Is she okay?*"

"Yes, of course. She's been asleep for hours."

"Go check on her."

"Crawford—"

"Just do it." Reining in his impatience, he added, "Please, Grace."

Fifteen seconds later, she returned. "She's in her bed, fast asleep."

He took his first steady breath since discovering the vandalism. "Is your house alarm set?"

"You know Joe."

"Keep it set. Even during the day."

"What's the matter? Has something happened?"

An explanation would only support their argument that he was dangerous to be around. "A daddy thing," he said, forcing himself to give a light laugh. "Moment of panic. You know how it is. Sorry I bothered you. Good night."

He disconnected and, when he did, he became aware of a noise outside. Quickly but quietly, he went down the hall and into the living room. Slipping his pistol from the holster at the small of his back, he peeked through a front window and saw a shadowy form approaching the porch.

Crawford turned on the outside light and simultaneously flung open the door.

The man halted and shielded his eyes against the sudden glare. He blinked Crawford into focus. "Hey, Crawford."

He was a professional server whom Crawford had used himself.

"I know it's late, but I came around earlier and you weren't here." With apparent reluctance, he withdrew an envelope from the breast pocket of his jacket and extended it to Crawford. As he took it, the server said, "Sorry, man."

Crawford didn't thank him, but he shook his head to indicate that it was unnecessary for him to apologize. He was only doing his job.

The server touched his eyebrow in a quasi salute, then turned and walked back to his car parked at the curb.

Crawford closed his front door. Considered an immediate threat to Georgia, he'd been served with a temporary restraining order. He glanced in the direction of her despoiled bedroom.

The irony didn't escape him.

As soon as her back hit the sofa, he flung open her robe, ruched up her t-shirt, and hooked his thumbs into the narrow band of her panties. They were off and flung to the floor within seconds.

She yanked his shirttail from his waistband and grappled with his belt buckle. More practiced at opening his fly, he pushed aside her clumsy hands and hastily undid the buttons. Together they shoved his jeans and underwear over his butt. A heartbeat later, he was inside her. Completely and solidly. Engrafted.

For five seconds—ten?—neither of them moved, not even to breathe, possibly because they couldn't quite believe that they'd reached this point of no return without kissing or wooing or foreplay.

Then he braced himself above her by placing one hand on the edge of the seat cushion, the other on the arm of the sofa behind her head, and began pumping into her. The angle of each thrust was perfect, the friction electrifying. Yet, greedy for more, she dug her heels in and tilted her hips up to amplify the grinding motion of his.

In a shockingly short time, she was gathering fistfuls of his shirt, then her hands moved up to his shoulders, where they held on, her fingers digging into the firm muscles. Her back arched and held in a silent plea for one more stroke…one more glide…one more…And she came.

The instant he felt her helpless clenching, he surrendered to his own climax. The intensity of it caused his arms to collapse. He settled heavily on top of her, pulsing inside her, his breath hot and damp against her neck as he groaned, "Christ, christ."

The echo of Crawford's grating voice jarred Holly out of the dream, which had been a startlingly lifelike reenactment, and her body had responded accordingly. Her heart was thudding. She was short-winded. Her sex was achy and wet and feverish.

Do you remember it like I do?

Throwing back the sheet, she got out of bed and went into her bathroom. She turned on the faucet and splashed cold water on her face. But it didn't wash away the memory of Crawford sprawled on her chest, his own expanding like bellows while he took a few moments to catch his breath. Precious few moments, however. Then he abruptly raised his head and looked directly into her eyes from a distance of mere inches.

Her hands now trembling with the memory, she turned off the faucet and dried her face. As she lowered the towel and saw her image in the mirror above the sink, she realized that this is the way she must have looked to him in that moment: hair straggling over her face, eyes glazed and dilated, cheeks flushed, lips parted in bewilderment over what had just happened.

Then as now, her nipples had been so tight underneath her t-shirt, so sensitized, that the abrasion of the soft cloth had been enough to send tingles through her. If he had touched them in that moment, brushed his tongue across them, even fanned them with his breath, her heart might have burst from the pleasure.

But he hadn't. He had broken that moment of shared wonderment by slipping out of her and levering himself off the sofa. That's when she was struck with the enormity of what they'd done, the sheer calamity of it. Frantically, she'd pulled down her t-shirt and crammed the hem between her thighs. She rolled onto her side and drew herself into a ball. But there was no cause for modesty, because, by then, he was making his way out, his boot heels thudding against the hardwood floor.

Of all the factors relating to that event, the one that surprised her most was her own spontaneity. She hadn't paused even long enough to ask herself *Should I or shouldn't I?* She had simply acted on a propulsive desire without giving any thought to the wrongness or rightness of it.

Which was unlike her. Following her father's abandonment, her mother had relinquished all major decision making to her. Bearing that much responsibility, she had carefully weighed every decision. She couldn't afford to make one wrong turn, because her future, as well as her mother's, had depended on correctness.

There had been no place in her life, ever, for caprice.

As she gazed at her reflection now, she realized that, despite the consequences that might arise from that one rash act, she didn't regret it as much as she should. Had she been her careful and cautious self, she would have missed those thousands of incredible physical sensations. She would have missed those erotically charged moments measured by the cadence of their hard breathing. She would have missed the utter wildness of it, the untempered carnality. She would have missed…him.

Better to be remembering it now with a trace of regret than forever regretting that she had denied herself the experience.

But he would always be the man she had compromised ethics for. And to him she would always represent the system standing between him and his child. His parting words to her last night had cut to the quick, but they had summed up the hopelessness of their situation.

After showering and dressing, she went into the kitchen to find Marilyn already there, sitting at the dining table, which she'd turned into a temporary workspace for herself. They exchanged good mornings, and when Holly asked Marilyn how she'd slept, she guffawed. "Some bodyguard I am. I went out like a light. What time did you get home?"

"Around ten thirty. I had a police escort all the way to the back door, then they parked at the end of the drive."

"They're still there. Did you happen to watch the news last night?"

"No."

"They've got another person of interest. His name is Chuck Otterman."

Holly stopped in the act of pouring herself a cup of coffee. "Are you certain?"

"Heard it again this morning. I thought the name sounded familiar, and guess what?" She tapped a sheet of paper with a list of names on it. "He's contributed to your campaign."

"Yes, I know. I've met him." She realized now why Crawford had asked her about the man, seemingly out of the blue. "What are they saying about him?"

Marilyn filled her in and summed up with, "Frankly, I don't think it amounts to much. He came forward of his own volition. A guilty person wouldn't call attention to himself. And what could he possibly have against you?"

"Nothing that I know of."

"I think the media just got wind of his sneaking away from the courthouse and made more of it than is there." Marilyn pointed at the chair across from her. "Sit. Let's talk."

Holly sat.

Marilyn clasped her hands together on the tabletop. "You shot down—maybe not the best turn of phrase—my idea of using the Texas Ranger somehow to—"

"I stand by that decision, Marilyn. He's got enough on his plate."

"Holly, he's a poster boy."

"For?"

"For long and lean, badass lawman. Your description 'cop-like' didn't include the chiseled chin, the cheekbones, and the fact that he's a hunk."

"Honestly, Marilyn. How old are you?"

"Never too old to notice. I Googled him last night. Do you know his history?" Before Holly could reply, she began citing what she called Crawford's "exploits," including Halcon.

"And he's not just a shoot-'em-up. Practically single-handedly, he busted up a kiddie porn ring run by a preacher and his wife from right here in Podunk, but they had customers all over the world. Even had the feds singing his praises."

She sat forward, leaning into the table. "He's smart. He's tough. He was rude as hell to me, but I'll forgive him that because he has this remarkable soft spot for his daughter. His *orphaned* child. He was in your courtroom fighting to regain custody of her, *when*..."

She paused for dramatic effect. "When he's called upon to save the life of the judge who might very well have ruled against him." Spreading her arms wide, she exclaimed, "It's Hollywood. It's chivalry and valor. People will eat it up. But we've got to serve it to them."

"I've recused myself from his custody case."

That blindsided Marilyn. "What? When? You did? Want to tell me why?"

"No."

Holly's succinct but firm reply left Marilyn with no wiggle room for argument. Tactfully backing off that, she picked up a pen and began using it to beat out a rapid tattoo on the table.

A full minute elapsed, then Marilyn tossed down the pen and smacked her hands together. "Actually this is even better. Yes! As the presiding judge, you were limited as to what you could say. Now that you won't be hearing his case, you can be subjective. You're free to talk about him in any terms you choose."

Holly sighed. "Marilyn—"

"I know you don't want to expose his daughter to the media. I get that. Besides, I doubt the grandfather would permit it. He wouldn't even listen to my pitch. But what if we—"

"Wait. Back up. You tried to pitch this idea to Joe Gilroy?"

"About half an hour ago."

Holly looked down at Marilyn's cell phone lying on the table between them.

Marilyn said, "I Googled him, too, and had their home number in no time. Not that it did me any good to call. The instant I introduced myself and told him who I was, he hung up on me. But we can still cash in without using the little girl. We can—"

"Excuse me for just a moment." Holly pushed back her chair and stood up.

"Where are you going?"

"I'll be right back."

Holly left Marilyn dictating notes into her cell phone. When she returned a few minutes later, Marilyn was still at it. She completed her thought, then clicked off the phone. "I've come up with some ideas just off the top of my head. We don't have to implement all of them, but... What's that?"

Holly sat Marilyn's packed suitcase near the back door. "Don't you recognize it?"

"You're moving me out?"

"No, I'm firing you."

Marilyn's lips went slack.

"I appreciate everything you've done, Marilyn. You were worth every penny I've paid you up to this point. But the lengths to which you'll go to win the election are repugnant to me." When she saw that Marilyn was about to speak, she held up her hand. "Argument is futile. Our association ends now. Please clear the table before you go. Have a safe drive back to Dallas."

Neal was waiting in the corridor outside the ME's domain when Crawford arrived a few minutes before nine o'clock. Neither spoke. Crawford took up a position against the wall and just looked at the other man.

Finally Neal said, "The PD is all abuzz this morning."

Crawford turned away to look down the long hallway, currently deserted. Neal didn't take the hint. "Is it true you got served a TRO?"

"Yes."

"Did you threaten your father-in-law?"

"No."

"You're capable of violence. I have firsthand experience."

Crawford brought his head back around and caught Neal swabbing his lower lip with his tongue. "But I don't give advance warning of it," Crawford said. "Sort of defeats the purpose."

"You're destructive," Neal said, gathering angry momentum. "That little stunt you pulled last night with the TV station set this investigation back—"

"What *investigation*, Neal? You're soft on the one thing we have going."

"Otterman? The chief—"

"Awww. Did you get called into the principal's office?"

"I got reamed."

"For letting this case congeal on your tidy desk?"

"For your unsubstantiated allegations—"

"I didn't allege a goddamn thing. True or false, Otterman came to us and admitted to talking a cop into letting him leave the courthouse. Huh? True. True or false, I asked him to take a look at Rodriguez, and he said okay. Also true. What did I allege?"

Neal remained silent but irate.

Crawford took a breath and assumed a more concili-atory tone. "Look, you want me to talk to the chief and take full responsibility for any backlash over Otterman, I'm happy to do that."

"Hell. No. I don't want you talking to anybody. Something about you just naturally pisses people off."

"And here I was hoping to get elected homecom-ing king."

"Who trashed your house?"

The flippancy of Neal's question grated the part of him left raw and exposed by the vandalism. But he replied with a forced nonchalance. "The PD really was abuzz this morning, wasn't it? Forget holding seminars on home security. Y'all ought to conduct them on gos-siping effectively."

"Wasn't gossip. It's a matter of record. You called the police to your house. Responders filed a report."

Crawford knew the chances of catching the intruder were slim to none. Anyone committing a crime that specific, that targeted, knew what they were doing, and it was doubtful they'd left incriminating evidence behind. Even so, the room was being dusted for prints this morning.

The vandal had entered through a window in Geor-gia's room, but a flashlight search of the area outside it hadn't yielded much. One of the officers had theorized that the culprit had been looking to steal something that he could swiftly pawn for drug money. "When he found dolls instead of electronics or jewelry, he got mad and went a little crazy."

Crawford didn't agree with that theory, but he hadn't argued. He'd called in the police only so there would be a record of the break-in if ever he should need it, say for an insurance claim.

"Any idea who did it?" Neal asked him now.

Crawford wouldn't have answered anyway, but he was spared the need to. "Here's Otterman."

The man stepped off the elevator and strode toward them, looking as robust and arrogant as he had the day before. The only difference was that he was dressed in work clothes. The legs of his khakis were stuffed into boots that were caked with mud. He stopped a few feet from them, his eyes as hard as drill bits as he addressed Neal. "Are you so desperate for leads that you had to put my name out there?"

Neal quailed. "No one from our department referred to you as a person of interest, Mr. Otterman. That was the reporter's inference. He's since been corrected and promises to recant."

"For all I care he can refer to me as Jack the Ripper. It doesn't change the truth, which I told you yesterday. The only skin off my nose is that reporters are calling me for comment when I've got a tight schedule, a busted piece of equipment, and a crew standing around scratching their balls while I'm down here with you." He checked his wristwatch. "Can we get on with this so I can get back to work?"

Crawford was standing near the large red button next to the double doors. He pressed it and they were buzzed in. He stood aside and let the other two go in ahead of him, Otterman looking straight ahead, continuing to pretend that he didn't exist.

Neal had notified the staff that they were coming and asked them to be ready. Dr. Anderson was otherwise occupied, but one of his assistants was there beside the table. Once they were in place, he respectfully folded back the sheet.

Crawford kept his eyes on Otterman, who, in spite of his repeated denials of knowing Jorge Rodriguez, instantly gave himself away. Crawford saw the man's gut quicken with a sharp indrawn breath. He blinked several times, then hastily looked away.

"Mr. Otterman?"

He recovered himself so rapidly and so well that if Crawford hadn't been watching for signs, he would have missed them. When Otterman replied to Neal's discreet prompting, it was as though he had dropped a welder's mask over his face. His transformation was that sudden. His expression was closed, unforgiving, unrevealing.

He said, "I don't know him."

Chapter 20

———◆———

Crawford drove straight from the morgue to the courthouse. Neal had arrived moments ahead of him. When Crawford walked into the CAP unit, the detective was smoothing down his necktie as he lowered himself into his desk chair. His maddening calmness infuriated Crawford.

He strode over to the desk. "He was lying."

"I would have laid odds you'd say that."

"I *saw* it, Neal."

"You saw what you wanted to see."

"The signs were there. Plain as day. He recognized Rodriguez immediately, dammit. Even you couldn't have missed his reaction."

Neal shot him a fulminating look, but Crawford sensed he wasn't quite as indifferent to Otterman as he pretended. "You did notice, didn't you?"

"A flicker," Neal admitted. "Nothing to get you this excited. Maybe he and Rodriguez had been at side-by-side urinals."

"And maybe Rodriguez was part of a plot."

"Plot? We haven't established a plot. Suddenly this is a conspiracy, and Chuck Otterman is behind it?" He laughed shortly, then his eyes narrowed on Crawford. "Why are you so keen on him?"

"Why aren't you?"

"Because there's no evidence that points to him," Neal said, raising his voice. "No motive. Nitpicky things like that which are essential to upholding our system of justice. Even if they're no big deal to you, they are to the DA."

He was right, and Crawford had nothing to counter with, but he wasn't throwing in the towel, either. "I still say he's playing us. He made a preemptive strike by coming in here and staging the honest citizen, *mea culpa* scene. Smart move. By telling us himself that he was there, rather than letting us find out on our own, we're less likely to suspect him."

"I *don't* suspect him. We dug and found nothing remotely connecting him to Judge Spencer except a donation to her campaign."

"Maybe we dug in the wrong place."

"On that point, I couldn't agree with you more. We're digging in the wrong place." Neal's cell phone chirped. "Excuse me." He answered and listened for a moment, then said, "Hold on." He covered the mouthpiece. "My wife. Our youngest is throwing up." He swiveled his desk chair around to face the window, giving Crawford his back.

Crawford walked over to the makeshift coffee bar, which amounted to a Nixon-era machine and fixings. He poured tepid sludge into a Styrofoam cup, then used his burner phone to speed-dial Smitty.

The club owner answered with a grumbled, "Who's this?"

"Just checking to see if my phone is broken or something."

Recognizing his voice, Smitty swore. "You said to call if I had something. Have I called? No."

"There's a guy I know at the IRS—"

"I swear!"

"—who actually gets off doing audits."

"Honest to God, the object of your affection hasn't even been to the club—"

"Tickled Pink?"

"None of them. Not since you were here. Proving what I've said all along. You're a jinx."

"Have you talked to anybody about him?"

"You think I'm crazy?"

"I think you're scum. Have you?"

"I've put out some feelers, okay? Nothing's come back."

Just then Matt Nugent entered the room, bringing with him several files. He looked excited. Crawford glanced over at Neal, whose back was still to the room.

"Do better, Smitty, or I'm gonna have to alert the vice squad to that underage girl you've got dancing."

"Shit! How'd you know about her?"

"I didn't."

Crawford clicked off, pitched his cup of coffee into the trash can, and deftly intercepted Nugent. "Morning, Matt. Neal's on the phone. Whacha got there?"

"Nothing."

But Crawford could tell by Nugent's bobbing Adam's apple that it was something. Giving the young detective no time to protest, he forced him to execute an about-face and steered him back into the corridor. He moved them out of earshot of other police personnel and, before Nugent could stop him, plucked one of the files from his collection.

"You're not s-supposed to see those," he sputtered as Crawford opened the file.

No, he was quite certain Neal hadn't wanted him to see these. The photographs were grainy, blurred, apparently taken with a telephone lens of a moving object:

himself. They documented his comings and goings over the past twenty-four hours. On foot. In his truck. Arriving at the courthouse. Leaving it. Sitting at the bar where he'd nursed a bourbon. Being served a TRO beneath the beam of his front porch light.

He couldn't believe he hadn't picked up the tail, but he hadn't been expecting one, hadn't been looking for one. Chalk up a point for Neal.

As he flipped through the eight-by-ten printouts a second time, he asked, "The photographer didn't happen to catch the son of a bitch who tore my little girl's room all to hell, did he?"

Crawford's tongue-in-cheek inflection escaped Nugent, who answered seriously. "Neal already asked. No."

Although Crawford was seeing things through a red mist of outrage, he knew that his reaction would be reported to Neal. Exercising control and care, he lined up the edges of the printouts, replaced them in the file, and returned it to Nugent. "Whoever the guy is, he does good work."

Nugent said miserably, "Neal's gonna have my head."

"Don't worry about it. If it comes to that, I'll tell him I bullied you into showing me. He'll believe that."

"Thanks." He hesitated, then said, "I don't get why he had you tailed, anyway."

"I don't get it, either, Matt."

They reentered the CAP unit. Neal was still talking on his phone, so he didn't notice Nugent's nervousness as he sat down at his desk and booted up his computer. Crawford was trying to process what the surveillance signified and how to confront Neal with it, when the office line on Neal's desk rang. Automatically Crawford answered.

"Crawford Hunt."

A perky feminine voice said, "Oh, hi. This is Carrie Lester."

Crawford's eyes cut to Neal. "I'm sorry, who?"

"I'm Neal's wife. We haven't met, but of course I know who you are."

Crawford stared at the back of Neal's head while his wife inadvertently trapped him in a lie. "I hate to bother you," she said, "but I've been trying to reach Neal, and his cell phone is going straight to voice mail. I wonder, is he around?"

※

When Crawford walked in, Holly's assistant looked up from behind her desk, registering surprise. "Mr. Hunt?"

"Is the judge here?"

"She came in about ten minutes ago."

"Would you please tell her I'm here? There's been a development in the case I need to discuss with her."

She used a desk phone to communicate with Holly, and a few seconds later, she opened the door to her private office and looked at him expectantly. "Good morning."

"Hi. I apologize for not calling ahead."

"You need to see me?"

"Right away."

She stood aside and motioned him into her office. "Mrs. Briggs, hold all my calls, please." She closed the door and turned to him.

Today her business suit consisted of black pants and a black-and-cream striped jacket. The top underneath matched the light stripes and had a row of tiny pearl buttons down the center of it. As enticing as that view was, he kept his gaze above her neckline.

"I'm sorry for what I said last night, that I'd have Georgia if it wasn't for you."

"Sadly, it's the truth, though."

"Maybe. If you split hairs. But I was mad over something else and shouldn't have taken it out on you. Anyhow..." He left it at that and so did she.

"Were you served?" she asked.

"Within minutes of getting home. I had an eventful night."

And he knew he looked it. It had been well into the wee hours before the patrolmen wrapped up their investigation of the vandalized room and the perimeter of his house. After they left, he'd lain awake, mulling over the destruction, wondering who had done it and, much more worrisome, why.

Having gotten only a couple hours of sleep, there were dark circles under his eyes. He hadn't bothered to shave and had only towel-dried his hair. His shirt and jeans were clean, but he was wearing yesterday's wrinkled sport jacket, which he'd lifted off the back of the dining chair as he passed through the kitchen on his way out.

"Did something else happen last night?" she asked.

"I'll get to that. First, I gotta ruin your day."

"A development in the case? That wasn't just something you told Mrs. Briggs so you could apologize?"

"Unfortunately, no. I came to give you a heads-up."

He propped his hands on his hips and looked down at the floor, wishing a script had been etched there for him to follow. But there wasn't. He had to come up with the words to tell her, and he figured the blunter the better.

"Neal's been having me followed." She opened her mouth to speak, but he said, "Wait, hear me out. That's not the worst of it. He's got pictures. I don't know how long the surveillance has been going on, or how thorough it's been, but I wanted to warn you that you might be featured prominently in some of the shots." He nodded toward the three tall windows behind her desk.

"I don't know for sure because I only saw a sampling. I've used these guys myself and know how resourceful they can be. If the tail saw me come up here last night, if he got pictures through those windows, then we're blown. You and me together."

Together up against the edge of her desk, his hands all but cupping her ass as they leaned into each other and crotch-bumped. Even a camera lens would have steamed up.

"At least we didn't kiss," he said. "He didn't catch us in a lip-lock, but I don't think anyone could mistake… well…you know."

Their gazes held, then hers dropped to his mouth, then lower to the center of his chest. "Why did Neal have you under surveillance?"

He'd been expecting an accusatory outburst. Momentarily taken off guard by her question, he made a dismissive waving motion with his hand. "He's got this notion that I was behind the courtroom shooting."

"*What?*"

"Crazy, I know. But with my ruination in mind, he's running headlong down a dead end. Meanwhile." He told her about Otterman's reaction to seeing the corpse. "Neal didn't want to admit it, but he noticed it, too."

"I'm not defending Chuck Otterman," she said. "I don't know him well at all. But that's my point. Other than his modest contribution to my campaign, there's no connection. I would tell you if there were."

"I believe you. But it might be something you're not remembering, or something you don't even know. Maybe linked to the firm in Dallas?"

"I called to apologize for all the inconvenience this

had caused them. I was assured that my safety is their primary concern. But in any case, Chuck Otterman has never had any dealings with any attorney there, past or present, including me."

"Maybe they're holding back because of privilege."

"That occurred to me. I asked." She shook her head. "I believe they would tell me. This is a murder investigation, after all."

"Okay. But keep thinking." He waited a beat, then asked, "What are you going to do about the other?"

"You mean the photographs?"

"I don't know if there are any of you. But if there are, they'll be damaging."

"I'm no longer hearing your case."

"No, but it's still a murky area. That asshole Sanders could turn it into the scandal of the decade." He turned away from her. "Dammit, I should have stayed away from you. If I wind up costing you the election, I'll never forgive myself."

"Will you forgive yourself for saving my life?"

He came back around. "What?"

"Crawford, I was compromised the moment you leaped over that railing and shielded me from the gunman. No matter what's happened since, I could never have made an objective decision regarding the man who risked his life in order to save mine."

It sounded a little too pat, an honest but well-spun answer she'd prepared in anticipation of being asked a sensitive question about him. "Did you come up with that, or did what's-her-name?"

"I fired what's-her-name this morning."

That was surprising news. "How come? Her haircut?"

She laughed. "Reason enough. But we had a difference of opinion over how my campaign should proceed."

His cell phone dinged, signaling a text message. "Hold the thought." He opened his text page and stared in puzzlement at the still-frame picture of Georgia that appeared. He tapped the arrow to play the video.

Her giggles sounded throughout the chamber. He recognized the park setting, the familiar playground, the swing set. Georgia's blond curls caught the sunlight at the apex of each arc of the swing. Her small hands were clutching the thick ropes, her toes stretching out in front of her to reach as high as they possibly could. She was laughing happily.

The video ran for thirty-two seconds, and it was the longest half-minute of his life. The caption accompanying the video: "You're making this too easy."

He bolted for the door and nearly ripped it from the doorjamb as he pulled it open. Behind him, Holly cried out, "Crawford? What?"

"Call 911," he yelled as he blasted past her startled assistant. "Get police there."

"Where?"

"The park playground."

On the seemingly endless staircase that wound down four floors, he shouted for people to move aside and pushed those who didn't react soon enough out of his path. He leaped over half the treads. When he reached the lobby, he called to two deputies who were standing together chatting, "The city park. Now!"

He didn't wait to see that they followed as he barreled through the courthouse entrance and sprinted to the parking lot, fumbling with his key fob to unlock his SUV. He clambered in, started it, and pressed down on his horn to signal any other drivers in the parking lot that he was claiming the right of way.

On the city streets, his tires screeched as he wove in and out of traffic. Driving with his right hand, he reached through his open window with his left and attached the mag-mount cherry to the roof. Glancing in his rearview mirror he saw that the sheriff's unit was running hot behind him. He accessed his police radio and blurted out the basic info to a dispatcher.

He sped through the pair of stone columns at the entrance to the park and took the curving lane in a straight line, his accelerator mashed flat to the floorboard. When the parking lot adjacent to the playground came into view, he applied his full weight to his brake pedal, causing his SUV to skid the twenty feet. He rammed it into park and was out of it before it had shuddered to a complete stop.

He heard Georgia before he saw her. Her laughter was high and light, her giddy squeals piercing the heavy air. He rounded the trunk of one of the spreading live oaks and spotted her. She was standing on the merry-go-round, holding onto one of the T-bars, laughing as Grace spun her round and round.

Crawford fell back against the tree trunk and bent double, placing his hands on his knees, gasping for breath, tears of relief mingling with the stinging sweat that dripped into his eyes.

When he straightened up, he saw Joe Gilroy. He was leaning against his car where it was parked in the lane, his cell phone in his hand. He was watching Crawford. He smiled. "Thank you. I can now have you arrested."

Crawford's field of vision shrank to the size of a pinhead, and his father-in-law was at the center of it. He started forward in a measured but determined tread that must have signaled Joe to the rage that had turned his blood to lava. The older man straightened up and took a defensive stance.

Crawford charged across the remaining distance

between them, grabbed him by the front of his shirt, spun him away from his car, and shoved him so hard he stumbled backward, landing hard in the gravel.

"You've done it now," Joe growled. "You're going to jail."

"What kind of sick game are you playing, Joe?"

"Game? What are you talking about?"

"That video. Your cute little caption."

"You're crazy. I always said so. You've just proved it. I don't know anything about a video."

Crawford reached down for him, but one of the deputies who'd huffed up behind him, spoke his name in a cautionary tone. "Don't do it, man, or we'll be hauling you in."

Crawford heeded him, but he never took his eyes off his father-in-law. "Give me your phone."

"Go to hell." Joe stood up and dusted off the seat of his pants. "I'm collecting Georgia and Grace and getting out of here and away from you." Looking beyond Crawford, he said to the deputies. "What are you waiting for? I have a restraining order. Arrest him."

"Sorry, Crawford," one of them said. "Let's go."

Crawford didn't move. Still fixed on Joe, he repeated, "Give. Me. Your. Phone."

Joe glared at him with loathing and turned away. Crawford's hand shot out and grabbed Joe's arm. A struggle for possession of the cell phone ensued. The deputies scrambled to join in and, together, were able to pull Crawford away.

Neal's car came to a halt only a few yards from where he and Joe were faced off while he continued to struggle against the deputies' hold on him. Neal and Nugent got out on opposite sides. Another car pulled up behind Neal's. Holly alighted from it. In his peripheral vision Crawford saw flashing lights, signaling the arrival of more squad cars, which he himself had summoned during his mad drive here.

"What the hell is going on?" Neal asked.

"He attacked me," Joe said. "Arrest him."

Crawford, breathing hard, said, "He texted me a video of Georgia because he knew it would get me here. See for yourself, and tell me what you would make of it."

With a nod from Neal, the deputies let him go. He pitched his phone to Neal and gave him the security code.

Joe said, "I don't know what the hell he's talking about."

Neal pulled up the video text on Crawford's phone and played it. "Doesn't say who sent it. May I see your phone, Mr. Gilroy?"

Joe puffed out his chest. "If my word isn't good enough for you—"

"Mr. Gilroy?" Holly wedged her way between Neal and Nugent and came to stand in front of Joe. Her voice was soft, controlled, that of a mediator. "If this is only a misunderstanding, why not defuse the situation before your granddaughter notices the police cars and becomes frightened?"

"If she's frightened, it'll be his fault, not mine."

"Then you can take the higher ground."

His eyes narrowed on her. "You've got nothing to do with this anymore. I'm beginning to wonder why you recused yourself. Has he won you over to his side?"

"I'm on Georgia's side." She let that resonate, then said, "Please?"

Joe's eyes glinted with hostility and pride, but when Neal extended him his palm, he slapped his phone into it. "Your security code, please, Mr. Gilroy?" Neal accessed the text file and then checked his photo library. "It's not on here."

Holly, who'd also been watching the phone screen, looked up at Crawford and shook her head.

By now other policemen were converging on the group. Neal said to Nugent, "Tell them it was a false alarm. Send them away."

"This *wasn't* a false alarm," Crawford said. "You saw the video." Looking at Joe, he added, "He was on his phone when I got here. He could have deleted it."

Joe ignored him and addressed Neal. "I didn't shoot any video."

"Somebody did." Beside himself, Crawford plowed the fingers of both hands through his hair and held it back. "It was sent as a warning. If it wasn't you…" Recalling the angle from which the video had been shot, he scanned the surrounding woods. "He would have been over there."

He struck off, but one of the deputies pulled him back. "We got it, Crawford. You deal with this." He and his partner hurried away.

Neal asked Joe, "How long have you been here?"

"Close to an hour. We've had the playground to ourselves the entire time. Until he arrived." He gave a brusque tilt of his head in Crawford's direction. "He was driving and behaving like a maniac. He attacked me. Do your job, Sergeant Lester, and lock him up."

"*Daddy!*"

Georgia's glad cry stunned them all. They turned to see her running toward him, arms outstretched. Instinctually Crawford started toward her, but Neal stepped in front of him and planted his hand in the center of his chest. "Stop there."

"Screw that."

"If you go near her, I'll have to arrest you."

Crawford shoved Neal's hand away. "No, you'll have to shoot me."

Chapter 21

———◆———

Crawford pushed Neal aside and rushed to meet Georgia halfway. She tackled him around the knees. He lifted her up, his arms enclosing her tightly.

Her skin was hot and sticky from her recent exertions on the playground. He could feel her heart beating against his chest. He buried his face in her hair and inhaled her scent.

"Daddy, you're squashing me."

"I'm sorry." He allowed her to lean back but kissed her rosy face several times, and his kisses were enthusiastically returned. He stroked a few ringlets away from her damp hairline. "Have you been having fun?"

Grace gave him wide berth as she hurried past them, moving in the direction of the others. Crawford didn't care what was playing out behind him. Georgia was alive, untouched, unafraid, and that was all that mattered to him.

He carried her back to the merry-go-round, sat down on the metal disk, and held her on his lap as he idly pushed them around by digging his boot heels into the hard-packed groove encircling it.

While she chattered, he conducted an inventory of her parts and features to assure himself that all were intact and unharmed. He silently thanked God, whose existence he questioned but whom he strove to appease in exchange for Georgia's safety, health, and longevity.

"Are you listening, Daddy?"

"To every word."

"Who's that lady?"

He turned to see Holly walking toward them. "Her name is Judge Spencer."

"Like Judge Judy?"

He smiled and shook his head. "Nothing like Judge Judy."

He stopped the slow spinning so she could join them on the merry-go-round. As she sat down next to him, she said under her breath, "I got you five minutes." Then, "You must be Georgia. I'm Holly."

She extended her hand. Timidly, Georgia shook it.

Crawford whispered near her ear. "What do you say?"

"Pleased to meet you."

"I'm pleased to meet you, too. I've heard so much about you."

"You have?"

"Is it true that pink is your favorite color?"

Georgia's initial shyness evaporated. Having someone new to talk with unleashed an unbroken stream of conversation. "Do you like the slide or the swings the best?" she asked Holly.

"Oh, the swings by far."

"Me too. I like to go high. Daddy pushes me high, but I have to hold on real tight, so I won't fly out like he did when he was little and knock out a tooth that wasn't even loose. Show her, Daddy."

He complied, pointing out one of his lower front teeth to Holly. For Georgia's benefit, she inspected it solemnly. "That must have hurt."

"It was a baby tooth," Georgia informed her. "So one grew in its place, but you still gotta hold on tight to the ropes."

"I'll make sure I do."

They let Georgia direct the conversation, and it was as flitting as a butterfly. Holly subtly nudged his elbow when their time ran out. The five minutes had passed far too quickly.

For Georgia, too. She didn't take it well when he told her that it was time for them to leave. "Can we go get ice cream?"

"Not today, sweetheart."

"Please. Holly can come, too. Won't you, Holly?"

"I would love to, but I can't today. Maybe some other time."

Georgia was so disappointed, Crawford was afraid her whining would turn into crying, and, after today's events, if he saw a single tear, he would never be able to let her go. Lifting her off his lap, he stood her up behind his back. "Climb on. I'll carry you."

Riding on his shoulders was always a treat. She gripped handfuls of his hair as he walked in an exaggerated stagger back to the parking area. She was giggling when he swung her down. Kneeling in front of her, he ran his hands over her arms as though to convince himself yet again that she was safe and sound. "Be a good girl."

"I will."

He couldn't tell her when he would call, or when he would see her next, because he didn't know when it would be. He never made her a promise he couldn't keep. "Give me a kiss."

She bussed him on the mouth, then he clutched her to him for as long as he dared before releasing her. "Go on now. Grandma and Grandpa are waiting."

"You're quiet tonight. What's the matter?"

Grace looked across the dinner table at her husband, then got up and carried her barely touched plate to the sink. "Just thinking."

"About that business at the park? I could tell it upset you."

"Georgia was so unhappy when we left."

"She was fine until she saw him. Making people unhappy is his specialty."

Grace turned away and began loading the dishwasher. "I don't believe Judge Spencer would have intervened on his behalf if she'd thought Georgia would suffer any ill effects."

"I think something shifty is going on between the two of them."

Grace paused what she was doing and looked at him over her shoulder. "Shifty?"

"She went on TV and made him out to be a hero. Hours later she recused herself from his case. I think her objectivity has been compromised, all right, but not strictly because he saved her life."

"You think there's an attraction?"

"I hope the judge has better sense."

"Our daughter didn't."

He scowled. "Beth couldn't see past his appearance. But he showed his true colors today. By the time the rest of you saw him at the park, he had calmed down. When he arrived, he was rabid. Completely unhinged."

"In his place, wouldn't you have been?" Grace asked. "If you'd been sent a photograph or video of Beth with a caption like that, wouldn't you have been completely unhinged until you knew she was safe?"

"It's not the same."

"How is it different?"

"I wouldn't have attacked the first person I saw."

Speaking under her breath, Grace said, "That's another thing."

"Pardon?"

She flung down her dishcloth and turned to him. "All these years we've known Crawford, the dislike between you two has been there from the get-go. You've had arguments, running arguments that lasted for months. Not once," she said, holding up her index finger, "has a disagreement resulted in a fistfight."

Joe left the table and joined her at the sink. "What's your point?"

"It seems awfully coincidental that the first time Crawford has ever raised a hand to you, it happened within hours of your filing that restraining order."

"Which he validated by laying into me."

"But he never had before. There was no reason for you to file that restraining order, Joe."

"From where I'm standing, there was. Have you forgotten that he came here two nights ago—"

"And you exchanged words. Heated words, yes, but your shouting was just as loud as his. He didn't threaten you with bodily harm."

"I got the restraining order for Georgia's protection, not mine."

"That's crap. Pure crap."

"Where's this language coming from?"

"Crawford would never harm that child. You know that. I know you know that."

Unused to her having an angry outburst, he rocked back on his heels. "Do you want him to have Georgia, to take her away from us?"

Grace sighed. "It would break my heart to lose her."

"Then stop defending him. We're in this fight to

win." He poured himself a cup of coffee and carried it with him as he left the room, saying as he went, "Leave everything to me. I know what I'm doing."

Rather than reassuring her, that's what worried her most.

—————

Seeking solitude after leaving the park, Crawford drove out of town to one of his favorite spots. The natural lake was located deep in the woods, reached only by a narrow dirt road that petered out shy of the lake by thirty yards, which had to be covered on foot.

The isolated spot had been his haunt for twenty years. He'd discovered it shortly after moving back from California, where he'd lived with his mother and her new husband until he turned sixteen. Then he'd insisted on returning to Texas so he could attend and graduate high school in Prentiss with his original class-mates and friends.

His mother and stepfather had put up very little resistance to the idea. He figured they were as glad to get rid of his churlish self as he was to go.

His mother's sister had taken him in—because by then Conrad was well established as the town drunk, incapable of caring for himself, much less a teenager. As a means of trying to make up for her sister's neglect, his single, childless aunt had lavished him with attention and affection until the day she died. By then he was an adult and appreciative of her kindness. But while living with her, he had daily tested the good-hearted lady's patience by being not at all lovable. Along with typical teenage angst, he carried an additional chip on his shoulder (the size of Rushmore, according to Holly).

Because of his bad attitude, it had taken time to rees-
tablish himself with his classmates, form new alliances,
and acclimate to small-town life. Even after being accepted into the popular crowd, he remained defensive,
rebellious, and angry.

On days when his mood turned particularly dark,
he escaped to this spot and whiled away hours skipping
stones, taking out his nameless frustration on the mirror
surface of the lake. One day he threw rocks until his
arm gave out from exhaustion. Sitting down on the
muddy shoreline, he placed his head on his bent knees,
and wept.

By the time he had cried himself out, he realized that
he wasn't angry at his aunt's claustrophobic house and
her cloying affection. It wasn't his friends or coaches or
schoolwork causing him to be persistently aggravated
and annoyed.

He was angry at his parents.

Each had exed him off their to-do list, and they'd
done so in permanent ink. His mother had her life, and
it didn't include him. His father had no life beyond
his next drink. Crawford couldn't fix or change the
circumstances. This was a done deal. This was the
hand he'd been dealt, and it was up to him how he
played it.

He hadn't buried his anger in the thick mud that
day and left it there, forever forgotten. After all, real
life wasn't a fairy tale. His anger remained with him,
as indelible as his palm print. But he had chosen and
resolved that day not to let it destroy him.

The only time he'd violated that resolve was after
Beth died, and he was still suffering the consequences
of that lapse. He wouldn't let it happen again.

He drove back to town and went straight to the
courthouse, more determined than ever to get justice for

Chet, even for Jorge Rodriguez, who also was a victim of a tragic chain of events perpetrated by someone.

Crawford wanted that someone. He wanted him bad.

Neal was seated at his desk. He looked up, saw Crawford, and said, "I suppose you got my voice mail."

"No." He sat down across from the detective. "What did it say?"

"I asked you to come in as soon as possible."

"Sorry. I haven't checked my phone for a while. Something come from the interviews?"

"Nothing."

"How many more to go?"

"Done. Finished this afternoon."

"No red flags?"

"Nope. All were folks as honest as the day is long."

"Except the one who gunned down Chet."

Neal looked chagrined, but didn't say anything.

Crawford waited, then casually asked, "How's your kid doing?"

Neal gave him a blank look, then, "Oh, he's fine. Summer bug. Nothing serious."

"Hmm."

"You left the park in a hurry," Neal said.

After sending Georgia to rejoin her grandparents, he had walked to his SUV, climbed in, and, without explaining himself or saying a word to anyone, he drove away. He raised one shoulder in a negligent shrug. "You didn't shoot me. Nobody cuffed me, so I left. That video of Georgia scared the hell out of me. I needed some downtime."

"Where'd you go?"

"My secret. Did the deputies turn up anything in the woods around the park?"

"No."

Crawford hadn't expected them to. "Lots of trees

and brush to hide behind. Whoever shot the video could have come and gone without Grace and Joe seeing him."

"Any idea who that might be?"

"If I knew, he'd be in the hospital. Or a coffin."

"Comforting thought."

"True, though. And it brings me to something I want to bounce off you."

Crawford sat forward and propped his elbows on his thighs, tapping his chin with his thumb knuckles as he tried to put his thoughts into words, words that wouldn't cause Neal to nix them just to be contrary.

"Our case is stalled, Neal. Something you said this morning has stuck with me. We're digging in the wrong place. I've been thinking. Since the shooting, so many things have—"

"You're off the case."

Crawford went perfectly still as he met the other man's implacable gaze.

"That's why I called you to come in," Neal said. "I needed to tell you. It's effective immediately."

Moving slowly, Crawford sat up straight. "When did this come about?"

Neal shook his head as though the timing of the decision didn't matter. "You shouldn't have been involved in an investigation in which you're a material witness. The chief realizes that now. He's going to talk to your superiors and explain that it was only as a courtesy to Mrs. Barker—"

"Who's still a widow without closure. So why don't you want me involved?"

"I just told you."

"Rhetoric. What's really going on, Neal?"

"I'm not compelled to explain the decision."

"Not compelled. Translated, that means you don't

have the balls to tell me to my face. You'd rather be sneaky, put someone on my tail to take pictures."

Neal cursed under his breath. "Nugent."

"Don't blame the kid. I didn't give him a choice. Whose nephew is he, anyway?"

"One of the county commissioners," Neal mumbled.

Crawford laughed without mirth. "I was asking facetiously. Nugent should get out now. He's not cut out for this line of work." He paused for a beat. "Why'd you have me tailed?"

Neal didn't respond.

"Sorry to disappoint," Crawford said. "You didn't get any pictures of me doing incriminating stuff, did you?"

"I didn't get any pictures of a vandal breaking into your house, either."

Crawford just looked at him, then burst out laughing. "You think I trashed Georgia's bedroom after spending two weeks' paycheck and lots of time getting it ready for her? Why would I do that?"

"You don't need a reason to go on a rampage. You've got a short fuse. You react without thinking. You can't control your impulses or violent tendencies, as evidenced today at the park."

Crawford would be damned before defending a reaction that was in perfect keeping with the scare he'd received. Instead he went on the offensive. "You know, Neal, if you're going to lie, learn not to get trapped in it."

"What are you talking about?"

"That phone call today wasn't from your wife, and it wasn't about a kid throwing up. Who kept you on the phone for that long, very engrossed?"

Neal's face turned red, but rather than answer, he asked, "What did you really say to Rodriguez up on that roof?"

"You're still hung up on that?"

"It's a pretty damned important 'that.'"

"My vindictive son of a bitch of a father-in-law planted an idea in your head, and you seized on it."

"Answer the question."

"Should I call Bill Moore?"

"I don't know, should you?"

"You and I don't like each other. Never did and never will. Put that aside for a minute. Do you honestly think that I had something to do with the shooting?"

"What were you doing last night in Judge Spencer's chambers? An officer came to me this morning and reported seeing you storm out."

Crawford said nothing.

"She left a few minutes after you, and the officer described her as looking 'shaken to the core.'"

Neal didn't mention having pictures of them together, which was a relief. "Anything else?" he asked mildly.

"You made a big deal about a bruised knee. Who else but you says the gunman was kicked in the knee?"

"More still?"

"Lots more. You remain the only person who claims Rodriguez wasn't the shooter."

"If I was behind it, wouldn't I want everyone to believe that he *was* the shooter, seeing as how he's dead and can't deny it?"

"You would, unless…"

Crawford cocked his head as though to better hear the part that Neal had left dangling. "Unless?"

"Unless a connection could be drawn between you and Rodriguez."

"No such connection exists."

One corner of Neal's mouth twitched into a half smile. "I fibbed to you about that phone call because it was Chuck Otterman who called me. He said if you were around, I should pretend to be talking to some-one else. He said no doubt I had noticed his surprised reaction to seeing Rodriguez's corpse. I admitted I had noticed. He was calling to explain why he reacted the way he had."

"The tension mounts."

Neal didn't acknowledge that. "Although Otterman didn't know Rodriguez by name, he recognized him on sight."

Crawford snapped his fingers. "They were at side-by-side urinals."

Neal continued unflappably. "On or around one forty p.m. Monday afternoon, Otterman arrived for his ap-pointment at the DA's office. As he was going in, he saw Rodriguez on the courthouse parking lot." He paused, took a breath. "Talking to you."

Chapter 22

Two policemen in a squad car followed Holly home from the courthouse. She pulled her car around to the back of the cottage where she parked and got out. One of the policemen saw her safely inside, then returned to his car out front.

The moment Holly locked herself in, she shed her professional reserve and composure along with her suit jacket and high heels. She'd been keeping up appearances all day. Now, she gave over to her fatigue and despondency.

Greg Sanders's foretelling that she would "mess up" seemed disturbingly close to coming true.

Before leaving her office, she had received a reply email from Governor Hutchins. The best thing she could say about its content was that it was noncommittal. He neither commended nor chastened her for recusing herself from Crawford's custody case, saying only that, even though he was away, he'd been kept apprised of the ongoing investigation into the shooting and that upon his return from the conference, he wanted to discuss certain aspects of it with her.

The ambiguous tone of the email worried her. If he

was second-guessing appointing her to the bench, if he withdrew his support, it would be disastrous for her professionally, and even more crushing from a personal standpoint. She would have failed to live up to Judge Waters's expectations. She would have failed to meet her own.

The troublesome email had come on the heels of the incident in the park where she'd had the devil's own time negotiating those five minutes for Crawford.

"There's no question that this is in violation of the restraining order, Mr. Gilroy. He was very wrong to attack you. But look at them." She'd gestured toward the merry-go-round where Crawford and his daughter seemed to be discussing the sequin appliqué on her top. "Think how traumatic it would be for her to see him arrested and taken away."

To close the sale, she'd offered to monitor their conversation and set a time limit.

Further, she asked that when his five minutes were up, he be allowed to leave without being apprehended.

Both Mr. Gilroy and Neal Lester had balked at that. But she asked them to consider the situation. "That video struck fear in him. Despite the likelihood of being fined and/or arrested, he raced here, without regard to anything except Georgia's safety."

Joe Gilroy wasn't easily persuaded. "To hear you tell it, he would slay a dragon to save her."

"I believe he demonstrated that."

"Am I supposed to forgive and forget that he attacked me?"

She'd reminded him that he would have an opportunity to testify to the incident at the full restraining order hearing.

"Well, that's not good enough," he'd said.

He then had laid down the condition under which he

would give Crawford a free pass for today. "That's the only way he's getting off the hook for this."

Her choices were to accept his condition, or for Crawford to be shackled and taken to jail.

Now, as she trudged toward her bedroom, she felt as though there were an anvil hanging from her neck. When Crawford found out about her agreement with his father-in-law, he would hate her.

It would come as another blow to him, more severe even than the others. As she thought on it, she realized that the fallout from the shooting had been far more consequential to him than to her. Since Monday, he'd taken hit after hit, and, now, thanks to her, he stood to lose his child for good.

She might have been the intended target in the courtroom, but it was Crawford who—

Suddenly she stood stock still, her jacket and shoes dangling from hands gone listless. Mentally, she backtracked, rethought what had only now occurred to her, then dropped her jacket and shoes to the floor and quickly retraced her footsteps to her kitchen, where she'd left her handbag.

After retrieving her cell phone from it, her fingers couldn't move fast enough to punch in Crawford's number. It rang once, then went to voice mail. "Damn!" Again, with butterfingered haste, she accessed Neal Lester's cell number and called it.

He must have seen her name on his caller ID because he answered briskly, "Judge Spencer? Are you all right?"

"Perfectly all right. But I need to talk to you about Crawford Hunt."

"What a coincidence. I was just about to call and advise you to avoid him. I had him taken off the case."

With forced calmness, she said, "You are overreacting to what happened in the park. He—"

"It has nothing to do with that. Not directly."

"Then why have you removed him?"

"I have an eyewitness who can link him to Rodriguez prior to the shooting."

Her knees went weak. She leaned back against the wall and listened with mounting dismay as he explained what had taken place in the morgue that morning. "Otterman saw Rodriguez in conversation with Crawford outside the courthouse."

When she was able to find her voice, she said, "That can't be true."

"He's positive. He knew it in an instant but feared reprisal from Crawford, so he didn't blurt it out. He called later and told me in secret." He hesitated, then said, "I've wanted to ask you a question but hesitated because I felt it was inappropriate. Now I believe it's relevant. Judge Spencer, were you going to grant or deny Crawford's custody petition?"

"It is an inappropriate question. I can't discuss that."

"Well, I believe Crawford predicted that you would deny his custody. So he found a guy who nobody knew, who had fake IDs and little money. Someone desperate or easily duped, or both. He staged this attempt on your life. But his plan all along was to spring into action and take out the shooter. Whether you lived or died, he would have become a hero."

She denied it with the first inconsistency that came to mind. "How was he to take out the shooter when he didn't even have his service weapon in court?"

"He knew Chet would be down and could use his."

"That's even more outlandish. He would never have ordered the assassination of Chet Barker. He thought the world of him."

"That's true. But he loves his daughter more. He did all this for her, to get her. After his courtroom heroics, and all the accolades to follow, who would deny him custody?"

He was running with this hypothesis like a team of wild horses. Rather than be dragged along with him, she strived to remain rational and clear-headed. "Why would he cook up this elaborate scheme, then protect me with his own body?"

"To make it look good. But Rodriguez panicked and bolted before finishing you off and before Crawford could finish him. Crawford couldn't let him be captured. He chased him and caught up with him on the roof. He confronted him one-on-one even after other officers cautioned him against it."

"That seems more like courage than conspiracy."

"No, he wanted to see Rodriguez downed one way or another. The video shows Rodriguez freaking out the instant Crawford stepped out onto the roof."

Since she hadn't seen the video, she couldn't comment.

Neal pressed on. "For the sake of argument, judge, no one can substantiate the pierced ear thing, or that Crawford kicked the gunman. There's absolutely nothing to support his suspicion of Otterman, who just happened to appear minutes after I had expressed my own suspicion of *Crawford*. He saw an opportunity to create a distraction with Otterman. It backfired on him.

"And he's been unusually preoccupied with you. He told you first about the pierced ear, I believe to test your reaction to his claim that the gunman didn't have one. Remember, he's the one who insisted on putting you under guard.

"Initially, I mistakenly thought his obsession with you was sexual, but this development with Otterman casts it in a new light. He's keeping close tabs on you for a reason. Am I right or not that he devises excuses to be alone with you?"

After a moment, she said quietly, "If he's adapted a protective attitude I believe it's because he has a vested interest in my welfare. That's a common reaction from one who saves your life."

"Is that what you really think?" Neal asked softly. "Or are you just saying it?"

"I wouldn't say something I didn't believe."

"You would if you were frightened enough." He let those words hover, then said, "Judge Spencer, you've gone out of your way to publicly exonerate Crawford of any wrongdoing or recklessness. You went to bat for him today in the park. I'm wondering, has that been all for show? Are you taking his side to appease him?

"But before you answer, I should tell you that I know he went to your chambers after hours last night. He was seen leaving in a temper, and I'm told that you looked extremely upset when you followed a few minutes later. Be straight with me now, because I can't protect you otherwise. Has Crawford threatened you?"

The back of the house was in complete darkness. Holly climbed over the fence and then took a moment to catch her breath, although her heart continued to thud so hard it was painful. Cautiously she approached the back door. Through it, she could hear his voice. At her soft knock, he stopped speaking immediately.

A few seconds later, he opened the door. If he was shocked to see her, he didn't show it. His silhouette looked large and indomitable against the weak light from the ice dispenser on the refrigerator door. So far as she could tell, it was the only light on inside the house.

He brought his cell phone up to his ear. "I'll call you back." He clicked off and lowered his hand to his side. Otherwise he didn't move. His eyes were too hooded for her to gauge his reaction to seeing her on his doorstep.

She said, "You're probably surprised to see me here."

"You could say. How'd you get here?"

"I ran."

"Ran?"

"Jogged. It's only a few miles."

He assimilated that, then asked, "Are your guards bringing up the rear?"

"They think I'm still inside my house. I slipped out the back door, squeezed through the hedge, past the main house, to the street behind."

He stifled a sound that could have been amusement, but his voice was gravelly with anger when he said, "Neal's guy could be somewhere out there with his candid camera trained on this house."

"I'm aware of that."

"I don't think he got us last night, so why press your luck? Why take a chance on making the front page tomorrow?"

"Sergeant Lester told me you're no longer on the case."

"He tell you why?"

"Yes."

"And?"

"Chuck Otterman is lying."

He didn't say anything for a moment, then, "You sneaked out and ran all the way over here just to give me your vote of confidence? You could have called that in."

"I don't trust phones, to say nothing of phone records," she said, quoting him. "There's a lot we need to talk about, and I wanted to do it in person."

"I'm listening."

"I think I know why no clues have turned up

regarding the shooter's identity, why the detectives, you, everybody has met with nothing but dead ends."

"Still listening."

"The shooting wasn't about me. I wasn't the target. You were."

He still didn't move for several seconds. Then he reached for her hand and pulled her across the threshold. "Come in."

———◆———

"Crawford's been ousted."

"Be more specific."

Pat Connor glanced around cautiously, but no one could have overheard him except for the ever-present bodyguards, and they never registered interest or any other emotion. Nevertheless, he kept his volume low. "On a pretext, I dropped by the department to see if there was any new scuttlebutt. Man, was there. Neal's taken Crawford off the case. And get this. He's now a person of interest."

"For the shooting?"

"You got it."

The deep chest rumbled with suppressed laughter. "That boy's having a really bad day."

"I heard he went apeshit when he got to the park." Officially it was Pat's day off from work, but he'd been busier today than any in recent history. "That video wasn't easy to get, you know. I got chigger bites to prove it."

"You still have the phone you used?"

"No. I pitched it right after sending Crawford the text. It's at the bottom of the Sabine."

Actually that was a little white lie. The burner phone was hidden beneath the front seat of his car.

He had held on to it, just in case. You might say it was his insurance policy. Some people just weren't to be trusted. In particular, the man sitting across from him.

"Is he in lockup?"

"Crawford? No. According to the rumor mill, Neal played it by the book and suggested that he call his lawyer. Crawford told him to go fuck himself. Which a lot of people would like to tell Neal."

"He's a prick."

"No argument there. But he's smart enough to know that in a popularity contest between Crawford and him, Crawford would win hands down. Neal would be bad-mouthed for locking Crawford up while he's building a case against him, which most agree is horseshit anyway. Neal let him go, and, politically speaking, that was a sound choice." A bit uneasily he added, "Probably not what you wanted to hear, though."

"Actually it's precisely what I wanted to hear."

"Really? Why's that?"

"I'll acquaint you with my reason when I'm ready to. Thanks for the update."

Pat recognized the dismissal for what it was. He got up and walked away. He felt a powerful thirst coming on, because, the hell of it was, Ranger Crawford Hunt had always treated him decently enough. He felt bad for spying on him and setting him up to take a fall. Using that video of his little girl? That had been low, something Pat would never have believed himself capable of doing, no matter who'd ordered him to.

But he had a debt to pay, and if he didn't…

It didn't bear thinking about.

Crawford could see well enough in the dim kitchen to take a glass from the cabinet, fill it with tap water, and hand it to Holly. "I'd offer you something else, but I don't want to turn on the lights and give the shutterbug an advantage."

She had run from her house to his wearing a pair of old jeans with holes in the knees. A white t-shirt clung to her damp skin and outlined her bra. Her nipples made twin impressions that had captured and held his attention.

"Crawford, did you hear what I said?"

He brought his gaze up to hers. "You weren't the target, I was. It's not the breakthrough you thought. I reached that same conclusion myself several hours ago."

He told her about going from the park to the lake in the woods. "First, I had to cool down. Then I started at the beginning and thought through everything that's happened since the shooting. And it all related to me, not you. I was about to share my theory with Neal and suggest that we explore it, when he dropped his bombshell."

"May I sit down?"

"Sorry."

He indicated the dining table. They took chairs adjacent to each other, and when their knees touched, he kept his against hers. "You look great, by the way."

"I'm sweaty."

"I'm aroused. How did you come to the conclusion that the shooting was about me?"

"Much the same as you. I was thinking about all the hard knocks you've had since, how the repercussions of it have affected you much more than me. I called you first, but when you didn't answer, I phoned Neal. I only got out a few words before he hit me with his theory that you're the villain."

She repeated Neal's harebrained conclusions. "Thing is, I think he really believes it," Crawford said.

"I'm afraid so, too. He ended by asking if you had threatened me."

"To which you said…?"

"No. At least not in the way he meant."

He studied her shadowed face, that mouth, those eyes, the locks of hair that had shaken loose from her messy just-got-laid ponytail, and thought, *Damn*. He said, "We're in a dark, empty house. I've got a king-size bed and time to kill."

"Till what?"

"Till the Houston office calls me back. Or Neal shows up to arrest me. Let's go in the bedroom and take off all our clothes."

"Crawford, this is serious."

"I know." He sighed. "I'm trying to keep myself from strangling Neal for stupidity. I want to take a sledge-hammer to Chuck Otterman for lying. You can save two lives by going to bed with me."

"Are you positive Otterman is behind it?"

"No. He might have told Neal that he saw me with Rodriguez just to pay me back for getting his name in the news."

"You leaked that?"

"We needed a spark plug. It worked."

"But it made an enemy of Otterman."

"I think he already was. He didn't dress up in the white outfit, but I'd bet good money he was behind the shooting."

"But why?"

"Hell if I know. I've got people researching." He left his chair. "More water?"

"No thanks."

He refilled the glass anyway and brought it back to

the table. But he remained standing. "I've racked my brain. Swear to God, I'd never seen the man till he walked into the CAP unit yesterday. But it was like looking at a cobra. I felt a gut-deep revulsion. Fear. I don't usually get that."

"There must be a reason for it."

"I think so, too. I just have to find it. When you got here, I was talking to my buddy in Houston who—"

"Harry or Sessions?"

"You know their names?"

"I introduced myself."

"At the press conference?"

"At breakfast."

"Breakfast?"

"They'd spent the whole night sitting in their cars outside my house. The least I could do was cook breakfast for them."

Picturing that cozy gathering around her kitchen table, he put his hands on his hips. "Nobody mentioned that."

"They advised me not to."

"Did they say why?"

She just looked at him.

With more testiness, "Did they say why?"

"They said you were touchy about your women."

His jealous reaction was proof enough of that. Then he realized what she could infer from their remark. "Holly, I never told them that we'd—"

"I didn't think you had. But they seemed to know."

"I guess they could tell by the way I was acting."

"How were you acting?"

"Want the gutter term for it?"

She ducked her head and kept it lowered for several moments. When she raised her head, she resumed where they'd left off by asking what the other Rangers had reported to him.

"I asked them to look for any connection between Otterman and me. Or to Beth, the Gilroys, the DPS. So far nothing."

"Halcon?"

"First thing we checked because it makes the most sense. But during that year-long investigation, Otterman was working up in the Panhandle. He didn't take a day off for months either side of the shootout. No record of him ever being in Halcon.

"I thought maybe he wanted to avenge one of the bystanders who'd died, but he has no kinship or ties whatsoever to any of the casualties. Sessions is excellent at research, but he didn't find a thing. I was asking him to dig deeper when you showed up at the back door."

"What about other cases you've worked on?"

"I've gone back through years of records. But I trust my memory even better than I trust a computer. If Otterman had ever been a blip on my radar screen, I would remember the name. If not the name, the man. I'm dead sure of that."

"So maybe it isn't him," she said. "Maybe he just told Neal he'd seen you with Rodriguez to spite you. Having it reported that he'd left after the shooting had to have been embarrassing for him."

He gave a hard shake of his head. "He's not wired that way. He was pissed, but by no stretch embarrassed."

They lapsed into a thoughtful silence, then she said quietly, "I don't even want to suggest this. It's so egregious that I hesitate to—"

"You're thinking Joe."

Her shoulders sagged a bit, letting him know that he'd guessed correctly. "He wouldn't do this, would he?"

"Come here. I want to show you something." Taking her hand, he led her through the dark house to the door of Georgia's bedroom. He used the screen of his phone for illumination. "I think you can see well enough without more light."

She expelled a breath of disbelief. "What happened?"

"Neal didn't tell you about this?"

"No. My God, Crawford."

"It was this way when I got home last night. Everything was new. The makeover was going to be a surprise."

"Did you file a police report?"

"The whole shebang. They dusted for prints this morning, so it looks even worse than it did. I haven't had a chance to start the cleanup."

She went into the room and did a slow pivot, making small sounds of remorse as she assessed the destruction. She picked up the sparkly ballet slippers, the bands of which had been ripped off. "Who would do such a thing?"

"The same person who sent me that video of Georgia on the swing, looking so angelic, innocent, vulnerable. I haven't quite recovered from that yet." Every time he thought about it, his blood vessels throbbed with a combination of fury and terror. "Some sick fuck used my little girl to get to me. I want to kill him."

"How can Neal Lester possibly account for this?"

"He suggested that I did it myself."

"And texted yourself the park video?"

"I guess."

She placed the slippers on what was left of the dressing table and rejoined him in the hallway. "I don't believe your father-in-law would do any of this."

"He's told me he'll do whatever it takes to keep Georgia. Or, more to the point, to prevent me from having her. But, honestly," he said, gazing back into the room, "this doesn't fit Joe's profile." He clicked off his phone and replaced it on his belt.

"What are you going to do?"

"Wait on Harry and Sessions. See what turns up."

"What if Neal arrests you in the meantime?"

"His cover-your-ass MO is working in my favor now. He won't detain me till he has something to go on."

"So you wait."

"And do what I've wanted to do since you got here."

He slid his fingers up into her hair until his hands were closed around her head, then he tilted it and brushed his mouth across hers. "A word of caution, judge. Don't show up at my back door looking like you do unless you want to get manhandled." After thoroughly kissing her mouth, he moved to her neck, gently sucking her skin, tasting the saltiness of her sweat.

"Crawford…"

The moaned admonishment was so halfhearted, he continued, kissing his way past her collarbone to her breast. He nuzzled the tip through the damp cloth of her t-shirt.

She exhaled a sharp breath. "I woke up this morning dreaming about it."

He gently cupped her other breast. "Good dream?"

"Sinfully good."

"Holly Spencer, bad girl."

"I think you must be right. The dream was exactly as it happened. I was eager, and you were very… decisive."

The smile he felt in his heart never quite reached his lips because they were lowering to hers. "I had to be inside you. Just had to be."

He kissed her like she was a bad girl, taking her mouth with heat and hunger. He slid his hand past the small of her back into her jeans and, feeling nothing but smooth skin, palmed her ass and tilted her up against his fly. "All this would feel so much better without clothes on."

To his disappointment, she pushed against his chest, creating space between them, and turned her head aside. "You don't want to kiss me like this, Crawford."

"Hell you talking about? I want to kiss you all over." Each time she turned aside, his mouth followed hers. "I want to French kiss you all over." He withdrew his hand from the seat of her jeans and moved it around to her front, sliding it between her thighs and caressing her through the soft denim. "Here."

She stifled a groan of pleasure but pushed his hand away.

Frustrated and confused, he took a step back. Dammit, he knew she wanted him. "What, Holly? You're no longer my judge."

"It's not that...I..." She took a breath, pushed strands of hair off her face, and pulled herself up to her full height. Bolstering herself. "To keep them from arresting you today, I made a deal."

"Deal?"

"Your father-in-law insisted on it. I didn't want you to go to jail," she said, almost on a sob.

"What deal?"

"I agreed to testify for the plaintiff at the full restraining order hearing. I'll have to bear witness to you assaulting Joe Gilroy today."

That hit him like a ton of bricks. He just stood there staring at her.

Looking anguished, she backed away several steps, then turned and hurried down the hallway, only to be brought up short when his cell phone rang.

She stopped, turned, and watched him yank the phone off his belt. Obviously she thought, as he did, that it would be one of the other Rangers with the requested update.

But it was neither of their names that appeared in the

LED. He snarled into the mouthpiece. "What the hell are you doing calling this number?"

"Am I speaking to the superstar lawman Crawford Hunt?"

"Cut the crap, Smitty. What have you got?"

"What I've got is a sorry-ass drunk out here who's in hock to me for his afternoon binge."

"Not my problem."

"Oh yeah, hotshot? Says he's your daddy."

Chapter 23

—————◆—————

As soon as Smitty told Crawford where they were, he disconnected the call. Holly was right behind him as he went down the hallway and into his own bedroom, where he pulled on a windbreaker to cover his holster. Sweeping his keys off the dresser, he stepped around her on his way out of the room. "You know your way home."

"I'm coming with you."

"Hell you are."

"I heard what the man said."

"Caps off a great day, doesn't it?"

"I know all about your father, Crawford."

"He's not a father, he's a drunk. I'm sure it's in my file." By now they had reached the back door. "Neal's surveillance is probably out front. If you go back the way you came, you should be okay. Be careful hopping that fence again."

"I'm coming with you."

He bent down, putting his face close to hers. "No effing way."

"Fine. Tickled Pink? I'll find it." She pulled open his back door and slipped through.

He would be long gone from the nightclub before

she could run home and then drive there, but the thought of her showing up at one of Smitty's joints alone… "Shit!"

He went after her and caught her mid-stride, taking her by the elbow and redirecting her toward his SUV. "This'll make for good color commentary when you testify against me at the restraining order hearing."

He boosted her up into the passenger seat of his SUV, then placed his hand on the top of her head and none too gently pushed her down below the level of the window. "If you don't want to give Neal's guy a photo op, keep your head down till I give you the all-clear."

Part of him had wanted only to provoke her, but the precaution wasn't wasted. As soon as he left his driveway, he spotted a car at the far end of his street pulling away from the curb. It followed at a discreet distance for several blocks as he navigated through his neighborhood keeping to the speed limit.

Then, "Hold on," he warned Holly as he rounded a corner and floor-boarded his accelerator. He didn't let up until he was certain that he'd lost the tail.

"You can sit up now."

He drove past the high school football stadium that marked the edge of town, then turned off onto a two-lane country road that wound through the woods. The pine trees lining it were as straight and closely spaced as the wall of a stockade. It was a dark night. The slender moon was obscured by a low ceiling of clouds.

Out of the corner of his eye, Crawford could see Holly only by the glow of the lights on his dashboard. She gripped the armrest when he took a steep curve without slowing down. "You could get a speeding ticket."

"A traffic violation on top of a conspiracy to murder. That would be just awful."

She whipped her head around and snapped, "You don't do yourself any favors, Crawford."

"Look, you don't like the way I drive? Tough. I didn't want you along."

"This isn't about your driving. I came along to try and prevent you from doing something you'll later regret."

"Like today when I knocked Joe on his ass."

"Exactly like that."

"I thought he'd sent me that video. Any parent who loves their child would have had the same reaction."

"I agree. I'll testify to that."

He gave a harsh laugh. "Save your breath, Your Honor. No matter what you say from the witness stand, I'm never going to get Georgia back." He turned his head. "Am I?"

She looked straight out the windshield and spoke so softly he could barely hear her over the truck's engine. "Ultimately, maybe."

"But not before more petitions, more hearings, more time spent without her."

"And most likely not without involving Georgia."

She glanced at him and their gazes held for several telling seconds. When he turned back, he gripped the steering wheel tightly. The lengths to which he would go to regain custody ended with Georgia being forced to choose between him and her grandparents. He would never put her through that.

He and Holly traveled the remainder of the way in silence, and soon a tacky neon sign signaled that they'd reached their destination. He made a hard left turn into the nightclub's gravel parking lot and drove through it to the back of the building.

Knowing of the misdeeds committed on parking lots at places like Tickled Pink, inside and out of vehicles,

Crawford thought it safer for Holly to come inside with him. He turned off the engine and opened his door. "I can't leave you out here, but I warn you, this could be a shocking eye-opener."

As though in defiance of the warning, she opened her own door and hopped down before he could come around and assist her out. They walked up to the metal door. He banged on it.

Smitty himself opened it. "'Bout fucking time. I—" He drew up when he saw that Crawford wasn't alone, and, in obvious recognition of Holly, flashed his rodent grin as he eyed her up and down. "This is a new look for you, isn't it, sweetheart? You ought to ditch the black robe for good."

Smitty's leer had him questioning the decision to bring her inside. "Lay off her."

"Don't mind him, honey," Smitty said as he stepped aside to admit them. Shooting Crawford a dirty look over his shoulder, he added, "He's a buzzkill."

He escorted them into his office, which was as disorganized as any of the others in which Crawford had met with him over the years. Oozing charm as oily as his hair, he held a chair out for Holly and offered her something to drink.

Crawford clapped a hand on the man's shoulder and forcibly turned him around to face him. "Where's the old man? I thought you'd have him here in your office."

"Tried to. But he's an ornery cuss. Short of having my bouncer get rough—and considering your daddy's age, that wouldn't look good to other customers—I left him where he's at. Been there since about three thirty. He's run up a tab to the tune of sixty-seven dollars and change. Said you'd cover it."

Crawford ignored the hand Smitty held out, palm up. "Let's go." He motioned with his head for Smitty to lead the way. "Lock yourself in," he said to Holly as he passed through the door, then waited until he heard the click.

He relied on Smitty's familiarity with the layout as he followed him through a maze of dark corridors until they reached the club proper, where the music's volume was physically assaulting. On stage, a girl was humping a brass pole. The clientele was rowdily encouraging her with whoops, whistles, and applause.

Smitty shouted above the racket, "Over there." He pointed to a table in the darkest corner of the room where a bouncer was keeping close watch over a slumped and motionless form.

Conrad's cheek was mashed against the sticky table-top. A string of drool clung to his slack lower lip. He was barely conscious, but when Crawford took him by the arm to haul him out of his chair, he came up swinging. The uncoordinated uppercut missed Crawford's chin by a mile. The momentum behind it would have sent Conrad sprawling if Crawford hadn't caught him.

He really didn't give a damn about how bad it looked to other customers for him to grapple with the old man. Within seconds, he had both Conrad's hands behind his back and was holding his wrists together in an iron grip. With his other hand around the back of Conrad's neck, he held him upright.

"How'd he get here?" he asked Smitty.

He jangled a set of car keys in front of Crawford's face. "Bouncer found them in his pants pocket."

The bouncer was a beefy guy with a shaved and tattooed head. "Bring his car around to the back door," Crawford told him. "It won't be hard to find. Bald tires, faded blue paint. And thanks."

He propelled Conrad across the club toward the

corridor through which they'd come. Conrad stumbled and weaved but Crawford somehow got him that far without him falling.

Smitty followed on Crawford's heels, yapping about the outstanding tab.

"Shut the hell up," Crawford said. "You'll get your damn money."

When they reached the door to the office, he called out to Holly, who unlocked and opened the door. Humiliated, he watched her face as she got her first look at the slobbering, reeking derelict who'd sired him. She didn't register the repulsion he'd expected, but rather concern for the way Conrad's head flopped forward when Crawford let go of his neck.

Digging into his pocket, he pulled out a money clip and handed it to her. "Pay him, please."

She took a fifty and a twenty from the clip.

"And a ten for the bouncer," Crawford said.

"I'll give it to him," Smitty said, reaching for the extra bill.

She snatched it out of his reach. "I'll see to it, thank you."

She seemed impervious to, and in no way intimidated by, the lurid pictures papering the walls. Instead, the way she looked at Smitty as she handed him the money to cover the tab, she might have been in court, rendering a life sentence of hard labor.

"Your customer is obviously intoxicated. Yet you've admitted to continuing to serve him, over a course of hours, sixty-seven dollars' worth of alcohol. Had anything untoward happened as a result of his inebriation, you could have been held responsible and criminally charged. The doors of this grimy establishment would have been padlocked. You were very fortunate this time. Mr. Hunt might be willing to overlook your negligent and potentially criminal disregard for his father's debilitation...in exchange for your discretion."

Smitty's brow was furrowed, but he translated the language well enough. He wet his lips nervously and said, "Sure, sure, judge. I wouldn't let on about this. Crawford's a friend. We go way back."

Crawford canceled that sentiment with a snort. "Hold the door so we can get out of here." After Holly went ahead of him, he hung back long enough to say to Smitty, "I don't care how far back we go, you breathe a word about her being here, and I'll rip your balls off."

Smitty gave him a sickly smile, as though he just might be taking the warning seriously.

Crawford managed to get Conrad to his SUV and into the backseat. The old man slumped sideways, his head coming to rest on the arm of Georgia's car seat. Crawford resolved to have it sanitized before he put her in it again. If she ever got to ride with him again.

The bouncer had delivered Conrad's car, and Holly had given him his tip. "Do you mind driving that?" Crawford asked of the roughly idling heap.

"Not at all." She walked around to the driver's side and got behind the wheel.

Mortified and angry, Crawford climbed into his SUV. Once on the highway, he maintained his speed so Holly would have no trouble following him. Besides, he was in no rush for her to see the squalid condition of Conrad's house.

When they arrived, she came over and handed him Conrad's car keys, plus his own money clip. "Don't forget this."

"Thanks. If you touched Smitty, you'll want to scrub your hands with disinfectant."

"But he was such a gracious host." She fluttered a

small piece of paper. "He sneaked me this while you weren't looking."

"What is it?"

"A coupon for the cover charge on my next visit."

"That lousy lowlife. I should turn around and—"

He broke off when Conrad opened the door of the backseat and got out. "I don't recommend Smitty's places. The dancers are only so-so and the restrooms stink worse than outhouses."

No longer drooling, reasonably clear-eyed, he was standing perfectly upright. He hadn't slurred a single word. He smiled. "*Surprise!*"

———

Conrad extended his hand to Holly. "Judge Spencer, I was hoping I'd have an opportunity to meet you. I'm Conrad Hunt."

She shook his hand. "Mr. Hunt."

"Thank you for driving my car home."

"You're welcome."

"I felt it best that I continue the act till we got here. Was I convincing?"

"Very," she said, laughing lightly.

Beaming her a smile, he said, "Come in, come in." He placed a guiding hand beneath her elbow and directed her toward the house. "Watch your step. I would have cleared a path, but I didn't know I'd be having guests tonight."

Crawford, having recovered from his shock, planted himself in front of them. "What the hell do you think you're doing, Conrad?"

"I'm showing some manners. Which is more than I can say for you."

"Why the act? What are you trying to pull?"

Conrad fanned the air in front of his face to wave away mosquitoes. "Bloodsuckers. The judge will be eaten alive if we don't get her inside."

He nudged Crawford out of his way and continued on, warning Holly again to be careful where she stepped. Bringing up the rear, Crawford muttered that Conrad had had years to clear the path to his door. The yard was still littered with junk, but he was shocked and relieved to find that the interior of the house, at least the rooms immediately visible as he went through the front door, had been tidied since his visit on Tuesday.

At some point during the drive from the nightclub, Conrad had tucked in his shirttail and smoothed down his hair, which had been standing on end when they left. He actually looked halfway presentable.

"I apologize for smelling like a distillery," he was saying to Holly. "The whiskey I didn't pour out under the table, I've been splashing on like aftershave. Please, have a seat."

He motioned her toward the sofa, over which an old but clean patchwork quilt had been spread to cover the stringy upholstery. Continuing to play host, he said, "Would you like something to drink?"

"No, she wouldn't."

Conrad looked over at Crawford and frowned at his rudeness. "I wasn't talking to you. And I didn't mean a drink drink. I was thinking along the lines of coffee or a Dr Pepper."

Holly spoke for herself. "I appreciate the offer, but no thank you, Mr. Hunt."

"Call me Conrad, and let me know if you change your mind." He sat down in his recliner, popped up the footrest, and wiggled his butt around to make himself comfortable, all the while smiling at her.

Then he noticed that Crawford had remained standing barely inside the front door. "Are you just going to stand there like a cigar store Indian? Why don't you sit down and try to be sociable?"

"I don't have time for a social call. I need to get Holly home before her guards realize she's missing."

Conrad looked at her with new interest. "You sneaked out of your house?"

"Something I haven't done since I was a teenager."

Laughing, he slapped the arms of his recliner. "I'm glad to hear you got up to mischief. I was beginning to think you were too perfect."

"Oh, no. I went through a very brief rebellious phase right after my father left, before I accepted my new role as head of the family."

"How come you snuck out tonight?"

Before she could reply, Crawford did. "She came to see me. We can't be seen together, so—"

"Why can't you be seen together? You're working the shooting case."

"Not anymore." Crawford gave him a condensed rundown of the day's events.

As he finished, Conrad was shaking his head with disgust, but the first words out of his mouth were regarding Georgia. "Your little girl come through it all right?"

"Yeah. Thank God. She was unaware of what was going on. Didn't see me whaling into her grandpa."

"You want my opinion, Joe Gilroy had it coming just for being Joe Gilroy."

Crawford glanced over at Holly before saying, "I'll pay for it. It might be a while before I'm allowed to see Georgia again."

Conrad cursed under his breath. "I can't believe he hit you with a restraining order."

"We're waiting on a date for the hearing. I'll fight it. But even if I win that battle, there's this other."

Conrad said, "Neal Lester is a pompous fool with lots to prove, which makes him a *dangerous* pompous fool."

"This wild hair he has about Crawford is ridiculous," Holly said.

"A wild hair underscored by Chuck Otterman's lie," Crawford added.

Conrad stroked his chin. "Why would Otterman lie to incriminate you?"

"I have no idea. Holly and I were discussing it when Smitty called to tell me that you were drunk and disorderly. What was that about? You've been drunk for real so many times, why the playacting?"

"Because I didn't want anybody to guess what I was really doing there."

"I'll bite," Crawford said. "What were you really doing there?"

"Spying on Chuck Otterman."

Crawford felt like he'd been clipped behind the knees. Was Conrad the missing link to Otterman that he'd been searching for? He walked over to the sofa and sat down on the arm of it near Holly. "You were spying on Otterman? Why? Did you ever prosecute him?"

"No. At least I don't think so."

"Then what do you know about him?"

"Only what I've read." He waited a beat. "Plus what I gathered from my personal experience with him."

"The surprises just keep coming. I didn't know you had any personal experience with Otterman."

"Well, there's a lot you don't know."

"Apparently. Tell me something I don't know, Conrad."

"I applied for a job out there at the man camp."

"When?"

"Last year. Wintertime. Don't remember what month, but it was cold."

"You don't know anything about that industry."

"I figured I could empty trash cans. They have a maintenance and sanitation crew."

"And you have a law degree," Crawford snapped. "Or did."

Conrad grimaced and looked at Holly with embarrassment. "Last winter was a low point, even for me. I was out of work for months. Electric company cut me off. I needed money to get my heat back on."

Shame unspooled inside Crawford. He hated that she was hearing this, but at least now he no longer had to dread her learning just how polluted his gene pool was.

"Did you get the job?" she asked.

"Didn't want it. While I was in the office filling out the application form, a truck came roaring up with an injured man inside. And by *injured*, I mean bad. His arm had been mangled by a piece of machinery. It was hanging on by a thread, literally. He was in shock. Seemed to take forever for the ambulance to get there.

"Meanwhile, Otterman went on a rampage, yelling at everybody. He ordered some men to get the truck cleaned out. Blood was sloshing in the floorboard, and that's no exaggeration.

"He told two other men to get back out to the rig where the accident had taken place and to fix whatever had malfunctioned before OSHA came calling. They were also told to pass out cash 'bonuses' to the crewmen who had witnessed the accident."

Crawford said, "He bribed them to go deaf, dumb, and blind when the federal inspectors arrived."

"Exactly. During all this ranting and raving, he didn't show an iota of concern for the man who was in danger of bleeding out. That changed when the EMTs arrived. It was like somebody had tripped a switch inside him. He put on quite a show. Saint Chuck. Benevolent and caring. All but laid on hands and prayed over the guy he'd taken no notice of up till then."

Conrad made a face. "Sickened me. Broke as I was and needing that job, I tore up the form, left, and never went back. I'd rather be a career drunk than work for a man that two-sided. If I was still a prosecutor, I'd be on him like white on rice."

"Looking for what?"

"Don't know," he replied to Crawford. "But I think Mr. Chuck Otterman must have a moonlighting business."

"What makes you think so?"

"When he's in these clubs—"

"Which clubs?"

"Like Smitty's places."

"You've seen him before tonight?"

"Lots of times." Conrad looked over at Holly and gave her a pathetic smile. "I've been known to patronize some of the seedier establishments around. But I've turned over a new leaf."

She smiled at him. "You're sober now?"

"Sixty-four days."

"Excellent start. Congratulations."

"I'm also gainfully employed."

"Where?"

"At the sawmill."

During their chummy exchange, Crawford had left his perch on the arm of the sofa and made a circuit of the living room. It was straighter than he'd ever seen it. He looked through the open doorway into the kitchen. The sink was clear of dirty dishes, the counter free of coagulated spills, the floor swept. On the surface, it appeared as though Conrad might truly be making an earnest stab at sobriety.

But his history didn't foreshadow success. Crawford had been disappointed too many times to believe that this new leaf would be any different from many others, so he doused his flicker of optimism and brought his mind back to Otterman.

Speaking his thought aloud, he said, "He supports local politicians and judges, but spends his evenings in strip joints."

"Where he drinks only moderately if at all," Conrad said. "He ignores the dancing girls. But he's never idle. He holds meetings like the ones he held today."

Crawford had already heard this from Smitty. "Who'd he meet with today?"

"It was a freakin' parade," Conrad said. "And, like anybody at a parade, I took pictures."

He reached into his pants pocket and withdrew a cell phone, which surprised Crawford, since Conrad had never owned one.

"Where'd you get that?"

"Winn-Dixie."

"When?"

"Yesterday."

"Why?"

Conrad looked at him with annoyance. "You want to see these or not?"

Crawford took the phone from him and accessed the photos gallery. "Why are you just now getting around to telling me that you have pictures of Otterman?"

"I was pacing myself. Besides, you kept interrupting."

As Crawford punched through the photos in the file, Conrad continued to talk.

"See the two guys sitting at the table nearest the booth? Bodyguards. I nicknamed them Frick and Frack, the shorter of them being Frick. But they're no-nonsense. Armed. I saw the bulges. They came in with Otterman, left with him, were very attentive the whole time he was there, didn't drink, weren't distracted by the show."

"Why would he need bodyguards?" Holly asked.

"Good question," Crawford said. An even better question was why Smitty hadn't mentioned Otterman being there today, knowing that Crawford would have paid him for that information. He would take that up with the slimy bastard later. Right now, Conrad had his attention.

"Men came and went," he was saying. "Otterman talked to each separately, and their conversations ranged in length."

"Did anything change hands?" Crawford asked.

"Not that I saw, and I was looking for things like envelopes of cash. Maybe the clubs are only used as a place to negotiate terms, and the transfers take place somewhere else."

Conrad could be right. Also, Crawford had done enough computer-age detective work to know that bank account passwords were as good as, often better than, legal tender. "Okay, go on."

"That's basically it," Conrad said. "He left with Frick and Frack. I put on my one-man show."

"Why didn't you just leave?"

"I was supposed to be drunk on my ass, remember? I was afraid if I tried to drive, they'd call the cops, who would either have thrown me in jail without administering a blood test, in which case I'd be stuck there, my phone confiscated. Or they'd have drawn blood, realized I was faking, and then what? Where would you be?" He grinned. "Told you I was a good snoop. You can thank me later."

The images taken by the cell phone camera were

grainy because of the dim lighting inside the club. Conrad had fiddled with the zoom periodically, causing some of the photos to be out of focus, and there were a couple of close-ups of his thumb. But Crawford had to give the old man credit for his ingenuity.

In several of the shots, he'd caught Otterman doing his trick with the coin. He recalled how Conrad had described him. "Two-sided."

He hadn't realized that he'd spoken the thought under his breath until Conrad called him on it. "Come again?"

"That thing he does with the coin—"

"He was doing that on the occasion I met him," Holly said and imitated the motion.

"He's two-sided. Can change personalities in an instant. Two sides of a coin. Is there a parallel, an inside joke he's playing on everyone?" Crawford shrugged over his own conjecture, then, looking back at Conrad, he asked, "No one noticed you photographing him?"

"With all those bouncing tits—" He looked over at Holly. "*Girls* to look at? No one was paying any attention to a hopeless drunk getting progressively plastered, which…" He placed his hand over his heart, saying to Holly, "I regret to say, I have a reputation for doing."

The old man's ability to charm her rankled, so Crawford focused on his task. Tapping on the next photograph, it immediately gave him pause. The man facing Otterman across the table was wearing a cowboy hat. The brim cast a shadow over his face, so nothing much was showing underneath it except for his hair. The way it was pressed flat against—

Hastily he applied his fingers to the screen to enlarge the picture so he could see the man's features better, and when he got a good look, he recognized him instantly. "Holy shit." He took in every detail, making certain that he was right before holding the phone down to where Holly could see it. "Look familiar?"

Without hesitation, she whispered, "That's the gunman in the courtroom."

"You're sure?"

"One hundred percent. I wouldn't know his face because of the mask, but the hair is exactly the same."

"That's what I noticed first. But we gotta be sure."

"I am."

"He's a cop."

She gave Crawford a swift glance, then looked again at the cell phone screen. "Yes! I've seen him in the courthouse. Never wearing a hat, though. I don't know his name."

"I do."

Chapter 24

———◆◆———

Crawford headed for the door.

Holly shot to her feet and went after him. "Where are you going?"

"To make some calls. Stay put. I'll be right back."

She watched him through the screen door as he leaped over the steps of the porch and landed in the yard, his cell phone already in hand.

"He's always been like that," Conrad said from his recliner. "Agile and quick as a whip, even as a baby. Took after his mother that way. She was a dancer, you know."

"A dancer?" Holly looked back at him from over her shoulder. "No, I didn't know that."

"She had a studio out at the strip mall, taught ballet and tap dancing. Jazz. All of it. Each spring, she put on this big recital at the civic center. Everybody in town went. Quite a show. Took months for ladies to sew all the spangles on the costumes."

Holly remembered the ballet slippers in Georgia's bedroom and wondered if that was a deliberate or subconscious link Crawford had formed between his daughter and mother.

Conrad was staring into space, sadness weighing down his facial features.

"She was beautiful and talented, and I guess that made her feel entitled to better. To more. She talked a lot about being unfulfilled."

Then he stirred, gathered himself, and gestured toward the yard where Crawford was pacing, his cell phone to his ear. "His mother and I were sorry excuses for parents. He turned out better than anybody had a right to expect."

"Better than he gives himself credit for," Holly said, speaking more to herself than to Conrad.

"You've come to know him well after only three days."

"Seems longer."

"When did you sleep together?"

She whirled around and looked at him with astonishment.

He chuckled over her guilty reaction. "Thought so."

"Mr. Hunt, Conrad—"

He raised a hand to stop her. "No explanation necessary. But I'm guessing that the timing of it was... problematic."

At her pained expression, he said, "Admit nothing, judge. I don't need to know. Don't *want* to know. I just hope it works out okay, because, as women go, he's had it rough. His mother ran off. His wife died." He paused, his gaze narrowing a fraction. "He loves that little girl of his. Be a damn shame if he lost her, too."

"It won't be up to me. I recused myself."

"Under the circumstances, that was the ethical thing to do. But forgive me for saying, you don't look too happy about it."

"I feel an obligation to people who've put their trust in me and my career. I don't want to let them down."

Studying her, he frowned thoughtfully. "This thing between you and Crawford, has it made you, or would it make you, an inferior judge? Would you be less good on the bench because of it?"

"No. In fact, I'd be better. He's made me realize and accept that gray areas do exist. I used to see only black and white."

"Go with that, Holly, and stop beating yourself up. I happen to be an expert on disappointing people, and I can tell you from experience that the more you *worry* about doing it, the more you do it. Fear of failing someone becomes self-fulfilling."

"I'll take that under advisement." They exchanged a smile.

Then he looked through the door at Crawford. "I'd like to see him happy."

"I saw him with Georgia for the first time today. While he was with her, he was happy, lit up from the inside. And why wouldn't he be? She's adorable."

"Is she?" In his rheumy eyes, a flicker of joy was almost instantly replaced by sorrow. "He won't let me see her."

It was plain to Holly how deeply that rejection affected him. "Perhaps he'll change his mind."

"No, no. I don't blame him a bit. I don't want my granddaughter to know me like this." He raised his hands to encompass himself and his environment. "An old alky fighting with every breath to stay sober? No. I don't want Georgia to have that image of me any more than he wants to expose her to such.

"No, if ever a day comes when he wants to acquaint her with her Grandpa Conrad, I'd like him to show her a picture of me from thirty years ago when I was feared by some of the meanest sons of bitches in this state. When I was the bane of the best defense lawyers, and had the utmost respect of judges," he said, adding a wink. "I'd like him to tell her about how I was before... Well, before." His smile was wistful. "I'd be proud for my grandchild to know me in that light."

———

Crawford looked back through the screen door and wondered what Holly and his old man were talking about with such absorption. Annoyed because he'd called the same number three times without success, he paced a tight circle as he redialed it once again.

"Come on, come on, jerk-off. I know you're there." This time the phone was answered with a timorous hello.

"Nugent?"

"Stop calling me. I can't talk to you."

"Where's Neal? I've tried every number several times."

"He checked out to go to dinner with his family."

"I don't care how you manage it, just find him, tell him he needs to get an arrest warrant for Pat Connor. Joseph Patrick Connor. He's on the list of PD officers who were on duty and inside the courthouse at the time of the shooting."

"I know. He was questioned and released."

"Erroneously. Text me Connor's street address. Also, tell Neal to get a search warrant for his home, car, everything. Are you getting all this? Write it down if you need to. Tell Neal to meet me at Connor's house with those warrants. I'll go on ahead, make sure he's there, and keep an eye on him till Neal arrives. And— this is very important—notify the sheriff's office that somebody needs to go out to the man camp and bring Chuck Otterman in for questioning."

"You're kidding, right?"

Crawford shouted, "Do I sound like I'm kidding?"

"Neal's already on the brink of firing me. If I tell him this came from you—"

"He's not going to fire you. You're a county commissioner's nephew. Don't forget to text me that address. I need it now. And if you screw this up, Neal will be the least of your worries because I'll throttle you myself. Get your butt in gear. Time to man up, Nugent."

Crawford disconnected, accessed Conrad's phone, and hastily emailed himself the photo of Pat Connor in conversation with Otterman. He strode toward the porch, hurdled the steps, pulled open the screen door, and with an underhand throw, tossed Conrad his cell phone. "Guess I owe you a thanks."

"Guess you do."

"It was a damn crazy thing you did. Risky. But it gave me the break in the case I needed. Thanks."

"I'm glad I could do something for you."

Father and son held each other's gaze for several beats, then Crawford reached for Holly's hand. "Let's go."

With her in tow, he walked hurriedly to his SUV. As he steered it down the potholed drive toward the main road, he told her that he had put things into motion. "We'll have Connor in custody within the hour. I predict he'll give up Otterman as leverage for a life sentence, because he faces the death penalty if convicted of killing Chet."

"You still believe Otterman was behind it?"

"Someone was. Pat Connor doesn't have the imagination or initiative to pull off something like Monday's attack."

"Assuming it's Otterman, how did he get Connor to agree to do it?"

"Otterman's got to be holding something bad over Pat's head. He knows where the body's buried. A gambling debt. Something. We need to find out what it is, so we'll have our own bargaining chip."

With that in mind, he reached for his phone and called Harry Longbow. Crawford told him that he had identified the courthouse shooter and gave him Connor's full name.

"Prentiss PD officer. A long-timer with low rank. Not even a beat cop any more. He provides security at the courthouse. Damn! I just remembered. He was one of the cops guarding Holly at the press conference the other day. Neal told me that all those officers had been cleared."

"Another confidence-booster," Harry drawled. "What's this Connor's beef with you?"

"I don't think he has one. Or with Judge Spencer. He's somebody's puppet."

"Otterman?"

"Top of my list. They had a one-on-one this afternoon in a strip joint." Crawford described the meeting. "I have the photo, which proves an alliance of some sort. I'm guessing it's unholy."

"You want me to research that?"

"Hate to dump it in your lap, Harry."

"You've got your hands full. Sessions is still working it, too. Hasn't come up for air in hours."

"Thanks. Start with recent deposits to Pat Connor's bank account that don't look like cop pay. The mother lode would be if you could trace funds of unknown origin to Otterman."

"I'm getting hard already."

"Rein it in. I doubt it'll be that easy."

"Me, too, but, you know, we can hope. Anything else?"

"Yeah. How was breakfast?"

It took Harry a moment to piece it together, then he sighed. "She told you?"

"Call me the second you have something." Crawford

disconnected and glanced over at Holly. "What did you and Conrad talk about?"

"How much he cares for you."

He made a scoffing sound. "That's a laugh."

"He didn't profess it in so many words, but the message came through loud and clear."

"Funny, I never got that message."

"Maybe you weren't listening."

He shot her an angry look. "And maybe he saw a gullible audience for his sob stories. Did he tell you he wasn't invited to my wedding?"

"No."

"Huh. That's one of his favorites. Beth urged me to include him. I refused. I told her that if he was sent an invitation, the *groom* would be a no-show."

Seeing the reproach in Holly's expression, he said sourly, "Before you go tearing up for poor Conrad, you should know why I was so dead set against having him as a wedding guest.

"See, over my objections, my aunt asked him to go with her to my high school graduation. He came, but he didn't see me walk across the stage and get my diploma. Before they got to the H's, he puked his guts up in the aisle of the auditorium. He was ejected by men he was cursing at the top of his lungs and trying to fight off. He created the biggest spectacle in commencement history, and that dubious record still stands."

"I'm sorry, Crawford."

"Doesn't matter." His flippancy only underscored that it did matter—a lot. She probably picked up on that. Feeling defensive, he said, "I'm telling you this crap for just one reason, and that's so you won't be taken in by Conrad's charm. Believe me, it never lasts long."

Since leaving Conrad's house, he'd had the mag-mount on the roof of his SUV and lights flashing behind the grille. But once he left the highway and neared her neighborhood, he turned them off. "No one needs to know where you've been tonight. Can you sneak back in?"

"I sneaked out. Drop me on the street to the south of the main house."

Taking the last corner with his headlights off, he rolled to a stop at the side of the narrow lane. Through the trees, he could barely make out the roofline of her cottage. He disliked the darkness and all the good hiding places in the surrounding shrubbery. "I should see you in, check your house."

"There's no need. There never was. I wasn't the one in danger."

"We could be wrong."

"I don't think so."

"Neither do I, but I won't breathe easy until Pat Connor and Otterman are in custody."

She placed her hand on his arm and squeezed it gently. "Be careful."

"I always am."

"You *never* are."

She said it with a teasing lilt, but he remained unsmiling as he removed his arm from her hand. "Save that for the hearing. You can swear to it under oath."

"Crawford—"

"I gotta go."

"Would you rather have been arrested in front of Georgia?"

"Now's not the time to talk about this."

"Then why'd you'd make that snide remark?"

"Why'd you make that deal with Joe?"

"Because he gave me two options, and both were crummy. I had to make a snap decision and act on it.

You, of all people," she said, jabbing the air between them with her index finger, "should relate to that."

Giving him no time to respond, she shoved open the passenger door, dropped to the ground, then slammed the door closed. She jogged toward the azalea hedge and disappeared into the foliage.

Dammit, he wanted to go after her, finish the fight, then get her naked and watch her boil over for a different reason entirely.

Swearing, he put the SUV into reverse and backed all the way to the corner.

Holly's cell phone rang just as she was unobtrusively letting herself in through the back door. She halfway expected it to be Crawford, calling to apologize, or to continue their argument. But the number in her LED wasn't his.

"Hello?"

"Judge Spencer, Greg Sanders."

The very sound of his voice made her shiver. "How did you get my cell number?"

"I have resources."

"Your client base."

Ignoring the droll remark, he said, "A lot's happened since our conversation at the elevator the other day. You've had a harrowing week. Did you get my roses?"

"A thank-you note is in the mail."

"You liked them, then?"

"They were thorny."

He snorted a laugh.

She wanted to hang up on him, but she wondered what was behind the unprecedented call. "We've exhausted the topic of the roses."

"You want to know why I called." She didn't reply. He went on. "I was summoned to lockup tonight to confer with a client. The place was hopping. Guess what the rumor mill is churning out tonight?"

"I'm sure you can't wait to enlighten me."

"Ranger Crawford Hunt, whose praises you sang the other day on TV, has been booted—pun intended—"

"Clever."

"—off Neal Lester's investigation. Furthermore, Lester was overheard suggesting that the next time he and Hunt talk, Hunt will probably want to have a lawyer present."

"I hope you're not calling me to ask for a reference."

He laughed, and she envisioned the large teeth and Mrs. Briggs's grandpa's mule.

"No, representing Hunt might be considered a conflict of interest, since you're so solidly in his corner, and I'm your opponent."

"I'm still failing to see the purpose of this call."

"Only to say what a shame it is that you've publicly defended the guy who's suspected of planning the shooting spree. Remember, I told you it was only a matter of time before you messed up. And did you ever."

"Surely you're not calling to gloat over an incident that caused the deaths of two men. Even you wouldn't be that obnoxious."

"No, what happened to Chet and that other fellow is a tragedy. But in light of recent developments, your exaltation of Crawford Hunt doesn't speak well of your discernment, does it?"

She had to bite her tongue to keep from revealing what she knew now about Pat Connor and Chuck Otterman. "I can't comment on an ongoing police investigation."

He guffawed. "How long are you going to hide

behind those skirts? Fact is, you put all your eggs in the wrong basket."

"Good night."

"Hold on. This turn of events has created an embarrassing situation for you. But there's an easy way out."

"I don't need a way out of anything."

"Nice try, but we both know better. Why don't you fade gracefully into the background and let me run uncontested? See? Win win. I get what I should have had in the first place, you get to save face."

"Don't call me again."

"This is a one-time offer. You should accept it."

"Or what?"

"Or I'm going to shred you. I'm going to find out what our tough Texas Ranger was doing up in your chambers last night. Yes, judge. There's scuttlebutt over that, too. By the time I'm done, you'll wish you'd never heard of Judge Waters. You'll be a speck in the history books of this county's courts."

He paused, took a breath, then in a patronizing tone, he said, "I'd rather it not come to that, and I'm sure you don't, either. So, what do you say?"

She didn't say anything. Effectively thumbing her nose at him, she clicked off.

Tomorrow, after Pat Connor was in custody and Crawford had been cleared of all suspicion, she would be vindicated.

But that was tomorrow. First, she must endure what she anticipated would be a long night.

As Crawford sped toward the address, which, surprisingly, Nugent had texted him, he left his SUV's emergency lights off, not wanting to announce his approach. Pat Connor had to be on edge, fearing that he would be found out. A nervous perp, seeing a cop and realizing the jig was up, could get trigger-happy. This was one time Crawford would wait for backup.

But his caution was unnecessary, because when he turned the corner onto Connor's street, it was alive with activity and ablaze with the flashing lights of half a dozen vehicles.

Neighbors, most dressed in nightclothes, were standing in their yards, talking among themselves, watching with curiosity as uniformed officers strung crime scene tape around the unkempt yard.

"Oh shit."

Chapter 25

———◆———

Crawford's purposeful stride quickly covered the distance to the open front door of a modest house where a patrolman had been posted to keep out anyone who didn't belong. He eyed Crawford warily and addressed him by name.

Crawford said, "Connor?"

"Found dead on his kitchen floor."

Crawford expelled a long breath and spat out an obscenity, but as he made to enter the house, the policeman took a sidestep and blocked him. "Lester ordered me to keep everybody out."

"I'm working with Lester."

"Crawford, the word going around is that you're implicated."

"The word going around has changed."

"Since when?"

"Since the courtroom shooter turned up dead on his kitchen floor."

"Pat Connor was the courtroom shooter?"

In answer, Crawford merely raised his eyebrows.

The patrolman looked around to see who might be watching, then said under his breath, "I never saw you."

"Thanks."

Crawford stepped across the threshold directly into a forlorn-looking living room. He noticed the gun belt lying on the coffee table, the service weapon still holstered. He registered the sagging curtains, the vintage easy chair positioned directly in front of the wall-mounted flat-screen TV, a side table cluttered with the detritus of a lonely life.

Noticeably missing were family photographs, books, plants, or signs of a pet. Connor was dead, but, by all appearances, he hadn't been living much of a life.

Without Georgia in his, this might be a crystal ball view of his future.

Made uneasy by that thought, he walked from the living room into the kitchen, where Neal was bent over the corpse and talking with Dr. Anderson who, despite his obesity, had managed to squat. Nugent was standing in the doorframe of an open pantry, looking distinctly ill at ease. When Crawford walked in, he gave a twitch and said, "Uh, Neal."

Upon seeing Crawford, Neal stood up slowly. "How'd you get in here?"

"Walked."

Neal let the smart-aleck remark pass. "I got your messages. As it turns out, the warrants for Connor that you requested won't be necessary."

"You discovered him?"

"As you see him." He stood aside.

Connor's body had crumpled, folding in on itself, his face to the floor. He'd been shot in the back of the head.

Neal said, "Two bullets. Close range. Somebody wanted him not just dead, but very dead."

Crawford took in the rest of the scene. An open can of Coke stood on the counter with a partially filled drinking glass beside it. A bottle of whiskey was on the floor near the body, tipped over onto its side. Particularly gruesome was the confluence of spilled liquor and blood on the grimy vinyl floor.

"Looks like he was pouring himself a drink and was unaware of his visitor," Neal said. "Either that, or he had enough trust to turn his back on him."

Crawford addressed the ME. "How long's he been dead?"

"Best guess, couple of hours." He reached for Crawford's hand. Crawford helped haul him up. He puffed a thanks. "I'll notify you as soon as I can be more precise on the timing."

"That his phone?" Crawford indicated the cell phone Neal was holding in his gloved hand.

"One of them."

"He had more than one?"

"The one with his official number was on the end table in the living room. It's already been bagged. I found this one in his pants pocket." He activated the phone, accessed a page, and held it up for Crawford to see the screen.

"The video of Georgia."

"Sent by text to your cell phone at—"

"I know what time I got it, Neal," Crawford said tightly. "I was there."

Sensing the tension between the two, the ME said, "Excuse me. I'll go check on the ambulance. Let me know when I can have him."

Following his departure, the other three were left in an awkward, almost hostile silence. Crawford was the first to speak. "Have you searched the house?"

"I have uniforms doing that," Neal replied. "Nugent made a walk-through as soon as we got here."

Nugent said, "I didn't find anything out of the ordinary."

"I wouldn't expect you to," Crawford said. "He left behind the evidence of the courtroom shooting. We'll be able to match his DNA to what we got off the painter's overalls and mask."

"What makes you think he was the courtroom shooter?" Neal asked. "You failed to elaborate when you called Nugent and threatened him to get his butt in gear, or else."

Crawford used his phone to open the email he'd sent to himself and showed Neal the picture of Pat Connor with Otterman. "This was taken earlier this evening. I instantly recognized Pat as the shooter."

"He was one of the officers guarding the judge during the press conference."

"A short while ago, I remembered that."

"You didn't have an epiphany then."

"He wasn't wearing a hat."

"And the hat made all the difference to you?"

"You're scoffing, but actually it did." To Holly, too. But he couldn't tell Neal that.

Neal continued. "It was Pat Connor who told me about your meeting in chambers last night with Judge Spencer. He saw you leave, hot under the collar."

Crawford remembered that a cop had been lurking in the darkened corridor as he'd left Holly's office. "Was he by any chance my tail taking the pictures?"

"No."

"Then what was he doing up there at that hour?"

"More to the point, what were you?"

He didn't answer that. "It should tell you something that, since Monday, Pat Connor had placed himself in our paths, mine and the judge's, when I hadn't bumped into him more than a handful of times in the past five years. He was keeping tabs on us. He was the shooter,

Neal. Same hair. Body type. Check his left knee. He's probably still got the bruise."

"I've already told Dr. Anderson to look for that. But even if Connor was our shooter, why'd he do it?"

"Somebody put him up to it."

"I agree. Who?"

"Best guess?" Crawford tapped the screen of his phone to pull up the picture again. "He was with Otterman. Early this evening. In a club called Tickled Pink."

"How'd you get the picture?"

"That's your question? You're standing three inches from a dead cop who had a covert conversation *today* with a man who by his own admission left a crime scene, *and that's your question*?"

Neal remained unflappable. "True to form, you're making a coincidence into a crisis, just so you can spring into action and dazzle us all."

"Fine. You don't want to soil your hands with something potentially messy like a corrupt cop schmoozing with a bigwig, give it over to me. Because I don't give a shit who I offend. I want the bastard behind Chet's death, and I think it's the same smug bastard who lied about me and Rodriguez. Soon as Otterman gets to headquarters, put me in an interrogation room with him. I'll wring his thick neck till he——"

"He's out of town."

"What?"

"He's gone fishing for the weekend. His secretary doesn't know where. She thinks somewhere in Louisiana. He'll be back on Monday. I asked her to have him call me if he reported in, but she doesn't expect him to."

Disbelieving what he was hearing, Crawford looked over at Nugent, who gave an abashed shrug. When Crawford went back to Neal, he regarded him with genuine perplexity. "You're content to sit back and wait until Monday?"

"Oh, not at all. I'll be busy turning your life inside out. I did obtain a search warrant, but it's for *your* house. Consider it served." He removed the document from his pocket and shoved it at Crawford.

Looking down at the corpse, he continued. "Connor sent you a video of your daughter. Was that intended as a wake-up call? A subtle threat? I don't know, but, knowing how you feel about her, it's definitely a motive. Can you account for your time this evening?"

He could. But not without involving Conrad and Holly. Instead, he tried to reach Neal in a way that Neal would respond to. "You're making a ruinous career choice here, Neal. Think it over very carefully before you decide to proceed."

"I've already decided."

"You're arresting me?"

"Not yet. I'm asking you to come down to head-quarters for questioning."

"This time I'll have a lawyer with me."

"Good idea. Turn around."

Understanding his intention, Crawford turned and raised his hands in the air. Neal pulled his pistol from the holster at the small of his back. "One sniff, you'll know it hasn't been recently fired."

"You wouldn't be that stupid. I know it's not the murder weapon."

"You're just being careful."

"That's right."

"Can I drive myself to the courthouse?"

"Sure," Neal said. Then to Nugent, "Go with him. Soon as CSU gets here, I'll be along."

Crawford gave the grisly sight on the floor one last glance, then left through the living room, Nugent on his heels. The patrolman at the front door said, "Every-thing okay?"

Crawford didn't bother answering.

———

Once in his SUV, Nugent riding shotgun, Crawford called William Moore. "Did I wake you up?"

"It's okay," the attorney replied with customary terse-ness. "I'll charge you my after-hours rate."

"Can you meet me at police headquarters in fifteen minutes?"

"What happened?"

"A Prentiss cop took two bullets in the back of his head. That's all I'll say now. I'm not alone."

"You're under arrest?"

"Not quite. Can you be there?"

"I'm not a criminal lawyer, Crawford, and that's what you need. I recommend Ben Knotts."

"That guy? Hell, no. I've seen him in action. I brought a case to trial, and Knotts defended the sleazebag who popped his girlfriend for horning in on his dog-fighting operation."

"Was the sleazebag acquitted?"

Crawford sighed and said grudgingly, "Have Ben Knotts call me ASAP."

He disconnected. Nugent, who hadn't spoken up till then said, "I probably shouldn't be telling you…I mean, I guess it should come from Neal."

"What?"

"Somebody IDed Rodriguez this afternoon." At a sharp look from Crawford, he rushed on. "Guy who owns a landscaping company in Lufkin had to fire him a few weeks ago, on account of—well, lots of DMV red tape after Rodriguez got a routine traffic ticket. That's when they discovered Rodriguez's documents were fake. Landscaper liked him, hated to let him go 'cause he'd worked for him for several years, dependable, all that. But he has a policy against hiring undocumented—"

"Why's he just now coming forward?"

"He's been on vacation in Colorado. Got back last night. Caught up on local news this morning. He emailed us a copy of the phony green card. Name on it is Jorge Rodriguez. Still not sure that was his real name. The picture, though…it's him."

"Did he have a family?"

"He lived with a woman. Two kids. Landscape guy doesn't know if they were married, but probably not. He's gonna pay for his burial. Said it was a shame."

It was a fucking shame that filled Crawford with incredible sadness. "I appreciate you telling me, Matt. Thanks."

Nugent tore at a loose cuticle with his teeth. "Why would you call about Connor, tell Neal to meet you at his house, if you knew what he'd find when he got there?"

"Doesn't make sense, does it?"

"Unless it's true what they say?"

"Who's they?"

"Everybody."

"What do they say?"

"That he's not seeing straight."

Crawford declined to comment as he pulled into a parking space at the courthouse. His phone jangled. "Must be the lawyer." He answered and told the caller to hold on, then said to Nugent, "Can you give me a minute?"

"I'll be right over there. And, uh, I'd better take your key."

Crawford pulled it from the ignition and handed it to Nugent, who got out and went to huddle beneath a shallow overhang above the building's side entrance. It had started to drizzle.

Crawford answered his phone. "Crawford Hunt."

"How does it feel?"

"Excuse me?"

"Your world has come crashing down around you, hasn't it?"

The hushed voice was full of menace, and Crawford recognized it immediately. "You son of a bitch."

The laugh that filled his ear was nasty with delight. "So many bad things happening to you. And guess what? There's even worse on the way."

The caller disconnected.

Crawford quickly checked the call log, but, as expected, it said only "Unknown" where a name and number should have been.

He sat there, wavering between rage and fear. From the day of the custody hearing, there had been a purposefully orchestrated dismantling of his life. Being suspected of Pat Connor's murder was just the most recent catastrophe in a carefully planned, destructive sequence.

There's even worse on the way.

Crawford knew down to his marrow that it wasn't an empty threat.

He stared through his rain-pebbled windshield at the looming structure of the courthouse. The upper floors were dark, but all the windows were alight on the ground floor where police headquarters were.

He looked at Nugent, shoulders hunched against the increasing rainfall, hands in his pockets, jiggling change like a man waiting for a bus.

Crawford's cell phone dinged. He checked the caller

ID and saw the name Ben Knotts, the recommended criminal attorney. He let the call go to voice mail.

After a few more seconds of consideration, realizing what he had to do, he banged his fist hard against the ceiling of his SUV.

———————

Neal pulled his car into an empty parking space, got out, walked briskly to the side entrance reserved for police personnel, and was surprised to find Nugent loitering just outside it.

"What are you doing out here? Where's Crawford?"

Nugent indicated the familiar SUV parked in the second row of the lot. "Talking to a lawyer. He put in a call on the way here."

"That was fifteen minutes ago."

Nugent checked his wristwatch. "Closer to twenty."

Neal looked at the SUV, seeing nothing in the darkly tinted windows except a watery reflection of the courthouse. "Goddammit!" He struck off running toward it.

"He couldn't have gone anywhere," Nugent called. "I have his key."

Neal jerked open the driver's door. Lying on the seat was a cell phone, along with the bulbs that belonged in the dome light and the twin map lights on either side of the rearview mirror. Otherwise, the vehicle was empty.

Chapter 26

————◆————

Holly was in bed but not asleep. She answered her phone after the first ring.

"You've shown a knack for sneaking out," Crawford said, sounding out of breath. "Think you can you do it again? This time in your car?"

"What number is this?"

"A burner phone."

"What's going on? Have you arrested Pat Connor?"

"That didn't go as planned. I need you to pick me up."

"Where are you? Where's your truck?"

"Sitting empty on the courthouse parking lot, and when Neal discovers me missing from it, he'll go mental, and then he'll put out an APB, and if I'm apprehended I go to jail. And I can't go. Not yet. Not tonight. Will you do it?"

She tried to process it all as rapidly as he'd related it. "Why would Neal put out an APB on you?"

"Connor's dead."

In clipped cop-speak, he described the murder scene. Amid her murmurs of disbelief, he continued in the same rapid-fire way. "I went there to arrest him, and instead wound up in Nugent's custody. I went quietly and was willing to go through the first round of questioning. But then I got a phone call."

"From whom?"

"I'll explain that when you get here."

She hesitated, and as though reading her mind, he said, "I wouldn't ask you to aid and abet, Holly. Timing is everything and, right now, this minute, I haven't been charged with a crime, and I'm not asking you to commit one. But I need a fair and impartial witness to something I'm about to do, someone with unimpeachable integrity who could later testify as to my motive for doing it."

"What are you going to do?"

He said nothing for several seconds, then, "Do you think I killed Connor?"

"I know you didn't."

"Do you think I was behind the courtroom shooting?"

"No."

"I'm under the Jackson Street bridge, eastbound side. Ten minutes. If you're not here by then, I'll know you aren't coming."

———

As he slid into her passenger seat, he said, "That was twelve minutes. I was getting worried." He turned to look out the rear window. The wet streets were dark, and no other vehicles were in sight. Which was why a man on foot, walking through the rain, would have attracted attention to any cop on patrol.

Besides, it would have taken him too long to cover on foot the distance he had to go. There was no time to waste.

She pulled back into the traffic lane. "I don't know where we're going."

"Turn around when you can. We've got to get on the opposite side of downtown, but keep to the back streets. How did you manage to get away without being followed?"

"I drove over ground through my backyard to the driveway of the main house. I went out that way."

"You really do have a knack. The next left will put you on Fair Avenue. Go south. I'll tell you where to turn."

"An hour ago, I told the police on duty at my house that I was retiring for the night. But if they notice that my car isn't parked in back, Neal will probably issue an APB for it, too."

"He will, but it won't do him any good. I switched out your license plates."

She glanced at him with disbelief. "What? When?"

"Tuesday night. Actually Sessions did, but I asked him to."

"Why?"

"You weren't taking the need for guards seriously. In case you shook them, I would have your new tag number. The unsub—even if he was a cop—wouldn't."

"I was never in danger."

"I didn't know that then. We'd only just discovered that Rodriguez wasn't the gunman. By the way, he's been identified." He recounted everything Nugent had told him. "He was probably in the courthouse to see about getting legal documentation, got nervous about possibly being deported, went up to have a cigarette while rethinking it."

"He wasn't involved."

"Not until he picked up that pistol." Crawford would forever regret that young man's fate, but for now he had to table his sorrow over it. Other matters couldn't be postponed. "At the second caution light, go left. Stay straight for about a mile."

"How did you get away from Nugent?"

"I disabled the interior lights and crawled out the tailgate. I feel bad about tricking him. He's a decent guy, just not good cop material."

"Why does Neal persist in considering you a suspect?"

"You can ask him that when he questions you."

"Do you think he will?"

"I know he will. Or he should. About three blocks ahead, take a right onto Pecan. What will you tell Neal?"

"That depends on what he asks me. But I'll have to be truthful."

"You haven't done anything illegal."

"No. Ill-advised, perhaps," she said, shooting him a small smile.

"Smitty's been put on notice. On pain of death, he won't talk about your visit to his club. Conrad won't. With luck, you'll be back to your house before it's noticed that your car's missing. If you are caught, you can say—truthfully—that a friend called and begged for your help, and you can't breach that friend's confidence. All of it the truth."

"You make is sound so easy. As I told you that night we met, you have more experience with crisis situations than I do. I'm an amateur. Greg Sanders urged me to cut and run before he shreds me."

After she told him the highlights of their recent conversation, Crawford muttered a few choice epithets. "He's bluffing, pushing your buttons to see how you'll react."

"Maybe. But apparently he has contacts within the police department who've been keeping him updated. He knew you'd been implicated in the courthouse shooting. By now he's probably heard about Connor. That will really make his day."

"Jesus, Holly, I'm sorry. I wouldn't have dragged you

deeper into this, but I didn't have time tonight to come up with a plan B."

"You've yet to tell me about the phone call that prompted this emergency."

"I'll tell you when we get there."

"Where are we going?"

"To my father-in-law's house."

She braked hard in the middle of the street and turned to him with dismay and anger. "No wonder you're just now telling me that!"

"I'm only going to talk to him."

As though he'd told her he was going to beat the living daylights out of Joe Gilroy, she kept her foot on the brake and shook her head firmly. "Whatever you have in mind, I can't be a party to it."

"I'm not even armed. Neal took my pistol." He motioned her forward. "Drive."

"Absolutely not."

"Fine. Thanks for the lift."

In a flash, he was out of the car and running as fast as he could in cowboy boots to cover the remaining few residential blocks. The Gilroys lived in a well-established neighborhood of older homes situated on large lots with carefully maintained lawns and mature trees. Holly followed him in her car, but she was forced to keep to right angles while he cut diagonally across driveways and yards.

When he reached the Gilroys' house, he ran along the side of it toward the rear. He heard the squeal of Holly's brakes, her car door being shut, her running footsteps slapping the wet pavement of the driveway.

He reached the back door mere seconds ahead of her. He raised his hand to knock, but she rushed up behind him and grabbed his forearm in a two-handed grip. Her breath coming in fast pants, she said, "Crawford, whatever you're thinking of doing, don't. I beg you. For Georgia's sake."

The door came open suddenly. "What the bloody hell?" Joe Gilroy, standing behind the screen door, took in the situation at a glance. To Holly, he said, "I tried to tell you, didn't I? I'm calling the police."

"I *am* the police," Crawford said.

"You're a hazard. This time you go to jail." Joe turned away.

Crawford was vaguely aware of Holly losing her balance when he shook off her grasp, but through the screen, he could see Joe going for the phone, and he had to stop him.

He pulled on the door handle. Discovering it locked, he jerked on it repeatedly and viciously until the old-fashioned clasp gave way, then he flung open the door and rushed inside.

He was across the kitchen in two strides, snatching the cordless phone out of Joe's hand, and throwing it to the floor.

Grace appeared, her hand at her throat, crying out in alarm as the two men went at each other. Joe threw punches that would have leveled anyone weaker and slower to react. Crawford dodged the pounding fists and at the same time landed a few well-placed punches.

Holly cried out, "Crawford! Stop! Stop!"

Crawford saw that Joe was becoming winded and used that to his advantage. He drove his shoulder into the older man's midriff and pushed him backward until he came up against the counter, then planted his hand in the center of Joe's chest and lodged his knee up between his thighs.

Joe was red-faced with fury. His teeth were clenched. "I'm going to kill you."

"Maybe," Crawford said, breathing hard. "Later. But right now, you're going to get Georgia up—"

"Like hell I am."

He tried to wrestle free from Crawford's restraining hand, but Crawford jammed his knee directly beneath Joe's testicles. "You're going to get Georgia up and dressed and…and leave. Take her away from here, Joe. Please," he said, his voice cracking. "Get her away from me."

———

It never failed to freak Smitty out, this thing that Chuck Otterman did with the fifty-cent piece. It was like he was trying to hypnotize you or something, but it had the opposite effect on Smitty. Rather than lull him, it made him nervous as a whore in church.

Every time he came to this place, he dreaded it more, and always considered himself lucky when he was able to leave under his own power, drive away in his own car, all his parts still attached, his heart lub-dubbing in a more or less regular rhythm.

The only reason he risked coming here was because doing business with Otterman was so profitable. But their transactions required him to drive for miles through an eerie swamp, nary a light to be seen after sundown, to this fishing cabin that had probably been put together by a coon-ass using Elmer's and thumbtacks.

He'd once asked Otterman what state it was in, Texas or Louisiana.

"Are you into geography?"

"Not really."

"Then what difference does it make?"

The difference it made was a long list of federal crimes involving words like "interstate trafficking," but

Smitty kept his concerns to himself and had continued to make periodic trips to this old fishing shack way out in the middle of spooky-effing-nowhere.

The corrugated tin roof leaked. A bucket had been placed on the floor to catch the constant drip from the hard rain that contributed to the chilling atmosphere. The plunking sound the drops made as they splashed into the bucket was driving Smitty to distraction, but Otterman seemed unbothered as he set aside his coin and counted out hundred-dollar bills onto the table between them, forming neat stacks of fifty. When he had ten stacks, he passed them one by one to Smitty, who placed them in a pouch.

With a flourish, Smitty zipped it up and flashed Otterman a grin. "Those boys guarantee their product. You have any trouble with the guns, you be sure to tell me."

"You can count on that."

Otterman's tone wasn't the friendly kind that Smitty had been hoping for. Truth was, it had the undercurrent of a threat and made him need to pee. With false bravado, he said, "When you need more, you know who to call." And he winked. "Always a pleasure doing business with you, Mr. Otterman." He stood up.

"Sit down."

Smitty dropped back into his seat. For what seemed like an endless time, the only sounds in the room were the incessant drips, the rain striking the metal roof like a hail of bullets, and distant rumbles of thunder.

Finally, Otterman said, "Pat Connor. Know that name?"

"I don't believe I do."

"Prentiss policeman."

"Oh well, no wonder." Smitty shot a laugh over his shoulder at the two men standing behind him. "I don't have many friends among enforcers of law and order."

"Earlier this evening, Connor met with me in your crappy nightclub."

"What about?"

"A couple hours later, he died in his kitchen."

"Ticker gave out?"

"He was shot dead while pouring himself a drink."

Now Smitty really had to pee. "You don't say? Huh. I hadn't heard that. The clubs don't close till two a.m., so I don't often see the evening news."

"He was discovered too late to make tonight's news." Otterman glanced up at the man standing at Smitty's right shoulder. "But I have it on good authority that two bullets were fired into the back of Connor's skull."

Smitty whistled, or tried to. His lips were too rubbery to pucker. "That ought to do it, all right."

"To have been executed like that, Connor must have let down someone who was counting on him to deliver. Money. Goods. Information. Something of value like that."

Smitty actually flinched when Otterman suddenly sat forward and leaned toward him across the table. "Do you know Crawford Hunt?"

He screwed up his face as though thinking hard. "Crawford Hunt, Crawford Hunt. The name sounds familiar, but I can't quite place him."

Otterman said mildly, "Take your time. Think about it."

After a few seconds, Smitty pretended to have suddenly remembered. "Oh, yeah. Wasn't he the guy—"

"The Texas Ranger."

"Right, right," he said, snapping his fingers. "Wasn't it him who was in the courtroom when it got shot up this week? Is that who you're talking about?"

Otterman flipped the coin, caught it and formed a fist around it, then leaned even closer toward Smitty. "You're a pimp, a crook, and a creep. The only reason I tolerate your company is so I don't have to personally deal with the backwoods, redneck lowlifes around here who supply surprisingly good guns.

"But if you ever lie to me again, not only is your lucrative sideline with me finished, I'll also burn your ratty clubs to the ground, and then stick the barrel of one of those pump-actions up your anus and pull the trigger."

Smitty swallowed and bobbed his head in complete understanding.

Otterman sat back and calmly resumed rolling the coin across the backs of his fingers. "Let's try to have an honest conversation. I'll go first. After I left your club tonight, Crawford Hunt was seen there. In your company, Smitty. He also had a woman with him. They carried somebody out."

"His old man. Who's a sorry drunk. If you were from around here, you'd know the history. Anyway, tonight, he was worse off than usual. I had to call Crawford to come get him and cover his tab."

"That's it?"

"That's it."

"You have no other dealings with Crawford Hunt?"

"Shit, no. I hate his guts. A few years back, he busted me for public lewdness. A guy can't get a blowjob in his own car?"

"Who was the woman?"

"Can't remember her name, but she could shrink-wrap your dick."

"The woman with Hunt, you idiot."

"Oh. The judge."

"Holly Spencer?"

"She doesn't look like any judge I ever faced. Firm tits, smokin' ass."

Otterman didn't react for several seconds, then he cracked a smile that sent chills down Smitty's spine. "You're the expert on that."

He forced himself to chuckle. "Well, I reckon everybody's gotta be good at something."

Otterman's smile relaxed until it was no more. "The boys will see you out."

With no more notice than that, "the boys" jerked him to his feet with such force his teeth clicked together. He was supported between them as they dragged him toward the door.

It occurred to Smitty in a moment of blinding, terrifying clarity that he'd forgotten the money pouch, and that, this time, he wasn't leaving the fishing shack under his own power.

———

Crawford's plea to his father-in-law had left the four of them in a bizarre freeze-frame. He was the first to move. He turned his head and looked at Holly. In a gruff voice, he asked, "Are you hurt?"

Astounded by the sudden turnabout, she looked at him with bafflement. "Hurt?"

"You lost your balance on the step."

"Oh. No, I'm...I'm okay."

Still holding her gaze, he said, "You understand now why I wanted you here, to see this, hear it."

"I believe so."

"I still want custody of Georgia. This doesn't change that." Turning back to his father-in-law, he said, "We'll continue our fight, Joe. Once all this is over, we'll pick up where you threw that last punch if that's how you want it. But you've got to get Georgia away from here tonight. Right now."

He lowered his knee so that it was no longer wedged between Joe's thighs and withdrew his hand from the man's chest. Having seen for herself the ferocity of Joe Gilroy's hatred for Crawford, Holly halfway expected him to launch another physical attack. He didn't, but his facial features remained granite hard, his eyes piercing.

He said, "I'm not going anywhere until you tell me what this is about. What's happened?"

Rain had plastered Crawford's hair to his forehead, but he seemed impervious to it and his wet clothes. "I know who the courtroom shooter was. So does Holly."

Joe's eyes cut to her. "It's true," she said. "I identified a Prentiss police officer as the gunman."

"How'd you figure it out?"

"Too long to go into," Crawford said. "But an hour or less after we made this discovery, he turned up dead. Murdered inside his house. And it wasn't pretty."

Grace made a mournful sound. "Let's all sit down. I'll make coffee."

"There's no time for coffee, Grace," Crawford said. "Start gathering up only what you'll absolutely need to take with you."

"For how long?"

"I don't know. A few days, maybe."

"Hold on, Grace," Joe said when it appeared that she would do as Crawford asked. "I haven't heard anything that compels me to pack up my family and sneak out of town in the middle of the night like a band of gypsies."

"Can't you for once just do something without having to be the fucking commander?"

Holly took a handful of Crawford's shirt and pulled

him backward, then stepped between him and his father-in-law. "Mr. Gilroy, Mrs. Gilroy," she said, turning her head to include Grace, "we've concluded that I wasn't the intended target in the courtroom. Crawford was."

Joe glanced beyond her toward Crawford. "That doesn't surprise me. But why, specifically?"

"Do you know a man named Chuck Otterman?" Crawford asked.

"I've heard of him, sure. Runs the drilling outfit? What's he got to do with it?"

As concisely as possible, Holly explained the situation. "Crawford has Texas Rangers in the Houston office trying to determine what the connection is and why Otterman would conspire to have him killed."

Crawford took over for her. "In the meantime, he called me."

That took Holly aback. "The phone call you mentioned. It was Chuck Otterman?"

"I recognized his voice." He repeated the brief conversation. "He said there was worse coming my way, and I take that threat seriously. Everything else he's done has been a sick warning. The park video, trashing Georgia's room, and—"

"Trashing her room?"

"Joe, we can't explain it all now," he said impatiently. "Bottom line, Neal Lester, for reasons of his own, and, in part, thanks to you, is trying to pin all this on me."

"All I did was ask—"

"I know what you asked, and it was bullshit. But Neal has run with it. I slipped away tonight, but if he finds me, he can hold me for forty-eight hours before charging me, and if I'm in lockup, I can't protect Georgia, and I go a little crazy when I think of Otterman getting near her. Touching her."

"This threat you say he issued—"

"I don't say it, he did it."

"Okay, but he didn't mention Georgia."

"Dammit, Joe, are you willing to risk her life just to win an argument with me?"

"Don't lay any of this on me," the older man shouted back. "It's a mess of your own making."

Crawford closed his eyes briefly, and when he re-opened them, they were bright with an intensity of feeling. "You gotta know how hard it is for me to come here and ask you for a goddamn thing, but you must put our quarrel aside and get Georgia out of here." The older man opened his mouth to speak, but Crawford headed him off. "And it's gotta be now."

Holly divided a look between the two adversaries, still facing off, each as unbending as the other. Taking matters into her own hands, she walked over to Grace. "If you'll show me where things are, I'll help you pack."

———

While Grace, Joe, and Holly hurriedly collected and packed essentials, Crawford moved from room to room, checking the street out front as well as the back of the property, watching for the stealthy approach of police-men or squad cars, because he figured Neal would eventually think to look for him here.

And so might Otterman or his emissaries.

At some point, Grace brought him a towel. He'd dried off as well as he could while remaining vigilant.

"Daddy?"

When Georgia spoke his name, he turned away from a window overlooking the street, and the sight of her caused a pinching pain in his heart. Holly had quietly gathered articles of clothing from her drawers and packed them in her suitcase, but they'd waited until the last possible moment to wake her up and get her dressed.

She looked sleepy and uncertain as she gazed up at him. Mr. Bunny was clutched to her chest.

"Grandma said we're going on a trip. I don't want to."

"Sure you do." Crawford picked her up and hugged her close. Her arms closed tightly around his neck, her legs around his waist.

"Can I go to your house?"

"Not this time."

She laid her head on his shoulder and turned her face into his neck. This was tearing him apart, but he had to be the grown-up, the brave one. He infused his voice with false enthusiasm. "You're going to have a great time."

"That's what Holly said."

"She's right. Grandma and Grandpa have lots of fun things planned. But you have to be a good girl and mind everything they say. Okay?"

"Why can't you come?"

"Because I have to work. But I'll be thinking about you the whole time, and wishing I was with you." He felt her chest hitch with a small hiccup that presaged tears. He told himself she was crying from sleepiness, from being startled awake and confronted with a situation that was out of the ordinary and beyond her understanding. But whatever the reason, he couldn't bear parting from her when she cried.

Rubbing circles on her back, he murmured into her hair, "Come on now. You're going to be all right. Let's get you into the car."

"Will you carry me?"

He squeezed his eyes shut to keep his own tears inside. "You bet."

Holding her tightly against him, he carried her through the house, now dark, and into the attached garage, where Joe was placing her suitcase, the last of the luggage, into the trunk. When he would have walked past Crawford without saying anything, Crawford addressed him.

His father-in-law stopped and looked at him.

"You're the only person I trust to do this, Joe. I know you'll protect her as fiercely as I would."

Joe held his gaze, gave a curt nod, then got into the driver's seat.

Without further delay, he carried Georgia to the backseat door, which Holly was holding open for them. He settled Georgia into her seat. When she started to reach for the straps, he said, "Let me buckle you in this time."

"Mr. Bunny, too."

"Of course." He clicked the fasteners and made sure they were secure, then placed his hands on either side of her face and pressed his forehead against hers. "Be sweet for Daddy."

"Okay."

"I love you."

"More than anything?" she asked, repeating what he often said.

"More than anything." He kissed her forehead, her hair, her cheek, and finally her lips.

But when he tried to back away, she reached for him. "Daddy? Where we're going, will you be there tomorrow?"

"Probably not tomorrow."

"When?"

"As soon as I can get there."

Then before he let her forlorn expression change his mind about the necessity of this separation, he kissed her again, quickly stepped back, and closed the car door. She placed her hand flat against the window glass. On the outside of it, he kissed her palm, then aligned his large hand with her tiny one, and they stayed that way until Joe backed the car out.

Chapter 27

W here will they go?" Holly asked as Crawford hustled her into her car.

The street was empty. Nearby houses were dark. From all appearances, no one had noticed their brief visit with the Gilroys. Even so, Crawford was scanning the area, alert to the motion of every leaf, the spatter of every raindrop.

"Grace's sister recently remarried after years of widowhood. She lives with her new husband in a retirement community outside Austin."

"They're in for a long drive."

"Five hours, give or take. Rain may slow them down. I hope Georgia sleeps most of the way."

"I don't know how you said good-bye to her without cracking."

"I don't know how I did, either." He stared vacantly for a few seconds, then cleared his throat and indicated her ignition. "Get going. I need to be well away from here before Neal comes looking."

"He's called me." Steering with her left hand, she used her right to pull her cell phone from the front pocket of her jeans and passed it over to him. "It had been vibrating, but I ignored it. I checked it while Grace was getting Georgia dressed, but I didn't listen to the messages."

"He's left two," he said. "And you have one text, but it's from Marilyn."

"Why would she be texting me?"

"Want me to read it?"

"Please."

He pulled it up. "It says, 'WTF is going on?' Wording doesn't sound like she's trying to mend fences."

"Call her for me, please."

He used the phone to make the call, but it went through the Bluetooth speaker of the car. As soon as Marilyn answered, she blared, "Holly, thank God you called. I've been worried sick."

"Why?"

"That detective called me. The tight-ass. Lester? Anyway, he was at your house and—"

"At my house? When was this?"

"One vodka and three cigarettes ago. He asked if I'd heard from you, and I told him no, that you were no longer my client, then he told me that you were missing and feared that you'd met with foul play. That's how he put it. He mentioned the murder of a police officer. I've been going crazy here. Where are you? Are you all right?"

"Yes, I'm fine."

"You're not being made to say that under duress, are you?"

"No. However, I can't talk now. There's uh, uh…a situation that I really need to attend to. I apologize for the scare and appreciate your concern. Truly."

She was about to disconnect using the button on her steering wheel, when Marilyn said, "The uh, uh situation involves him, doesn't it? And don't you dare insult me by asking who. The shooting was only the first shock to your system, wasn't it? Mr. tall, blond, and badass was another."

During the course of their conversation, Holly had been keeping her eyes on the road. Now she flicked a gaze over to Crawford, who was sitting as still as a stone beside her, his eyes fixed on her, taking in every word.

"Your silence is screaming at me, Holly," Marilyn continued. "And what I'm hearing is conflict of interest, circumspection versus lust, a moral and ethical dilemma in spades. All of which are right up my alley!" she chortled. "I can't wait to tackle them."

"I fired you, remember?"

"Yes, but now I get why. You were protecting him."

"From *you*."

"Right, but I can back off that."

"Listen, Marilyn—"

"No, you listen. You're an excellent judge, Holly. Dedicated and idealistic. You actually believe in what you're doing. And that's not just me trying to woo you back, I happen to mean it. You should be in that job."

"After this week, I'm afraid Governor Hutchins will rethink his endorsement. Greg Sanders has suggested that I make a graceful exit to save face."

"No way in hell. The governor's blessing is a stroke we can always use, but I can get you elected without it. Hell, I might even do something totally revolutionary in politics and awe the voting public with the truth.

"Sometimes that's actually the best approach. Hide in plain sight. I'll be thinking about our strategy. In the meantime, tend to this 'situation' with the Texas Ranger. He's a rude bastard, but he definitely has appeal. When you need me, I'll be ready."

After the disconnect, she couldn't avoid Crawford's grin. "You called me tall, blond, and badass?"

"I didn't, Marilyn did."

"Will you hire her back?"

"I don't know. More importantly, did you hear the part about Neal being at my house?"

"Yeah." His grin faded as he sighed. "I should have left you out of this, but I couldn't rely on Grace to back me up. Joe could've browbeat her into claiming that I had relinquished Georgia to them without any stipulation that it was temporary.

"I needed you there, but I hate further involving you in what Joe correctly called a mess of my making. Although hell if I know what I did to piss off Otterman, a man I'd never even seen before he walked into the police station."

He leaned his head back and closed his eyes. Looking at his profile, she was struck by how utterly fatigued he appeared. There were dark crescents under his eyes. The hollows beneath his cheekbones were more pronounced than usual.

She asked, "When did you sleep last?"

"I don't remember."

"You're exhausted."

"Joe's no pushover, and I've fought him twice today. Then the episode with my old man. None of my run-ins with him are easy. But what really took it out of me was having to tell Georgia good-bye."

"Which you've also done twice today."

"Both times wrenching. Tonight was different, though. She sensed something was wrong. I goddamn hate that she's worried. I couldn't promise her when I would see her again, and the fact is..."

"The fact is?"

"If Otterman has his way, I never will."

Suddenly, he sat up straight and opened his eyes, the darkened sockets making them look extraordinarily bright with resolve. Thumping his fist on his thigh in time to his words, he said, "I can't let that happen. I may not regain custody of her, but I'll go to hell and back before checking out on her."

"What are you going to do?"

"Stay alive. Stay underground long enough to get Otterman before he gets me."

"How do you intend to go about that?"

"That's the tricky part. I'm working on it."

"You could turn yourself in to Neal. Enlist his help."

"No way. He's bowed his back on Otterman."

"Maybe he's changed his mind."

"I can't chance it. I'd be hamstringing myself."

"There's nothing I can say that will change your mind?"

"Sorry, Holly, no."

She pulled the car over to the side of the road and turned to face him. "Then you need to get out."

Crawford watched Holly's taillights disappear, then struck off walking swiftly, hoping to blend into the darkness and keep from being seen. First order of business was to find shelter from the rain. He covered a couple of blocks before coming upon a vacant house with a "For Sale" sign in the yard.

Crouching against the back wall of the open carport, he called Harry Longbow and woke him up.

"Sorry, man," the other Ranger said around a yawn, "still haven't turned up squat. Not a thread connecting Otterman to you, or to anyone close to you. But I had to get some shut-eye. I called to let you know that I was taking a break, but got your voice mail."

"I had to leave my phone behind."

"Aw, hell. That doesn't sound good."

"Pat Connor's turned up dead, and Otterman issued me a threat."

Harry grumbled, "There goes my nap."

Crawford gave him the rundown. "I got Georgia out of town. That was top priority."

"Where're you and the judge now?"

"She's on her way home."

"What about you?"

"If you don't know, you can't tell. It will occur to Neal to ask if you've heard from me. I'm surprised he hasn't called you already. When he does, you can honestly tell him that you don't know where I am or what my plans are."

"I'll bring Sessions up to speed, so he won't be taken unawares."

"Thanks."

"Maybe you ought to let the prick take you into custody. Jail's at least safe."

"It's also sorta confining."

"There's that."

"How's the major taking it that I'm implicated in a murder?"

"Says it's about the deepest bullshit he's ever had to wade through. He's calling Neal Lester bad names, and he hasn't even met him yet."

Any other time, Crawford would have laughed. But the situation was no laughing matter. "I'm attributing Chet, Rodriguez, and now Connor to Otterman. A body count of three, just this week. I want this son of a bitch, Harry."

"I'll get right back on it."

"No, finish your nap. Otterman is probably regrouping tonight, too. He had a busy day. The park video. The titty bar meeting."

"The execution."

"He didn't shoot the video and he didn't pop Connor. He doesn't do his own dirty work. He's got Frick and Frack."

"Who're they?"

"A pair of bodyguards. And then there are the Pat Connors."

"Facilitators too dumb to say no to him?"

"Too scared, maybe. You know what this is feeling like? Organized crime shit."

"I'm liking this asshole less and less," Harry said.

"Me too."

"Keep your head down."

Crawford gave him the number of his burner phone, then used it to make another call and impatiently counted the rings until Smitty's nasal twang instructed him to leave a message.

Crawford said only, "You know who this is. Call me back, or your shriveled pair are history."

He clicked off, checked the time, then pulled up the collar of his windbreaker and plunged into the rain.

Chapter 28

————————

Wen you told him to get out of your car, he didn't put up an argument?"

"At first," Holly admitted in reply to Neal's question. "But I told him I would take him absolutely no farther. He got out. I drove home."

When she'd arrived, Neal Lester and Matt Nugent were sitting in an unmarked sedan at the end of her driveway. She drove around back and entered her house through the kitchen door, then met them at the front.

As she ushered them inside, she said, "I spoke to Marilyn. She told me to expect you."

She'd offered to make coffee, which they declined. They'd taken seats in the living room and for the past twenty minutes she had been recounting everything that had happened since getting the call from Crawford.

"He didn't tell you what he was going to do?"

"'Stay alive.' Those were his words. For his daughter's sake, he wants very much to live. Having seen her safely away, he was much calmer than he'd been an hour earlier. When he called and asked for my help, he sounded desperate."

Neal said, "He was. He had just escaped from police custody."

"He told me that he drove himself to the courthouse and was willing to cooperate. He hadn't been handcuffed. He hadn't been arrested or read his rights." She paused and looked at the detectives expectantly. "Unless he was lying to me."

"He wasn't. We didn't do any of that," Nugent supplied and, when Neal shot him a withering look, he added, "Which is why I figured he could be left alone to talk to his lawyer."

Neal said, "If all he wanted to do was get his daughter out of harm's way, why did he fool Nugent and abandon his car? Why didn't he tell me about this phone call that caused him to take such drastic measures?"

"He was afraid you wouldn't believe him. I think he was probably right." She paused to let that sink in. "He was afraid that every minute spent on sorting things out was another minute that his daughter's life was in danger."

Defensively, Neal said, "Nobody else heard this mysterious phone call, did they?"

"I was with him when it came in," Nugent said.

"But he told you it was the lawyer."

"Have you spoken with the attorney?" Holly asked.

Ready with the answer, Nugent said, "Crawford had asked for a referral. Ben Knotts called him and got his voice mail. That call came in minutes after the one from the unknown."

She looked at Neal. "He asked for an attorney. Doesn't that indicate that he had every intention of going through the questioning process, and would have if not for that threatening call from Chuck Otterman?"

"No one has ascertained that it was Otterman," Neal argued. "The call from the unknown could have been a solicitation. He used it to trick Nugent."

Holly said, "If the call was a trick and the threat a

fabrication, why would he have implored his in-laws to immediately leave town with his daughter? They will corroborate that's what happened."

"Mr. Gilroy already has."

Nugent's statement left Neal no choice except to elaborate, although he did so grudgingly. "After dispatching a patrol car to their house and having it reported that nobody was at home, I called Joe Gilroy's cell number. I had it from interviewing him after the shooting."

"He confirmed what I've told you?"

"To the letter. There's still no love lost between him and Crawford, but Crawford convinced him that the girl needed to be moved without delay."

"I was similarly convinced," she said. "Unlike you, I believe Mr. Otterman is culpable."

"That video seals it," Nugent agreed.

"Shut up, Matt," Neal snapped. "It doesn't seal anything."

Holly didn't reveal that she knew the origin and content of the video to which Nugent had referred, but she looked at Neal and raised her eyebrows inquisitively. Stiff-lipped with resignation, he said, "Crawford has a video of Pat Connor in conversation with Chuck Otterman. He claims it was shot at a local bar early this evening."

"That's why Crawford left his cell phone behind," Nugent said. "So we'd have that video."

"He left his cell phone so we couldn't use it to track him," Neal said with asperity.

Holly asked, "Does Mr. Otterman have an explanation for this conversation with the murder victim?"

"He's out of town. We're trying to locate him."

She looked around her living room. "Forgive me, but you seem much more preoccupied with locating Ranger Hunt."

"Because he skipped out on a homicide investigation. And even if he's cleared, he's dangerous and irresponsible. I shouldn't have to remind you of that. You've seen him in action."

"Yes, I've seen him in action saving lives and protecting others. Are you sure that your disapproval of his methods, compounded by your personal dislike, hasn't clouded your judgment?"

"Are you sure hormones haven't clouded yours?"

Nugent made a choking sound.

Neal's glare stayed fixed on her. "I think you keep defending him because you're just a little attracted to him, Judge Spencer."

"Well, you're wrong, Sergeant Lester. I defend him because I believe he's right. And I'm not just a little attracted to him, I'm *very* attracted to him. The attraction is inconvenient. Until I recused myself from his custody case, it was unethical. It has the potential of causing me embarrassment and possibly costing me my job, making Crawford Hunt an unexpected complication in my life. But it does not make him a murderer. It does, however, make you a fool for pursuing him instead of the culprit." She stood up. "Is there anything else?"

Neal was still seething as she saw them out. She watched until they drove away. Only then did she close the front door and go around the room turning off lamps. After making sure the house was secure, she went into her bedroom and, as she closed the door, leaned weakly into it and pressed her forehead against the cool wood.

From behind her, one strong arm encircled her waist and firmly positioned her backside against an unquestionably aroused man. He gathered her hair in his fist and moved it aside so he could plant a hot kiss beneath her ear, whispering, "Well, Your Honor, guess you told him."

Chapter 29

———◆———

Crawford slid his hands beneath her top and unhooked her bra. Reaching around to her front and up into the cups, he took her breasts into his palms. His fingertips played over her nipples. Holly's whimper of pleasure melded with a whine asking for more.

He turned her to face him, rid her of top and bra by pulling them over her head together, and before her hair had settled back onto her shoulders, his mouth was fastened to her breast. She clasped his head between her hands as he drew on her with such fervor, the sensations were like sparks of electrical shock.

She didn't want him to stop, but his wet clothing was an aggravation to both of them. He broke away from her to shed his windbreaker. He unbuttoned the first few buttons of his shirt, and then, because that was costing precious time, he pulled it over his head.

She didn't dare turn on a light and risk him being seen by her guards, but she wanted to know him. Placing her hands on his chest, she felt a dusting of hair and nuzzled it. His nipples were hard. She swept her tongue across one, causing him to hiss a swear word as he worked open the buttons of his fly.

She reached into that widening wedge, feathered

her fingers through the coarse hair, then closed her hand around him. His head dropped heavily onto her shoulder.

As she explored, his panting breaths fell hot and moist on her skin.

He was incredibly hard, the skin stretched tight along the shaft, the tip smooth and full to bursting. The pad of her thumb collected a drop of semen, spread it in deft circles until he puffed a profanity and moved her hand away.

Crossing his arms beneath her bottom, he lifted her and carried her to the bed. When she was lying on her back, he worked her jeans and underwear down her legs. Once they were off and out of his way, he got onto the bed, standing on his knees between her thighs, which he pushed back toward her chest.

Then they both went completely still. For several moments, their heavy, irregular breathing was the only sound in the room, in the world. She sensed his movement before she felt his hands on the backs of her calves. He squeezed them, familiarizing himself with their shape. He caressed them up to the backs of her knees where he outlined her kneecaps with his thumbs before covering them with his palms.

Her breath hitched when his hands moved again, this time sliding up the insides of her thighs, slowly but purposefully opening them, opening her, for his descending shoulders, head, mouth.

The heat of his mouth encompassed her. For precious moments, he did nothing else. Just that. Just there. A gentle suction held her with motionless and incredible intimacy. Until gradually he began to make love.

Each brush of his lips, every whisk of his tongue elicited a quickening of her entire body. Whenever his mouth withdrew to take a love bite from her inner thigh or to plant a kiss on her mound, her back bowed, her hips thrust upward in a restless, desperate yearning for him to find the one spot he had kissed around but had yet to touch.

It wasn't until she groaned his name that he obliged her, but tantalizingly, applying his tongue so softly, so exquisitely that her breaths evolved into moans, and her body drew up tight. Attuned to her, he centered the caresses, concentrated them into ever-shrinking spirals, until the sensations painted onto her coalesced into a burst of pleasure so intense, she couldn't contain it.

He levered himself up and, with one strong thrust, he was inside her, appeasing her craving to be stretched, filled. He trapped her orgasmic cries inside a kiss and then let her drift down and rest while he sipped at her earlobes, her eyelids, her lips.

Her mouth opened beneath his, and the sweet kiss turned evocative. His tongue coupled with her mouth as his hips engaged in an erotic rhythm. He moved in and out of her in breath-stealing juts and glides.

Each stroke brought her closer to another orgasm, and when she was once again on the brink, he slid one hand under her bottom to hold her in place as he targeted several rapid thrusts that sent her over. Then he buried himself deep.

His climax was shattering, long, intense.

Eventually they recovered, but when he would have left her, she murmured a wordless complaint and he resettled heavily atop her.

Speaking low against her neck, he said, "Where'd you learn to fuck like that? Law school?"

"No, here. Tonight."

She felt his smile against neck. Levering himself up, he looked into her face. "That night, after the shooting, and we were talking there in the hallway of police headquarters?"

She nodded.

"This is what I was thinking about," he said, and made a nudging motion.

"You weren't!"

He gave a purely masculine and unrepentant shrug. "You were so buttoned up in your dark suit and blue shirt. Held together so tight. All the time I was trying to make conversation, I was wondering, 'Just how tight she is.' Thinking about it was driving me crazy."

"You hated me."

"I did. Didn't stop me from wanting to fuck you." He rubbed his lips across hers, which had parted in shock. "I also thought it would never happen. Not in a million years."

"A million years or a few hours. I was easy."

He left her and, falling onto his back, he said, "In no way has this been easy, Holly." Raising his head, he looked down the length of his body. "I can't even get naked first."

He remedied that by tugging off his boots and socks, then working off his wet jeans. Before tossing them to the floor, he removed a pistol from the holster clipped to the waistband.

"You told me you weren't armed."

"When I told you that I wasn't. I borrowed this from Joe." He sat the pistol on the nightstand.

"Borrowed?"

"If he misses it, I'll beg forgiveness." He lay down and drew her to him. Now skin to skin for the first time, he passed his hand over her bottom and gave a grunt of satisfaction. "Better."

"Much." She plucked a few strands of his chest hair. "I didn't know this was here."

"Do you mind it?"

In answer she rubbed her cheek against it, then pressed a kiss on the warm skin underneath. "How long had you been inside the house?"

"When Neal and Nugent left? About ten minutes."

"Ten minutes!"

He fondled her breast, asking thoughtfully, "Am I ever going to see these in the light? They feel great. What do they look like?"

"The plan was for you to wait until they'd gone before you came in."

"I was getting soaked. Besides, I wanted to hear what they had to say."

He'd been surprised when she'd stopped the car and abruptly told him to get out. Then she'd outlined her plan, and, as she'd told the detectives, he had initially resisted the idea of her sheltering him overnight. But she had finally made him see reason. Every other place he could go would be watched—he couldn't just wander the streets in the rain, and he needed rest and refueling.

The agreement had been reached about a mile away from her house. He'd had to go that distance on foot while she returned home and confronted the detectives.

"I stopped on the way to make a couple of calls," he told her now, "but got here and let myself in—"

"Remind me to relock that window."

"I got here in time to hear that you're *very* attracted to me."

"I told you I wouldn't lie to the police."

"So it's true then?"

"True." She could tell by his grin that he liked hearing that. "It was Marilyn who put me into mind of hiding in plain sight."

"Please," he groaned. "Don't mention her. I don't want to lose what I've got going here." He captured her hand, sucked her thumb into his mouth, making it good and wet, then dragged it down and pressed it against the crown of his penis. "Work that wicked magic again." He closed his eyes and exhaled deeply as she began a gentle, rotating massage.

In a whisper, she asked, "Who did you call?"

"Hmm?" His hand closed around her breast, but in a comfort-seeking way.

"You said you stopped and made a couple of calls."

"Harry," he mumbled into the pillow.

"What did he say?"

"That feels so good. Don't stop."

She smiled. "I doubt Harry said that. Who was the second call to?"

"Smitty. I've gotta find him and kill him tomorrow."

"Don't. You'd go to prison. They wouldn't let you wear your boots in prison, and I like your boots. They have character. They're well worn, not new and shiny. And you'd probably be made to wear your hair short in prison. It would be a shame to waste all this unruliness." She ran her fingers through the thick strands. "The truth is—and I'm very into telling the truth, you know—there's nothing I dislike about you."

He responded with a soft snore.

———

Chuck Otterman rarely stayed in the fishing shack overnight. It boasted even fewer creature comforts than his trailer at the man camp, although there was a double bed behind a plywood wall, where he occasionally caught a few winks. He never slept more than four or five hours a night, anyway.

After dealing with the nightclub owner, he'd dozed, but had gotten up before dawn. While making coffee, he received a text notifying him that Neal Lester had called the office at the man camp and had impressed on the overseer left in charge that it was urgent he speak to him.

Staring out into the heavy rain as he sipped his coffee, he thought that perhaps he should assuage the detective's anxiety. He used an untraceable cell phone to place the call.

"Hello?"

"Sergeant Lester? Chuck Otterman. Is it too early to call? I understand you've been trying to reach me."

"Where are you, Mr. Otterman?"

"Hell if I know." He lowered his voice as though he didn't want to be overheard. "Some colleagues over here in Louisiana invited me for a fishing weekend. I met up with them in Lake Charles, then we drove for hours. Far as I can tell, we're in the middle of nowhere. It's still dark, and they're already on the water. Thank you for giving me an excuse to beg off."

"What time did you meet them in Lake Charles yesterday?"

"I'm sorry?"

Lester repeated the question.

"Late. After dinnertime. Why?"

"A Prentiss police officer named Pat Connor was killed last night."

He was quiet for a moment, as though taking that in. Then he breathed a sigh. "I understand now why you've been trying to reach me. I met with the man right before I left town."

"At a gentleman's club called Tickled Pink."

"Oh, so you already knew. You must've questioned the owner. Smitty something? He's a cockroach. He scuttled over while I was there to ask if everything was to my liking."

"We want to question him, but so far we've been unable to find him."

Otterman chuckled. "That could be a problem."

"Why do you say that?"

"Because from what I understand, he tries to stay under the law's radar. He's probably as crooked as a dog's hind leg."

"What were you doing in his club with Pat Connor?"

"I often meet with people there."

Lester cleared his throat. "That doesn't seem like your kind of meeting place, Mr. Otterman."

"The oil and gas industry has its opponents, from powerful politicians to crackpots. A goodly number of local businessmen and government officials support our exploration, but they don't want to advertise the fact. They refuse to meet with me in my office at the camp, they certainly don't invite me to theirs, so we meet at that seedy club."

"I'm still not sure I understand."

"It ensures discretion. Anyone in that place can't tell who he's seen there without giving himself away, can he?"

The detective seemed to ponder that. It was a time before he said, "Pat Connor was a cop, not a businessman."

"He had heard—through the police grapevine, I suppose—about me seeing Crawford Hunt with that man Rodriguez."

"How did that relate to Pat Connor?"

"I don't know. He asked to speak with me privately. The only reason I agreed to the meeting was because he told me he'd been on duty in the courthouse on Monday. I thought maybe he had something to contribute or to ask me about that. But when I arrived at the club, he was in no condition to talk about anything. He was already drunk. He rambled. He sweated."

"Sweated?"

"He wasn't in uniform. He was wearing a cowboy hat and kept taking it off to blot his forehead. He was anxious. Paranoid, actually. After about ten minutes, I'd had it. He was wasting my time. I told him to get to the point or get lost. He got lost."

"He left?"

"I thought he was too drunk to drive, and offered to let one of my assistants take him home. He said no thanks. In hindsight, I should have insisted. He shouldn't have been behind the wheel. Was anybody else hurt?"

"He didn't crash his car, Mr. Otterman. He was murdered at home."

"Jesus! When you said he'd been killed, I assumed…Jesus."

"During his paranoid rambling, did he mention having any enemies?"

"No, but apparently he had at least one." He let that resonate before continuing. "Did he have family?"

"He was a bachelor. Lived alone."

Otterman didn't remark on that. He didn't ask if there had been any witnesses or if any evidence had been found at the scene because he wasn't troubled about the crime being traced back to him. Men he used for jobs like this didn't make mistakes. If they did, it was their last one. Case in point: Pat Connor.

After another stretch of silence, Lester said, "I understand you'll be back on Monday."

"Around noon."

"You were one of the last known persons to talk to Connor. Would you come to headquarters so we can get an official statement?"

"Of course." Then, "Forgive me, Sergeant Lester, before you go, I must ask." He rolled the coin across the backs of his fingers. "Do you have any reason to believe that this officer was another casualty of the courthouse incident? I mean, is it possible that he was silenced for something he knew or saw?"

Stiffly Lester replied, "I can't discuss an ongoing investigation."

"Right. Of course."

"I'll see you on Monday, Mr. Otterman. Until then, what's a good number for me to call if I need to contact you?"

"Use the number at the camp. Someone there always knows how to reach me."

He hung up before the detective could say anything more. He caught the coin in his fist and banged it down on the table. "The final nail," he said around a smile. It was now only a matter of time.

———

Crawford came awake with Holly curled beside him, facing him, her face close to his on the pillow, her thigh snug between his. They still lay on top of the duvet, but at some point after he'd fallen asleep, she had pulled a throw over them.

When she did, he had awoken, lifted her thigh over his hip, and slid into her. Being sheathed in her had brought a drowsy erection to a full one. Invitingly, she moved against him, took him deeper. He exerted just enough motion to create an erotic ebb and flow until they came together. Instead of fireworks, it had been as comforting as a warm bath.

He hadn't even opened his eyes. Not a word had been spoken. But it had been intensely intimate, and, beyond feeling good sexually, he had felt an inner contentment that he'd missed during the years of sleeping in an empty bed and waking up alone.

Now, gazing into Holly's face, looking incredibly peaceful and trustful in sleep, he felt a welling of tenderness for her and, with it, a primal surge of ownership. He wanted this woman. He wanted to claim her. He wanted to keep her. He couldn't.

But he was here now.

He pulled back the throw. The daylight limning the window shutters was new and fragile, but he could see well enough, and all the parts of her that he'd imagined or felt in the dark were prettier than he'd envisioned.

Dipping his head to her breast, he gently sucked the delicate pink tip into his mouth. As he tested the texture of it with his tongue, she stirred, sighed his name, and rested her hand on his head.

"I finally get to see you naked in the light."

"And?"

"I wish I'd burned all your clothes while you were asleep."

She laughed softly. "You're not so bad looking, either."

She leaned over him and kissed the center of his chest, his navel. Scooting down, she ran her hands over his thighs and when she found the two scars on his calf marking the entry and exit wounds of the bullet that had passed through, she kissed them and spoke softly of how grateful she was that it hadn't been worse.

"What if you had died that day?" she asked, looking up at him with liquid green eyes. "I'd have never met you."

The emotional catch in her voice touched him deeply. "Come here." He cupped her underarms and pulled her up over him until his mouth could take hers in a ravenous kiss. Gradually, mouths still eating at each other, he rolled her onto her back and stretched her arms above her head.

He kissed his way down the undersides of both arms as his hand reshaped her breasts, then rode the contours of her rib cage down to her abdomen. Her breath stuttered against his lips when he trailed his fingers back and forth across the hollow between her hip bones, then through her pubic hair. It was blond and soft. And beneath it, she was silky and wet.

He sank his fingers into the fluid heat and returned his mouth to her breasts. Noticing a rosy abrasion, he asked, "Is that a whisker burn? You should have told me."

"I didn't care."

"Now?"

"I don't care."

"I'll be gentle."

The merest flick of his tongue elicited a reaction. "Okay?"

"Yes," she gasped.

"Again?"

"Yes."

The carnal exploration of his fingers soon had her writhing sexily, and he knew she was close. He stretched above her and brought them eye to eye. "I want to watch you lose it."

He was stingy with the pressure of his thumb on the outside, drawing out the pleasure, holding off until she released a low keening, and then he curled his fingers forward inside her, creating a gentle squeeze between the two pressure points.

She clamped her lower lip between her teeth. Her back arched as she raised her hips and ground against his hand. Into her ear, he poured a litany of love words, sexy words, dirty words. Finally she coasted down, and her lazy eyes fluttered open.

He laid a soft, tender kiss on her lips. "Beautiful."

"You are." She reached up and pushed her fingers into his hair. "And much sweeter than you let on."

"Me, sweet?"

"Hmm. With your daughter. With me." She outlined the shape of his lips with her fingertip. "You're not so tough."

"Say things like that, you'll ruin my reputation."

"I promise not to give you away if you'll kiss me again."

"Thought you'd never ask." He obliged her, sending his tongue deep into her mouth and savoring the taste he was coming to know, to need.

When they pulled apart, she rocked against his erection. "That's going to leave a bruise on my stomach."

"We can't let that happen, it being such a pretty stomach and all. Any ideas?"

She crooked her finger for him to lower his head and then she whispered what she had in mind. He looked at her in shocked wonder. "Have you been spying on my wet dreams?" He focused on her mouth, on that full lower lip, and when he placed the pad of his thumb in the center of it, she stroked it with her tongue.

In a voice thick with arousal, he said, "I need to shower first."

They showered together, and the soapy navigation they conducted over each other was inquisitive, extensive, and ended with him leaning against the back of the shower, one hand braced on the tile wall and the other on the glass door, hanging on for dear life, praying that he would survive the avid action of her mouth.

She got out first, dried, and wrapped herself in the

familiar robe. "I'll make breakfast." She left for the kitchen.

He toweled off and moved around the bedroom gathering his clothes and putting them on. They were uncomfortably damp, but they would have to do. He was slipping Joe's pistol into the holster when Holly returned, carrying a cup of coffee.

"This will get you—" She stopped when she saw that he was fully dressed except for his windbreaker. "What are you doing?"

"I need to go before it gets any later."

"Go where?"

"I don't know yet."

"You don't have a car."

"That's a problem I've got to fix."

"Crawford!" she exclaimed.

He pulled on his windbreaker. "What?"

"You can't just leave on foot."

"That's how I got here."

"What are you going to do?"

"I told you last night. Stay alive. If I can."

"Get Otterman before he gets you."

"Or Georgia." He hated even voicing the possibility, afraid of making it an omen. "Because if Otterman wants to get to me, he'll eventually go after her. And the surest way to protect her is to remove him from the planet."

"You would kill him?"

He just looked at her, then away, saying, "I can't do anything until I find him."

"When you do?"

"I'll have to wait and see."

With a solid thump, she set the cup of coffee on the dresser. "What are you going to do?" she repeated, enunciating each word.

"Stop asking, Holly," he said with matching testiness. "I won't tell you."

"Is it lawful?"

"Mostly."

Her brow was knitted with worry and rising anger. "You don't trust me?"

"I trust you completely. I trust that you'll always tell the truth. Which is why it's better for me that you don't know everything. About anything. If you have a problem with that—"

"I have a problem with you taking on Otterman by yourself."

"That's the way I operate."

"Which is the height of arrogance and conceit."

"Yeah, well, think what you want about my ego. I know why I'm doing this, and I've gotta get at it."

He moved toward the window, but she stepped in front of him. "If you break the law, you'll destroy any chance you have of getting Georgia."

"Your deal with Joe destroyed any chance I had."

"That's behind this morning-after mad dash? You're angry?"

"No, I'm not angry." But his near shout sounded angry, so he lowered his voice to a more controlled volume. "Could I fuck you like I did if I was angry?"

"Last night you said you hated me and still wanted to."

"But I wouldn't want to wake up with you. Yeah, the sex was great. But I liked waking up next to you almost as much. If circumstances were different—"

"What circumstances, Crawford?"

"Lots of circumstances."

"Specifically. Otterman?"

"That's the most immediate circumstance."

"I agree, so why not call Neal Lester? I'll own up to sheltering you. Talk to him, reason with him lawman to lawman. Together, playing by the book, you'll go after Otterman."

"Okay, say we luck out and get him behind bars by nightfall. He signs a full confession of all his evil deeds. Then what? *Our* problems will still be there."

"Back to those unspecified circumstances."

"All right, I'll name you one. You crossed a line with me." He motioned toward the bed. "Your job, your career, the thing you hold most dear, wouldn't be in jeopardy if not for me."

"No one knows about us."

"Yet. But secrets like this have a way, Holly. You're not so naive as to think we can keep a lid on it." By her silence, he knew she agreed. "Say the secret that we've slept together remains intact, and you lose the election anyway, we'll always wonder if it was because of our association. I couldn't live with costing you the judgeship. Could *you*?" He shook his head. "There are some things you and I just can't get around."

"The biggest one being that I stand in the way of you getting Georgia."

He spread his hands as though to say, *See?* "We're each other's worst enemy."

"You weren't concerned about any of this last night."

"I was. I just wanted you too bad to let the issues stop me." Before she could offer a comeback, he said softly, "They didn't stop you, either."

The fight went out of her. "True. Because I had begun to think, hope, we could overcome these obstacles."

"Some, maybe. Not all."

She looked deeply into his eyes and said quietly, "Beth?"

That hit him unexpectedly, and his heart bumped, then began to beat erratically. "What about her?"

"You tell me." Looking wounded, she glanced down at the tousled bed. "Was she in there with us?"

"No. *No*." He combed back his hair with his fingers and drew in a ragged breath. "Christ, don't think that. It's not that at all."

"Is that the truth?"

"Yes. I swear it."

With alarming intuition, barely audibly, she said, "Just not the whole truth."

No. Not the whole truth. The whole truth would doom him.

He came toward her slowly and placed his hands on her shoulders, turned her and gave a gentle push, so she landed facedown on the bed.

"Crawford?"

"Shh. Listen."

Crouching over her, he ran his hands up the backs of her thighs, over her bottom, along her back, his thumbs tracing the corrugation of her spine. Then covering her hands with his, he interlocked their fingers and nuzzled her hair, which was sweet smelling and still damp from their shower.

"Holly, if I could, I'd be falling crazy in love with you. I'd have you in my life, my house, my bed. My heart." When she moved as though trying to turn over, he pressed her down more firmly. "*If* I could. But I can't."

Gradually, he let go of her hands, eased up, and pushed himself off the bed. "Tell them I came in through your bedroom window, overpowered you, and stole your car. It's all true."

Chapter 30

———◦———

He'd filched Holly's car keys from the pocket of her jeans, which were still crumpled on the floor beside the bed. He remembered her telling him how she'd driven her car across her backyard, past the main house, and onto the next street without her guards out front being any the wiser.

Before Holly would have had a chance to raise the alarm, he was out the elderly lady's driveway and winding his way through town, avoiding the thoroughfares. Sooner or later, he would be caught.

But later, he hoped.

As he drove, he called Joe Gilroy's cell number. Grace answered. "Where's Joe?" he asked.

"In the shower. He told me to listen for the phone."

"Everything okay?"

"Neither of us has slept much, but we're all right."

"How's Georgia?"

"Still asleep. She got upset last night, wondering why we're here. She kept asking if you'd know where to find us."

He had to talk around the lump that formed in his throat. "If she asks again, tell her I'll always be able to find her."

"Do you want me to wake her up so you can tell her that yourself?"

He was tempted, but it would be selfish of him. Hearing her voice would make him feel better, but it would increase Georgia's homesickness and add to her anxiety over the unusual situation.

"Thanks for offering," he told Grace, meaning it. "I trust you to keep her reassured."

When she expressed concern for him, he hedged, mumbling that he was fine. "I hope all this will be over soon and you can come home. I can't thank you enough for doing this."

"Be safe, Crawford."

"You too." He clicked off before she asked questions he wouldn't know how to answer.

But Smitty might.

He hadn't responded to the voice mail message Crawford had left last night, which was a dead give-away that he knew something he didn't want to share. But before Crawford could wrangle information from him, he had to find him.

Strip clubs looked desolate in the early hours of the morning, particularly a dreary, rainy morning like this one. He started with Smitty's establishment that was closest to town, but found the place dark and uninviting without its lurid flashing neon. The parking lot was empty. At Tickled Pink, the same. And the next one he checked was also deserted.

The fourth he'd never been to before. It was even more disreputable looking than Smitty's other clubs. This was a place for down-and-outers who had hit rock bottom. Its opaque windows, low roofline, and dirt parking lot, now dotted with puddles of muddy water, weren't inducements for fun-seeking people.

Crawford drove around to the rear of the building,

which was situated right on the edge of the forest. The trees and underbrush seemed to be encroaching on the squat structure with the intention of eventually overtaking it, perhaps to put it out of its misery.

Near the back door was an ugly gray car. Crawford rolled Holly's car to a stop, got out, and looked inside the other vehicle. A lot of trash, stained fabric upholstery, but nothing else.

He slid Joe's pistol from his holster. He'd already checked the cylinder, knew that there was a .38 bullet in each of the five chambers. Stealthily, he walked to the metal door. The doorknob was loosely fitted and had a standard lock. Crawford didn't even have to try hard to pop it using a credit card.

The door opened out. He pulled it toward him, creating a gap only wide enough to slip through, then closed it quickly, realizing that his silhouette made a large target even against meager, watery daylight.

Inside, the air was as dank as that of a locker room and smelled of booze and stale cigarette smoke. The darkness was absolute, forcing him to give his eyes time to adjust. He stood perfectly still and listened. He could hear the rain dripping off the eaves outside. Other than that, nothing.

"Smitty?"

His voice was absorbed by the darkness as though the building had swallowed it. Louder, he called the name again, without response. Turning on his cell phone was a risk he had to take. Without a light, he couldn't see his way any farther into the building.

The glow of the screen provided just enough light for him to make out his immediate surroundings. Dead ahead, liquor crates were stacked against a concrete block wall. An industrial mop bucket occupied a corner to his left. The mop was dry and covered in cobwebs.

To his right was a narrow passageway. He started down it.

The first door he came to was ajar. Just as he drew even with it, the cell phone's screen blinked off. Heart thumping, he waited in the stygian darkness, and when nothing happened, he turned the phone back on and gave the door a push with the short barrel of the .38.

His was the only image reflected in the mirror above the dressing table that ran the width of the room. He backed out and moved along the hall past a second door that opened into a phone booth–size restroom with a disgusting toilet and a stained sink.

The third door belonged to an office that resembled the others in which he had ambushed Smitty over the course of their association. The cramped room had a littered desk, beat-up file cabinets, overflowing trash cans, and walls papered with pornographic pictures.

And Smitty was there. On the floor.

Crawford hissed, "Son of a bitch!"

———

It was a familiar scene—she in her living room being questioned by Neal Lester and Matt Nugent. Only a few hours after she'd seen them off and joined Crawford in her bedroom, the detectives were back, and Crawford's whereabouts was once again the subject under discussion.

Neal asked, "You have no idea where he was going?"

"You've asked me that twice already," she replied. "If I knew where he was going, I would have told you when I called."

She had alerted him as soon as she reached her back

door and confirmed that her car was missing. "I caught a glimpse of taillights as he turned left out of the driveway of the main house. That's all I know."

"You didn't know he planned to take your car?"

"Only moments before he left. He must've gotten the keys earlier from the pocket of my jeans."

"How'd he manage that without you knowing?"

She looked at Nugent. "I wasn't wearing them."

"Oh."

It felt like betrayal, informing on Crawford to the police, to Neal especially. But he had to be found, stopped, before—

She didn't allow herself to think beyond that, to conjecture what might happen to him, or what he might do to Otterman. She vacillated between being furious at Crawford and fearing for his life. He would despise her for calling the dogs on him, but she'd rather have him alive and hating her forever than dead.

The two detectives were watching her as though expecting her to produce something more substantive. "Why aren't you out looking for him?" Frustrated by their inactivity, she left her chair, a hint for them to get going. "He's driving my car. Even if you don't know the tag number he swapped for mine, you know the make and model."

"I've put out an APB," Neal said. "But we wouldn't be in this situation if you'd told us last night that Crawford was here."

"You didn't ask me if he was here. I answered all of your questions truthfully."

"That's whitewashing, judge. Truth withheld is a lie. You deliberately misguided us."

"Because you wanted to detain him when you should have been following other leads, such as the nightclub video on Crawford's phone. He left it for you, practically a signpost pointing to Chuck Otterman for the murder of that policeman."

"We're trying to follow up on that video by tracking down a guy named Del Ray Smith."

Smitty, Crawford had called him, but she didn't let on that she knew that.

Neal yielded the floor to Nugent, who looked eager to be helpful. "He's the owner of the club where Connor and Otterman met. I went to the place last night and was told by an employee that Smith had left around ten o'clock. Nobody knew where he was going, but he didn't come back before closing. We've been trying to track him down."

"Without success," Neal said.

"Did you try the club this morning?" she asked.

"Locked up tight. He's not at his apartment. Car's gone, too. We've had a deputy watching the place."

Smitty must have left Tickled Pink shortly after she and Crawford had. But rather than dwell on him, she wanted to pound home the importance of Otterman. "Why would Pat Connor have been meeting with Chuck Otterman?"

"Mr. Otterman explained that."

Disbelieving her ears, Holly gaped at Neal. "You've talked to him?"

"Before dawn this morning. He had checked in with his foreman, who told him I'd been trying to reach him. He called me."

"He's still conveniently out of town?"

"Fishing somewhere in Louisiana. He couldn't be more specific. Friends drove him. He said he didn't know exactly where he was."

"He didn't know?" she exclaimed. "A man with his managerial personality didn't know where he was? You actually believe that, Sergeant Lester?"

Stung by her incredulous tone, he took a defensive stance. "He owned up to the meeting with Connor even before I asked him about it. He said they met at Connor's request. Otterman thought it might have something to do with the courthouse shooting. But he said that when they met, Connor was incoherent. Paranoid and anxious."

Thoughtfully, he added, "Everybody with a badge is taking Connor's murder—his execution—hard. First Chet. Days later Pat Connor. Even if the evidence bears out that he was the courthouse shooter, it's like there's a contaminant seeping through the whole law enforcement family."

"Crawford isn't the contaminant," she said.

Neal slid his gaze toward the hallway that led to the bedroom, but before he could speak aloud what his arch expression implied, her cell phone rang. She snatched it up. "Hello?"

"Judge Spencer? Harry Longbow."

She could have melted with relief. She mouthed his name to Lester and Nugent. "Have you heard from Crawford?"

"Not since last night. That's why I'm calling you. I thought maybe you two…He's not with you?"

Spirits sinking again, she explained the situation.

Having been brought up to speed, Harry gave a long sigh. "Lester and Nugent are on it?"

"They're still here with me, but they've put out an APB."

"And Crawford left your place at dawn?"

"Soon after."

"Hell bent on chasing down Otterman."

"Yes," she said with desperation. "He was dead set on going alone. I'm afraid for him."

"He can take care of himself. But I'd feel a lot better

if he had more reliable backup. You say Lester has already put out an APB for Otterman?"

"For Crawford."

"*Crawford?*" He muttered something she couldn't decipher, but his tone was disdainful. "It's Otterman he should be after."

"I agree completely. But Sergeant Lester spoke to Otterman this morning, and he had an explanation for that meeting at the nightclub." She related it, but the veteran Texas Ranger was no more persuaded of Otterman's innocence than she had been.

Harry said, "Smooth talker, but I ain't buying it. We don't have proof yet, but bits and pieces are starting to add up."

"To what?"

"Halcon. Crawford needs to know, like now. I've been calling this new number he gave me, but he's not picking up."

She sat on the edge of the chair she had recently vacated and rubbed her forehead. "Why wouldn't he answer?"

"Could be any number of reasons."

She wasn't deceived by his reassurance. He was as worried as she.

"But listen," he said, "if you talk to him before I do, tell him to get back to me or Sessions right away."

"Yes, of course. I will."

"And, just in case…I don't want to alarm you or anything, judge, but if Otterman thinks there's something between you and Crawford, you could be in danger, too."

"I'll take care."

"Do."

When she disconnected, Neal said, "Well? What did he say?"

She looked at him with reproach. "That he would feel a lot better if Crawford had more reliable backup."

"You're ruining my life!"

"Put the gun down, Smitty."

"I want to kill you."

"I want to kill you, too." Crawford reached behind him and groped for the light switch, flipping it on. Smitty was hunkered down beneath the desk, aiming a pistol at Crawford's midsection.

Calmly, Crawford thumbed back the hammer of Joe's revolver. "If I kill you, I'll be eradicating a moral abscess, and I've got law and order on my side. Somebody will probably erect a statue of me in the town square. If you kill me, you get the needle for taking out a law enforcement officer.

"That is if you even make it to death row," he went on conversationally, "which I doubt you would. Texas Rangers don't take kindly to fellow Rangers getting killed by anybody, but pimps and bootleggers really piss them off. Some of those boys wouldn't think twice about intercepting you on your way to trial, squashing you under their boots as you tried to 'escape,' and scraping you off like so much dog shit. It would save the state the cost of a syringe."

Smitty actually sobbed.

"For the last time, put the gun down."

His grip on it hadn't been all that firm or steady. When he let go of the pistol, it clattered to the floor. Crawford walked over and kicked it out of reach, then bent down and grabbed a handful of Smitty's shirt. He hauled him from beneath the desk and onto his feet, then shoved him backward into a chair.

"Your life is nothing to brag about, Smitty. How am I ruining it?"

"Pour me a gin."

"Not likely."

"Please. I'm shaking here."

He was. Like a leaf in a high wind. Even for Smitty, he looked a wreck. His comb-over was flipped the wrong direction, his clothes disheveled. However he'd passed the night, indications were that it had been long and tortuous.

Crawford took mercy, not because he felt sorry for him, but because he had no time to waste, and Smitty could backpedal, whine, and drag this out forever.

A Styrofoam cup on the desk contained an inch of coffee dregs. He emptied it onto the floor, then filled it with cheap gin from the bottle sitting on top of the file cabinet and handed it over. Smitty took a gulp. Before he could take another, Crawford reclaimed the cup.

"Please," Smitty pleaded. "I need that."

"I need answers. Why haven't you called me back?"

"I've been busy."

"You don't get another drink until you tell me something. Why were you hiding in here in the dark, with a loaded pistol, looking scared as a rabbit?"

Nothing.

"Were you hiding from me?"

"No."

"From who then?"

"Isn't that your phone ringing?"

"I'll get it later. You were supposed to be giving me stuff on Otterman."

"I forgot."

"Forgot?"

"I've had other things to attend to. I don't drop everything for you, you know. Oh, wait," he said, snapping his fingers. "I do. I did! Just last night, I dropped every-thing to let you know that your daddy was—"

"Shooting video."

"Huh? Video? That's against club rules."

"He shot video of a meeting between Chuck Otter-man and a cop—now a deceased cop." He noted that Smitty didn't register surprise. "Huh. I see you knew that already."

"So?" He wiggled in his seat, corrected the direction of his comb-over, and looked longingly at the cup of gin. "A cop getting whacked. Can't remember where I heard about it. There goes your phone again. You'd better get it. Must be important."

Crawford let it ring. "When I came to pick up Conrad last night, you failed to mention that Otterman had been in Tickled Pink all afternoon meeting with people, one of them the now dead police officer."

Smitty squirmed in his chair.

"You've got five seconds, Smitty."

"To do what?" he asked, his voice going shrill.

"To tell me what you know about Chuck Otterman."

"I don't know nothing!"

"Five."

"I swear. I…I see him talking to all kinds of people. I told you that already."

"Four."

He blubbered, "He'll kill me."

"That's why you were hiding under your desk? You're on Otterman's hit list?"

"No! I…I didn't say that."

"Why are you afraid of Otterman?"

"When I said he'd kill me, I was joking!"

"Three."

"I need another hit."

Crawford passed him the cup. He kept gulping for as

long as Crawford allowed before taking it back. "Why were you hiding in fear of Otterman?"

Smitty actually sobbed again. "He asked me about you."

Crawford kept his expression neutral. "Me?"

"Did I stutter?"

"When did he ask you about me?"

"Last night."

"Where?"

Smitty clammed up and shook his head.

Crawford tabled that question for the time being. "What did you tell him about me?"

"I sorta fudged."

"You lied."

Smitty heaved a sigh of confession. "He asked if I knew you. I pretended not to, but then—"

"You spilled your guts, because at heart, you're a chickenshit. We both know that, so tell me what you told him."

"Nothing important. I swear. He asked if I had, you know, dealings with you. I told him no. Told him that I hated you. Which is the gospel truth," he added with a glower.

"What else did he want to know?"

"That was it."

"Smitty."

"Crawford, let it go," he pleaded. "You do not mess with this guy."

"You don't mess with me, either. What else did you tell him?"

"Can I have a drink?"

"Depends."

Smitty hesitated, then said, "He wanted to know what you were doing at the club last night. Who the woman was. Like that."

"You told him it was Holly Spencer?"

"I was afraid they were going to feed me to the alligators. One piece at a time."

Crawford thought about that. "Otterman's supposedly on a fishing weekend. Is he in Louisiana? Is that where your meeting with him took place?"

"Aren't you listening? If I help you, he'll kill me!" he screeched. "Five, four, three, two. You can count down from a thousand, I don't care. I'm not telling you anything else."

Crawford eased back, shrugged. "Okay. Don't tell me anything else. I'll put you away for indecency with a child, compelling prostitution of a child, statutory rape. If it lasted more than thirty days, that's continual sexual abuse of a child. Let's see, am I leaving out anything? Oh." He gestured toward the wall of dirty pictures. "If you took pictures of her, that's—"

"She was sixteen!"

"A minor. Dancing naked, giving lap dances?" Crawford *tsk*ed. "Bad business, Smitty. A new low for you."

"She lied at her audition. Soon as I found out her real age, I fired her."

"How many times did you bang her?"

"I didn't!"

Crawford just looked at him.

Then with sullen defiance, Smitty grumbled, "You don't even know for sure there was a girl. It was a lucky guess."

"An educated guess."

"Where's your proof?"

"I'll shut you down while I search for some," Crawford said. "But I'm busy these days. It might take a good long while to collect evidence, track down the child."

"Child, my ass."

"I'll eventually find her, and, all that time, you'll be

languishing in the Prentiss County jail, shuffling around in house shoes, and trying to stay on the good side of the bubbas. Many of whom have baby sisters."

Stubbornly Smitty shook his head. "Threaten all you want. I'm not telling you anything more about Otterman, especially not where he's at."

Crawford's phone rang again. This time he answered. "Where you been?"

It was Harry. "You have something on Otterman?"

"A thing that bothers us."

"What?"

"He left a lucrative gig in the Panhandle to sign on with the outfit he works for now. Took a big pay cut."

"When did he make that move?"

"He was back and forth for a few months. Made the transfer permanent about the time Halcon went down. Which makes Sessions and me nervous."

It made Crawford nervous, too. In fact, it made him queasy. "The outfit is headquartered in Houston, right?"

"Right. Sessions is working a hunch," Harry said. "What sorta scares us? If this is revenge on you for something relating to Halcon, he's taken his sweet time. Which tells me, A, he's a planner. B, he's patient. And C—"

"He's ready to end it."

"In light of this week's goings-on? Looks like. Have you found out where he is?"

"Putting the squeeze on a weasel. Let me get back to you."

"Hold on," Harry said. "There's more."

"Shit."

"Yeah, I haven't even got to the good parts. After you stole the judge's car, she notified Neal Lester." He let that settle, and when Crawford didn't respond, he said,

"I know because I called her looking for you. Lester and his sidekick were at her house."

"Was she all right?"

"Shook up. She only ratted 'cause she's scared you'll get hurt, or killed, or do something crazy. And the worst of it, Lester's still gung-ho to pin all this on you."

"He can't be that stupid. That video of Connor and Otterman should have changed his mind."

"Uh, about that. Otterman trumped you."

Harry recounted the predawn conversation that Neal had had with Otterman. "Admitted to the meeting, played dumb about how Connor died."

Crawford swore. "Otterman's playing Neal like a fiddle."

"And it's working. He's issued an APB for you and the judge's car."

"Any more good news, Harry?"

"Pretty much it for now."

"Well, Neal's preoccupation with me is good for something. It's keeping a police presence around Holly."

"I'm glad of that, too. Oh, Sessions just rushed in, looking excited, and I don't reckon it's over wallpaper. Carry on with your weasel. I'll call you back. When I do, answer your damn phone." Then Harry was gone.

As Crawford clicked off, Smitty asked, "Who was that?"

"Another Texas Ranger. He advised me to stop screwing around, to go ahead and kill you for assaulting me with that pawnshop pistol. Good riddance, he said."

"I didn't assault—"

"I don't want to kill you, Smitty. I'd rather get you sent up for all those first-degree felonies." Crawford leaned down over him. "But because I'm such a nice guy, maybe I could persuade the DA to go light on you, seeing as how she sought employment and lied at her audition. But I'll do this only if you tell me where this place is in Louisiana."

"I never said there was a place in Louisiana." Smitty reached for the cup of gin.

Crawford backhanded it to the floor. Bending down closer, he said, "You're actually gonna continue holding out on me when I can set you up on play dates with every perv in Huntsville for the next ninety-nine years?"

Smitty whimpered. "Look, Crawford, swear to God that all I did was pick up cash and drop it off."

Crawford hadn't even asked Smitty if he had business with Otterman. The mention of cash was a slip of the tongue that he tucked away for future reference. "Where is he?"

"First, I want to get something in writing about…about the underage girl thing."

"First, you'll get my boot up your ass. Where is Otterman? Name the town."

"There isn't a town."

"*Nearest* town."

"She looked twenty-two. Twenty-five! One look at her, no jury would convict me."

"Smitty."

"I need a guarantee."

"Scout's honor."

"Not good enough."

"Scout's honor that when I *do* find Otterman, which I will eventually, I'll make sure he knows that you were the one who pointed me in his direction."

Smitty groaned and clutched his crotch like he had to pee. "Prentiss."

"What?"

"Prentiss. That's the nearest town."

"He's not in Louisiana?"

Miserably, Smitty shook his head. "It's this side of the state line. Just barely."

"But in Texas?"

Smitty wiped his runny nose on his sleeve as he nodded.

Crawford grinned. "Perfect."

Chapter 31

Crawford wanted to talk to Holly, but he called Neal instead, who answered with a rude "Who's this?"

"You need to get an arrest warrant for Chuck Otterman, and I don't care who you have to blow to get it."

"For what?"

"Start with conspiracy to murder, then fill in the blank. Pat Connor would be the most expeditious. I've got someone who'll turn state's witness against Otterman if we strike the right deal."

"Del Ray Smith?" Neal asked, scoffing. "Way ahead of you, Crawford."

Shit!

"Sheriff's deputies found him duct-taped to a chair in the office of one of his clubs. He accused you of police brutality and stealing his car, which appears to be the truth, since Judge Spencer's had been dumped there, and his was gone. They've been grilling him good, but he refuses to tell the deputies why you strong-armed him and where you went when you left."

Smitty would give it up. He always did. Crawford's time just got shorter to find Otterman before the cavalry was dispatched.

He said, "Stop screwing around with Smitty. You've got the video of Otterman and Connor."

"Which is evidence of nothing except a conversation, and no ADA is going to hang their ambition on that."

"It's a start. It's enough to bring him in, put him on the spot, make him explain that meeting."

"He already has. I questioned him about it early this morning."

"Oh, I heard all about your little chat. Civic duty Chuck came clean before you even asked. Didn't that smack of manipulation, Neal?"

"This call smacks of manipulation."

Mentally cursing, Crawford tried to think of a way to shake him. Then he remembered Smitty's admission of being a cash courier. "Otterman's dirty. Into more than drilling for gas."

"Like what?"

"I don't know yet."

Neal gave a skeptical grunt. "Try harder, Crawford."

"What's that mean?"

"According to Judge Spencer, your buddies in Houston are close to linking Otterman to Halcon. Maybe it's not Otterman who's dirty. Maybe it's you."

"Otterman might think so."

"Why would he?"

"I don't know that, either."

"Or you're not telling me."

Crawford came back angrily, "I'll tell you this much. From the courtroom shooting forward, this has been about me. Otterman and me. But it started with him, because I'd never laid eyes on the man until he sauntered in that day. He sought me out, not the other way around. And even though you poo-poo it because you don't want to believe it, I think there's a lot more to him than his hale-fellow-well-met bullshit act.

"And if you hadn't wasted so much goddamn time wanting to believe that I was the perp, we'd know what he's about, we'd know what he had on Pat Connor that cost him his life, and we'd have this son of a bitch behind bars.

"Your past mistakes are history, Neal, but what holds for your *future* is that if any harm comes to my little girl or to Holly Spencer, I'll ruin your lofty career plans by telling everybody how bad you fucked up because of the juvenile grudge you bear me. Then I'll rip your head off your shoulders. If I'm dead, 'my buddies in Houston' will likely do it for me."

Neal didn't say anything, but Crawford sensed him fuming.

He pressed on. "Georgia's out of Otterman's reach, but keep people on Holly. In *sight* of her at all times. And just so everything's neat and tidy when I catch up to Otterman, get that goddamn warrant."

"While you're doing what?"

"While I go fishing."

He clicked off and tossed the cell phone into the passenger seat of Smitty's car, in which also lay Smitty's nine-millimeter. Crawford was grateful for the additional handgun, but it and Joe's revolver were all he had. Depending on what he found when he reached his destination, that might prove to be insufficient firepower. Otterman had at least two of his heavies with him. *I was afraid they were going to feed me to the alligators*, Smitty had said. They. Probably Frick and Frack.

Fortified with a couple more shots of gin, and threatened with being taped to a chair, Smitty had drawn Crawford a crude map. "After three or four miles on that state road, you'll come to a sign advertising taxidermy. It's got an armadillo on it. Hook a left. If you miss that sign, you're good and screwed, because you'll never see the turnoff without it. Past that point, if the roads have names or numbers, I don't know them."

Once he got the map, he'd taped Smitty to the chair anyway, knowing that sooner or later someone would come looking to question him about Pat Connor's being in Tickled Pink hours before he was murdered.

Crawford was lucky to have gotten away before they'd arrived, and wished it had taken a little longer for Smitty to be found. The best he could hope for now was that Smitty would hold out on the deputies who were questioning him. This time, his whining and bargaining could buy Crawford valuable time.

Smitty had warned that he was sending him into the boondocks, and at least about that he wasn't lying. Crawford had gone five miles on the state road before he spotted the landmark taxidermy sign marking the turnoff. It led to seemingly nowhere.

A swampy wilderness stretched endlessly from both sides of the narrow road. The terrain was waterlogged, overgrown with vines, forested by trees struggling against suffocation from the Spanish moss that hung from their branches in large clumps. Cypresses were rooted into the marsh by knobby knees that poked up out of the viscous surface.

The winding road barely qualified as such, and intersected with dozens of others that looked similarly difficult to drive on. Without the map, Crawford could have driven for days, going in circles, having to backtrack. Either Smitty deserved credit for his powers of recall, or he deserved to die for sending Crawford on a wild goose chase.

He'd soon know which.

Calculating that he was about a mile away from the spot marked with a large dot on Smitty's map, he pulled the car off the road, far enough for the wild shrubbery to provide some concealment, but not so far that it would get stuck in the spongy ground. He might have to leave in a hurry.

He put Smitty's pistol in the holster at his back but kept Joe's in hand as he set out on foot.

Smitty had said the place was inside the state line. Crawford hadn't seen any indication that he'd crossed over into the neighboring state. If this ended with an exchange of gunfire, it would be a lot more convenient if his badge made him official.

But, at this point, even an important detail like jurisdiction wasn't going to stop him. He was determined to reach his self-proclaimed enemy ahead of everyone else because this was a personal fight, instigated by Otterman. Crawford feared learning what had inspired the man's hatred, but he had to be the first to know.

Even if it killed him, he had to know.

The road was an ochre-colored mire. Crawford stayed off it to avoid exposure and imprints of his boots, but slogging through the bog and underbrush was a workout that soon had his clothes drenched with sweat. It had stopped raining, but the low ceiling of gray clouds threatened to unleash a downpour into air already saturated with moisture. Beyond an occasional splash, a rustle, a desultory birdcall, the swamp was noiseless and oppressive. Yet it teemed with unseen and menacing life forms.

He had about reached the conclusion that he would have to go back and kill Smitty after all, when a rusty tin roof came into view. He crouched and waited, fearing that his progress might have been noticed and monitored, but after five minutes, he continued on, moving closer to get a better look.

Smitty had described the place as "nearly falling down." Indeed the weather-beaten frame structure looked on the verge of toppling off its rotting pilings into the sluggish creek.

If it had collapsed, it would have taken Chuck Otterman with it.

He was sitting in a ladder-back chair on the porch beneath a deep overhang. The railing on which he'd propped his feet was listing, and only about half its spindles were upright, but he looked as arrogant as a king on a gilded throne, angled back, puffing smoke rings that held their perfect shape until they were absorbed by the thick air.

Crawford was close enough to smell the cigar.

The two men he recognized from Conrad's video were occupying opposite corners of the dwelling. One was keeping an eye on the creek side as he pared his fingernails with a knife. The other was doing nothing except leaning against the exterior wall, idly picking at his sideburn while watching the road. Within his reach was a shotgun propped up against the wall.

Otterman finished his cigar, then lowered his feet from the railing and stood up. He stretched and spoke to the man watching the creek, although Crawford was too far away to catch what he said. He did hear the squeak of the screen door hinges when Otterman pulled it open and disappeared inside. It slapped closed behind him. His sentinels remained in place.

Crawford backed away, careful not to create any more of a stir than necessary.

He didn't breathe easily until he'd covered at least a hundred yards. By the time he got back to Smitty's car, he was dripping sweat.

But rather than feeling depleted, he was energized. Adrenaline was like rocket fuel pumping through him. The hell of it was, he had to keep that rush under control until dark. It was said that he was impulsive and reckless. That could be justifiably argued. But he wasn't suicidal.

He thought about summoning Harry and Sessions. He knew they'd waste no time joining him, but he didn't want to drag them into a showdown where jurisdiction was uncertain. He also wanted to know if the hunch that Sessions had been following had panned out, but if he called about that, they would pressure him to tell them where he was and what he planned.

Then, too, he dreaded hearing where Sessions's hunch might have led.

He considered calling Neal to ask about the arrest warrant, but he was going to make his move on Otterman with or without it. If later he had to defend his actions, he could say truthfully that he'd acted on the assumption that a warrant had been issued, based on his last conversation with the lead investigator.

He considered changing his mind about speaking to Georgia. He longed to hear her voice. She would tell him she loved him, and he would know that she spoke the unqualified truth. There were no filters on or conditions to her love. He would like to hear the words from her again. But if he called, she might ask him for promises. He wouldn't make promises to her he might be unable to keep.

He wished he could roll back the clock and relive those first few minutes when he woke up feeling Holly's breath on his face, her body warm and soft against his. He would welcome a do-over of those brief moments of contentment. *I wish I still had it to look forward to,* she had said of their quickie couch sex. He wondered if she felt that way now.

God knew she shouldn't. There were so many things to apologize for, he wouldn't know where to start. If not for him, the shooting would never have happened.

Her life would never have been endangered, her career would be on solid footing. Did the minutes of bliss they'd shared make up for the crap he'd left her to deal with? Only she could answer that, and he couldn't possibly blame her if the answer was *no*.

Deciding against making any of those calls, he removed the battery from the burner phone and settled in to wait for darkness.

After the two detectives left Holly's house, she fretfully wandered from room to room as though looking for direction or insight into what she should do. Her car was found and returned to her, but her feelings of uselessness and fear for Crawford's safety increased the longer he remained unaccounted for.

At noon, she switched on her television, wondering what was being reported on the news. The lead story was Pat Connor's murder. Video shot outside his residence showed CSU personnel carrying out labeled bags.

"This is the second Prentiss law officer to be killed this week," the reporter said solemnly. "Although the two crimes are unrelated, the grieving among—"

"Unrelated?" Her angry shout echoed through the cottage.

She hurriedly dressed for the office and drove to the courthouse, her escorts following closely in their squad car. She eschewed the slow elevator and took the atrium stairs, the officers tripping along behind her.

Mrs. Briggs was startled by her sudden entrance and even more startled by her request. "Call the TV station in Tyler. Ask to speak to the reporter who broke the story about Chuck Otterman, and when you get him, tell him that if he'd like an exclusive interview with me to be here in an hour." She paused, then said, "And see if I can possibly speak to the governor."

"When?"

"Now."

She went into her private office and paced until her desk phone rang. "Governor Hutchins is on the line," Mrs. Briggs told her.

Holly took a deep breath and pressed the lighted button. "Governor Hutchins, I know you've just returned from the conference. Thank you for taking my call."

He conveyed his sadness over the terrible event that had taken place in her court and asked after her well-being. When she had assured him that she was fine, he reluctantly mentioned the "unpleasant aftermath."

"That's why I'm calling, governor. I'm about to grant a TV interview, which no doubt will have a ripple effect that could reach as far as your desk. I wanted you to know about it in advance."

She talked for five minutes without interruption. When she finished, he said, "Essentially, what you're saying is that the investigators are barking up the wrong tree."

"Yes, sir. When this interview airs, my judgment will be brought into question. I've already been accused of being too personally involved with Ranger Hunt."

"Is that the case?"

"There is a strong emotional pull, yes." She gave him time to process that and make of it what he would. "But it hasn't blinded me, sir. What's become perfectly clear is that an equally powerful prejudice *against* Ranger Hunt is hampering the investigation. I fear this personality clash is preventing justice from being done for the murder of Chet Barker and now Officer Connor. No matter what the repercussions might be to me and my career, I'm compelled to speak up about it."

During the ensuing silence, Holly held her breath. Finally, he said, "Be careful how you phrase it."

The TV crew arrived within forty-five minutes of Mrs. Briggs's call, and twenty minutes after that, the reporter had his exclusive. Ten minutes after the crew had gathered up their gear and left her chambers, Neal Lester barged into her inner office, looking ready to explode.

"I'm sorry, judge. He—"

"It's all right, Mrs. Briggs."

Her assistant backed out, but left the door open.

Neal said, "You could have given me fair warning. A news team arrived downstairs asking me for a follow-up sound bite to your interview."

"That sounds only fair. Why are you upset?"

"Why'd you offer them an interview in the first place?"

"Because Greg Sanders has been suggesting that 'in light of a chain of tragic events all relating to me,' I should do the public a favor, withdraw my name from the ballot, and give him a free pass to the bench. I wanted people to know that I have no intention of doing that."

"I don't care about you and your election. What did you say about Chuck Otterman?"

"The reporter asked if I thought he had anything to do with the courtroom shooting death of Chet Barker. I told him that since it was an active investigation, I couldn't comment, then referred him to you for statements regarding Monday's tragedy as well as last night's murder of Officer Connor."

"Effectively linking the two incidents, and linking both to Otterman." His shout rattled the chandelier.

She didn't offer a comeback.

"Did the reporter ask you why your *boyfriend* skipped out before he could be questioned about Connor's murder?"

It was a struggle, but she kept her temper under control. "He asked if Crawford Hunt was a person of interest in Connor's murder. I said that I hadn't heard that term applied to him. Which I haven't."

"Not yet. But it's a fact that he eluded the authorities with your help. It stretches credulity that he over-powered you and stole your car."

"That's what happened."

"Tell me where he is."

"I don't know."

"Don't insult my intelligence."

"I'm beginning to doubt your intelligence, detective."

"Where is he?"

"I don't know!"

Suddenly behind him, the two familiar Texas Rangers appeared. Harry Longbow politely excused himself to Mrs. Briggs. "We need a word with the judge."

He and Sessions edged past Neal into her inner office. Harry then shoved the detective back through the door and slammed it in his face. She knew from their grave expressions that something was terribly wrong. Weakly, she said, "Crawford?"

"What you just said, is it true? You don't know where he is?"

"I swear I don't."

"You haven't heard from him all day?"

"Not since dawn. I'm desperate to talk to him."

"Yeah, us too."

"You told me he gave you a new phone number."

"We've been calling it for hours. Keep getting noth-ing. Tried to locate it using triangulation. Either he's not close enough to a cell tower for that to work, or he's taken the battery out, or both. Anyhow, we decided to drive on up here, thinking maybe he's in trouble and needs our help."

"Judge," Sessions said, speaking for the first time. "Look, we figure y'all got a thing going, and, far as we're concerned, that's good. But you're not doing Crawford any favors by keeping what you know to yourself. So, if you know where he was headed this morning, you need to tell us."

"All I know is where he left my car."

"Where was that?"

She told them about Smitty.

"That must be Crawford's weasel." Harry hitched his head toward the outer office. "Guess he's gotta be in on this." Sessions opened the door and signaled for Neal to join them. As soon as he crossed the threshold, Harry said, "Tell us about this Smitty character."

Neal gave them Smitty's basic bio. With obvious resentment, he added, "He's been thoroughly interrogated but refuses to disclose anything. He says Crawford will kill him, if Otterman doesn't kill him first."

"Well, he might be right," Harry said. "About Otterman anyway."

Sessions said, "Let us have a crack at him."

"That won't do any good," Neal said. "You won't get anywhere."

"Well, we gotta try," Harry said.

His somber tone made Holly's heart clutch.

"We discovered why Otterman's holding a grudge against Crawford," the Texas Ranger said. "The boy's walking into way more than he's bargained for."

Chapter 32

Crawford had decided to wait until full dark to make his move. But the choice of when to act was taken from him when he saw headlights cutting through the swampy landscape, approaching from the direction of the fishing cabin.

With no time to spare, he knocked out the dome light of Smitty's car, crawled over the console, and got out on the passenger side, closing the door behind him. The auto came into sight just as he plastered himself against the trunk of the tree nearest the car, making himself one with it in the darkness.

The car went past, then the brake lights came on as though the driver had just noticed Smitty's car. Crawford took a tighter grip on Joe's revolver, not daring to breathe, as he waited to see if the driver would continue on, or get out and investigate.

He couldn't tell how many people were inside the idling vehicle, a late-model, foreign-made luxury sedan. The windows were darkly tinted, but even if they hadn't been, the gloomy day had turned into a black night. He could barely see his own hand in front of his face.

Then an interior light came on as the driver's door was pushed open. Crawford recognized the man behind the wheel as the bodyguard who'd been trimming his fingernails. Frick. He got out and stood there in the wedge of the open door, looking around, wary and watchful.

"Yo! This is private property."

Getting no response, he left his car in the middle of the road, motor running, and walked slowly toward Smitty's. Crawford noticed that he kept his right hand lowered, holding it close to his thigh. That's where his weapon would be.

He approached the car from the rear on the driver's side. As he inched forward, he gradually raised his right hand and kept it extended in front of him as he jerked open the driver's door. When nothing happened, he ducked his head inside to take a look, and that's what Crawford had been waiting for.

He pounced and was on the guy before he had time to react to the rustle of foliage. Crawford clamped the back of his neck, pushed his face into the driver's seat, planted his knee between his shoulder blades, and jammed the barrel of Joe's .38 behind his ear. "If you want to live, drop the blade."

Just as Crawford had assumed, that's what he was carrying. A man who uses a knife to pare his fingernails likes knives.

The man hesitated, his hand still gripping the hilt of the switchblade.

"You can try," Crawford taunted softly, "but your brain will be mush in milliseconds. Are you that fast?" He let him think about it for about two heartbeats, then said, "Drop it into the floorboard now."

The man did as told. He asked, "Are you Hunt?"

"Pleased to meet you."

He gave a nasty laugh. "Otterman's waiting. He's gonna kill you."

"Ya think? Too bad you won't be there to see it."

———

"What the fuckin' hell?"

Chuck Otterman was slicing into a thick juicy steak when the sudden blare of a car horn arrested him in motion. He dropped his knife and fork onto his tin plate, grabbed his pistol, and stamped over to the screen door.

He recognized the approaching car as the one belonging to him, sent on an errand only a short time ago. It was skidding over the slick, muddy road, fishtailing crazily as the driver sped headlong toward the shack, horn still blaring.

Otterman's second bodyguard stood poised on the top step of the porch, double-barreled shotgun in one hand, his other shading his eyes against the headlights, which, on bright, were blinding. "What the hell's he doing?"

The car came to within thirty yards of the shack where it braked so suddenly, it slewed hard to the right, nearly going out of control and into the creek, before sliding another few yards and shuddering to a stop. The horn went abruptly silent.

Then nothing.

After several moments of ominous silence, the bodyguard looked toward Otterman for instruction.

"Well, don't just stand there." Impatiently he motioned the man forward.

The bodyguard clumped down the porch steps and walked purposefully toward the car, calling out the name of his confederate as he went. But as he got closer to the car, his stride slowed and became less confident.

He shaded his eyes again. "Doesn't look like there's anyone behind the wheel."

"Have you lost your mind?" Otterman said. "What the hell are you talking about?"

The bodyguard went closer, then reached from a careful distance to open the driver's door. He turned back to Otterman, saying stupidly, "Nobody's in here."

"It didn't drive itself," Otterman snarled. "Turn off those goddamn headlights."

His man did as told, and the surrounding area was once again pitched into darkness. The only light for miles originated from the bare bulb dangling from the ceiling above the table where Otterman's T-bone was growing cold.

He called to the bodyguard, "Got a flashlight with you?"

"Yes, sir."

"Look around."

Otterman backed into the shack, returned to the table, and yanked on the dirty string to extinguish the overhead light. Now the blackness was absolute except for the occasional sweep of the flashlight beam through the trees.

He felt his way back to the chair he'd vacated and sat down. Barely able to detect the outline of the screen door, he fixed his gaze on it and waited, letting his eyes grow accustomed to the darkness. He no longer saw the flickering of the flashlight. He could hear the tick of his wristwatch, nothing else.

Then from the direction of the creek two gunshots were fired in rapid succession. Only one of them from the shotgun.

Otterman remained as he was, motionless, and only mildly curious to see who would walk through the screen door. The more time that passed, however, the surer he became that it wasn't going to be his bodyguard, who would have been using the flashlight to find his way back.

Ten minutes elapsed before Otterman felt the shift of air signaling that someone had gotten into the cabin by a means other than the door. Probably he'd come in through a window in the partitioned-off section where the bed was. Otterman had to hand it to him— he was good, so stealthy Otterman hadn't heard a sound.

Otterman yanked on the string above his head. When the lightbulb flashed on, it shone down on him, his uneaten steak, and the man who was seated adjacent to him at the table, bound and gagged, the barrel of Otterman's .357 pressed against his temple.

At the sight of him, Crawford was stopped in his tracks.

Otterman said, "Well, you finally made it. Your daddy and I were getting worried about you. Weren't we, Conrad?"

———————

The two Texas Rangers were granted time alone with Smitty in an interrogation room. Three and a half minutes after they went in, Sessions came out, saying to Neal in passing, "He made a mess on the floor. You're gonna need a mop."

"Did he tell you where Crawford is?" Holly asked Harry as he emerged behind Sessions, who was already pecking out a number on his cell phone.

"He drew us a map."

Nugent asked, "How'd you get it from him?"

"He struck up that chorus about Crawford killing him if Otterman didn't, and I told him those were possibilities, but I was a sure thing, and poked my six-shooter in his ear."

Neal said, "I don't approve of your methods."

"I don't give a fuck."

"State troopers are rolling," Sessions reported as he

ended the brief call. "I told them the general vicinity. One of them knows where this taxidermy sign is. They're gonna meet us there. They'll notify the Prentiss SO and sheriffs of neighboring counties since the loose bladder in there didn't know exactly which one this place is in. Just in case it's in Louisiana, authorities over there are being alerted, too."

Harry looked at Neal. "It's outside PD jurisdiction, but if you want in on the party, follow close."

"Tell them about the fingerprint," Nugent said, virtually loping to keep up as the group made their way toward the side exit of the courthouse.

Neal said, "A fingerprint lifted from the back of a dining chair in Connor's kitchen belongs to a man in Otterman's employ. Match came up immediately. He has a list of priors. Illegal possession of firearms. Assault. Suspected but never charged in two execution-style homicides."

Harry looked at Neal and smirked. "Too bad Crawford's not here to say 'told you so,' but he wouldn't anyway, 'cause that's too much like something you'd say."

Sessions was the first to reach the exit door and held it open for the others as they filed through. Last in line was Harry. He stopped and turned to face Holly, who had kept pace with them.

The Ranger took her by the shoulders. "Judge, ma'am, this is as far as you go. I've got your cell number. I'll call you as soon as we know something."

Beneath his heavy hands, her shoulders slumped with disappointment and resignation. "Please be careful. And I want to know immediately...whatever," she finished tremulously.

"Understood. Oh, and sorry about the f-bomb. That guy gets under my skin." He released her and hurried to catch up with Sessions. They climbed into an SUV similar to Crawford's and sped away. Neal and Nugent peeled out after them.

Holly counted to ten, then ran to her car and followed.

———

Upon seeing his father, Crawford's heart lurched.

Conrad's feet had been tied to the front legs of the chair with what looked like fishing line. His hands were secured together behind his back. A rolled handkerchief cut like a bit through his mouth and was knotted at the back of his head.

But it was Conrad's eyes that disturbed Crawford the most. They gazed up at him with shame, hopelessness, and remorse.

Otterman said, "I don't have to tell you, do I?"

Crawford dropped Joe's revolver to the floor. "Cut him loose."

"You wouldn't come in here with just one handgun."

Crawford reached toward the small of his back.

"Easy," Otterman warned.

Crawford removed Smitty's nine-millimeter from the holster. It joined the other on the floor.

"Kick them away."

He did.

"Thank you."

"He doesn't need to be gagged anymore. Take it off him."

"Not until you and I have discussed some things." Otterman used his foot beneath the table to push out a chair for Crawford. "Sit and place your hands down flat on the table."

Crawford did as told. "You can point the damn pistol at me now."

Otterman grinned, but kept the gun against Conrad's temple. "Your father's a coward."

"Like that's news?"

"I had him picked up this morning, and I'm told his efforts to defend himself were pathetic. His house was described as a rat hole."

"Worse than that."

"Oh, you're going for indifference." He barked a laugh. "Won't work. You care for him or you wouldn't have rushed to his rescue last night."

Still feigning detachment, Crawford said, "I did it for me, not him. I don't want everybody knowing what a worthless drunk my old man is."

"But everybody already does."

"My cross to bear."

Otterman regarded Conrad with scorn. "Just now, he could've warned you by making some kind of sound, even with the gag. But he knew if he did, I'd blow his brains out. So he sat there as mute as a stump and let his son walk right into his own killing."

"I'm not dead yet."

Crawford's words carried a sinister implication, but Otterman remained unfazed. He tipped his head in the direction of the creek. "My man?"

"Resisted arrest."

"Dead?"

"He didn't take me seriously."

"And the other one?"

"Sent his regrets."

Otterman cracked a smile, or what passed for one. "I was told you're a smart-ass."

"Who told you that?"

"Friend of mine." This time the smile that spread slowly across his face was intolerably smug. "A very *close* friend who knew you well."

His gloating caused a leaden sorrow to seep out of Crawford's heart and spread through the rest of him, but he kept his expression as blank as possible, unwilling to give Otterman any advantage over him.

If he let emotion dictate his reaction to anything—*anything*—Otterman said, he and Conrad were as good as dead. Their survival depended on cold calculation, not emotional reflex. He had to play this out smarter than Otterman did.

"You're also remarkably predictable," Otterman continued.

"How's that?"

"My man's shotgun would have been too bulky for you to sneak in through the window, but you would have kept the other's switchblade. You probably thought I'd forgotten that, but I hadn't. I've been watching for it. You will regret later that you didn't use it sooner. And, I believe, despite your best effort to appear unconcerned for Conrad here, the only reason you haven't is because I've still got this pistol at his head.

"Now, remove the knife from wherever you hid it—I'm assuming your boot—and, with the blade end pointed toward you, set it on the table, then return your hands to it, palms down."

In his mind, Crawford was chanting swear words, but he remained calm as he reached into his boot, slid the knife from it, and followed Otterman's instructions. Otterman picked up the switchblade and tossed it out of reach, along with the steak knife he'd been using.

Crawford turned his head and spotted where they'd landed against the far wall, leaving him no hope of reaching them. As he came back around to Otterman, he made brief eye contact with Conrad. "Bringing him here was a wasted effort," he said to Otterman. "He's got nothing to do with anything."

"No?"

"No."

"Was it a coincidence that he and I were in the same nightclub yesterday?"

"He's a drunk. He'll drink wherever he happens to land."

"Well, it doesn't matter if that was coincidence or not. He's helped to pass the time while I was waiting for you. See, here's where your predictability comes in. I knew I wouldn't have to bother coming after you, not after you'd seen Pat Connor's video of your kid. Bet you shit when you got that text."

Crawford kept his features stony.

"And," Otterman continued, "I knew the pimp would crumble under pressure and point the way here. All I had to do was sit back and wait, knowing you'd show up and bring the fight to me. And here you are."

His complacency was almost more than Crawford could stand, but he forced himself to keep still and maintain a conversational tone. "What kind of deal have you got going with Smitty?"

Otterman made a derisive sound. "He's only a messenger boy."

"Between you and who?"

"Rednecks with more cousins than teeth. I doubt many of them can read, but they supply surprisingly good quality weapons."

Guns? Otterman was about *guns*? Crawford's brain kicked into high gear, but he tried to act as though this was common knowledge. "The feds are on to you, Chucky. ATF is—"

"Your bluff is no more convincing than your indifference." Otterman flashed an evil grin as he picked up the coin that had been lying beside his plate and began rolling it over the back of his left hand while still cradling the .357 in his right.

"Nobody is on to me, Ranger Hunt. Eventually you might have picked up on my profitable sideline. No matter how well one covers his tracks, there's always a trail, which is why I moved around so much in the early days of my career. You've proved yourself to be good at finding those trails, even from your computer desk. You're almost as good at detection as you are at shoot-'em-ups.

"But you've been so preoccupied lately with Georgia. Pretty name. Pretty little girl. You've also been spending time with Holly Spencer, lady judge with a smokin' ass, who's gone on TV singing your praises. You don't have to tell me what's going on there, but I think I can guess." He bobbed his eyebrows. "In any case, your mind hasn't really been on your work lately, has it?"

At the mention of their names Crawford's blood ran cold. Still, he kept his features schooled. "Enlighten me," he said. "Smitty buys the guns for you and takes a percentage when he delivers?"

Otterman laughed. "Would you trust that lying turd with a cache of expensive and highly marketable weapons?"

"Good point."

"Take another guess."

"Smitty never touches the guns, he only launders the cash through his clubs."

"I never touch the merchandise, either."

"I see," Crawford said, even as he was beginning to. "You're merely the conductor. Others are playing the tune. Even while busy gun trafficking, you hold down a full-time job and still find time to make speeches to pillars of the community about economic growth."

"See how well it works?"

"Flip sides of the coin."

Otterman looked down at his left hand and smiled. "You're thinking way too hard. This is merely a habit. Don't read any symbolism into it."

"Who do you sell the guns to?"

"Well, up until four years ago, I had a very good customer. The individual who knew you so well."

The cogs in the wheels of Crawford's brain clicked into place and suddenly it all made sense. "Jesus Christ," he whispered. "This is about *Fuentes*?"

"He was as obsessed with you as you were with him." He chuckled over Crawford's evident surprise. "You didn't know that? Guess you're not so smart after all. Fuentes was, but he didn't really have to be all that savvy to spot you. You don't exactly fit the profile of a feed store clerk.

"He marked you as soon as you got to Halcon. You fascinated him. See, my *amigo* Manuel bought into the image of the Old West Texas Ranger. He loved the myth, the lore. It was a bit disappointing to him that you got around in a pickup truck instead of on horseback.

"Anyway, he knew you'd make a move. He just figured you'd have better manners than to come after him at his niece's party. As it turns out, that was a fatal miscalculation on his part. You weren't so mannerly after all."

"I cut off the head of the snake."

"Killing the whole damn thing." His composed recitation came to an abrupt end as he banged the tabletop with his fist, rattling the tin plate. "You robbed me of a good thing."

"This is payback."

"This is only the start of it," Otterman said. "First, you'll watch him die," he said, tipping his head toward Conrad. "Then"—he winked—"I have a few other entertainments planned. I know how much you care for the women in your life."

Crawford's gut clenched with revulsion and fear, but he kept his head in the game. Either he or Otterman would die soon. If he got lucky and it was Otterman, he wanted to know as much as he could about him and his criminal activities.

Redirecting the conversation, he said, "After I blew Fuentes to hell, you signed on with the outfit in Houston."

"To keep closer tabs on you. You moved to Prentiss to be closer to your kid, and I asked the company for a transfer here. Since then, I've bided my time."

"Why not just take me out right away? A drive-by. An ambush in my house like Connor. Why the masquerade?"

"You underestimate your star power. No ordinary, painless shooting for you. I wanted your death to be spectacular. When I heard about your custody hearing, I cooked up the plan with Pat Connor. Scheduled my appointment with the ADA just so I'd be there to see your bullet-riddled body zipped up in a bag."

"Didn't happen."

"No. The dumb fuck missed. Got scared. Ran." The harsh, angry features smoothed out. "But," he said in a lighter tone, "actually it turned out better. It's been fun watching you squirm this past week, seeing you scared."

Crawford didn't give him the satisfaction of knowing how effectively his revised scheme had worked. "What would you have done if Connor had been caught?"

"Well, ideally, he wouldn't have made it out of the courthouse alive. In a building crawling with cops, I figured somebody would cap him, perhaps even the bailiff he killed. But I wasn't worried about him being captured. If he'd fingered me, who would have believed that I was involved? You've had some experience with that yourself, right? People disbelieving allegations about me?"

Crawford didn't reply to that. "Why Connor?"

"You pick a guy who everyone sees, but no one is looking at. He's coasting through life. You offer him a little excitement in his otherwise dull routine."

"I appreciate the lesson on how to corrupt, but how'd you get him to agree to the assassination attempt?"

"He'd made some contacts for me with those coon-asses selling guns. Worked okay for a while, and then Pat helped himself to a piece of my pie. Like I wouldn't notice. Stupid mistake. But I didn't kill him, because it's always helpful to have a plant in the local police department. It's even better if the plant owes you a favor for sparing his life." He shrugged. "His usefulness ran out."

"None of this comes as a major revelation," Crawford said. "Except that you did all this to avenge Fuentes."

"What did you think?"

"I thought…" But he stopped there, never wanting to speak aloud what he had feared most: that Beth had somehow been at the heart of Otterman's revenge.

Refocusing on him, Crawford said, "I thought your vengeance had a measure of honor behind it. Twisted valor, maybe, but at least *some* sense of valor. I thought this was revenge for one of the party guests who got killed in Halcon, or maybe one of the officers who died."

"Why would I give a rat's ass about any of them?"

Crawford looked deeply into the other man's eyes. Or tried. They were impenetrable. Dead. There was nothing behind them. He understood now that's why he'd had such an instantaneous aversion to him. His eyes were soulless. The loss of a beloved woman, or friend, or relative wasn't behind his vendetta. Merely greed for money. And power. That's what really got Otterman off—playing with people's lives. "My mistake," Crawford said. "You wouldn't give a rat's ass. I gave you credit for being human, when all you are is a criminal, getting back at me for blowing away your business partner."

"It took me years to win that cocky little bastard's confidence. Years more to establish a monopoly with him. Then you came along, and ended it in a five-minute gunfight."

"Actually it was seven minutes."

Otterman caught the coin in his fist and banged it against the table again. "Seven minutes that cost me millions of dollars."

"Gee, that must've cut deep."

On the last word, Crawford gave the rung of Otterman's chair a hard shove with his foot and sent it over backward. Taken off guard, Otterman's index finger contracted around the trigger of the .357. The shot sounded like a cannon and blasted a hole through the roof.

As Crawford lunged across the table, he grabbed the fork from the tin plate and, following Otterman down, plunged it into the side of his neck. He'd aimed for the carotid, wasn't sure he'd hit it, so he pulled the fork out and stabbed him again, and a third time. When arterial blood spurted, he pushed off him and wrestled the pistol from his right hand.

Otterman's eyes weren't so soulless after all. They were now wild with panic as he dropped the infernal coin and, with both hands, futilely began trying to stop the geyser of blood from his neck. The dropped coin rolled across the floor on its edge, then got lodged in a crack between the uneven planks.

Crawford aimed the pistol down at him. "Just so you don't go anywhere while you're dying…" He shot him in the kneecap. "Courtesy of Deputy Sheriff Chet Barker."

Crawford was deaf to Otterman's gurgled screams as he went over and got the switchblade off the floor. He used it to cut through the knot holding the gag around Conrad's head.

"Good work, son," he panted as he spat out the handkerchief.

"You all right?"

"Roughed up a bit, but basically okay. I think my wrists are bleeding."

The fishing line had dug deep into the flesh, breaking the skin. As gently as possible, Crawford cut through the binding, then freed Conrad's feet from the legs of the chair, and helped him to stand up.

As he shook feeling back into his hands, Conrad said, "My dog and pony show last night did you some good, huh?"

"It did me a lot of good."

Crawford saw the flash of pride in Conrad's eyes even as he snorted with self-derision. "Got me kidnapped, although I put up more of a fight than he let on. I guess it's true what he said. I could've made some sounds to warn you of what you were walking into, but—"

"He would have killed you without blinking."

Conrad laughed. "I'd be no great loss. I kept quiet because I had to see for myself that one of those assholes outside hadn't killed you. I wanted to make sure you were okay. For a few minutes there…" Then he shocked Crawford by pulling him into a hug. It was clumsy, awkward for both of them, but it counted. They thumped each other on the back.

As they broke apart, Conrad smiled up at him, and Crawford saw tears standing in his father's eyes.

Then Conrad's gaze suddenly snapped to Crawford's right. Realizing in an instant what it must signify, Crawford reacted, bringing the pistol up as he spun around. There was an eruption of gunfire.

Otterman never felt the bullet that finished him.

Nor did he hear Crawford's anguished cry. "Dad!"

Chapter 33

Holly followed the caravan of official vehicles as far as they would allow. By the time she reached the turn-off, designated by the now well-known sign, the road had been barricaded and only personnel with official business were being allowed beyond it.

Even some law enforcement officers with no specific reason for being there were prevented from going farther, and they began unsnarling the traffic jam caused by converging vehicles. The congestion had made it difficult for ambulances to get through. No one Holly asked knew the number or nature of the casualties for which the ambulances had been called.

She and spectators drawn to the emergency had parked along both shoulders of the backwoods state road. There she paced, clutching her cell phone, willing it to ring. She had called Harry, Sessions, and Neal in turn, leaving voice mails for them.

Of course, it was Crawford's voice she wanted most to hear, but she didn't have the number of the burner phone he'd been using to communicate with Harry…until he had stopped communicating.

When her phone finally did ring, Neal Lester's name appeared in the LED. Breathlessly, she answered.

He said, "I'm calling on Crawford's behalf."

"He's all right?"

"He's fine, just occupied."

Her sob of relief was so forceful, it hurt her breastbone. "You swear? He's all right?"

"Yes. He's been talking everybody through what went down. It's a madhouse."

"I know. I'm here."

"Where?"

"Here. Parked on the shoulder just west of the turnoff."

He paused briefly, then said, "I'll meet you at the barricade. Five minutes."

Even on foot, she made it there before he did. He pulled up in his sedan on the other side of the barricade, got out, spoke to one of the officers keeping people out, and ducked under the barrier to reach her.

"What are you doing out here?"

"I couldn't just go home and sit. Tell me what's happened. Has Otterman been arrested?"

"He's dead. Bullet to the head. Knee shot out. I'll spare you the more gruesome details."

"Crawford...?"

"Yes."

She clung to every word as Neal described the situation. When he stopped to take a breath, she said, "The Rangers had discovered Otterman's connection to Manuel Fuentes. That's why they were so anxious to reach Crawford."

He nodded. "Otterman admitted to Crawford his illegal gun trade. The bodyguard Crawford stuffed in the trunk of Smitty's car was mad as hell for being wrapped up in duct tape, but he fared better than his coworker, whose body was found half in, half out of the water. Dead. After hearing about his buddy, and the carnage inside the shack, he was more than willing to open up about the gun running."

The word "carnage" caused her to shudder. "But Crawford's all right?" She couldn't have confirmed it enough times.

He averted his gaze. "He is. But, well, his father didn't make it."

She fell back a step. "*What?* Conrad was here?"

"You know him?"

"Tell me!"

He told her about the abduction. "The guy locked in the trunk said they had picked up Mr. Hunt early today, brought him here. He had deep ligature marks on his wrists and ankles. Otterman finished him off. Crawford is…" He looked aside and shook his head.

She covered her mouth with her hand. "Can you take me to him?"

"No. Even if I could, I wouldn't. You don't want to see him now. Trust me. He went a little crazy when he heard you were in the vicinity. He's—" Whatever Neal was about to say, he changed his mind. "You should go home, Judge Spencer. He's going to be tied up for a long while yet. Wait for him to contact you."

Since Crawford hadn't called her himself, she had little room to argue. Neal was about to turn away, when she stopped him. "Thank you for coming to tell me all this in person. I wouldn't have wanted to hear it over the telephone."

"I felt I owed Crawford a courtesy," he said, looking uneasy. "Owed one to both of you." He gave her a brusque nod and ducked beneath the barricade.

She walked back toward her car, resentful of the chaos going on around her—the endless number of official vehicles with their obnoxious flashing lights reminded her of a garish midway. The clustered bystanders were swapping rumors about the body count, speculating on who had died and who had lived to tell about it. She wanted to scream at all of them to shut up.

When she reached her car, she got in and laid her forehead on the steering wheel.

"Drive, judge."

Nearly jumping out of her skin, she whipped her head around, gasping his name when she saw the amount of blood soaking his clothes.

The massive red stain was fresh enough to show up shiny in the kaleidoscope of flashing red, white, and blue lights around them. His eyes glinted at her from shadowed sockets. His forehead was beaded with sweat, strands of hair plastered to it.

He remained perfectly still, sprawled in the corner of the backseat, left leg stretched out along it, the toe of his blood-spattered cowboy boot pointing toward the ceiling of the car. His right leg was bent at the knee. His right hand was resting on it, holding a wicked-looking pistol.

He said, "It's not my blood."

"I heard."

Looking down over his long torso, he gave a gravelly, bitter laugh. "He was dead before he hit the ground, but I wanted to make sure. Dumb move. Ruined this shirt, and it was one of my favorites."

Up ahead, officers had begun moving along the line of spectator vehicles, motioning the motorists to clear the area. She had to either do as he asked or be caught with him inside her car.

"Sergeant Lester told me that you'd—"

"Shot the son of a bitch? That's true. He's dead. Now, drive."

God bless her, she didn't argue. Without further discussion, she started the car, then pulled it onto the road.

"You should be more careful about leaving your car door unlocked," he said. "But I'm glad you did."

"Where do you want me to take you?"

"Head toward Prentiss. I'll direct you from there."

Now that they were clear of the congestion, he sat up and placed the pistol on the floorboard. "I wonder if Joe's missed it yet."

"Do you want to talk about what happened?"

"Otterman killed Conrad. I killed Otterman. I thought he was done for, but...He knew I had extra weapons. Why didn't I check him for another?" He planted the heels of his hands against his eyes that stung with unshed tears. "I shouldn't have kept him from seeing Georgia."

"Conrad, you mean."

"That was hateful. Spiteful. I was angry at him for so many years. I—" He stopped, unable to go on.

Holly, speaking quietly, said, "He understood, Crawford."

He lowered his hands from his eyes and met hers in the rearview mirror. "He understood and agreed with your decision. Sometime I'll tell you what he said about it, but now's not the time. Shouldn't you go back?"

"They got what they needed from me tonight. We're picking back up in the morning. I wasn't doing Conrad any good. One of the EMTs told me that media was already camped out at the hospital, waiting for the ambulances to arrive. I just couldn't face all that right now."

"They'll be looking for you. At least call Neal." When he didn't respond, she offered to call for him.

Reluctantly, he nodded. "I guess you should. I hate

to think of all that personnel wasting time searching for me."

She punched in the call and put it on speaker so Crawford could hear. As soon as Neal answered, he said, "Crawford's vanished. Nobody saw him go. He didn't tell anybody—"

"He's with me."

"Why doesn't that surprise me?" he muttered. "Where are you?"

"He said you were resuming in the morning."

"Seven thirty."

"He'll be there." She clicked off. "I think he's worried about you."

Crawford scoffed. "He's only worried he'll catch heat for being wrong. Anyway, thanks for doing that."

"Don't thank me."

Taking him completely by surprise, she steered sharply off the highway onto the shoulder, got out, and opened the back door. Practically crawling over him, she placed her hands on either side of his head and drew his face to hers.

"Holly, I'm a mess."

"I don't care. I can't wait any longer to touch you."

They kissed openmouthed and deep. When they finally broke apart, she continued to run her fingertips over his face as though to assure herself that he was really there. With emotional raspiness, she said, "I thought you might die."

"Honestly, I thought I might, too."

He palmed the back of her head, tilted it, and they kissed again; he broke it off before he wanted to. "The reason I split? This investigation will tie me up for hours, days, weeks, and I've *got* to see Georgia. If you don't want to take me, I'll find some other way to get there. But I am going to see her."

"You want to drive to Austin tonight?"

"They're not in Austin. Grace doesn't even have a sister."

The attractive log house belonged to friends who attended the Gilroys' church. It was used as a weekend getaway. The pine-studded lot was situated on a lake about twenty miles south of Prentiss. Joe had suggested it as their hiding place, and Crawford had thought it sounded ideal.

He'd lied about where they were going because of its proximity to Prentiss. And to Otterman. He had kept it from Holly in case she was ever pressured into telling someone what she believed to be the truth.

Together they walked up to the front door. He knocked softly. A few moments later, the light above the door came on. Grace gave a startled scream when she opened it and saw Crawford.

"It's not my blood." Grace looked anything but reassured as he and Holly stepped inside and she saw his mud-crusted boots and jeans, the pistol he was holding at his side. "I want to see Georgia. But I need to wash up first."

"Back here."

She led them down a hallway and into a sizable den, comfortably furnished, with a wall of windows overlooking the lake. Joe was reclined in a leather chair, wearing a headset, watching TV.

Grace spoke his name loudly enough to override the TV audio. He turned his head in her direction, then did a double take when he saw Crawford. He bounded out of the chair as he ripped off the headset. "Holy hell!"

For the third time, Crawford said, "It's not my blood.

It's my dad's, actually. He's dead." While his in-laws were trying to absorb that, he said, "But so's the bastard who killed him."

"Otterman?"

Crawford nodded. "But I killed him with his own pistol, not yours. I took this the other night. It was never fired." He set the pistol on an end table. "Can I borrow a shirt?"

Grace, still looking stunned, left and returned shortly with a plain white undershirt, the kind Joe wore year-round. She showed Crawford into a powder room. After closing the door, he looked at himself in the mirror above the sink, and the image was shocking, frightening.

But he didn't dwell on how ravaged he looked. He removed the bloodstained shirt and washed his chest and hands. Tap water mingled with his father's blood, forming a red whirlpool that eventually faded to pink. As he watched it drain, tears dripped from his eyes. He splashed his face with cold water and raked back his sweat-soaked hair.

When he came out of the bathroom wearing the white t-shirt, he said to Grace, "If I could bother you for one more thing. A paper bag. I need to save this shirt in case it's needed as evidence." When that had been seen to, he asked, "Where's Georgia sleeping?"

Joe thrust his chest out, taking an all too familiar combative stance. "That restraining order is still in place."

Grace shot him a quelling look. "Joe, for godsake."

She led Crawford from the main room and back down the hall, stopping outside a closed door. "I'm truly sorry about your father."

"Thanks."

He let himself into the bedroom and closed the door.

There was a nightlight, by which he could see Georgia sleeping on her side, Mr. Bunny hugged against her. He didn't want to wake her up and get her excited to see him, only to have to leave her again, and, in any case, the filth on him would ruin the bed.

But he knelt beside it and couldn't resist hooking one of her curls with his little finger and raising it to his lips. To keep her safe, he would have killed Otterman or anyone else a thousand times over.

He watched her sleep, smiling as he listened to her soft snores, which he would have recognized anywhere in the world. Her sweetness and innocence were like a balm to his punctured heart. After about ten minutes, he whispered that he loved her, kissed the lock of hair again, then tiptoed out and pulled the door closed behind him.

The other three were waiting for him in a strained silence. Holly looked particularly anxious about his state of mind. Grace sat as rigid as a two-by-four, her features frozen with tension.

Joe unleashed the anger he'd kept bridled up till now. "How dare you come here, looking like you climbed out of a charnel house."

"It's just not in me to fight with you tonight, Joe." He nodded Holly toward the door.

"Congratulations on getting the bad guy," Joe said.

"Thanks. 'Night, Grace."

"How many rules did you break in order to get him?"

Crawford stopped, turned, and, feeling incredibly weary, faced his father-in-law. "A few. I bent others. But I'll be damned before I apologize for it, especially to you. Otterman spent four years plotting this, and he wasn't going to stop until he killed me. Or people around me."

"I gave you a second pass on the restraining order because of the threat he posed to Georgia."

"I've thanked you for that, and my gratitude is sincere. So why are we having this conversation? Let's go, Holly." He took her arm.

Joe, however, wasn't willing to call it a night. "You'll be a hero again tomorrow."

"I know how that galls you. I don't like it, either."

"You expect me to believe that?"

"The only thing I expect from you, Joe, is to be a horse's ass, even on a really, really bad night."

"I just want you to know that I'm not backing down from my fight to keep my granddaughter."

"See you in court."

"And you won't have *her* on your side."

Holly, to whom Joe had been referring, stepped forward. "Please don't talk around me, Mr. Gilroy. If you have something to say to me, I'm right here."

"You made a deal with me. Don't forget that."

"I haven't forgotten it. Crawford is aware of it. When I take the stand, I'll testify to the truth."

"You will, *he* won't."

"Crawford wouldn't lie under oath."

"He's been lying under oath since we started this mess. He's living a lie."

Crawford noticed the triumphant gleam in his father-in-law's eyes, and in that instant, in that moment of raw clarity, realization struck. "Jesus." His head dropped forward until his chin almost touched his chest. He pressed his hands against his temples.

"Crawford?" Speaking his name with obvious concern, Holly placed her hand in the center of his back. "What? What is it?"

He lowered his hands, raised his head, and walked slowly toward Joe, searching his eyes, and reading in them the fact of the matter. "You know." He delved deeper into Joe's indomitable gaze. "You've always known, haven't you. It was your silver bullet."

No longer looking so self-satisfied, the older man said querulously, "I don't know what you're talking about."

"Oh, yes you do," Crawford said softly. "When were you going to use it, Joe? When no other options were left open to you?"

"What are the two of you talking about?" Grace asked.

Crawford said, "You want to tell her, Joe?"

The older man made a dismissive gesture. "He's talking nonsense."

"No, it makes perfect sense," Crawford said. "Until just now, you didn't know that *I* knew. You've been waiting for just the right moment to spring it on me."

"Knew what?" Grace asked with increasing impatience.

Joe looked over at her, and his jowls relaxed. The fire in his eyes dimmed. He looked like a commander who'd been trapped in his own well-set ambush.

Grace said, "Joe? What?"

But when her husband didn't say anything, Crawford gave her a sad smile, then looked into Holly's eyes. "I'm not Georgia's father."

Chapter 34

Holly's lips parted in disbelief.

Grace covered her cheek as though she'd been struck.

Joe walked over to the recliner and sat down heavily.

Crawford addressed Holly. "Under oath, I never referred to her as my daughter. You can check court transcripts. I never even refer to her that way in conversation. Other people do, and I never correct them, so technically, I guess that's lying, because I didn't father her."

"How long have you known?"

"Since she was a year old. Beth told me the morning I left that last time for Halcon. She didn't want me to go. I insisted that I had to, that I had a job to finish. The argument turned ugly. She wanted to hurt me in the worst possible way. And she did."

Grace, openly crying now, covered her mouth to hold back a sob.

"Who was the father?" Holly asked.

"Nine months, give or take a week, before Georgia was born, I was supposed to have come home for a weekend. At the last minute, something came up, I had to stay in West Texas. Beth was furious. She rounded up a few girlfriends and they went out. Got a little crazy.

She met this guy at a bar and slept with him to punish me. Two weekends later, when I did come home, we had lots of makeup sex, so I had no reason to think the baby wasn't mine. Beth chose her moment to tell me."

"Which is why I question it," Holly said. "Maybe she made all that up, just to try to keep you from going after Fuentes."

Crawford looked over at his father-in-law, and, feeling the weight of Crawford's stare, he said, "It's true."

"And you've kept this from me?" Grace said.

"Beth came to me in confidence," he said defensively. "She found out she was further along in the pregnancy than she was supposed to be, realized what had happened, panicked. She came to me asking what she should do. She was upset with herself. Mortified, actually. She didn't want it to destroy her marriage. She wanted *you*," he said to Crawford, "so I advised her never to tell you. Until now, I didn't know she had."

Crawford said, "She claimed she'd never seen the guy before that night, and never saw him after. Didn't even remember his name. Is that true?"

Joe gave a curt nod. "It was a classic one-night stand."

That relaxed the tension that had been gripping Crawford for days. "I hoped she was being truthful about that. This past week, there were times when I wondered if Otterman had been the man."

"Oh, Crawford." Holly reached for his hand and squeezed it hard.

"Actually, that's what I feared most. My biggest relief wasn't seeing him dead, but learning that he had nothing to do with Beth, nothing to do with Georgia." His voice cracked when he spoke her name. "I ventured a lot of guesses about Otterman, but that was the worst of them. I don't know how I would have borne knowing that… Well, it doesn't matter now."

He walked over to where Grace was sitting and hunkered down in front of her, covering her tightly clasped hands with his. "Don't ever think badly of Beth. I had made her unhappy. She made one misstep. She loved Georgia. She loved me. I know she did.

"Just a few days after that quarrel, she got the call that I'd been wounded. Maybe she felt like she'd jinxed me, caused me to get shot, something. I think that's why she was trying so hard to get to me that night. She wanted to make things right between us."

"Would you have forgiven her?"

"Yes. I have forgiven her. Because I loved her, too. As for Georgia, she became mine when the doctor handed her to me seconds after she was born. I couldn't love her more if I had fathered her."

Joe stood up. "But you didn't. She's our blood, not yours. So many times, I've wanted to hit you with the truth. I hate that you denied me that pleasure."

"*I* didn't." Crawford came to his feet and faced him. "Beth did."

"You thought it was your secret to keep, and you've kept it."

"To protect Beth from being scorned. By you and Grace, by anyone."

"Who do you think you're kidding?" Joe sneered. "You sat on it because you know that this gives us a stronger claim to Georgia."

Crawford was determined not to let the conversation spin out of control. Besides, he was too weak and weary to fight another fight. Quietly, but emphatically, he said, "Believe what you will, Joe. I kept Beth's secret because I didn't want the truth to reflect badly on her. I also wanted to protect Georgia from any kind of cruel backlash." He paused for a beat, then added, "What you do with it is entirely up to you."

The older man's expression and body language remained unyielding.

Crawford picked up the sack containing his shirt and reclaimed Holly's hand. They left the room together, went down the hall, and out the front door, where he stopped to face her.

"Now do you understand why I said I couldn't have you? I meant everything I said in there about wanting to protect Beth and Georgia. But Joe's right. I also knew that if the truth about her parentage became known, I was sunk. So, yeah, I lived the lie. It didn't bother me, not in the least. Till I met you. You're grafted to the truth. Your lifework is to seek the truth. Living that lie suddenly mattered. And it mattered huge."

She had listened intently, and when he finished, she said, "I do understand the dilemma you faced. But let's not talk about it anymore tonight. I just want to hold you." She wrapped her arms around his waist, then flinched away from him and brought her hand from behind his back. It was stained red. "Crawford, this is fresh blood!"

He gave a sheepish shrug. "Some of it was mine."

"Ready?"

"Yes, Daddy."

"Keep your eyes covered till I tell you."

He guided Georgia down the hallway to the open door of her bedroom, positioned her, then said, "Okay, you can look!"

She lowered her hands and began to squeal as she hopped up and down. "That's gonna be my bed?"

"It's all yours. This is your room from now on."

She turned and hugged him around the knees. "Thank you, Daddy! This is the best surprise ever!"

He returned her hug, then nudged her into the room. "Go check it out."

She went directly to the ballet slippers and tutu.

He had replicated everything that had been destroyed. The vandalism was attributed to Pat Connor. That was only one bit of the wealth of information supplied by the surviving bodyguard as part of his plea bargain.

From him they also learned that Chuck Otterman, by working for several companies over many years, had created a complicated relay system of weapons trafficking that might otherwise have taken years to discover, and even longer to unsnarl and prosecute the participants. The guard also identified the roughnecks who played active roles in that sideline, and exonerated those who were clueless to it.

Many of Otterman's local weapons suppliers were busted by a joint task force of officers from several agencies, state and federal, including Harry and Sessions out of Houston, and Crawford out of his office in Prentiss. As it turned out, cousins of even the tightest clans would rat each other out. It was surprising how cooperative they became when faced with felony charges. And Harry's six-shooter.

Holly joined him at the door of Georgia's bedroom, setting her pink suitcase just inside it. "I think she likes it."

"How can you tell?" he asked, smiling over Georgia's enthusiastic *ooh*s and *aah*s as she moved from one treasure to another.

"The trunk of my car is packed with stuff. Where are you going to put it all?"

"We'll find room. Maybe she'll cull some of it." He placed his arm around Holly's shoulders and kissed her brow. "Thanks for doing that, by the way."

He'd accepted her offer to pick up Georgia at the Gilroys' house and deliver her and her belongings to his. "It wasn't too bad."

"Joe?"

"Coolly polite. Grace got teary-eyed, but she was smiling and enthusiastic for Georgia's sake. It helps that she'll be keeping her after school every day."

He had told his in-laws that he would get Georgia to school each morning, but that he needed someone to pick her up and watch her until he got home from work. When he asked Grace if she would be interested, she had wept and gratefully accepted the proposal.

"It's a good arrangement," he said to Holly now.

"It was kind of you."

"I know how hard it was for them to give her up. Seeing them every day will help Georgia with the transition, too."

The restraining order had been revoked. That hearing had never taken place. When the custody hearing was rescheduled with another judge, Joe didn't use his silver bullet. Crawford figured Grace had forbidden it. He also reasoned that Joe, who'd had ample opportunities to confront him with the truth, hadn't because, he, too, had wanted to protect Beth and Georgia from any hint of scandal.

However, true to his word, Joe hadn't given up without a fight. He argued against Crawford's ability to parent Georgia as well as he and Grace did.

Holly had been subpoenaed, and had truthfully testified to his losing his temper and assaulting his father-in-law. But during cross examination, Bill Moore had made certain that the judge heard from her the extenuating circumstances that explained and justified his behavior that day in the park.

The judge took it all under advisement, and, after

three tortuous days, Bill Moore called Crawford. "You got her. Congratulations. Don't fuck up."

Heart bursting, he said, "For this call, you can bill me double."

"Don't think I won't."

Watching Georgia now, testing out the bed by bouncing on it, he asked Holly, "Why do you think the judge ruled in my favor?"

"He was won over when you said there was a big difference between a father and a daddy. You'd had a father. You wanted to be Georgia's daddy." She hesitated, then said softly, "I went by his grave yesterday and left flowers."

"How'd you know where it was?"

"I checked at the cemetery office."

She had wanted to be at the burial service, but Crawford wouldn't hear of it, saying her attendance would raise eyebrows and beg explanations.

Only a handful of people attended the graveside service. Crawford notified his mother in California. She sent her condolences and a scrawny spray of flowers. A few men from the sawmill came, and one of Conrad's legal colleagues from back in the day. Harry and Sessions surprised Crawford by driving up from Houston for it. Neal and Nugent were there, Nugent fidgeting.

Throat tight, he said to Holly now, "You wouldn't think I'd miss him, but I do. He was never around, but I knew he was *there*. I grieve him, and all because of those last few seconds of his life. He hugged me. We smiled at each other. I don't recall that happening since I wasn't much older than Georgia is now."

"He died doing something for you, and that was important to him. I think you need to hear what he told me that night."

She related their conversation. "He ended by saying

he would be proud for Georgia to know him as he was in his heyday."

Crawford, his voice gruff with emotion, said, "I'll tell her about him, when she's older and can understand, and I can figure out a way to say it all. I'm not very good at stuff like that."

"That is so untrue. Chet's eulogy was beautiful."

He'd served as a pallbearer and, at Mrs. Barker's request, he'd delivered a brief but heartfelt tribute.

"Will you ever tell Georgia about her parentage?"

He replied without hesitation. "Definitely. At the very least she should know that she has the medical and genetic history of only one parent. I'll tell her when she's old enough to understand all the implications."

"The most important one being how much you love her. When Beth told you she wasn't your baby, you could have rejected her."

"Not a chance in hell. I know what it's like to have parents wash their hands of you. I vowed then that Georgia was never going to feel like she'd been discarded."

"That's why she'll love you so much."

"She's crazy about you."

"Is she?"

"Holly said this, Holly said that. Where is Holly's house? Can Holly come with us?" He looked down at her. "Honestly, I'm a little jealous."

For weeks leading up to the custody hearing, his life had been as he'd predicted—consumed by the fallout from the Otterman denouement. He and Holly had talked daily, sometimes several times a day, but had refrained from seeing each other. Each was still under close public scrutiny. He'd been far more concerned for her than for himself.

"I won't let you lose the election because of your association with me."

But once the custody ruling had been made, restrictions no longer applied. They began appearing in public together. When this was slyly remarked upon by Greg Sanders, Marilyn issued the statement she'd prepared for the eventuality. It described their "growing friendship" as "one happy outcome of the crisis situation they had shared and survived."

She'd been retained to see Holly through the election, on the condition that Crawford and Georgia not be exploited. So far, she was abiding by that condition.

"I spoke to the governor today," Holly told him now.

"What did he have to say?"

"Nothing about me. All about you. He wants to meet you."

Crawford looked down at her skeptically.

"I'm serious. He called you a favorite son of Texas. Asked if your gunshot wound—" She stopped and glared up at him.

"I knew it was only a flesh wound."

"No, you didn't."

"I had stuff to do that night before going to the hospital."

Still looking put out with him over his self-diagnosis, which had cost him a loss of blood and the threat of serious infection, she said, "Governor Hutchins wants to shake your hand. He stands solidly behind his decision to appoint me."

"You're a shoo-in."

"If Sanders beats me, I'll start a practice here in Prentiss."

"You'll win. You have the PD's endorsement."

They'd made their peace with Neal Lester. Neal had cornered Crawford one day in a corridor of the courthouse and manfully apologized for letting personal feelings get in the way of the investigation. "I screwed up."

"Keep doing what you do, Neal," Crawford told him as they shook hands. "Departments need cops like you to balance out the cops like me."

Now, drawing Holly closer, he said, "You also have the backing of Prentiss County's criminal element. Smitty called me today. He wanted to know when you're going to redeem your coupon."

"I can't believe Judge Mason granted him bail."

"He's a small fish. The authorities are after bigger fish, and Smitty knows it. He'll plea-bargain himself out of any serious jail time. Actually I hope he's not in for long. He's useful. Never mind that he's a damn douche bag."

"Shh. Watch your language."

"Sorry. He's a regular douche bag."

Holly laughed. They resettled their attention on Georgia as she squirmed into the tutu. "You should bring her to the courthouse one day soon. I could give her a tour of the courtroom and take her up to my office."

"She'd like that. A few days ago, she asked me if you wore a robe like Judge Judy. I told her yes. What I didn't tell her was my fantasy about *dis*robing you."

"Oh?"

He moved them out of sight of Georgia, and situated her between him and the adjacent wall, where they'd stood before and kissed under much more desperate circumstances.

"In my fantasy," he said, "you've got nothing on under your robe."

"And you discover this how?"

"I'll show you when we act it out." Their smiles met, meshed, and as he nudged his way between her thighs, the kiss intensified.

"Daddy?"

Holly tried to spring apart from him, but he held her close, keeping his arms looped around her waist. "She had just as well get used to it," he whispered. Then to Georgia, "Yeah, sweetheart?"

She walked into the hall, wearing her tutu, tiara, and ballet shoes, carrying her new doll. Taking in the scene, she said to Holly, "You have to be careful not to hug Daddy too tight because he's got a big Band-Aid around his tummy."

"I'll be careful, I promise."

"Okay. Can we make sundaes now, Daddy?"

"I promised sundaes, and I always keep my promises."

"Can Holly stay?"

He looked deeply into her eyes. "Can Holly stay?"

She replied, "Holly can stay."

Acknowledgments

I want to thank the Honorable Diane Haddock, Associate Judge, District Court 233rd, Tarrant County, Texas…

…first for being a fan, then for becoming a friend, and, as I was writing this book, for providing me with valuable information. Please don't hold her accountable for any mistakes I made.

And my family joins me in extending a special thank you to Parrie Jane Carroll, who served as my personal assistant for twelve years. They didn't seem as long to me as they must have to her! She managed to keep our lives in order with admirable patience, poise, grace, and seeming ease, when we all know full well we're virtually unmanageable. She is missed, but has earned every moment of a peaceful retirement.

About the Author

Sandra Brown is the author of seventy-five *New York Times* bestsellers. There are more than eighty million copies of her books in print worldwide, and her work has been translated into thirty-four languages. Four of her books have been made into films. In 2008, the International Thriller Writers named Brown its Thriller Master, the organization's highest honor. She has served as president of Mystery Writers of America and holds an honorary doctorate of humane letters from Texas Christian University. She lives in Texas.

sandrabrown.net
Twitter @SandraBrown_NYT
Facebook @AuthorSandraBrown